D0246527

We hope you enjoy this book. Pl[...]
renew it by the due date.

You can renew it at www.norfolk.gov.uk/libraries or
by using our free library app.

Otherwise you can phone 0344 800 8020 -
please have your library card and PIN ready.

You can sign up for email reminders too.

Also by Christobel Kent

The Crooked House
The Loving Husband
The Day She Disappeared
What We Did
A Secret Life

★

A Party in San Niccolo
Late Season
The Summer House
A Florentine Revenge

the widower

Christobel Kent

SPHERE

SPHERE

First published in Great Britain in 2021 by Sphere
This paperback edition published by Sphere in 2022

1 3 5 7 9 10 8 6 4 2

A CIP catalogue record for this book is available from the British Library.

ISBN 978-0-7515-7659-7

Typeset in Bembo by Palimpsest Book Production Ltd, Falkirk, Stirlingshire

Printed and bound in Great Britain by Clays Ltd, Elcograf S.p.A.

Papers used by Sphere are from well-managed forests
and other responsible sources.

Sphere
An imprint of
Little, Brown Book Group
Carmelite House
50 Victoria Embankment
London
EC4Y 0DZ

An Hachette UK Company
www.hachette.co.uk

www.littlebrown.co.uk

For my children

Go, his voice whispers to me through the house's corridors and passages, from behind its green, musty overgrown windows, through cracks and skirtings: *go.*

What are you waiting for?

And I am going, going. Chased down, out of breath, of strength and I know the end is waiting for me there, just there, impatient behind the door. I take what is left to me of courage – mighty – to push it open, and now there I lie, curled on the tight bend of the stairs. The skirt is rucked up high on my thighs but I don't pull it down. I gaze up, blind, into the world that has narrowed to enclose me and then to let me go.

Go, gone, then: at last.

Die in spring, that's my recommendation. Violets in the mossy edges of the grass, the white narcissus-like stars, while the green is new and bright and the air smells – of heaven.

1

I'd never had a garden before I came here, before Evan gave me one.

But it won't be spring, it will be autumn – because my time is run out, the moment has come. And there he will be, Evan, standing – proud, shy, aloof – on the edge of it all, as he always does. He won't take the drink they bring him on the tray: he will be standing very close to the rustling reeds beside the rising brown of the water, as if he'd like to step inside them, to walk away from it all and into the tide to meet me. His eyes will look sore with crying: he will rub at them and his guests will see, the others who've congregated on the lush autumn lawn for me, one by one they will turn and look at him and whisper their sympathy.

He might nod stiffly if approached. He's grieving, they will think, of course they will: he's the widower. I was the focus of his life, of his every effort, and everything he did was for me, perhaps they will say that. People do, at funerals. And in a sense, it will be true.

Will some of them turn away and say something different? Did anyone see, where all his pleasure and his pride really lay: in my suffering? I don't think he'll be afraid of that. He'll invite them all, secure in the belief that if they did see or guess, guilt will silence them; in the knowledge that he knows more than they do, that he understood me better.

He will have an answer for every qualm, every question. The grieving lover, who didn't see it coming. Except he did.

Evan, who knew, and made sure I didn't, who watched it coming and watched me run in circles, tighter and tighter, trying to get away.

And Jamie. Where will Jamie be? In his father's arms?

No, in Rose's, because she might be heedless, thoughtless,

irresponsible, but she'll come, for me, and for my Jamie. Three years is a long time but she'll still be my Rose, I've always held on to that, whatever happens.

And she'll be holding on to *him*, my son, looking awkward – oh Rose, not like that, he'll struggle. *It's the sister*, they'll mutter, eyeing her up openly. She'll look older, of course. She'll be brown from those years under a foreign sun, the long hair I used to comb will be bundled on the back of her head, her slim clever fingers – I don't know if she'll be strong enough. What does she know about babies, about small boys?

Jamie won't be struggling, though. He will hold on tight, he'll cling with his little hands – and I hope Rose will smile down at him as I used to, I hope that will come back to her, the memory of my face when I would take her and carry her for hours, my precious baby sister. *There.*

So they'll watch her, they'll mutter, 'What kept her away all this time, too good for us, was she? Where was *she* when her sister needed her?'

I'd like to run in between them – see me, I am the fog that will drift up, cold and grey, on the autumn tide – shouting back, *she didn't know. She didn't know. Leave her be, she would have come, if she'd known.*

And will she ask questions, now she has come? Or will she let it lie?

I wonder if any of them will talk to her, the few, the dwindling few, who have anything to say. Will you, Lindsay and Annie, Martha and Gerald? Or will you look across at Evan, and let it lie, too?

And if she does begin to ask, what then? What will happen to my little sister, then?

3

Chapter One

Five days earlier

Ah, shit.

Rose stood very still under the vaulted girders of the airport, and recognised no one. Bright, at least: the late sun streamed down in broad shafts on the crowded concourse, which was just as well as she was under-dressed for an English October.

In Rome it had been ten degrees warmer, and raining. The plane had sat on the runway for forty minutes for some unspecified delay while she watched the rain through the small smeared window, watched it spatter up from the puddles that formed and ran into each other on the cracked concrete. And now here, unexpectedly, was sun.

There was a bottleneck where Rose stood, in the corralled space exiting the big Arrivals hall, and there was a blur of motion beyond it. Groups breaking apart and re-forming, coming up the ramp from some underground car park, a gang of lads with backpacks, a hen

5

party with wheeled suitcases rumbling. Rose shivered, pale and goosepimpled under her tan, with every turn of the huge revolving door that brought them in and disgorged them.

Meet and greet.

It's not for long, not forever, just the funeral, then maybe— but even as she turned, Rose felt the future slip away from her, uncertain. She didn't know if he was the kind of man to come with a placard, but she supposed he'd know her. She could hardly remember him, although the last time she'd seen Kate, he'd been there. Two and a half years ago, she'd been home for a dental appointment, a day and a half, an Airbnb because they had no home any more. Kate had heard she was back and breathless on the phone with suppressed excitement had inveigled her to a pub near her flat. Rose had thought it was to meet the new boyfriend but it had been to tell her that she was pregnant.

'He's shy,' Kate had whispered, gesturing to Evan at the bar, who had spent most of the time getting their drinks, then engaged in a conversation with someone on the next table. 'And he thinks we should – you know. Make things up, or whatever, before—' and then had told her. Evan had kept out of the way. Kate had bossed and chivvied him, in such high spirits Rose had even borne it when she leaned closer and whispered, behind Evan's back, 'And what about you? You mustn't leave it too late.'

Kate. Kate.

There'd been one photograph of him – of Evan, small, stubbled, dark-eyed, very, very serious, at Kate's shoulder after the baby was born – but when the time came she couldn't find it again on her phone. She didn't know if Kate had photographs of *her*, Rose, about the place because she hadn't ever seen it. In her old flat there'd been several, one of the sisters hugging, an unusual moment because Kate was too no-nonsense for hugging.

Growing anxious, Rose looked around for the thousandth time, feeling the tide of guilt and grief that threatened to knock her off her feet, on to her suitcase, to just sob. To cry and cry and cry.

There was Facebook, of course, but Rose had stopped doing that, stopped looking, she'd told Kate that it was because social media was doing her head in, that people were leaving in droves, not just her, the digital detox. There had been only so many pictures of beaming babies she could take: Deb – her best friend in Italy and the most sensible person Rose knew after Kate – had said, confidently, 'Is because she is an older mum. She know she won't have any more, so—' and had shrugged. Deb was the same age as Rose: thirty-four.

'We probably count as geriatric too,' Rose had said to that, closing the page.

After that, Kate had emailed the odd picture. Chatty emails, about how hard Evan was working, about gardening – but not for a while. Rose thought it had been months but when she looked back it had been more than a year, since the last one.

There'd been phone calls, although too often it would be when Rose was about to go in to a lesson or out to meet someone for drinks. Students, or Deb. Still, Rose remembered Kate had been worried about Evan working so much, but on the bright side she had Jamie, she had her longed-for baby. Pregnant at thirty-nine, just when it was almost too late and of course, as always, Kate was going to do it her way. Home birth, all that. There had been showdowns with the medical authorities. Rose had tuned out: it had been Kate, being Kate.

They were going their separate ways. It happened.

Not this, though, *this* didn't happen. Shouldn't happen. Dead at forty-one.

Rose hadn't looked back at the emails. She was scared to, right at this moment, was the truth, she was scared to hear Kate's voice, that kind chatty voice, just wanting the time of day and Rose hadn't given it. Time would come when she could: people said that.

Her phone blipped and she pulled it out of her pocket in a hurry, she saw the Italian word and froze − but it was Deb. *Arrivata???* it said. Rose tapped in, *si,* in answer, and sent it. Deb was a big bright breezy woman but she was terrified of flying. Rose knew she had been sure, this morning when she said goodbye, that they would never see each other again.

Admit it: she'd resented him, the man she was waiting for, hated him, even, Evan Lloyd, for taking Kate away from her. Evan, Kate's man − lover, husband, now father of her child, all the things she couldn't imagine Kate having − looking back nervously at the bar two and a half years ago, the small shy man who'd found her, uncovered her, married her swiftly, discreetly, without need of family fuss, given her the baby she'd longed for just in the nick of time; Kate, the big sister to whom, under normal circumstances she could have been the one to run if lost, if

8

unhappy. Except that when eventually sulky Rose had decided she'd like a look at her big sister's happy life after all and returned to the Facebook page, Kate, it seemed, had detoxed too. There were no endless pictures of the little family, Jamie and Kate and the stepdaughter, what was her name – shit, she'd better remember, Clara, Serena? – there was no Facebook page.

Evan. Kate's husband, now her widower, because Kate was dead.

And then and there on the bustling airport concourse among the placards and the rumble of suitcase wheels Kate's face was suddenly in her head, so vivid Rose had to squeeze her eyes closed. Kate pushing her glasses up her nose as a teenager, Kate frowning as she laid out Rose's bank statements on the kitchen table when Rose had decided she ought to get a mortgage – *that* had never happened, although Kate herself had been a home-owner by twenty-three – Kate watering her windowboxes in the little first-floor flat in a sunny street in Brixton.

Jesus fucking Christ, thought Rose. If the fucking man doesn't arrive soon I'm going to start snivelling right here in arrivals over my burst-open suitcases, self-pity or not.

'Rose?' Hesitant. Anguished.

The voice was behind her. She turned, ready to hate him all over again because this was *his fault* – and there he was.

It had been late, when Evan had called, a week earlier. Rose had scrambled out of bed, dropping the phone, groping for the bedside light, staring puzzled at the unknown number. Mumbling her name.

She hadn't taken a sleeping pill. She was grateful for that, later.

'I'm sorry, have I woken you?' came the voice and she'd known, from the low, hopeless voice that this was something horrible. 'It's Evan. Evan Lloyd.'

For a second she didn't know who that was, and then she did.

Evan didn't tell her to sit down, though, as they were supposed to do, and she had found herself walking, in slow motion towards the window. 'Evan,' she repeated. 'Is everything all right?'

Walking, as if to escape. That old cowardly instinct of hers, to run away. To stare out at the old wall and the pines and the cars moving on the big road below, the outside world, anything but to focus on the matter in hand. And afterwards it seemed to her that she felt Kate even then, even before he spoke the words, felt that warm strong tug and Kate telling her, turn round and pay attention. Telling her not to moon out of the window. *Listen, Rosie, listen.*

'I'm so sorry,' he said, and said it again, twice, three times, until his voice disintegrated and Rose barged in.

'Is it – the—' for a second she couldn't remember the baby's name, 'Jamie? Is it Jamie?'

'No, no,' his voice rising, lost, and then she heard him make a ragged effort. 'It's not Jamie, Jamie's – he's fine – it's Kate.'

A silence, like a deep, dark well, and Rose could hear her own ragged breathing. 'Kate?' a silence. '*Kate?* Is she – what—'

He said it, then, but she couldn't hear, the words split

10

something open, black rushed in with a roar and he had to say it again. 'Kate's dead.'

A ragged breath, she didn't know if it was his or hers.

'She died, Rose,' he said, and she heard her own disbelief, her own denial in his voice, he sounded incredulous.

'*No*,' she said, 'what? *What?* She can't be, she was only—' Only forty-one. 'Was she in the car? Was it an – an accident?' Kate driving in the middle of the night was an outlandish idea, a frightening one.

And he – Evan, whose name had meant so little to her before that night she had barely remembered it if asked – began to tell her. When he said that Kate had in fact been dead for four days – four days, four days, during which time Rose had been walking and talking and drinking coffee and grousing over glasses of cold Frascati to Deb about work or money or men – she had let out a great sobbing gasp. She heard his silence.

'What day?' She couldn't fix anything in her head, time whirled around her.

'Sunday night,' he said, his voice very quiet.

'I don't understand,' she said stubbornly.

He cleared his throat. 'Early Monday morning, as a matter of fact, three ten in the morning—'

It took her a while to understand that it had not been an accident. Not in the car.

'It was the weekend,' whispering, desperate. 'I should have understood how sick she was. The surgery was closed. I thought it could wait – she said she didn't want to go to Casualty.'

'Sick? She was sick?' Thinking of all those stories, of

11

children brought too late to Casualty, of meningitis, of sepsis. 'What—'

'We didn't know,' and something broke from him, he restrained it in time. 'We didn't *know.*'

The words struck against her like doom.

'It all came on so fast,' he said. 'I – I – wanted to know what had happened,' he said. 'It was so sudden – she hadn't been feeling well but we – she—'

'She never liked doctors,' Rose had said suddenly, remembering. Since – since. Doctors always brought bad news: Mum coming back pale-faced with her diagnosis. All those days and nights with Dad in hospital.

'I wanted to get the results – the preliminary results of the post-mortem because otherwise – it made no sense. I wanted to know before I phoned you. Is that mad? Maybe I was wrong. I don't know. And I didn't – I couldn't bear to—'

'It's all right,' said Rose, numb, although it wasn't. It wasn't.

'Will you come home?' he said then, breaking in on her, breathless. 'Will you come home, Rose?'

Standing there in front of her view of streetlights and Roman brick and the green velvet of the umbrella pines, she had thought he was asking her if she would come back for the funeral. She hadn't known what he was asking.

'Yes,' she said, 'I'll come home.'

Chapter Two

Big emotional Italian Deb had burst into tears immediately, where Rose had stood, dry-eyed in front of her. They were in the park, above the city, and it was raining. You could cry and cry and cry and then what? You couldn't cry for ever. Kate was going to be gone for ever.

'Cancer? *Cancer?*' Deb had a hand on each cheek, eyes wide in horror. Kate had come to see Rose only once in Rome, a weekend just at the beginning. 'Like your mum?'

Rose said, 'Mum died of cancer, yes.' She felt dumb, stupid. 'I don't know what kind, Kate never – we never – I was twelve.'

'Yes, I—' Deb checked herself, looking stricken. 'I'm so sorry.'

Rose felt something, a trembling. It had been so long ago. It had seemed to take up all her childhood, their mother's dying: Rose had been barely a teenager when it finished. She didn't think about it.

For the first time she wondered if Kate thought about it – about her. Kate had been twenty, Kate all through it the one herding her out of the way, taking her to school, sitting with her when she couldn't sleep. She'd never talked to Kate about Mum since she died and now that made her feel as though she might be sick – but still she couldn't cry.

'Ovarian,' Rose said. 'That's what the post-mortem said. It can go undetected – and some women—' she stopped. 'I can't,' she said. 'Deb, I can't.' Took a breath. 'The funeral's next week.'

Dad had died nine years after Mum, of drink. Kate had sewed her a beautiful black dress for his funeral, that she'd never worn, because she hadn't gone. It had been that – and clearing the house – that had cooled things between her and Kate, turned them stiff and awkward. Kate wanting to keep everything and Rose wanting to throw it all away. Burn it. Kate firm and practical, Rose peevish and hysterical. And there was the beginning of the rift that Evan had wanted to heal.

It had been healing, quietly. It had. Jamie and Evan and a happy family.

She'd kept the dress: folded in tissue, it lay in the bottom of her suitcase on the wardrobe in her flat.

'I've got to go back,' said Rose, arms wrapped around herself.

'Of course,' said Deb, looking flustered and anxious. 'The funeral – do you want me to come with you?'

'No,' said Rose quickly. The thought of nosy warm Deb among them, whoever *them* turned out to be, Deb asking why no one was crying, looking at sausage rolls

14

and clingfilmed sandwiches with incomprehension. 'The truth is, I don't know how long I'll have to stay on.' She hesitated, uncomfortable. 'I suppose someone's got to help with the children, for – for a few days, at least.' Not meeting Deb's eye.

The rain seemed to have stopped but the air around them up here above the pollution was hung with a kind of sparkling moisture, pink and gold as if all the colours of the city were being refracted through it. Somewhere across the rooftops bells began to ring, one set off another and then the air was full of it. Leave here.

'Yes, well,' said Deb, and out of the corner of her eye Rose saw her looking slightly stunned, wide-eyed. 'I thought there was only one child.'

'Jamie's the baby,' said Rose stiffly. 'Well, two, is that a baby? He, her husband – he had a girl from his previous marriage, she's—' she cleared her throat, feeling like a fake and fraud, because of all the stuff she had no clue about. 'I don't even know how old she is.' A slender watchful child, a girl with long straight hair cradling Jamie in her lap, but that was an almost two-year-old image. 'Ten, twelve, something like that. She's called Serena.'

'Right,' said Deb, and Rose could hear her trying to silence her alarm. 'I'm sure you'll – you're quite right to—'

'I'll be crap at it,' said Rose, and she felt heat in her cheeks, she felt the threat of the same tears of rage she'd spent her childhood spilling, not grief, anger, anger. 'I'll be shit, but there's no one else. So I'd better go.'

'You won't,' said Deb, 'you won't be crap.'

Rose stared out over the city. 'How could it have

15

happened?' All of it was inside her still. 'I can't even iron properly,' she said and the bells were stopping now, one by one, falling away. The city spread out, far off towards the horizon there was a break in the cloud where it turned pink and yellow and suddenly she couldn't stand to look at it any more.

'She was still breastfeeding him,' she said, and Deb's face was pale, and then, to stop seeing that picture, 'Will you help me pack up the flat? I don't know if – when I'm going to be coming back.'

'It'll be all right,' said Deb, faltering. 'You'll come back.'

'Only one way to find out,' Rose said, trying to smile. The rain began again.

In the car they sat in silence, Rose upright in the passenger seat with her hands clasped round her handbag in her lap. For the moment small talk, at any rate, seemed impossible.

The sun was setting behind them as they headed east from the big white airport across bleak flatlands. Three years in the hot bright south, pink and yellow condominiums and noise and old ladies jabbering and the smell of coffee issuing from bars, and home all looked very green and very empty and very quiet. Houses dotted here and there, small and secretive, hidden away in clefts and corners and behind hedges. She'd forgotten that.

'It must look very different,' said Evan as they came on to a stretch of motorway, the flicker of streetlighting coming on in the dusk, keeping his eyes on the road. She darted a glance at him, then over her shoulder where the baby – almost two, Jamie – was asleep in his

16

car seat, mouth just open, tearstains on his sore-looking cheeks.

Evan had been holding him when Rose turned and saw him and she must have let something show in her face – her fear, that looked like anger – because he had begun apologising stiffly, something about not having been to the airport before, and Jamie having to be woken. 'We're not airport people,' he'd said, helplessly. Avoiding her eye. 'Weren't,' rubbed his eyes, 'we never even got away for a weekend together.'

It had overwhelmed her, the flat exhaustion on his face, the whole world of their life together she had known nothing about, the child asleep on his shoulder. Kate was dead – how – and she was angry and what was she doing here? She knew nothing. She knew how to teach English to teenagers, and that not very well. She was appalling at teaching the five year olds, they ran rings round her and grimaced and teased her and their parents thought she was—

She'd apologised. 'I could have taken the bus, it was thoughtless.'

A sad, small smile. 'With all that stuff?' Gesturing at her suitcases in disbelief. 'You wouldn't have got to us before midnight, and the bus stops three miles from the house.' Rubbing his forehead: he had bags under his eyes.

He was small and wiry, his eyebrows thick and dark and meeting in the middle over brown eyes, dark hair on the arm that held Jamie in place as he struggled. And then he sighed. 'Let's go, shall we? I don't even know if I can find the car again.'

17

There on the echoing concourse with the people shoving past them Jamie wouldn't look at her. Diffidently Rose had put a finger to his small clenched fist, and he'd shifted, pulling the hand away but she could see one eye now, blue under a silky fair wisp of hair, regarding her from his father's shoulder. Feeling something ball up inside her as she met the steady look, the wet-lashed eye. Then he turned his face back into Evan's neck.

'He'll – he'll get used to you,' said Evan now at the wheel, looking straight ahead still.

'I should have come and visited sooner,' said Rose.

'You look a bit like her,' gruffly. 'That's bound to help.'

Do I? Furtively Rose peered at herself in the wing mirror. She'd spent most of her life thinking no one could be less like her than her sister. The thing inside her balled tighter. *I miss her. Too late.*

Outside the sun was almost completely gone and the fields stretched grey and lunar to either side of them. 'Where's your—' she checked herself. 'Where's Serena?'

'She's with a friend,' said Evan, clearing his throat. 'She didn't want – she gets sick in the car. You'll see her in the morning.'

Serena hadn't wanted to come. 'How – is she?' asked Rose. Stupid question, of course: she realised she knew nothing about the previous marriage. Now was not the time to ask. There was a silence and then he sighed.

'God knows,' he said. 'God knows.' He cleared his throat again. 'It's always been her and me. She's – used to that. I had to keep her, you see, I wasn't letting anyone else – I told them all, a man can be the parent—' he broke

18

off. 'The funeral's on Friday. I told you that on the phone, didn't I?'

'Yes, you'll have to let me—' but the glance he gave her silenced her.

'It made Kate so happy, finding you,' she said instead, the words coming from nowhere. 'Having her family, you know, at last, I think she thought it would be too late.' Feeling herself out on a limb in the dark because after the silence it felt like she was saying too much and besides she hadn't spoken to Kate in more than a year and hadn't seen her in three.

'Do you think so?' he said, the briefest glance at her and there was the sigh again, a long, broken sound. 'Do you really? I wish I knew.'

And then neither of them said anything, muffled in hedgerows that opened out to more endless flat fields, passing through closed-up, dead-looking villages of ugly bungalows, then there was a scattering of travellers' caravans, a dog ran across the road, abruptly Evan braked and turned and they were bumping down an unmade track, potholed gravel lit only by their headlights.

Through scrawny hedge to either side of them Rose glimpsed the gleam of something and she sat forward, peering through the glass of the side window, her back turned on Evan. There was a sliver of moon behind trees, an opening and a glimpse of an unearthly sort of landscape, flat and grey, glistening snail-trails she couldn't identify dusted here and there with grasses leading to a dark horizon. Behind her there was the small sound of a window being lowered and a cool breath of the outside on the back of her neck and she smelled something distinct and strange and wild.

The sea. She could smell the sea.

She turned back, not knowing yet what the question was on her lips and he nodded to her, smiling at last, and the car came over what felt like a low bridge, round the brick side of something large and unlit and pulled up in a gloomy cluttered yard. Behind them Jamie stirred and began the syllable as if it had been running in his head all this time. 'Mmm-ma- ma—' Not yet crying. Rose felt her hand go up to him and as it did, time loosened, the future rearranged itself.

'We're here,' said Evan, reaching a hand round and setting it on Jamie and abruptly he subsided, and was quiet, open-eyed. 'We're home.'

Chapter Three

I've got such plans. I know what we'll do with that big dark back room, a fire burning and a long patchwork table in there and women sitting around it, talking. Telling our secrets.

There couldn't be a more perfect house, could there? A sanctuary, a retreat. We'll have book groups, we can sit in the green room looking out over the grass, there'll be wine, there'll be Evan rolling his eyes as he brings us something delicious from the kitchen.

Jamie interrupting us, Serena joining us, when she's older. She's got brains – she sees things. She just needs to learn to see through other people's eyes and a book does that. If it's any good. She needs to come out of herself. It must have been hard for her. It must have been terrible: I tell her, *it happened to my sister, too.* It happened to Rose. Of course I was older, I could process it. That's what a psychotherapist would say, isn't it? You're older, you process it. Too young when you lose your mother and it's like radiation, it gets into your bones where you can't get it out again.

Will Serena like Rose? It's hard to tell. They're dark horses.

Rose woke from a dream of Italy, of Roman trees against a sunset, a man whispering to her, as Italian men did, as he passed. She stirred, frowned in her sleep.

And then abruptly she was awake. She didn't know what had done it: she'd dreamed a sharp noise, a shout, but the house around her, dim and muffled, was quiet.

The room was very cold. The smell that had come in through the car window last night was in the air and she still couldn't identify it, a damp briny smell, vegetable and mineral together.

She'd gone straight to bed the night before. They'd come in from the cluttered yard through one room smelling of smoke, then a dim kitchen, bumping against chairs, past a back staircase, into a hall she knew was big because of a change in the acoustic. She listened again now: perhaps that was it. Perhaps a chair scraping in the kitchen had echoed up here. The thought of the big strange house around her set up a vibration of panic – because it had felt vast in the dark, labyrinthine, big and untidy, damp and spidery and full of other people's things. Rome was another world, unreal already, a holiday.

'You're sure you don't want anything to eat?' Evan had sounded helpless, pausing in the dim room they moved into after the smoky room, an untidy kitchen with a long window and what looked like a toolbox spilling its contents out on a table. So helpless that she had almost put out a hand to him there in the dark but something told her not to.

She'd told him, no, she just wanted to sleep and she had, she had wanted to get her head down and close her eyes before the strangeness of being here in the middle of nowhere with a man she didn't know overwhelmed her.

Jamie hadn't woken when they pulled up, and they'd left him there while they unloaded. She'd paused, something tugging at her, her part in this, and she'd set down the bag she was carrying and said, 'Can't I – couldn't I—'

'He'll be fine,' Evan had said gruffly. 'Time enough to get to know them in the morning.' Obedient, she'd moved off, following him through the cluttered yard, a smell of refuse there.

And now it *was* morning. She groped for her phone at the bedside table, the beaded lamp brushing at her. Seven. So early. But it can't have been much past nine when she went to bed. She noted that there was no signal in the bedroom, and that her phone was almost out of battery. She got out of bed and immediately barked her shin against something hard.

Damn it. Damn the strangeness of it. Gingerly rubbing her shin she stood, and tried to orientate herself, and there it hung, the dress she'd never worn, on the back of the door. She had put it there in the dark, quickly, not wanting to look at it, at the painstaking darts and gathers, the tiny covered buttons. She looked away, now.

Last night Evan had led her round a galleried landing, not quite dark because a glass cupola rose above the big hall and the pale diffuse light revealed outlines here and

23

there, a balustrade, cornices, the height at which they crept around the big echoing hall. He had paused in front of one of the doors they passed so abruptly she bumped against him and he said, curt as he shifted away, 'Bathroom.' They stopped at the last door, where the gallery ended and when he pushed it open she saw there was a light on at least in there, someone must have turned it on for her or he must have thought ahead. A little Tiffany-shaded bedside lamp with beads hanging from it, it hardly illuminated anything but a corner of a faded blue bedspread: with a pang she recognised the light from Kate's old flat, one of the first things she'd bought for it.

She'd turned to say goodnight, but he had already taken three steps back away from her, mumbling something about the morning and she had been too tired even to make an answer.

There was a big window, shuttered, on the wall opposite the bed. Rose groped her way across the room in the light coming through the cracks and when she got to the window fumbled with the big iron latch across the shutters. She felt a cold marshy draught, then it swung down with a squeaky rasp that made her hold her breath, and turn. Behind her the shutters creaked ajar.

No sound – well, not quite. There was a far-off sound, a rushing, like water, from somewhere beyond the glass. But the house was quiet. *So Jamie slept this late, at least,* Rose thought, turning back to survey her room, illuminated by the shaft of light that fell between the shutters. The bed she'd slept on – soft and lumpy at once, her back reminded her with a twinge – was covered with a cover of faded blue velvet, crumpled pillows. Around it wallpaper

24

so old and bleached-out it could have been original, a pale greenish striped and curlicued design puckered with damp here and there and in a corner above the window beginning to peel down away from the wall.

They must have still been sorting it out, thought Rose, perplexed, putting her hand to the wall and feeling it powdery with something, not dust, chalky and damp, something like mould – because although Kate liked old stuff she liked things bright and clean, too, she liked order and efficiency. The money from Kate's flat couldn't have gone far enough, they must have taken another mortgage, they must have been doing it piecemeal— Rose shifted and saw something she recognised. A writing desk she remembered from Kate's flat, a roll-top with little drawers and pigeonholes, her pride and joy, she'd sanded and restored it and it had sat in the sitting room of her tiny flat, the last place she'd lived.

Crossing to it Rose pushed at the rolled shutter, but it was locked: so were the little drawers. Something crept at her back; Rose shivered in the draught and turned back to the window. Carefully folding back the shutters so as not to repeat the clatter of the latch for a second the morning light dazzled her, she must be facing due east because it was the actual sunrise happening right in front of her. She shaded her eyes with a hand and saw it through the wavy old glass as if she hadn't seen the sun come up, it seemed to her, ever before.

Except for a single dead tree, distinct and incongruous as a branched sculpture far out on the flat, there was nothing but marsh and sea, grey-green and silver, between her and the horizon. Between her and the fiery sun it was all water and light: it was like being on the edge of the world.

It was so beautiful for a moment it filled her head, everything else in there displaced, all the unease, all the questions. He'd brought her here. He'd brought Kate here.

And there on the floor by the bed were her bags, two bulging suitcases that represented her whole life. A week ago she'd had a job, a flat. Two weeks ago Kate had been still alive – and then it all flooded in and she sat down against the suitcases in the cold room and put her face in her hands.

Rose knew why Kate wouldn't have told her. She knew. Kate never said anything that wasn't positive. Don't worry people. *Not even her husband? The father of her child?* Manage. Keep your surfaces clear and your windows washed. Bake and sew, keep busy, craft classes, childbirth classes, yoga.

Don't worry Rose, out there behaving like a nitwit, casually foolish about relationships, a student barely out of his teens here, a married man there. She hadn't known he was married, of course, but that just made her more stupid. Rose, fancy free: don't burden her.

Kate wouldn't have told her there was something wrong, until she was sure. Rose could imagine her own side of the conversation: panic, truculence, insisting Kate went to the doctor so she, Rose, wouldn't have to worry. If only they'd had that conversation. If only Kate had phoned.

Rose should have phoned *her.* Sitting there on the cold, dusty floor holding on to her suitcases like they were going to save her, Rose flushed, angry, guilty,

And then, as clear as if she could hear it, she knew

26

what Kate would say to *that*. Yes, you should, but you didn't. Impatient, kind. *Grow up, Rose.*

Her eyes were still dry. She held it at bay.

She realised she'd been waiting for someone to tell her, as if this was a job, how long the contract was for.

Then she heard a sound. There was a sound.

By the time she pulled jeans on, a jumper over the T-shirt she'd been sleeping in, and got out on the landing the house had gone quiet again. She pushed open the door Evan had indicated as the bathroom, and realised she hadn't peed since she got off the plane last night.

Sitting, taking in the dingy room that smelled of ancient damp carpet, where a Victorian radiator sat rusting under a big window so beaded with condensation between thick ancient curtains she couldn't see out, unable, for the life of her to see Kate in this house before realising she hadn't locked the door (lazy, used to living alone) – the sound came again. A babble, not quite words, tremulous, rising. After a moment's panic she thought: *Jamie, of course.* She wasn't used to the sounds children made.

No one knows, though, do they? How to be a parent. Till they have to. And flushing, running the tap – all sounds loud in the echoing house, a great gushing chain-pull cistern, the clank and gurgle of pipes – she hurried out on to the landing to see Evan emerging on the opposite side holding the baby. Jamie.

She walked towards them, holding out her arms and Evan put Jamie into them. Easy as that.

Chapter Four

When Kate had come to see her in Rome they'd shared Rose's crap sofa bed, Kate fussing but not complaining. Suggesting this and that: a tablecloth, more tea towels, a shade for the light. Three years ago. Before Jamie – even before Evan, or at least, she hadn't mentioned him.

She *had* mentioned babies, bringing Rose a cup of tea where she sat propped up on pillows with last night's make-up still on. Sleeping on a sofa bed at your age; Rose knew what Kate was thinking. 'It's just I'd like to see you settled,' Kate said, perching beside her. 'Don't you think Mum would? And I wish I'd—' wistful then, 'well, anyway.'

Invoking Mum. It always rubbed Rose up the wrong way, Kate speaking for Mum, Kate who had known Mum seven whole years longer than Rose and therefore was the expert.

How could two daughters be so different? Dad – drunk – would say he was sure one of them must have come from the milkman. Peering balefully as if he couldn't work out which of them he wanted to disown.

Kate had not gone to university because Mum had been ill and then Dad was off the rails, had stayed close to home and worked as a legal secretary: she had saved enough for a deposit on a mortgage by the time she was twenty-three. Bought her own small flat in a nice modest bit of South London while Rose flitted from job to job after graduating.

Kate's life was so full of activities, she didn't allow for any suggestion that it might not be all she wanted, but Rose saw why she was single, even if Kate didn't. The activities were yoga and stitch and bitch, knitting and patchwork, old-school, worthy, useful, and dominated by women. And if there had been any men, Kate did give something off, competence, or an eye for failings, that would have made plenty of men nervous. She, Rose, had managed a couple of boyfriends at least, although lowering your standards did tend to guarantee that.

Kate had just always been there, solid, uninteresting, good-humoured, reasonable, good at sorting life out. And now Rose would never know what she'd been thinking, all that time.

Kate's visit to Rome, Rose knew, had been an attempt to restore things between them after the shitstorm of Dad's lingering, unpleasant death – Kate had gone every week to mop him up, Rose had walked out the first time he called her a little bitch, and had got a six-month job in Paris. By the time she got back, he was dead.

But every time Rose started to explain herself, defend herself – not that anyone asked – it came out wrong, it came out angry and defensive. And the only defence in fact that she had was that Kate was so good at everything there was no space for any contribution from Rose. Nothing she did could look as selfless or honourable, or even as competent. Kate restacked the dishwasher after her and cleaned her loo. There had been moments, in the soft Roman rain falling through the roof of the Pantheon, of quiet but in the end the trip had been, at best, an uneasy truce.

And then, six months after that visit, Kate had the man, and then the baby. Rose had come back, and had met them in that pub.

This is Evan, he builds eco-houses. If she'd imagined the man for Kate, he might well have done something like that, but he wouldn't have been Evan. He'd have been the lone man who goes to yoga or knitting, meek, eccentric, a wearer of vegan shoes.

Rose had always thought she was the interesting one: in the aftermath of Kate's death it seemed not so, it seemed the opposite of the truth. All that had been unknowable about her big sister was magnified now she wasn't there, would never be there again to ask. *What did you think? What was it like?* Rose could see her there in her neat bright little flat over her patchwork, could see her that last time, after they'd got back from the pub and said goodnight to Evan, Rose tucked up on that other sofa bed under a clean crisp ironed duvet with a glass of some ancient liqueur she'd forced out of Kate. She could see Kate laying the stitching down a second in response to something Rose had said and just looking off into the distance.

She couldn't remember what it was she'd said, not the minute after she'd said it probably. And now she'd never know.

They were in the kitchen. The toolbox she'd glimpsed last night was still there on the long-scarred pine table, along with newspapers. A high chair was clipped to one end of it. There was a stainless steel sink heaped with dishes and a long rather beautiful, very grubby window over it, through which a thin sun shone. Rose gazed at it, and the pale clean English sky she'd forgotten about.

Along one wall were rows and rows of servants' bells, some with faded labels still beneath them, hand-painted. MORNING ROOM, read one. Surreptitiously Rose extracted her phone: *No service*.

'The house is amazing,' Rose said. And it was. The ceilings – almost all of them with patches of damp, some with lath showing through where plaster had fallen away – must be twenty feet high. It was another world, an old world of servants' parlours.

Evan still hadn't shown her around – would he ever? He didn't seem the type, already – Rose hadn't been outside, but she'd seen enough just walking downstairs, through the big hall with its worn dark red turkey-carpet, past the bare wood of the back stairs. She'd come down the big staircase very gingerly, because she'd been carrying Jamie. She was fairly sure she'd never even held a child before beyond passing Deb's niece to its mother in Italy.

A kettle was gurgling on an ancient solid fuel stove, one of those great ranges, grubby-looking and as old as the house. There was a baby's bottle on the side, and a box with a picture of a baby on it. Rose was surprised by Jamie's weight: gingerly she shifted him to her hip and he clung to her sleeve but didn't wriggle.

'The house?' said Evan, glancing round the room. 'It's an interesting place. Kate— it was going to be Kate's project. We liked the peace and quiet.'

'Yes,' said Rose uncertainly. Really? She'd never known Kate live anywhere but a city, although she did love nature. Had loved. There had been walking holidays in places like Greece, looking for wildflowers among elderly hikers. She leaned down to peer at the box, feeling Jamie move with her, like she'd seen baby monkeys do, clinging. 'I'm no expert,' she said, straightening with a rueful half-laugh, 'but I don't think he needs baby milk any more.'

Evan half turned from her, rubbing at his face fiercely as if trying to erase something. 'Right,' he said indistinctly, his shoulder still facing her. 'She was – Kate was feeding him herself, you see, even though he's almost two. I told her she needed to wean him—' and he sighed, shakily. 'I thought it might be better – the teat, you know, more like her—'

'It's all right,' said Rose suppressing the thought that came to her, the image of Kate's head bent over her baby, because if she didn't – well. Rose wasn't the one should be crying. She spoke firmly, reassuring. 'I can see why.'

Jamie was heavy against her now, a thumb in his mouth and his head against her chest. Her shoulders were beginning to ache.

'It was an old rectory,' said Evan, abruptly. 'Belonging to the water board, because of the weir.'

32

'Ah,' said Rose, 'yes. That's the noise.' She had stopped hearing it, but as he said it there it was, all the time.

'It's back there,' said Evan, gesturing towards the kitchen window and the yard beyond it. 'We'll have to—' correcting himself, 'we always said we'd have to be careful when Jamie's a bit bigger. There's water everywhere. It comes up around the house with the tide.'

'What about — is it Serena? Your daughter?'

'She can swim,' said Evan, passing a hand over his eyes. 'I taught her myself when she was tiny.'

Something in his voice steered her away from the subject. 'A rectory — you mean, like a vicarage? So there's a church?'

'The church subsided, there's bits of it left over towards the weir. But they must have built this place on sounder ground, or something, because it's safe enough.'

So far Rose had only seen what she'd glimpsed from the bedroom window: reeds and marsh, a scrubby wind-blown hedge, something that looked like the parapet of a little bridge. 'Subsided?' she said. The thought was vaguely unsettling, the idea of a whole church being absorbed into this wide flat landscape.

'There was a very high tide, coinciding with a big storm,' Evan explained, weary, but turning back to face her at last. On her shoulder Jamie let out a little sound, half a sob, half hiccup, stretching a small hand at the sight of his father's face. Evan didn't seem to see, his face blank with tiredness. 'The church collapsed and bit by bit was washed away or sank into the mud. It's almost all mud, you see.'

'You haven't been sleeping,' said Rose, 'have you?' She wasn't used to being the one who was in control, or sensible, or monitoring others' wellbeing beyond staying away from anyone with a cold. It was the weirdest feeling, a kind of stirring of Kate in her. Evan just shook his head, not so much in confirmation as dismissal.

'Look,' she said, gaining courage. 'You go back to bed, why don't you? I mean – Jamie seems all right with me for the moment, doesn't he? I can—' she looked around the kitchen which seemed to contain hardly anything food-like, and swallowed the qualm, 'I can get him some breakfast, you know, make myself a bit at home.' He stared at her, swaying slightly, his eyebrows knitted and dark and said nothing.

For a moment his tiredness was gone and he seemed to be observing her with a kind of calculation that she didn't understand.

And then he sighed, and something extraordinary happened. He smiled.

'You are like her,' he said. 'After all.'

Chapter Five

Rose didn't remember what words Kate had used to tell her that Mum was dying. At twelve, she certainly hadn't registered the detail beyond cancer, that had gone too far, that had spread. And when she should have been grieving, she had been only angry.

Mum had always been a stiff, capable person, not demonstrative, a hard worker. Kate had a bit of that – a lot of that. But she tried to understand people, at least. Mum wasn't into that, it was her way or no way, and she hadn't told anyone about the lump until it was too late. Rose had gleaned that much from overhearing adults' conversations, as she hid under a trestle they'd laid against the wall in the village hall where they'd had the wake, the over-sized damask tablecloth hanging down to conceal her. Beyond it she could hear Dad getting steadily drunk. She'd been a small twelve but still too big for that kind of behaviour, gangly little legs up by her ears under there in the dust but she didn't care, let them drag her out.

She'd heard Kate calling for her, plaintive, at one point and had taken satisfaction in keeping to her hiding place. Kate had been nineteen. She had a car: she was one of them.

Evan had bumped off down the drive in the car.

God, I was a little shit. Watching Evan go, Jamie heavy against her, that was what Rose thought while also thinking how old and knackered the car looked and remembering Kate's little shiny car, one of those that looks like it's a toy with big goggling headlights and a jaunty rear end. The car bumping away from her now down the road was about fifteen years old, a stripped-out orange estate, bare metal on the back and a scrape down one side.

She could hear the clamorous rush of the water, beyond the bins and shed and tangle of undergrowth that enclosed the yard. Jamie looked asleep when she squinted down at him: he *felt* asleep, inert as a sandbag, but when she'd made a move to lower him into the cot – Evan had showed her where that was, a room on the corner of the house opposite to hers containing the cot, a chest of drawers and a narrow bed that was obviously being slept in – he had stiffened immediately and clung with that monkey instinct.

Evan had shrugged apologetically. 'He doesn't like to be left,' he said. But he made no move to help her.

'That seems natural,' she'd said, settling him back against her again (his eyes drooping immediately shut, his thumb planted back in his mouth) while also wondering how – when, *if* – she would be able to get to the loo again, or make a cup of tea. If there *was* any tea.

He was going to get Serena, he said, then he'd take her on to the site for a bit and they'd be back for lunch.

Serena, twelve years old. Rose's age when— Jamie sagging against her was one thing, somehow Jamie seemed to know her already. But an angry girl on the verge of adolescence – well, that was karma and no mistake. Rose sighed and – reaching under Jamie's warm weight with difficulty – felt in her pocket for her mobile. She'd dug out her charger to boost it but still no signal.

The air was cool and damp: she'd turned back at the door in search of something to wrap Jamie in, and found a little padded coat hanging just inside that she tucked around him and stepped outside. There were birds too, somewhere, in the big clump of trees into which the orange car had disappeared. A fresh wind was coming at her round the side of the house and hoisting Jamie higher, her feet bare in a pair of wellingtons – Kate's flowered ones that had been sitting by the back door, still with the traces of dried mud of a last walk – tentatively Rose set off to explore. She skirted the house, passing the short drive that had led off the bumpy track.

They had come over a bridge last night – that wasn't her imagination. A little abbreviated bridge, with a mud and reeds under it, a bit of bubbled brown water swirling: she wondered if that was what Evan had meant by the tide coming up. Rose had no clue what high tide would look like, she wasn't a country person, she'd never lived by the sea. Beyond the little — what was it, a moat? — stood a blank, windowless brick building with chained double doors whose purpose was unclear, some kind of machine house perhaps, connected to the water board. Was it even worth it? Trying to get to know stuff?

Rose had never been in a place like this before. The big old house in its time warp, untouched, unmodernised: it did seem as though before Kate and Evan came to reclaim it it might even have been abandoned. Built for a church that no longer existed, surrounded by water, by the silvery uncertain colours of a mud and sea and sky, a mirage, on the edge of the world.

She could ask Evan, but there were too many questions. And he seemed so far to be a man of few words: she couldn't tell if that would change. Grief battened you down, she knew that much. You needed time.

Rose skirted the grey brick flank of the house, a patch of scrubby grass, the corner of an overgrown veranda and then — oh, then. Then she saw it, saw why Kate had come, and willingly, not just for the strange bleak otherworldly marsh stretching to the horizon, not for the fresh wet air and the wide white sky because you needed protection from those things, and here it was.

The house stood in front of her square and beautiful, tilting a bit but somehow nobler, more likeable for that, battered but still standing. The windows were long and lovely, five across the top, french windows to either side of the front door. The old white veranda ran the whole width of the frontage, red tile cracked and rippling under it and the big twisted grey trunk of a wisteria climbing in and out of the wrought iron.

38

Stepping back on the uneven spongy lawn Rose made a sound under her breath, of wonder, and stumbled. Against her Jamie jerked awake.

'Be – be – be,' he said, gesturing, one cheek pink where it had rested against her, a tuft of hair sticking up wild from his round golden forehead. He set his head on one side, examining her.

'Breakfast?' guessed Rose, and he looked at her wonderingly, as if there was something in her voice he knew.

The front door wouldn't budge. It might be locked but it was certainly swollen beyond opening in its frame, so Rose went back round to the yard, and the low kitchen door.

In the kitchen she set him gingerly in the high chair, which he seemed to accept, though his eyes followed her unwaveringly. She opened the fridge and recoiled: it smelled stale, old. A tub of low-fat spread, a cracked piece of cheese in greaseproof paper, an open packet of ham, the meat's edges curling inside the plastic, some yellowing broccoli. Rose got out a carton of milk that seemed at least to be within its sell-by date, sniffed it warily and decided it was acceptable.

Rose closed the fridge door and there was Jamie, still looking at her steadily. When he saw the milk he began to bounce in the little high chair vigorously, one arm raised, one finger pointing. A cupboard: containing tins and jars, and two packets of Weetabix. Right.

Rose found a bowl in a pile on the draining board, fished out a little plastic spoon with a bear on it from a tangle of cutlery. Jamie watched her expectantly as she put a Weetabix in the bowl: she reached for another, and he smiled and bounced. It seemed to be a game: but when she raised a spoon to his mouth he turned his head away. A game she didn't know – and for a second Rose felt an abrupt ebbing of the energy that had got her this far, on the aeroplane, down the bumpy road, into the strange bed and out of it again.

'I don't know how to play,' Rose murmured, through gritted teeth and she saw his eyes uncertain, his face just on the edge of crumpling, his mouth beginning to turn down, and she jumped up, to avert it. Looked around the room, saw a jar full of implements, bread knife, potato masher, wooden spoon.

She held it out to him and he took it without hesitation. Wooden spoon. It might not be exactly the usual game – but it was a game. He brought it down on the table and she slipped a spoon of mush between his lips. For a second he stiffened, contemplating outrage, but then the wooden spoon came down again. Despite herself Rose smiled, he swallowed.

After about half the mush had gone down he reached for the teaspoon and she gave it to him with relief, and rose to put on the kettle. The room had warmed up, the big stove was cold but the sun was higher in the long window and it shone pale on the cluttered table.

As the kettle boiled Rose began with the washing up. Located a dishwasher, stacked it with what she could from the sink, ran a bowl of hot water that set pipes clanking and groaning, located plate cupboards, cutlery drawer, bins. Those were behind a door that led into a cold window-less room with a stone floor that she worked out was some kind of larder and they at least were orderly: organic, paper, plastics, in a neat row. It made sense that someone who built eco-houses would pay attention to his recycling. But the rest of it? The sink piled with dishes, the crumbs on the surfaces? Something hovered, ominous, like a shadow in the corner of her eye that disappeared when she turned to look at it.

In his chair Jamie babbled to himself, but he didn't cry.

Ignoring the sense that she was out of her depth, Rose found rubber gloves under the sink, and as she pulled them on she became aware of Jamie pausing in his industrious mess, of his eyes on her, that look again, as if he recognised something.

What must he be thinking? Did he think his mother was hiding somewhere, did he think she'd come back? She tried not to think of the last days. Of Kate lying in a bed in a bedroom Rose hadn't yet seen and was not sure she did want to see.

Teabags? She peered into a cupboard and a stack of Kate's crockery, at least, a whole dinner service of Cornishware, that blue-and-white striped stuff she had loved and had always displayed proudly. Rose straightened and looked around, because a big kitchen like this could have a dresser. Should have. She'd have thought it would be the first thing Kate would have done.

'Tea?' she said to him, and he tipped his head to one side, pointing at the kettle. 'Clever boy,' she said, and lifted the mug, but he just bounced and grinned.

Moving aside some baking trays to get to the back of a dusty half-empty cupboard under the window, she saw it. Kate's tea caddy and the sight of the little red-and-yellow tin, which she remembered Kate finding at some bric-a-brac stall years ago, a little tin with a black-and-white cartoon cat on it – stopped her in her tracks. She sank down on the floor, hugging it. *Kate*, she whispered to herself, *Kate. Where have you gone?*

From where she sat she could see Jamie's little round legs swinging beneath the table. She twisted the lid of the caddy: it stuck, the old tin must be rusted, but with an effort, Jamie's eyes curious on her, his hands reaching impatiently for it, she felt it loosen.

She'd registered, if she thought about it, that what was inside didn't feel like tea leaves nor bags, it had been something more solid, something that bumped. Perplexed, wondering only where the teabags *were* if not here, she peered down into the little tin.

It was hard to get her fingers inside, the opening was smaller than the tin: Rose turned it upside down and shook. *Was it – was it—* she'd seen a tight roll of something.

She stared, and the sound of rushing filled her ears, the water through the weir that she still hadn't seen, or her own blood drumming.

It was money.

Chapter Six

From Rose's earliest memories of her, Kate had been good with money. Interested in it. She liked piling up pennies. Dad had a drawer where he used to chuck his change, carelessly, and Kate would retrieve it. If jars filled up with change she would snaffle them. Rose remembered sitting beside her in her room as patiently she counted and sorted.

Kate had always had a post office account: Saturday mornings Rose would tag along with her, she'd have been just starting at school and Kate twelve or so and already the instructor, the teacher, together they would go along with Kate's haul – of pocket money, scavenged change, then once she was fourteen the earnings from her paper round, Saturday job. She would watch as Kate passed it across the counter and remembered thinking even then. The postmistress approved of her, wholeheartedly; so did Mum.

Dad was wary round Kate, always had been even when

Mum was alive, as if he knew his older daughter was on to him, and after Mum died he avoided her, he even went so far as to refuse to answer the door to her when she buzzed round in her little car, already in her first job, already renting. Rose remembered him trying to borrow money from Kate the first time he was laid off: he only tried once. Remembered hiding in her room as she listened to the conversation at the foot of the stairs because he had let her in that time, just not past the doormat. Hiding in an agony of wanting Kate to give him it so the argument would stop and at the same time wanting her to stand up to him. Kate had stood up to him.

Kate had asked him to let Rose live with her right after Mum died and he'd refused. Why hadn't she just left? She should have done. She should have left him there to drink himself to death on his own: as it was, she'd counted the days till she was grown up and then a couple of years later he was dead. Kate and her flat, bought – she'd let slip in an unguarded moment – in the hopes of Rose coming to live with her, or just – hastily covering up the slip – just, you know, a back-up plan, in case.

Rose had never gone to live with her, beyond the odd night in university holidays. It had worked too well, Kate's shepherding and sheltering and subsidising: Rose had been all too keen to shrug it all off and run away.

They'd sold the house. Rose had come back from Paris and poked through the remains of their childhood. It hadn't been worth much, an ex-council, two up, two down was all Dad had ever managed and the mortgage, they discovered after his death, had been interest only.

Kate had fussed over that too, angry at his fecklessness, *Who gets an interest only mortgage*, angry that he hadn't cared enough to leave them anything. That had been the cracks between them. 'It's only money,' Rose had said and Kate had turned on her, eyes flashing, as if she'd been insulted.

Deep down, Rose knew money mattered. It did. And she knew, she knew now at any rate if she hadn't before, that she could only turn her nose up at money while Kate was there, safe and clever and responsible.

By the time Rose heard the sound of the car bumping back down the track, she'd been listening out for it for at least an hour.

Jamie was asleep when she heard it: he'd been off for ages. Rose had seen a grubby off-road buggy leaning in the boiler room and strapped him in, on some vague idea that this sent small children off. All the time she kept thinking, *if Kate was here*. If Kate was there she'd have given Rose every tiny detail of Jamie's routine, nothing would have been left to chance. Evan had told her almost nothing.

It started well: he'd strained towards the buggy when Rose carried him in there in search of it but when she set him down and tried to strap him in he strained just as hard to escape. She pushed him, yelling and struggling against the straps, over the little bridge. There Rose hesitated: there was the sound of the weir one way, and in the other direction the outside world. She chose the outside world.

After about fifteen minutes Jamie fell asleep, tearstained, but she went on walking, thinking. If she went straight back now she wouldn't be able to think, the house would overwhelm her, its secrets, its beauty. The road was rough and potholed, the hedges fell away, she walked for more than half an hour and still there was no sign of any other habitation, nor a main road – nor a phone signal. It was more than flat, there was a sunken quality to the landscape, the ridge of a dyke rising a little way to one side, on the other the shining mud of the estuary with the rising tide tracing a snaking path in from the horizon.

The normal thing to do would have been to put the money back where she found it. The honest thing to do – but it wasn't as if Rose was going to keep the money, or spend it. It was their money, Evan's little family's money and – and.

It was Kate's money. It was so clearly, to Rose who knew Kate inside out, better than anyone, Kate's money. It was in her own little caddy, it was bound neatly in a hair elastic. Her little stash: it didn't surprise Rose that she was still doing it, partnered and settled down she may have been but Kate had always been a person of routines and habits, she had always known the right way to do things, the safe competent way. Money had got Kate out of the shit after Mum died and Dad went off the rails – Kate's money had got Rose out of the shit too, come to that.

Rose had three hundred pounds in her bank account, and that was it. Her last month's pay. The boss at the school, Carlo, had been nice enough: he liked her. He immediately told her, take time off. Till Christmas, at least and then we'll reassess. No offer of compassionate leave or pay but that didn't surprise her: it was a small operation.

The fact remained, she had barely enough money to buy a plane ticket back there.

The roll had contained five hundred and thirty pounds, mostly in small notes. Rose had taken it out of the tin and before she could think about what she was doing stashed it in the cloth tote she used as a handbag, which as she pushed Jamie was in the netting slung beneath the buggy. The air was soft and mild.

This had been Kate's life. Kate had pushed this buggy down the lane away from the house. Had she been looking for mobile signal, too? There was none. Kate had stashed money away. And as Rose put these things together she got a pulse, like a signal picked up from a faraway star. *Hello*, it said. *Hello, Rosie.*

By the time they got back to the house it was almost midday, Rose was worn out and starved. Leaving Jamie sleeping in the buggy at the back door, she went inside, stopping, turning, going back for the cloth bag. Almost immediately she was through the back door into the cluttered room where the boiler sat cold and silent, the house closed around her, not clamouring but whispering.

The kitchen cupboard where she'd found the money was still standing open and hastily she closed it. She looked around, wondering, trying to block out the house's murmur, not to hear what it might be saying. *Go away* – or *come inside*. Just a kitchen and already marginally cleaner than Evan had left it, order beginning to be restored, nothing to alarm her.

Was Evan like Dad? Rose was trying to make sense of Kate hiding money, as she had used to do from their father, so he wouldn't spend it on drink.

Here – the nearest pub must be miles and miles away, and in all the cupboards she'd opened there had been no sign of booze. In the kitchen, where the light from the long window was ebbing and the air around her turning cool, Rose turned, looking. No whisky, no gin, no wine-rack: no cans in the recycling. Unless you could suspect total abstinence – and the daughter of an alcoholic could suspect anything – Kate hadn't been hiding money to keep Evan out of the pub.

Just Kate's old frugal hoarding instincts then. Maybe. Rose kept turning, then stopped.

There was a calendar on the wall, beside the Aga: still on September and stepping up to it, turning the page to the right month on some feeble instinct for reasserting order, it occurred to Rose with a start – although it wasn't marked, of course it wasn't, women marked up calendars not men and this wasn't a date Kate would have known – her own funeral.

There was a jar of pens on the side beneath the calendar and picking one up Rose wrote the letter 'K' on the date. Hesitated, and put the pen back.

Had Evan made any arrangements, at all? Nobody had turned up, bringing casseroles, like they did when people with dependants died, nobody had called. Would people come here? People who'd known Kate: new friends, old friends. Panic jumped in Rose's chest as she contemplated the still untidy kitchen: she should have asked him. Not for the first time she felt how crap she was being, as a sister: she'd always taken the back seat, sulky, sullen, she'd always left it to Kate. Kate had organised both their parents' funerals: for Mum she'd fussed and bossed as Dad banged off the walls. For Dad she'd been colder, stiffer, but still organised. Phoning people, booking the hall, making sandwiches.

She went back out to check on Jamie and listened. The sound of the rushing water: could she hear a car? She strained, wasn't sure. Jamie'd be all right. Wouldn't he? He was small, he'd forget Kate, as long as someone – well. As long as someone took her place: Rose shrank from the idea that that someone was her. She was dreading meeting Serena.

As she stood there, something changed. The sun went, abruptly, dipping behind a big rusty-looking tree, a yew, and Rose felt a chill, and in the same moment remembered the money, in her bag, on the table and hurried back inside.

There was no sunshine in here, either, and the chill deepened. Picking the bag off the table, clutching it to herself, Rose turned to walk further into the house. If they were coming back – this was her chance, to explore.

Beyond the kitchen door was an odd dark kind of lobby, with more bells high on the wall and a green baize door. As it opened, letting a dim light in from the big dark red hall, Rose saw that there was a narrow panelled door in the wall in the in-between space: giving it a little push it opened a crack on what she saw was a back staircase, curving narrowly up, away from her, worn wooden steps, a thin iron rail running up a whitewashed wall. She let the door fall back and went on into the hall but the picture of that narrow space stayed with her, almost as if someone had sat there on the stair and looked back at her, an invitation to play hide and seek.

The green baize closed soft behind Rose, and she tiptoed on, from door to door. There was a large sitting room opening off the far side of the hall, with long windows, the light greenish and almost obscured by an overgrown climbing plant. Two old-fashioned sofas in faded loose covers, also greenish, furniture she'd never seen before. Kate had only ever lived in a one-bedroom flat, though, her stuff would have been swallowed up in a place this size.

Of course Kate wanted to come here, to run away with him. Of course. Kate must have been waiting her whole life for someone to tell her: forget patchwork and jam-making, come and live with me on the edge of the world. Of course her little sister wouldn't understand, until she did.

At the back of the hall was another big room, cavernous, heaped with shapes under dustsheets, some large canvases and a long window that might have caught the sun at this hour but it was so tightly shuttered Rose couldn't tell. Gingerly she lifted one of the dustsheets and saw Kate's old treadle sewing machine, black and gold, on its cast-iron stand: Rose set her hand against the cold metal but it told her nothing, except maybe that when you had to lug a Jamie around all day you didn't get much sewing done. She let the dustsheet drop back over it.

Retreating back into the hall, by day she could see that the old red carpet was nearly worn through: it was in shreds on one or two of the wide stairs. Rose took them two at a time, wanting to escape the dim cold of the ground floor, the shadows and dust, wanting to get some height. When she got to the top Rose could feel her heart beating fast, from the hasty climb and something else, she was aware of listening out, trying to hear over the rushing of the weir, in case the car was coming back.

It was barely warmer on the gallery: there was a draught coming in from somewhere and still no sign of sun. It seemed perverse to build a house with its back to the light for most of the day unless trees had grown up, like in *Sleeping Beauty*, to block it. Rose padded quickly to her own room, pulled out the suitcase she had not yet unpacked, got out the roll of money and stuffed it inside, down, to the back. And pushed the suitcase back under, far enough so it wasn't visible, heart thumping as she stood back up. She wouldn't think about it. What she had done. No one would know.

It was grey in the room now, not bright. The unmade bed looked cold and untidy, the little shut-up writing desk a reproach: and as she stood in the doorway the sashes of the long window overlooking the grey-green marsh rattled in the wind, and she thought of Jamie, outside. Just five minutes more. While she was alone.

The door facing hers at the far end of the gallery Rose knew was Jamie's, or Jamie's and Evan's – the nursery, she'd seen it last night. One other door, between her and Jamie. It was locked. Rose felt a curious sensation, irritation turning to something else, the sense of being unwelcome, a stranger. She wondered if Evan would have an explanation, would laugh it off. She couldn't imagine how she would put the question.

51

Unsettled, Rose made as if to go back down, then paused. The back staircase must come up, somewhere, the odd, intriguing little back staircase. But she heard the car, then, and ran.

Chapter Seven

Evan looked around at the kitchen, dazed.

'You didn't have to—' his voice cracked.

'It's no problem,' she said softly.

Jamie had still been asleep when the car pulled up: she'd stood beside him as it approached, one hand on the buggy. She could see Evan's face through the windscreen, pale and taut, as the car turned, to come over the little bridge. He looked like a man trying to overcome something, trying not to show pain. The things she needed to ask him ran in her head, and she quailed.

Beside him, as the car hit a pothole, a smaller figure jolted in the passenger seat, the oval face white and set, centre parting, staring at Rose.

'You must be Serena,' said Rose, awkwardly, as the girl climbed out, hugging a scruffy backpack covered in badges. She was slight and small for twelve, smaller than Rose remembered herself being. Her face was still a child's face, not an adolescent's, and obstinately blank in response to Rose's tentative smile. Evan was at the back of the car: when he came around it he was carrying supermarket bags. 'I'm Kate's sister Rose,' she said.

'You don't look like her,' said Serena, expressionless, holding her ground.

'Our dad always used to say I was the milkman's,' said Rose, stupidly, the joke that never was a joke was even less of one under the circumstances. Evan had been wrong, she felt dully: kids didn't lie. Serena looked up at her father as he came around the car, a mute demand in her eyes.

To cover up the moment Rose leaned down to her in a hug that was immediately awkward because Evan didn't move his hand and the girl didn't drop her backpack: brief as a result but long enough to feel how fragile the kid was, the narrow shoulders, skin and bone. And so stiff under the embrace that Rose felt herself flush as she straightened and Evan sighed and said, 'Why don't you unpack that bag, Serena?'

She ran off without a backward glance. It occurred to Rose that one of the locked rooms must have been hers.

'I'm sorry, she's—' he broke off, looking away. 'You'll have to make allowances.' He shifted, uneasy, as if there were admissions he didn't want to make.

'It's fine,' said Rose quickly, warmed by his loyal silence. 'It's horrible for her. And besides you should have seen me when I was that age.' And flushed again at the look of gratitude Evan gave her.

'I need to ask – I need to ask you about the funeral,' she said quickly.

'What about it?' he said stiffly, turning away to inspect Jamie, whose face looked pale now to Rose, his lips as colourless as his cheeks but then he gave out a little sigh and turned in the buggy, rubbing his forehead against the nylon and settled back into sleep. Reluctantly Evan looked back at Rose.

'I—' he said, agitatedly, 'I don't—' and walked past her abruptly, into the house. She followed.

'Who have you invited?' she said, to his back. 'Is it— you said the crematorium – will people be coming here afterwards? Do I need to help with – food or anything?' She hesitated. 'Drink?'

Evan stopped dead in front of her, in the kitchen and she could see where he was looking. At the calendar, as if in all the busy kitchen that was what hit him straight away: coming round him Rose saw he had turned very pale.

'I was trying to help,' she said, faltering, fumbling in her pocket for a scrap of tissue.

Overhead footsteps skittered, like a bird in the roof, or mice, and for a moment he just stared, his eyes burning black in his blue-pale, unshaven face. Then abruptly he put his hands up and the voice that came out was muffled.

'It's all right,' he said through his hands and his voice sounded so hopeless, so sad, that all the indignation, the anger, the fear Rose had been feeling evaporated. 'I'm sorry,' he said. 'I'm sorry.' He dropped his hands. 'I thought – I didn't want anyone else there at all, just the children and me, just— Then Serena made me – she said we had to.' He cleared his throat and sat at the table, pushing things aside, setting his elbows on the wood and his forehead in his hands. Tentatively Rose pulled out a chair and sat beside him.

'Sometimes I think she's still here,' he said, not looking at her. 'Sometimes I think—' and one eye blinked, then was hidden again. 'Sometimes I think if we just sit tight, she'll come back.' He sat up, put his hands flat on the table and said, 'Is it called denial? I don't want a funeral at all.'

The house was silent around them. Rose let out a long breath. 'So Serena – so you've told people.'

'They knew,' he said, shortly. 'You can't keep things quiet round here. In the town, I mean. Once the doctor – the funeral director—'

'Well, of course,' said Rose, shocked. They'd passed through the small town, the dirt road down to the house a half-mile beyond it. She remembered a dark high street, a few shop fronts, a pub. A quiet, innocuous place. 'But her friends—'

'Yes,' he passed a hand through his hair, distractedly. 'There's people coming. To the crem. I don't know how many.'

'And back here, afterwards?' She didn't know why she was pushing it, when it was obvious he would rather be dead himself: it wasn't her thing, either, not Rose's. Organising wasn't her thing, never had been. Kate would have wanted it, though. That certainty hung there, between them: she didn't need to say it. If Evan knew Kate like she did—

'I suppose so,' he said, dully. He did know, then.

He gestured at the bulging supermarket bags on the floor. 'Serena made me buy a whole lot of stuff,' he said, frowning fiercely downwards. 'I don't know what the hell to do with it.'

Rose swallowed. 'Leave it to me,' she said.

There'll be lunches, on the grass, under the big walnut tree. Like abroad, like in summer, like on holiday. Long tables, an old white tablecloth, glasses and silver and a napkin by each place, roses in pressed glass vases. Lettuce from the garden, strawberries and cream.

People will come, the distance won't matter to them after the first time. Friends will come. They'll bump down the lane complaining about coming to the ends of the Earth but when they see it they'll gasp. The magic of the tide coming up and almost cutting us off, the flowerbeds overflowing, lavender and jasmine and herbs, wicker chairs on the veranda. They'll take photographs, they'll tell people about it. *Kate and Evan's place, what a house, what a setting.*

And Serena helping, because she'll come round, she'll stop hating me. Jamie carrying chairs out, when he's big enough. He's strong already, I can feel him struggling. Getting too strong for me.

Of course they'll come, Evan says, pulling me close to him, *of course they'll come, if you want them. But I only need you.*

Chapter Eight

He mentioned it the next day, as Rose was about to go to bed. After a day spent gingerly going through the motions, establishing some kind of delicate balance under whose influence they could all pretend a terrible thing hadn't happened. A day being nice.

In the morning, after she'd heard Evan take Jamie downstairs Rose had tiptoed along the gallery, past the wide staircase. The door next to hers was Serena's, she knew that now, because Serena had banged the door shut on her last night. The next one was still locked. And opposite it where the gallery turned and ended was the narrow door half hidden in panelling, to the back staircase. Then Evan had called up to her and she had had to hurry downstairs.

The afternoon had passed in a blur. Lunch had been bread and cheese in a space cleared on the cluttered table, eaten hastily while Jamie slept on outside, under the walnut tree. Serena had sidled up, hovering at the table, seizing a plate as if planning to make away with it, saying something about schoolwork but Evan had stopped her, she heard a whispered, weary plea from him and after a sulky glance Serena sat. She nibbled, head down over her food, for five minutes then was off again, the green baize door closing behind her with its soft whump.

'Has she been off school for—'

'Since Kate died,' said Evan, pale-faced, standing to clear the plates. 'I'll do that,' she said gently, reaching for them.

The whole meal had taken less than ten minutes. This wouldn't do, would it? And again Rose had that sense of Kate stirring in her, Kate's determination to get started on a project, her no-nonsense. 'I remember—' and Rose hesitated again, the stack of plates in her arms. 'Being that age. Everyone seems against you.' She said, 'I don't know if you know but – I was her age when our mum died.'

Rose wished she hadn't said it: *me, me, me. It's not about you.* She blundered on. 'I just wanted to get on with my life, you know, back to my mates, back to normal life.' *Normal life*, she thought, as if she didn't know what the words meant.

'Yes.' He was avoiding her eye. 'But she's—' his voice was low, indistinct, 'she seems almost – vindictive. I know children can – that grief can show itself in complicated ways. But she seems – sometimes I think she's glad Kate's dead.' He glanced up at her from under fierce brows and she was struck by how helpless he seemed.

'No,' Rose said, almost in a whisper, faltering. Cleared her throat. 'I – it can look like that,' she said. 'It can seem like anger. She feels – abandoned.'

Evan searched her face. 'Do you think so?' he said, and she heard the need in his voice. 'I just – I don't want school psychologists on at her. Teachers, you know. Misunderstanding her.'

'I get that,' she said, with feeling, remembering. Those curious looks, the pity in a school nurse's eyes that had made her want to smash things.

'She's agreed, anyway.' He sounded worn out. 'She'll go back after the funeral.'

'I'm not telling you what to do, Evan,' said Rose gently, noticing that the dark blue sweater he was wearing was frayed at the cuffs, like a nervous, nail-biting child's.

'It's OK,' he said, rubbing his high forehead, brown from the sun. 'I wish somebody *would* tell me what to do.'

And then Jamie had woken up, and by the time she got back into the kitchen with him – red-cheeked and furious from finding himself strapped down – Evan was nowhere to be seen. Telling herself it was good he trusted her on her own with Jamie, Rose started all over again. Finding somewhere to park him, trying to tidy – the plates she'd begun to clear were still sitting there on the table – hunting down the baby food she'd found while unpacking the supermarket bags. She found herself muttering to Kate, in her head. *How the hell. How the hell.*

Kate would have managed this, wouldn't she? But then she'd got ill. It was hard enough when you were fit and healthy. The thought was so awful, of Kate, struggling, that Rose had to push it out of her mind. For a moment she glimpsed her old life, Rome, the neat little bedsit, the view of pines, the sound of scooters, the dirt and noise and it seemed like a faded photograph from someone else's life. She got a damp cloth, and a spoon, and sat. Jamie grinned.

She could hear them, upstairs, as she spooned the baby food into him, a tussle of some kind. Voices not raised – but insistent. When Jamie started to turn his face away Rose, unable to ignore the muttered conversation, stepped out into the corridor, on bare feet. Down the narrow space and into the wide, lofty, dim hall, a green gleam leaking in through the curved windowlight over the door. The smell of damp and salt and musty hangings.

And then there was the bang of a door and footsteps and she had flown back, to find Jamie trying to lever himself out of the chair.

In her arms he struggled, then turning himself into a dead weight, arms up over his head, insisting on being lowered to the floor.

Jamie could walk. Stupidly, that hadn't occurred to her, but as he set off for the door it was incontrovertible. Not even tottering, running, heedless of obstacles as Rose tried to catch up so that, mercifully, he fell at the first hurdle which was a still full bag of shopping. She swept him up and carried him back outside. There was grass there.

It had been a nice afternoon, mild and still, a kind of warm haze over everything as though pollen was floating in the air. She'd set him down and lain back: silence except for the rushing of water. Rose closed her eyes for a second – no more, before the meaning of the sound had her jerked upright, and there he was, heading for the reeds. *Jesus.* Surrounded by water: every mother's worst nightmare.

61

Running, grabbing, turning – and there was Evan coming round the house.

After that, she'd stayed inside, in the dim green sitting room where a pile of toys sat behind one of the sofas. Door closed. Jamie didn't seem discontented by his confinement but he had stood a long time at the long french window, hands smearing the glass. Serena, coming in wordless, had relieved her at around six, swinging Jamie effortlessly on to her hip and laughing into his face. Ignoring Rose.

She'd come out into the hall almost gasping with her freedom, and wanting to be outside again. The big front door didn't open from the inside, either, wedged solid with the damp. Evan was in the kitchen, chopping something: he had said, rather grimly, that he would cook.

'Can I— do you need a hand?' she said, reluctantly. Was this how the days would go? No. Evan would go back to work, Serena would go back to school. She would be here alone. She pushed that image away, too: there was no point, absolutely no point in mapping it all out, planning her escape already. And anyway – none of them knew how things would pan out. One day at a time.

Was that how Kate had got through the days? Feeling – whatever she had been feeling. Rose imagined a deep pain, a twisting, a nagging pain, she visualised the tumour and her hand went down there, into the tender hollow below her hipbone. Ovarian cancer: one of the silent ones. The silent killer. Had Kate told herself, you've pulled a muscle?

'Evan?' she said, patiently.

After a moment's thought, a blank look, Evan smiled,

a thin sort of smile. 'No, thanks,' he said. She bobbed an awkward goodbye and left.

Once outside Rose walked the perimeter of the garden, barefoot, to get the measure of the water. It was tricky to gauge: water seemed to be everywhere. Where there had just been a muddy puddle under the bridge was now a widening greyish pool, popping with bubbles on the edge. There was a large lawn in front of the house, roughly square with a stone sundial at the centre, along its edges a couple of scrubby bushes, some dug flowerbeds – but when Rose came close it was obvious the water had made inroads here, too. Saltwater: some of the plants were blistered and stunted, some of the bulbs had been dislodged, sucked out by a high tide she supposed although she couldn't see those waters now, only sedge and sea-lavender beyond the flowerbed.

There were tall pale rustling reeds along one edge of the lawn, the longest edge, exactly the direction in which Jamie had run the moment she set him down. Coming close to the rushes Rose could feel it underfoot, cold mud squeezing between her toes, and she took a step forward, unsteady, parting the tall stems. More water than mud, rising to her ankles, but another step and she could see what she already knew was there, the creek running beyond the reedy border. A gleaming bank of mud and what had looked like a trickle from her window as the sun came up was a broad brown stream now, flowing steadily and silently. She could see where it ran past the side of the house and disappeared into a thicket, towards the roar and rush of the weir. She backed out of the reeds, grateful to feel the grass and something firm under her feet.

Rose could see now that there were iron railings between the side of the house and the river, at least, although what good they were against a high tide or an ingenious toddler, she didn't know.

And there was the house facing her, its eyes the tall elegant windows, with the paint flaking from their fine glazing bars, and again she felt what Kate must have felt, seeing it, wanting it, whenever *it* had been – she hadn't told Rose about it, by then they'd been barely communicating – that they'd come to view. Rose only knew when the little change of address card arrived, a year ago: she should have phoned, she should have texted, asking to visit, to come and look over this place – but she hadn't. And Kate hadn't invited her.

But Rose could imagine it, Kate – lover of history, of rolltop desks and dressers and Agas, nooks and crannies and secrets and gardens and challenges – standing here where Rose stood now, thinking of the Victorian rector walking to a long-gone church, the tide sucking at its foot – and his wife in rustling crinolines. There must have been a moment when Kate realised the challenge was too much, it was too big, too strange – and she was too sick.

The misery, never far away, stirred, and under it, the questions. How could this have happened? Why had she gone quiet?

As the windows looked back at her, their dark panes silvered with the sky's pale reflection Rose had the weirdest sense that this house had done it to her, it was somehow envious, malicious – and then she stumbled, heard herself make a sound because someone moved, behind the glass.

Oh – there were two faces, one above the other, like a little totem in a downstairs window. For a moment she didn't know them, they were strangers, and then she did. Jamie, his little white starfish hands flat on the pane and above him the pale watchful oval of Serena's face. Her eyebrows were dark and precise like her father's. She hurried, ungainly, towards them, making herself smile and thinking, why did they come here? Why didn't Kate think of the dangers?

At the window Jamie had begun to smack his little palms against the glass: from above him Serena, unsmiling, leaned down to grasp his wrists.

What she hadn't thought about were the long, long hours to fill. She had an idea. 'Should I give him a bath, maybe?'

They were in the green sitting room, her and Serena and Jamie. But given her determined ignorance of little kids and the shock of the burden already that Jamie represented, even when things evened out and the funeral was over – Rose was surprised to find she didn't resent him at all. In fact when she thought about the room without him – the house, the *family* – without him she felt a sudden sharp sensation almost like fear and stepped quickly over to him, leaning down to pick him up, to feel his wriggling weight. She could feel Serena's eyes on her, contemptuous.

It was almost seven. Evan had lugged in a sack of some kind of fuel for the Aga, like fat pellets.

'Does your dad like cooking?' she said, hugging Jamie against her. He writhed. Serena shrugged.

'Well, he had to,' she said. 'You know.' Her mouth in a line. She was a beautiful kid, thought Rose, even sulky as she was, hostile as she was. Her face perfectly symmetrical, her eyebrows dark fine arches, her skin a kind of creamy olive colour.

'Yes,' said Rose, then, on impulse, she said, 'Does your mum – do you—'

Do you see your mum?

But she didn't get that far. Serena's eyes grew huge and black, a peat stream, her face like stone. 'Don't you, don't you—' her voice was choked, and Rose couldn't tell if she was angry or upset or what but hastened, trying to put it right.

'I'm – it's none of my business—' she saw Serena was trembling and moved towards her, awkward with Jamie in her arms, tried to free an arm to put around her but Serena only stepped abruptly away from her and they both stopped, a foot apart. 'I'm sorry, Serena,' Rose said, trying to make her voice soft, to brush it all away, 'I'm sorry.' Gave her a quick pat on the shoulder. 'Maybe you could introduce me to the bathroom?' Meaning, a room with a bath: the one Evan had indicated the night before had been a loo.

Serena stomped ahead of her up the wide stairs and shoved the door at the top of them open, standing back. A big tub, streaked with rust and limescale but clean, stood in the middle of a room with bare boards and another of those long windows. There was a sort of sideboard with a stack of what she assumed were nappies, and a changing mat on it.

'You can't fill the bath more than this high,' Serena said, stepping over to it to indicate six inches or so, 'it goes cold after that,' and Rose's heart sank. She loved a bath as much as the next girl who'd spent three years marooned in a foreign country with only showers, but she didn't love sitting in just six inches of water.

'Thanks,' she said, but Serena was gone.

There was a towel – but it occurred to her she should find something for Jamie to wear after it. Rose set Jamie down and immediately he tottered to the bath's edge and began to slap his small hands on it. Hurrying along the landing to Jamie's room she could hear them arguing again. The sound was muffled by the green baize door that divided the kitchen from the rest of the house but she could hear small tight angry sobs.

Oh shit, Rose thought, stopping in the doorway, *her mother's dead, isn't she? That's it.* They must have assumed she knew. Maybe Kate had told her, and she'd not listened to any of it, not the detail of how they met or how she fell in love – especially not that. *Miserable little sod, you are.*

There was a small chest of drawers in the room: the first drawer she opened, though, contained adult clothes, Evan's, tidily put away. A big jersey: she could smell him on it; a smell of leaves, the outside, wood fires. The realisation made her stiffen, guilty although at what she wasn't quite sure – at her own nosiness. She pushed it hastily closed again and found Jamie's things in the next one down, a stack of vests, little trousers, pyjamas, neat and ironed. It occurred to Rose that Evan must have had him in the same clothes for days because Kate must have done this, it was Kate all over. Colour co-ordinated, even, sleeves

67

folded underneath and a sweet, cosy smell. Kate's smell: the washing liquid she'd always used, since year dot. Rose found herself kneeling, bowed over the open drawer, she lowered her face a second to the pile and breathed it in then started back embarrassed, because what if someone came in?

Because if someone came in they would only think – only think Rose was grieving? Or an old maid stealing someone else's life, her child. Rose didn't know what Kate had said about her to Evan. Shaking her head over her thoughtlessness, and how she would end her days alone. And she didn't know why she wanted to bury her face in the little pile of wool and cotton. There was a shriek from along the landing and she grabbed some garments at random and hurried back but at the sight of her he grinned as if he'd played a trick on her, and sat down with a squelch on his padded backside.

It turned out to be a good idea. Jamie was clean – she'd never changed a nappy before but at least there were some disposables as well as the stack of cloth ones – and just about buttoned into pyjamas and by the time she got to the foot of the stairs, he was falling asleep on her shoulder. The kitchen was warm – much warmer than upstairs – the table had been cleared and laid with the blue-and-white plates and Serena was sitting at it, bowed over a book.

'I could have done that,' said Evan, turning at the stove, an anxious line between his brows. The air smelled of unfamiliar spices, something musky and middle eastern.

'Well, you were busy,' said Rose, smiling. Serena's head didn't move, but she didn't turn a page, either. 'That smells nice?' she ventured, and hurried on, 'It's good for us to get used to each other, anyway.' Realising as she said it that the time she would stay was extending, out of sight. She sat down carefully, so as not to wake Jamie and Serena's head jerked up.

'You should put him down,' she instructed.

'In a minute,' said Evan, gently. 'I'll take him in a minute.'

The cast iron pot was set on the table, Jamie was taken from her by Evan and it was just her and Serena. Serena looking at her across the table with a steady contempt. 'What are you reading?' Rose asked: Serena tipped the book's cover up to show her and she was startled to recognise it as hers, a book that had sat on her own childhood shelf and – she thought – Mum's before her. An old book about growing up a girl, a cloth spine.

'That's—' Kate must have given it to her to read because it was inconceivable that Evan had – or perhaps Serena had sought it out herself – and Rose felt the budding of a tear, hot in the corner of her eye.

'It's only because there's no internet,' said Serena, holding her gaze and the sensation receded.

With a shock Rose realised that she hadn't even asked about internet. Something about the house, about Evan, had forbidden it. 'But how do you—' puzzled. 'How do you do your homework, that kind of thing?' She felt Serena's beady black eyes on her, almost merry now, almost enjoying her tripping over herself for not wanting to do the wrong thing. From upstairs came a small wail, then silence. 'I mean, isn't it all online these days?'

'I download things at school or ask for printouts,' said Serena, something hasty about her response, about the glance flicked to the green baize door.

'Dad talked to them about it, how it wasn't right that everyone had to have internet. And there *is* internet, actually. It's just . . .' and she drew herself up stiffly, lips in a tight line, and said, '. . . it's better not to have it on all the time. *Kate* said that. Dad says that and I agree with him.' Head up, insufferable. But it was the first time she'd used Kate's name. 'So he turns it off.'

Rose was thinking. Wondering. Did that sound like Kate? She had never been anti-internet, a real pro at Facebook, at the beginning, anyway. Maybe it was Evan, he'd converted her. Certainly Rose didn't want to get her phone out in front of him, let alone to ask like a sulky teenager how she was expected to log on. If she knew where the router was, she could – when everyone was out she could – but she stopped herself. This wasn't her house, not her rules.

'Yes,' said Rose. 'He's probably right. Kate was right.' She swallowed. 'It was your idea, your dad told me,' she said, 'to have people back here, after the funeral.'

Serena flushed, pinpoints of colour. 'So,' she said. 'So what? You have to do it. Dad's just—' and then they heard him coming along the corridor and she clamped her mouth shut.

The meal was eaten in silence, except for Rose's inquiries about Jamie, and his routine, and getting him to sleep, answered in monosyllables by Evan. The food was unfamiliar, but good. Couscous or some kind of grain like that, with peppers and cinnamon and cheese crumbled on top of it: covertly Rose eyed Serena for disobedience but she ate doggedly, head down. But then Evan rose to stack the plates, and Serena scraped back her chair, grabbed her book and stalked off, her departure unremarked except for a clenching of Evan's jaw that Rose just caught as she got to her feet to give him a hand.

There were pans too big for the dishwasher and Evan stood helpless now with one in his hands; over the drying rack lay a pair of stiffened rubber gloves, their yellow mildewing. 'I'll do it,' she said, picking up the gloves. Kate's gloves. She saw his eyes on them, she felt his stillness beside her. She put a hand to his arm tentatively.

'I – I—' she heard his voice shake, she felt him stiffen under her touch, and she took her hand away. 'I'm sorry,' she said again. 'I'm sorry, I just want to do her justice. To do things the way she would have wanted them done. We'll – we'll get through it.'

He turned his face to her then, the dark eyes that turned down at the corners, his hair unruly, and she had the impression for a fleeting second that he wanted to touch her, she wasn't sure how, to put his head on her shoulder. But then the moment was gone.

'Thank you,' he said, with a smile that trembled. And then a sigh that filled his chest. They washed up together in silence, Evan at the sink and Rose drying, trying not to think of going to bed, another night, another day.

'I think I'll turn in,' she said, at the green baize door when they were done. It was not even nine o'clock. Evan nodded.

'I'll—' he looked around vaguely, 'I'll listen to the news,' he said, 'or something.' She saw the hollows under his eyes, and knew he wouldn't go to bed for hours, wouldn't sleep. She turned to go and he said something

71

else after her, something she thought was, *you can go and see her.*

Rose turned back. 'Serena?' she said, not understanding. And he was a ghost himself in that moment, looking back at her, a dark lost creature, hands helpless at his sides.

'Kate,' he said. 'You can go and see her.' With a shock Rose felt a prickle at the back of her neck, she felt her mouth open. 'In the funeral parlour,' he said, and there was something like a plea in his voice, a longing. 'I – I—'

'I can—' Rose couldn't complete the sentence.

'You can view the body,' his eyes held hers, lost. 'Tomorrow. They say you can view the body.'

'I'd like to do that,' she found herself saying, 'Goodnight, then,' pushing the door open and walking into the dark red-carpeted corridor before she could change her mind. Closing the door to her room carefully behind her, something brushed against Rose, her cheek, her hand, and in the dim room she paused a second, breathing the ghost of an old familiar scent. She felt her mouth open and then she realised it was the dress and quickly she turned away, into the room.

In the night she heard someone cry out, but when she roused herself, startled in the dark strange room, it was quiet again. It took her some time to get back to sleep.

Chapter Nine

I do, I want to be a writer. Doesn't everyone? Make the story that your life should be, dish the dirt, or just share it all, what you see through your window. I see the dark tree where the bird sits making its nest, I see the brown water of the estuary, I see the cracks, down there in the red tile under the veranda.

When we came to see the house I wanted to sit on that veranda, I was going to work on that front door till it opened and I would take my breakfast out there, a little coffee pot, a warm roll with marmalade, rain or shine. Serena would smile at me. I didn't know it would be neither rain nor shine most of the time but cloud and mist, the sea fog rolling in over the marsh, nothing visible beyond the brown tips of the rushes.

But begin at the beginning. If you know where that is, of course. When you sit down to write so many complications appear, like knowing where you came from or where you're going, let alone what it is you want to say.

Love, of course. I would write love stories, and I think

Rose would laugh, which is why I wouldn't show them to her: Rose isn't always kind, you see. She gets her own back for never being the first one by being cruel whenever she can. Is that true? I don't know if it is. She just hasn't grown up enough yet, she's thoughtless. I could tell her, love stories make the world go round. There's a market for them. And she'd sulk, because she'd know I was right.

When she comes, I'll show her my stories.

Rose decided I was not the love type a long time ago, because I was the mum type: maybe I was, even when I thought I'd never be one, that no one would see me like that. There was no one for me because I was too sensible, too careful, too self-reliant. *See, Rose! I stopped being so careful and there he was.*

We met on a fun run. *You can't put that in a story*, she jeers at me, I can just hear her. *What, with pink tabards and lycra?* Well, then, Rose it can be a diary, instead. A charity run, for cancer. He was there because of his wife, I was there because of Mum. You have to love a man in a pink tabard: he didn't seem to care. His trainers were very old and he looked like no one looked after him but he was doing his best.

Serena was there too. Standing at the finish line. I can't remember now, if she was all alone.

Rose stood on the pavement in the morning chill and looked. MARSHALL AND DAUGHTERS, FUNERAL DIRECTORS. It was on a side road to Heydon's High Street, next door to a charity shop. All funeral parlours looked like this: black-and-gold Victorian signage, a dusty window containing an urn and some plastic flowers. There was no call to modernise this business. It wasn't going to go online, after all.

74

Why was Kate in there? It was all wrong.

The heavy bicycle was parked round the corner, chained to a lamp post: Heydon was too old-fashioned for bike racks. Evan had been apologetic, but he needed the car, he was going into work. The bicycle had been in an outhouse, a big shed under trees alongside the water: it had one of those child-carrying boxes on the front. Not just the bicycle, either: a workbench on one side but on the other, as Rose's eyes grew accustomed to the light, she saw things she recognised. A wardrobe that had come from Dad's house, an old brass bed Kate had bought with practically her first pay packet. Boxes: one of them open, revealing books, their pages curling in the damp.

'I know,' Evan had said, his voice coming from behind her in the doorway. 'I know. We had such plans for this place. And in the end, what with Jamie, we hardly got around to unpacking.' He looked around helplessly. 'I don't know what to do next,' he said, in a voice so low she hardly heard it. 'All her stuff.'

She wheeled the bicycle out: it needed oiling, the chain was stiff with rust. Kate can't have been on it for months. 'How— those last months,' she tried, but the face he turned to her was so full of pain she stopped.

Breakfast had been toast and the dregs of marmalade from an ancient jar, Serena spooning cereal into her mouth hurriedly as if someone might take it away from her. She was skinny, all elbows and knees: Rose noticed that the book was still there, at her elbow. Jamie truculent, shoving away the bowl Evan put in front of him, rubbing his eyes with grubby fists.

'Did I— did he wake up last night?' she said. Serena's

head bobbing up then down, taking the book back on to her lap and silently slipping away again, the shush of the heavy door closing behind her. Rose watched her go, wondering. 'I thought I heard him.'

Evan sighed. 'Sorry,' he said, 'he's pretty good usually.'

'No, I—' she felt herself flush. 'He didn't disturb me.'

Rose had woken to a quiet house. Padding along the gallery, pausing to listen at Jamie's door, she had found herself at the back staircase. *Why not*, she thought, *why not?* And pushed the little door open.

It must have been a service staircase, although it was so narrow it was hard to imagine a tray being carried up it; Rose wondered why neither Evan nor Serena had mentioned it, unless it was too impractical, or dangerous – or perhaps it was one of those oddities in a house you just forgot about when you didn't use it. It didn't feel dangerous, exactly, although the wood was smooth with age, it was so tight a space that it would be hard to fall, in fact, but halfway down Rose found herself stopping, with the weirdest feeling that she wasn't alone, as if she'd heard something, in case someone might murmur to her, Kate walking down behind her, her hand brushing the faded peeling floral of the Victorian wallpaper. *Rose, Rosie-posie. Keep going.*

She hadn't been at all frightened: in fact when she got to the bottom and the narrow door let her out into that space between the green baize door and the kitchen she had wanted to turn around and go back inside, to listen, and hide. But instead she had gone into the kitchen, where light shone through the long window.

The shopping Evan and Serena had done the day after

Rose arrived had been haphazard, pretty much what Rose would have expected of a distraught man and a twelve-year-old girl – other than the absence of booze, that was. Crisps, Coco Pops, carrots, hummus, a sliced loaf. She was looking for coffee: she hadn't had any, she realised, since leaving Italy and she could feel the lack of it, after the disturbed night, in a tight little headache setting up, for the day.

Feeling the lack of coffee – they didn't drink it, Evan had told her, apologetic, when he found her opening cupboards – Rose had said perhaps she could buy some in town, which was when he told her he needed the car.

'You're going to work?' Rose said, taken aback. Then, dubiously, 'What about— I can take the – well, I could take Jamie with me, at least.'

Evan's face was pained, set. 'To the funeral parlour?' He shook his head, frowning. 'It's all right. I can take them both in with me for a bit. You can't be our slave, Rose.'

Rose didn't know if he'd called her by her name before. 'It's fine—' she tried, but he was firm.

'I can take them in, after all, I'm the boss,' he said, wearily. 'Really, it's OK, they're not your children.' Seeing her face perhaps, he said, 'I mean, I'm so grateful for – but they're not your responsibility.'

'Your business, it's eco-houses?' she said, wanting to stop his apologies, and he brightened, at last. She'd seen some brochures on the side when she'd been trying to clear the table, the night before, a line of austere wood-lapped buildings on the edge of marshland.

'That's what they call them,' he said. 'It's more compli-cated than that really, but yes. Carbon neutral sustainable housing. Alternative heating and power sources.' He reached for one of the brochures then, holding it protectively as if not sure whether to show her.

'Is that how you met?' she said then hurriedly, because the question exposed what strangers they were, for the hundredth time, it seemed. 'I can't remember. Kate was always interested in that – stuff,' she went on awkwardly, 'I mean, that kind of issue.'

Evan didn't seem to notice, nodding, a smile turning to something further off, something lonely. 'She was amazing. She was always so – supportive.' And he focused again, on Rose, a warmth in his face she hadn't seen before, the glow of something remembered. 'She was so determined it was going to work.' Rose shifted guiltily, remembering her impatience, at those early emails from Kate, talking about Evan's work, smug marrieds, she'd thought, complacent, virtuous. She hadn't been responsive, or interested – and Kate had stopped mentioning it.

'I'd love to see the houses,' she offered now, wanting to keep him like this, his edge – the brittleness that frightened her, as if he might shatter – gone.

But, 'Really?' he said, suddenly stiff, prickly, as if he suspected her of pity, or just was used to sceptics.

'Yes,' she said stoutly, then, 'well, sometime. When – when all this—' and had started clearing the table again. Jamie had gone quiet, watching them from his high chair.

He'd offered her the bicycle, then, awkward, and they'd come outside to the shed, Jamie on Evan's hip now, eyeing Rose with a sulky look, as if she'd abandoned him, rearing away from the bike as if it was his enemy. 'It's a bit of a

78

monster,' Evan said, and it was, cumbersome and covered with dust. She regarded it.

'I can do a bit of shopping, after,' she said, trying to sound cheery, and abruptly horrified at what she'd said. After she'd viewed the body. But again Evan hadn't seemed to notice.

It had taken an age, the road was unmade for something like three miles, the bicycle was heavy and the front box made it heavier and awkward to steer. Rose ground on, feeling a fraud, but the day was clear and bright, the hedges full of birds and the landscape completely flat. So flat that it was impossible to get a sense of what lay beyond the foliage, until Rose turned a bend on to the main road. There was the slightest incline, a break in the hedgerow and the marsh lay spread out, as far as the horizon.

Looking back she could see a grey-brick corner of the house, far off. She realised the extent of its isolation with a shock: it was right on the edge of things. She had the sudden memory of herself on that secret staircase, listening, waiting for a word from Kate as if she lived in those walls still, behind the peeling paper, marooned like a hermit or a nun. Who would have built it there, and a church too, there where the land was hardly land?

Evan had said something the night before about the marsh, having been reclaimed once then left to flood again and she recalled the black silhouette of a tall dead tree that was visible from her window.

MARSHALL AND DAUGHTERS. There was a buzzer: Rose pressed and waited in the cool morning. A woman went past walking a dog, very slowly, and although she didn't turn to look at her Rose felt herself watched. Maybe it

79

could go online, after all, maybe people could shop around, for whatever the choices were, the pink satin, the brass handles, she thought with a sudden access of savage rage – at whom? It wasn't the funeral parlour's fault Kate had died any more than it was the doctor's fault she had developed ovarian cancer, invisible, silent. But she needed to be angry. And they were so slow.

In her pocket her phone blipped: she'd almost forgotten the sound, it seemed, and she got it out to see a message from Deb, sent yesterday. Before she could read it the door opened and a woman in a black ill-fitting suit and tie was standing there: hurriedly stuffing her phone away Rose identified herself. The woman gave a little old-fashioned bow and shook her hand: her face was soft and creased with kindness and Rose felt herself subside, obedient, grateful that this was someone's job, that they'd seen it all before.

Rose followed her down a nylon-carpeted corridor, lined with certificates. Hands folded respectfully at her crotch, the woman asked if Rose wanted someone with her or— Rose shook her head, and waited politely for her to go.

Kate had gone to see Dad, in the chapel of rest on a busy South London road. Rose had never asked her what it was like, what she thought, and Kate hadn't divulged any of it. Rose still remembered her face, though, pale and closed, afterwards.

The room was small, with patterned carpet, more brightly lit than Rose had expected, like a waiting room in a private hospital except that at the far end on two trestles draped in dark red nylon was the coffin. There was a smell Rose couldn't identify, didn't care to identify, of chemicals and air freshener. She hung back: it didn't look like she had expected, somehow. Then, making herself take a step, then another, she saw – she wasn't looking inside, not yet, although it was there, the face was there, the profile against white cloth was there – that the coffin was made of an unusual material. Not the standard polished pine, brass handles; this was something more matte, plain and dull.

If Rose had thought about it, and she hadn't – it only occurred to her now, because why would you talk to your sister about her funeral arrangements when she was forty-one? – she would have thought Kate would have wanted something pretty, like wicker. Kate loved all things pretty, once she'd had a bike basket threaded with silk flowers: that memory came out of somewhere long forgotten, when she'd been at school, Kate still at home. Rose put out a hand to the weird thing in front of her, so weird, so blunt, so plain: it was a kind of cardboard. Not so crass as wine-box cardboard, higher tech, it would have to be – and she stood very still – it would have to be stronger than that. She put out a hand to touch it and the movement brought her close, at last, and there was Kate.

Her eyes were closed. Perhaps they did that. It was Kate, and not Kate. There was her mouth, her cropped dark hair. There was some make-up on her, her skin was an odd colour, but there was her small straight nose. Her cheeks, though. Her neck. She was much thinner: a life spent unable to resist biscuits, a life spent baking in a warm kitchen, had ended this way.

Kate.

She didn't know if she'd said it out loud or not: she leaned down, she leaned close. *Oh Kate.*

'Come back.' She had said that out loud, if only under her breath, and of course Kate didn't answer. There was not a hint of Kate's smell, of gingerbread and soap, it was gone: tentatively she put a hand to her sister's cheek and found it cold, inanimate, like putty. She lay there, inscrutable as she had never been in life, Kate who would argue and explain you into submission, comfortable, reasonable, bossy, infuriating Kate. Kate, the open book, had been closed. Kate was silenced.

Chapter Ten

There was no sign of the car when finally Rose ground back down the track and the brown pool beneath the small bridge was a puddle again, and a scurf of bubbles and scum in the grass. She climbed off the bike and wheeled it round to the back door, listening: there was the sound of the water across the weir but the house was blank and quiet in the sun.

The ride back had been even slower than the ride out: Rose guessed it was five miles, and with a heavier load it wasn't something you'd want to do every day, unless you had to. She couldn't help wondering, when Kate had last done it, and if it was wrong to want to know.

Let me know you're all right.

Deb's message had been sent last night. Rose had remembered to look back at her phone only when she turned the corner and saw the bike and knew, if she turned around, the funeral home would be out of sight. Until that moment it had seemed important to keep walking, not to look back. She had wanted the whole place to be gone, beamed up in a column of light or burned to the ground, the awful carpet, the horrible cardboard coffin, and the face inside it, the face that was both Kate's and really, really wasn't.

She didn't know why she'd gone to the Chapel of Rest. She'd thought Kate might have some message for her – just the sight of her familiar face, one last time – but there'd been nothing. There was this thing they said, about people looking as if they'd found peace. Kate hadn't looked like that.

Rose knew she had gone because Kate had done it for Dad: because Kate thought it was the right thing to do.

The woman undertaker had been waiting at the door. 'There's the book of condolence,' she said. 'If you want to look at it.' Rose had stared at her blankly.

'Am I supposed to sign it?' she said and the woman had smiled kindly.

'Well – if you like,' she said. 'But the condolences are for you. For her loved ones.'

There was so much Rose didn't know: it was another world, the world of the bereaved, a place of grey perms and tearooms and grandparents and plastic flower arrangements. Obedient, Rose let herself be shown to a lectern where the book sat open, a kind of visitors' book. There were five or six signatures and the phrases that came from that same antique place, *deepest sympathy*. Rose scanned the names with a kind of reluctance, the thought of those people she didn't know, scrawled signatures she didn't recognise but then one message stopped her, unsigned.

84

I'm so sorry, dearest K, all my love. Was that an 'L'? That message was different, it wasn't to the loved ones at all, it was to Kate herself, saying the thing Rose should have said, longed to say, wanted for a second to run back into the room and whisper into the cold cheek. *Dearest.*

And why would you sign it, if it was to Kate who, if magic and ghosts and the afterlife existed, would know who you were, anyway.

Beside her the Marshall daughter, hands still respectfully folded, had cleared her throat. 'I expect you'll meet them all tomorrow,' she said confidentially, as if she knew the impulse that had come over Rose and was stepping forward to keep her to the proper path, and Rose had taken it as her cue, and fled. The funeral loomed, all those people she didn't know and would have to meet. The house where she was still a stranger.

The pavement outside was deserted: the charity shop still closed, the dogwalker gone.

Rounding the corner Rose stopped in the sunshine, and looked at her phone. *Let me know you're all right.* Leaning against the bicycle in the quiet street, she called back. Deb's first lessons were at five in the afternoon and she knew where her friend would be, at the table in her little flat doing prep, coffee pot at her side. So far away.

There was a flood of recriminations, expostulations, *why on earth didn't you,* but weirdly the picture of Deb refused to come into proper focus, her voice sounded so far away, echoing down the line, her accented English that had been so familiar sounded now too foreign in this little dull side street. The old life, the faded photograph that was her past – and she supposed this was home now.

Rose had begun dully to explain the situation, the internet, the lack of signal, the isolation, all Evan and Kate's way of living. The router hidden away out of sight somewhere: not in any room she'd been in, so far. She heard Deb go quiet, waiting for her to finish, and she petered out.

'No phone signal – and no internet?' said Deb, her voice ominously level. 'Really? Couldn't he—'

'I'll ask him,' said Rose. 'I haven't even really got round to asking him anything— fixating on being able to get online, it doesn't seem right. When he's – they're – in this state. They seem completely shellshocked.'

She heard Deb draw a breath. 'It's not like you're going to be internet shopping, Rose,' she said, her voice rising. 'You need to keep in touch with people, with your life, with your real life. And what if the children were ill, or—'

'There's a landline,' said Rose, because she'd seen it, a telephone in the hall, so antique it even had the curly wire. 'I can call you on that.'

'Oh, sure,' said Deb, and that tone got through, the sardonic forthright Deb. 'Like when we were kids? And your parents listening in?' Rose heard an explosive sigh. 'Aren't you so lonely, sweetheart? No people, no traffic, no bars, Jesus, it sounds absolutely like the middle of nowhere. And your sister—' she hesitated. 'Darling, you've lost your sister. You need people around you.'

'I'll talk to him,' said Rose, 'I'll ask Evan,' but in that moment Deb wasn't comforting her, she was haranguing, and Rose felt the strangest urge to hang up on her and get back there. Back down the track to the quiet, just the birds and the rush of the water, and the soft voices on the back staircase. But Deb was her friend, she reminded herself with an effort, Deb needed to be answered.

'I'll work out when the internet is on and we can fix up a Skype call,' she offered. Silence. 'Maybe tomorrow,' she said. 'After the funeral. OK?' The narrow street was so quiet: it stretched away from her, net-curtains all the way down to a soft grey blur that was the estuary.

'The funeral's tomorrow?' said Deb, and her voice was too low, too careful, too sympathetic.

Rose felt that itch of impatience again, 'Yes,' she said, stiffly, 'yes, it's all right, I'll—' but Deb interrupted her.

'Call me when you get back there. OK? On the land-line, then I'll know the number, I can get in touch if I need to.'

'OK, yes,' said Rose. 'Sure. I will, look, thanks, Deb. I've got to go.' And hung up, before Deb could say anything else.

And now she was back at the house in the mild sunshine, but the idea of calling Deb filled her only with reluctance. A foreign call, at Evan's expense? When there was obviously no money to spare and he seemed to keep tabs on everything that happened in the house – and she still didn't really know if she was family or guest?

Wheeling the bike back into the barn she stood there, looking around. The boxes of books and the little cupboard and chair Kate had painted and stencilled herself: there was a hush in here, dust motes drifting in a shaft of sun. Rose took a step towards the cupboard and then heard a sound, quite distinctly, a breath behind her, a kind of sigh. She whirled around, and stupidly she knew she had been going to say Kate's name – now when she knew exactly how dead Kate was, how dead, how gone. And yet. And yet. In that moment something seemed to be gathering itself, drawing darkness from the cobwebbed corners of the dim old barn and if she stood there another second it would smother her. For a brief horrible second, she thought: she didn't just die. Something – the black thing that lives here – something killed her.

Twisting around in a sudden desperate rush to get out of the place, Rose was thrown off balance, and stumbling over one of the boxes that had bulged open in the damp at her feet she fell with a painful clatter against the bike, its pedal gouging her shin. She scrambled and was outside, the rush of the water in her ears and taking gulps of damp air. Around her the air glittered and whirled, and was still: the contents of the barn receded, into darkness.

Limping and shaky, Rose made her way back across the yard: as she lifted the latch of the back door she realised she had forgotten to ask about a key but it was unlocked and the now familiar smell of the boiler room greeted her, of cold ashes and something like paraffin. She felt suddenly sure she'd seen a first-aid box, an old-fashioned tin one with a red cross painted on it and there it was, in the murk above a stack of wood. Rose reached for it, clambering and suddenly there was someone, between her and the kitchen, a shadow of a person, a ghost.

Twisting awkwardly Rose felt the wood pile give way under her and she was down again.

'What are you doing?' came the voice, imperious, unsympathetic, from the doorway. It was Serena, wearing an odd get-up, a home-made-looking floral dress trimmed with lace that was tight under the arms.

'I cut myself,' said Rose, trying to sound rueful, struggling upright. 'Was that you, in the barn?'

Serena examined her with black eyes. 'I heard something and I came down,' she said, her gaze level. 'Dad says it's safe out here but I don't believe him.' Rose heard something else, like a threat, in the words.

'You stayed here on your own, though?'

Serena shrugged.

'I'm not frightened,' she said, indifferent. 'If there was anyone I would be able to scare them off.' Rose believed her.

'Does it— do you stay here on your own a lot?' she asked and saw Serena's face darken: she wasn't stupid. Absolutely not stupid.

'Why? Are you going to tell on Dad to the—'

'Don't be silly,' said Rose hastily and regretted it as Serena's eyes turned blacker still. 'No, I just – I just—' she sighed. 'I'm sorry, Serena, that came out wrong. I'm not some kind of spy, I'm just trying to understand how it all works. Your life, out here. So I can be useful.' And so I can make sense of it, she thought; so I can understand the life Kate chose, out here in the middle of bloody nowhere.

Serena's thin arms were folded across her front now and Rose saw the seam had split under one armpit. 'Well, there was Kate until – until two weeks ago, so I wasn't on my own,' she said. 'Was I?'

Her steady insolent hostility almost took Rose's breath away: she felt herself on the edge of fear. Rose was standing

89

now, leaning against the doorframe with Serena staring up at her. She was only a few inches shorter than Rose, she would be tall, Rose found herself thinking. Her mother must have been – but she sensed the last person she should mention at this stage was Serena's mother. 'I was looking for some antiseptic, or something,' she said. The blood on her calf had congealed, but it was throbbing.

Serena gave the old tin box a quick look and turned on her heel. 'It's not in *there*,' she said with disdain. 'I'll show you.' She ran, on thin bare dusty feet, ahead of Rose, into the hall, up the stairs. Plodding, Rose followed, Serena turning, dark-eyed and inscrutable, to look down over the gallery balustrade at her.

The first-aid box was in the bathroom: a plastic tub that Serena, standing in the middle of the room, held out to her. It contained an ancient bottle of iodine, some squares of gauze and a roll of plaster-tape and nothing else: no painkillers, no indigestion tablets, no allergy relief.

As Rose, having run her leg under the tap, applied a clumsy dressing Serena sat on the edge of the big old bath, her skinny legs stretched out in front of her from the too-short skirt, watching her.

'There's blood on you,' she said with satisfaction, pointing, and looking down Rose saw it on her skirt. 'If you want to change I can show you where the washing machine is. 'You'll need to know, won't you? If you're staying, that is.' Jeering at Rose for being out of her depth, for being the wrong person. Her rudeness was palpable, but you couldn't snap at a child who'd lost a mother. Two mothers. And trusted no one.

'I *am* staying,' said Rose, but Serena had turned on her heel.

As Rose walked along the gallery to her room, though, she could hear the girl's soft light footsteps padding behind her and when she got into the bedroom and set her bag on the bed, there Serena was again, standing in the doorway. She opened her mouth, and closed it again. Knelt at her open suitcase and got out another skirt, she'd last worn at Christmas, Christmas in Rome wandering in the rain along the wide green river. Kate had texted her, on the day. It occurred to her now, the faded skirt in her hands, that Kate must have walked a long way to find the signal to send the text, and Rose couldn't even remember what she'd said in answer. *Have a good one yourself.* Or something offhand and cold.

'This was always going to be your room,' said Serena, from the doorway in her precise cool little voice.

'What?' said Rose.

Serena regarded her, twisting a strand of hair round her finger. Her skin was sallow, she was almost ugly.

'Kate said,' watching Rose for a reaction. 'She always knew you'd come, she said you'd like it here. She said this was going to be your room because it had the best view.' She was looking at the bed, the little Tiffany lamp on the bedside table with a strange look of feverish suppressed excitement.

'I—' Rose choked it off, holding herself very still, because she could hear Kate saying it, looking out across the marsh and saying it fond and wistful, and she could see herself in Rome, drinking at the bar, dressing up for the *passeggiata*. Pleasing no one but herself.

'You didn't come, though, did you?' Serena didn't wait for an answer, she was wandering past her instead, light-footed and casual, into the room, to the window, without asking permission. Her stubby-fingered hand rested on Kate's desk, and she turned, her back to the light.

'Most of her stuff is still in the barn but she wanted this put in here specially for you, to do your writing.'

'My writing,' said Rose, and her voice sounded odd, choked: Serena looked at her, her interest sharpening.

'She said you were a brilliant writer and one day you were going to be famous.'

In her last year at school, moody and introverted, Rose had written poems and the English teacher, wanting to encourage her, had collected them into a little pamphlet. Two short stories in her twenties, both rejected by magazines.

'I don't think so,' said Rose, stiffly, countering that needling little voice in her head that Serena seemed to be able to hear too.

Serena shrugged, crafty.

'Well, she did say it, you can ask my dad if you don't believe me.' She knew Rose wouldn't do that, already she knew.

'It's locked,' she said, and Serena shrugged again, looking away. 'Kate was the one,' said Rose. 'She wanted to be a writer.' Surprising herself: it was a fact she had forgotten but it came to her now, and that seemed to keep happening. If anyone had asked her about her family she'd say her parents were dead and then sum up Kate in a couple of words, *mumsy, practical*. Big sister. But other things came tiptoeing back to her now Kate was gone. The endless intent reading, pushing her glasses up her nose, the scrawling, the scrapbooks, the diaries, the orderly book-shelves in her room.

Serena screwed up her nose: the fact didn't serve her, she dismissed it. 'She told me you were always the bad one, too,' she said.

'Like you?' said Rose, smiling and Serena's eyes turned flinty-black.

'I'm not,' she said. 'I'm not like *you.*'

I give up, thought Rose, and sighing – weary, hopeless, at her wit's end in the battle she couldn't win – stood up and held out a hand to Serena. 'Don't let's – don't—' she said, taking a step closer, close enough to touch the soft worn fabric of the little girl's dress Serena was too big for. 'We're both sad, Serena.' Serena pulled her arms across herself and said nothing.

Gently Rose set a hand on each side of Serena's narrow midriff, that sat several inches below the gathered waist of the little dress: she felt how thin the girl was, how tense. 'I like your dress,' she said. 'It looks home-made, did Kate make it for you?' Serena's eyes seemed to grow larger, Rose could almost see herself in them, but she pushed on, testing the instinct that had got her this far. 'I used to do that, when I was – your age. I liked finding my old things and—' And suddenly Serena's head darted close, chin thrust out, so quick and aggressive it might have been a snake striking.

Rose gasped and in the same moment the sound came, a new sound, above and behind the distant rush of water, it was the noise of a car's engine that came and went over the uneven ground of the track. And Rose steadied herself and the dangerous thread that had hung there, the gleam between her eyes and Serena's, was gone.

And Serena pulled back, white-faced, tugging at the skirt. 'She didn't – I was just—' she said, 'seeing if it—' She turned to the window then to the door, her narrow face drawn tight and she was running for the door, tearing at the dress so sharply to get it off that it tore behind and Rose saw the sharp little wings of her shoulder-blades, the knobbed ridge of her spine.

'Serena,' she said, fearful, 'I'm sorry, I didn't mean to—' But the girl had fled, and by the time Rose got to the door the gallery was deserted, the sun must have gone behind a cloud because the light through the cupola turned grey and the empty hall below yawned dark red in the sudden gloom.

Then she heard the crunch of the car's tyres coming over the little bridge and round the house, loud and close – and it all began again.

Chapter Eleven

I must dig out my patchwork basket. I don't know what's come over me. Jamie's sleeping now, and there are the evenings. Well, for the moment.

All those colours, between me and the horizon, grey and green and brown and silver, that's what makes me want to get started: Evan said it would be like this. That what I needed was a place like this and I would see the direction I needed to go. Of course patchwork's not his thing, sewing: when we were in the flat he'd laugh when I had the basket out, all the cottons, all the colours, when I spread things out on the kitchen table. *Little House on the Prairie*, he'd say. If he tried it though, he'd know, the calm that comes over you, with all of it ordered under your fingers, under control.

Of course, he does understand, really. Because his work's the same, he knows that, we're kindred spirits. I mean, designing a house and getting right in there on every detail like he does, fitting the houses together, giving each one the right space, the right setting, it's a craft just like jewellery or dressmaking. *Women do things on the scale they're allowed*, Mum said that to me once.

And I said something like, *Houses for men, sewing for women? The world's changing, Mum*. And she looked at me.

Not so much, Katie, she said. Not long before she went. Before she – died.

She was always unhappy with Dad, but she stayed. I don't know if Rose knew that.

We needed space. It's why we came here.

There was Kate, curled tight in a ball, compact as a baby in the womb but it was Kate, her bright dark eyes, her smile. The dream was so vivid it woke Rose up, scalp tingling with it. The horror of it. Kate trapped and dying. Why hadn't she asked for help?

The room was dim around Rose but the musty smell, the droop of the curtains in the damp, the sound of the water – hadn't it driven Kate mad in the end? Or had she managed to ignore it? – told Rose where she was. Her heart was pounding, it refused to slow down, and thinking of Kate going mad didn't help. In a few short hours, she would be at her sister's funeral.

Move, Rose told herself, and she did, flinging herself out of bed. So much to do.

The house was silent as she tiptoed along the gallery in the T-shirt she'd slept in, past the wide staircase yawning up at her from the dark, paused at the nursery door. She didn't know if Evan was in there, on the narrow bed, lying beside Jamie: there was no sound. It was early: the sky through the cupola was that grey-blue between dark and light.

The dream was still there. Like something from *Alice in Wonderland*, a cat coiled on herself, smiling. Kate had always been a cat person and as she opened the little secret door to the back staircase Rose realised for the first time that there were no cats here. Even in her London flat she'd had one and here, where it would have been so easy— The door closed behind her and she was in the narrow warm space. There was no light on the staircase but what filtered up from below was a soft red darkness.

Where are you?

It was here Rose felt Kate, here on the narrow tight-coiled stairs. It was why she'd walked past the wide sturdy burgundy-carpeted staircase, the stairs the vicar would have used, his crinolined wife on his arm. As the door closed soft behind her she wondered for a second, why and how they'd gone, those long-dead inhabitants of this strange old house.

She took a step down, suddenly unsteady, and the space closed in on her. Was it here she'd seen Kate in her dream, curled in this tight corner? Other voices whispered in the soft dark. Rose put out a hand to each side of her to steady herself and feeling the uneven walls beneath the old wallpaper told herself it was her own blood in her ears she could hear, or the rush of the weir, as she edged down towards the light, and as she reached the doorway the sound seemed to shift sideways and was gone, like smoke up a chimney.

On the kitchen table were the remnants of last night's

supper. Rose began swiftly to clear up: bending to stack the dishwasher it occurred to her that she should have got dressed first. But it wasn't yet six: ten minutes and she'd run back up.

The night before. Her stomach fluttered, anxious, at the memory.

She'd made pasta. There was a supermarket in Heydon and she'd bought tomatoes, bacon, olive oil, dried chilli to load into the bike's child-carrier. She'd never seen such a contraption before but then no one would sail into the traffic in Rome with a child on board. The barrow bit looked home-made. There were two seats in it, but she couldn't imagine Serena co-operating to squeeze in there with sticky-fingered Jamie. Maybe Kate had had a way with her, or Evan did.

She'd bought booze, too: Evan had helped her unload it. Three bottles of red, three of white and then to be on the safe side, a bottle of supermarket gin and some tonic. She had no idea how many people would come to the funeral because when she'd asked, Evan had just shrugged, helpless.

'It'll have to be enough,' he said, frowning down at the gin. Then, 'It's not as if people come to funerals to get drunk, is it?'

Rose had laughed before she realised it hadn't been a joke.

'You must let me give you some money,' he said, anguished.

'Oh,' Rose said, 'well – no. I mean, I've got enough to last me until—' She hadn't dared check her bank balance, had just offered the card but the payment had gone through. And until what? 'Until I go back,' she said, bravely, before backtracking. 'Or, or, get another job or something.'

Evan had fished a crumpled tenner out of his pocket, and then a fiver. She'd hesitated, but taken it. It felt weird – but she couldn't do anything else. Money was money: without money, it dawned on her, stuck here with the children and no job, she would have to ask Evan every time she needed to buy anything.

And then she remembered the fat roll of cash, stashed in her half-full suitcase, under her clothes. Not hers, not hers to spend: maybe she could open an account with it, for Jamie.

But for the moment, booze was booze: with the sauce bubbling on the stove and Evan out of the room some-where with Jamie she had poured herself a quick, stiff gin and tonic. She'd even bought a lemon. She'd stood over the sauce, downed the drink in two gulps and washed up the glass before she heard him on the stairs. She didn't even need to think about why. Booze cost money, Evan liked to keep a clear head, and gin and tonic belonged to a world he had renounced. He and Kate.

The thoughts had come crowding right in as the alcohol hit her stomach, all the eager curious thoughts that the dull daytime sensations kept out. All day, all week, the heavy thud of Kate's absence had blocked anything petty out, anything trivial or fun, gossip or checking herself out in the mirror: her absence for ever.

Inappropriate thoughts: what had their sex life been like, Kate's and his? Because they'd had one, they had Jamie to show for it. Evan was so contained, and so serious.

Whether the dress Kate had made would still fit, for the funeral, and who was going to be there and would there be anybody – *anybody* – she could talk to about how weird this all was?

Then slipping into old habits, booze always did that. Old lovers. What were they doing now, where did the married one live with the wife he'd never mentioned until the end – then she'd slipped the glass into the sink and a moment of clarity dawned, a space opening in her head where those men had been, the faces blurring. None of them had been the one. She ran the tap.

And as Evan walked back into the room, her thoughts loosened by the buzz of the gin, and as she told herself, *Whatever you do don't have a drink at the funeral*, she had remembered what she'd been supposed to do.

He was holding Jamie: she saw him survey the room, saw him look at the half lemon on the chopping board, inquiring, and then she saw him shift Jamie as if he was about to give him to her: Jamie's arms beginning to stretch out.

'Can I ask a favour?' she said quickly, forestalling Jamie by taking his little pudgy hands and moving them up and down, nodding and smiling.

'Of course,' said Evan but there was something cool and wary about the way he spoke. He shifted Jamie back round again, away from her. Defensive. 'I've been thinking, if you're not happy being stuck out here, there's always—'

She'd already slipped in the question about the internet just after they'd got back, out in the yard with Serena's beady eyes upon her, amused or contemptuous or both, that she was the one asking. Serena had reappeared in jeans and a T-shirt, no sign of the torn dress, before Evan had even climbed out of the car, shooting a warning look at her.

He'd answered, distracted, leaning down into the car. 'I switch the router on between six and seven every evening, it's a dreadful connection,' raising his head, turning to look at her. 'The bandwidth isn't generous, if Serena's on it then it's slow.' He straightened, apologetic, then frowned. 'Do you need the internet? You only need to ask.' Rose opened her mouth to say *An hour a day? Really?* But there was something in his tone, and she felt suddenly flustered, needy, assured him it didn't matter, she didn't need it, perhaps she could – and then Jamie had woken, red-faced and sticky and with his nappy needing changing and that had been that.

In the kitchen as dinner cooked, she had wondered if he could smell the gin on her when he said it. The drunk little sister out of her depth. She could ask him where the router was, do it herself. She knew she wouldn't.

'It's not that,' she said quickly, although even as she said it she was wondering, her thoughts slipping and sliding, what he had been going to suggest. 'No, I just wondered if I could use the phone? The landline?'

'Now?' he said, frowning. It was that frown. It made her feel like she'd asked something unreasonable, made her doubt herself, maybe she had. His house, his space, his phone bill. But just one call? She faltered.

'It's just that – I promised a friend I'd call her. Let her know how to contact me.'

He opened his mouth, a moment's hesitation. 'Of course,' he said.

The phone was in the cavernous hall, on a table beside the big front door that didn't open. There was a chair but she didn't sit down: lifting the phone she turned, and there was Evan standing there still, backlit in the doorway to the kitchen, as if making sure she found it. She smiled and he disappeared, but the green baize door stood open, and she could see his shadow, motionless.

It went to answerphone: she'd left it too late. Deb would be at dinner with her parents, and they were ferocious about mobiles at the table. She left the number.

'It's tricky,' she said into the silence. 'But the internet's up between six and seven in the evening as a rule, that's what I understand.' She could imagine Deb's incredulity. 'And with the funeral tomorrow—' Oh God, she thought, the gin again, oh God, oh God, Kate. She started again. 'I miss you, Deb,' she said unsteadily. 'I'll try you again.'

When she put the phone down and turned, Evan's shadow had been gone from the doorway.

Now in the thin early light, she grimaced. Dinner with her behaving all wrong, too bright, too loosened up, gaily talking about rubbish like who Serena's favourite boy bands were. She had flashes of Serena, beadily disbelieving across the table, pushing the *amatriciana* away, saying it was too spicy.

'Eat it, Serena,' he'd said and although his voice was mild, she'd lowered her head and begun to stab at it again, one pasta tube at a time.

It had been the gin, she thought now, opening the fridge to see how much of it she'd managed to squeeze into that small glass and frowned. The bottle wasn't in there.

She didn't have a hangover, just the ghost of a tightness

at her temples. All those questions. She made tea, and began boiling eggs for sandwiches and buttering bread. Opening a high cupboard in search of mayonnaise in the same moment she saw the gin bottle, incongruous among tinned tomatoes, and heard someone in the doorway behind her.

'I put it there to keep it out of Jamie's reach.' It was Evan, and his voice was dull. Letting the door bang shut hurriedly Rose stepped sideways, behind a chair, acutely conscious of her thighs barely covered by the T-shirt. He hadn't brought Jamie down and as she wondered what had woken him he stood just there, gazing at her unshaven, dark-eyed, and a bewildered look turning to something else. Haunted, desolate, his hands hanging by his sides.

'I thought,' he said, rubbing his eyes, 'I heard her — thought you were, I dreamed—'

'Oh,' she said, 'Oh, Evan. Oh, Evan.'

He didn't seem to notice what she was wearing, he didn't look down, and when Rose moved round the table to him and stopped, inches away from him he still didn't notice. He wasn't looking at her at all but somewhere else, somewhere over her shoulder to where she had stood. Rose couldn't come any closer: gingerly she put out a hand to Evan's shoulder as if he was sleep-walking and needed to wake up, and then exactly as she touched him his hand came up in a reflexive movement from his side.

As his hand moved it brushed against her where the T-shirt met her thigh and both of them moved sharply back from each other.

'I'm sorry,' he said and his eyes were wide with something, fear or something.

'I'd better – I—' she had said wildly, a sentence she was incapable of finishing, and fled.

It was waiting for her upstairs, as she shoved the door closed it swung a little, reaching for her with its soft hands, pleading. Rose lifted the hanger off the hook on the back of the door and held it up, feeling a great stone of misery behind her ribs. It would fit: any weight she'd put on in fifteen years had gone in the last few weeks. Kate had made her little sister a dress for her own funeral, and it would fit. And then Rose saw. She saw it.

She saw that where the tiny covered buttons fastened it at the front, down between the breasts, it had been slit. A long careful slit, barely fraying, down from the bodice to the belly – lower. Rose gasped, took a step back but still held on to it. *What. What?*

And there, where the slit ended was a bubble of red, a tiny bright bead of wax.

Chapter Twelve

She had a black skirt, and wore that, with an old cream silk shirt of their mother's that she and Kate had fought over once upon a time, so old it was going under the arms. Looking like a waitress but it didn't matter, Rose thought, none of it mattered, it was only a dress. But her mind roiled and turned: could it have happened by accident, long ago, and she hadn't noticed? Nothing about it felt accidental.

The crematorium was a low brick building beside a main road. Dreary clipped hedges, a large car park, squares of grass, one of which was patched and clogged with what Rose only realised were ashes when she saw a fat woman in a black coat unceremoniously emptying a plastic urn in a corner of it while a gaggle of middle-aged people waited for her on the gravel.

The service had been brief. Evan had only managed a couple of sentences before he faltered and went silent.

'You all knew Kate—' and he'd scanned the faces, his own white as a sheet. He'd shaved, and cut himself. He looked as if he was falling.

Rose, in the front row, caught only glimpses of about twenty people as they filed in, looked around the horrible room – a larger version of the Chapel of Rest with chairs that looked like they came from old people's homes and a chintz curtain behind the coffin – and recognised no one. A woman in a flowered dress under a shabby black coat looked at her intently, until she had to look away, scalp prickling with panic.

That morning, frantically sorting through her suitcase she'd heard a tiny sound and turned to see Serena in the doorway, again. Pinched and pale, the girl had said nothing and then gone. In the car she'd turned once or twice to check on them in the back seat but Serena was never looking back at her, she was staring determinedly out of the window, her reflection angry in the glass.

It wasn't till they were in the car that Evan had asked Rose if she wanted to say anything and she'd stared at him. *No*, was on her lips.

Rose didn't know the form. At Mum's funeral she'd run away and had to be brought back, only to hide under the table: she hadn't gone to Dad's at all. All she knew about funerals had come from the telly but she did know you were supposed to talk to people. To stand there in a receiving line like you were at a wedding, and let them talk to you, about what your person had meant to them.

Rose always said no. She always ran away. But before she could answer a text came in from Deb: *good luck*. And she found herself saying, *all right*. And when he faltered up she went to the lectern, looking back to make sure Jamie, asleep in the car seat, hadn't woken.

'None of you knows me,' she said, and the woman was looking at her again, in her flowered dress. 'Kate was my sister. She was seven years older than me.' She didn't know where the words came from but they came and the woman kept on looking steadily, as if to say, *I do. I know you.*

'When I was a kid—' she said. 'Once when I was a kid, I'd gone out and climbed a tree and couldn't get down and then I slipped. I couldn't shout for anyone—' *because Mum was already sick, because Dad would have belted her,* but they didn't need to know any of that and somehow she managed to keep talking without a pause. 'And I hung there, I must have been fifteen feet off the ground and I was terrified I was going to die and then Kate just ran out of the house and straight towards me and she got to the tree just in time and she caught me. And then she burst into tears.'

Did you see me? Did you see me out of the window? But Kate had shaken her head. *I just knew.*

They didn't need to know that either, this wasn't about her. Not about Kate always, always, *always* having been there for her. Whenever she was alone and sobbing over some bloke there had been Kate on the phone, as if she knew something was happening. *Just checking in.* And Rose had just thought she was being a nosy pain in the arse.

'She was so soft-hearted,' said Rose. 'She was so kind. She would do anything for anyone. She hated to see anyone frightened, or in pain.' On the benches, it seemed to her, all so still, no one was even breathing. Evan's head was down, down, from where she stood, elevated a little on the podium, she could see the white of his knuckles as he clasped his hands – but Serena was stiffly upright. She was staring back at her. Rose didn't know what she'd expected, except perhaps she had worried she might have gone too far and she didn't want the poor kid to have to cry in front of everyone – but that wasn't what she saw in Serena's face. What she saw was white rage, focused on her. Rose's gaze swerved, panicked, away and there was the flowered lady, looking back at her still, unblinking.

'I'm sure she'd want me to thank you all for coming,' she managed. 'And I hope we will see you later at – the house.'

Stumbling back to her seat she could hear the celebrant beginning to announce some hymn behind her and people stirred. She sheltered behind Evan in the front pew, reaching for Jamie who'd begun to stir in the car seat and clutching him. Hearing nothing, listening to nothing.

On her other side Serena sat bolt upright, not looking at anyone now. Staring at the coffin: when the hymn petered to a close and awful organ music had started and it had begun to move, if anything Serena had gone even more still, like something was holding her in its grip. Staring, staring.

And then they were leaving. It was over.

Outside people filed past them and Rose stood in an agony of obedience at the door, Jamie was awake and grizzling frightenedly, but he wouldn't go to Evan and she hung on to him for grim death. The people said things to her and she answered but she couldn't have recalled a word: she recognised no one. She was looking at the awful

108

ugly place and registering the fat woman with her urn and thinking, *This isn't where it ends. Surely, surely.*

'Where did Kate want her ashes to go?' she whispered to Evan, before she thought about it — *because why would Kate have said? She had no idea she was dying, she was young* — but it was too late. Following Rose's gaze, Evan looked aghast.

'Not there,' he said, white-lipped and she wanted to touch him then, to press his arm. Not there. Then he turned to her. 'Where's Serena?' He turned.

'Serena?'

Oh shit. Oh shit. Rose broke away from the line, feeling them watch her, Jamie heavy on her hip. The sky overhead was wide and pale and warm and she began to sweat. She could see Evan moving, jerky with panic, back into the crematorium and she was left here, weighted under Jamie, spinning round under the sky, looking, searching.

And then Rose saw her, across the far side of the crematorium standing in a tiled shelter a bit like a large bus stop where they put the floral tributes. Kate, plain as day, bending down among a clucking group of strangers to inspect the cards of condolence. Then when she stood and turned it wasn't her but there stood Serena behind her, at the back, arms folded across herself and exactly in the centre of the space as if presiding. Looking at Rose.

Then Evan was coming back towards her out of the crematorium, side-stepping a mourner and wordlessly Rose pointed to the shelter. He changed course. She watched them: Evan's head bent down at an angry angle, Serena unrepentant.

Jamie struggled in her arms and she set him down on the gravel. He began to totter, arms outstretched, back towards his father and Rose followed, in a daze. Because in those few minutes of fear under the wide hot sky, she had understood that it wasn't finished. Something had yet to play out, something that she had only sensed, that lived in the house's secret corners. That had watched Kate die.

When she focused again, Evan was walking back towards her.

'I don't know how long,' Rose muttered into the phone. There was a silence.

Messages and emails had come in all at once when she turned her phone back on but scrolling down through them what struck her was how little any of it mattered, or even needed to be read. Only Deb, dogged and anxious, needed a response. Her most recent in a string of texts was only a question mark, resigned and doleful and worried.

Rose was standing behind the hedge, not hiding exactly. Evan was putting the children into the car and she'd made some excuse. Left something inside.

'Not even an idea?' Deb wanted to know when she was coming back. One of her angry, sympathetic sighs came down the line. 'I don't understand,' she said, stubbornly. 'I just don't. This is the twenty-first century, and she wasn't living on her own.'

'I—' *It's complicated,* she wanted to plead. *It doesn't feel like the twenty-first century out there.*

'It isn't always someone's fault,' she said, miserable. 'It would be easier if it was. Look – he's heartbroken as it is.' She could hear his voice from along the hedge somewhere, sounding angry. 'I've got to go,' she said.

One car had got to the house before them when they bumped down the drive and across the bridge. A low dark car parked discreetly beside the brick pump house, someone sitting inside it. An Audi: living in Italy had meant she noticed a car's make, food and cars, favourite topics of conversation. She couldn't imagine Evan noticing such a thing.

When Rose had come round the hedge at the crematorium, her phone already safely in her pocket, she saw that Evan was on his, pacing. It was an odd sight, somehow: she realised she'd never seen him on it before, but as there was no signal down the track, she supposed that was why. Whoever he was angry with, was on the other end of the line. Inside the car she could see Serena's head, obediently motionless, Jamie strapped into his seat. 'No,' he was saying. 'I said no.' Then he saw her and turned his back and when he turned around again, he'd hung up.

As they had pulled away from the low grim building, in the rear-view mirror she'd asked timidly, who would be coming to the house. Evan had shrugged, not turning to look at her. 'It doesn't matter,' he said, dully. 'It's an hour out of their lives then they'll be off again.'

'Come *on*,' Rose said, surprised at herself. 'They cared about Kate.'

Rose wished she could remember the names of Kate's friends, from her patchwork class, from her book group, their names or even their faces. The truth was she'd thought they were all middle-aged and boring, women who sewed and cooked and went on protest marches and she switched off every time Kate mentioned them.

'Did they?' he said. 'None of them came to see us. To see her. I didn't invite them.'

'Was there a – a Hilary? I remember her talking about a best friend. One of those names that could be a man's or a woman's?'

'Lindsay,' came Serena's voice from the back seat, high and cold. Evan didn't look round at the sound of her name. 'Kate's best friend was called Lindsay, she told me.'

Lindsay. The L, in the book of condolence.

'Was she there?' Rose turned to look between the seats and Serena looked back, insolent. Shrugging.

'How would I know? I never met her.'

'Like I said,' said Evan, frowning. 'They never came.'

'So how did they know—' Evan just shook his head.

'Bad news travels fast,' he said. And the rest of the journey was accomplished in silence, except for Serena, in the back humming to herself, until they turned off the track and bumped down across the little bridge and saw the car.

'Trust Gerald,' said Evan, not troubling to slow down as he passed and through the dust the car threw up Rose saw a grey head in the Audi, a beaked sort of nose turn, mild, to look.

'Who's Gerald?' said Rose through the seats to Serena. Evan was already out of the car and walking back towards the Audi. Serena's mouth turned up, a little joker smile.

'Gerald,' she repeated, mocking, in a girlish voice that Rose recognised and yet didn't. Was that supposed to be Kate's voice? 'Gerald works for Daddy,' she said, turning bored when Rose just stared. 'His business-person. Partner.'

In the rear-view mirror she could see Evan standing

112

over the driver's door, talking down at this Gerald through the open window.

She'd made sandwiches, before they left, while Jamie howled upstairs where Evan had taken him to dress him, egg and tomato, ham. Putting wine in the fridge that morning Rose had seen the gin again and closed the door quickly. She'd cut the crusts off the sandwiches and laid a clean tea towel over them, three big platefuls, it wouldn't be enough. Leaning to look in the cupboard for the plates she'd thought about the money again. It would be useful, was the thought that came to her out of the blue now as she came back into the kitchen – a guilty thought. Useful for a cab to the station, for a train ticket or a plane ticket. What would five hundred and thirty pounds buy you?

By the time she got outside with a trayful of glasses and wine bottles there were a dozen people on the grass, and three more cars parked behind Gerald's polished Audi. One of them was the woman in the flowered dress, who immediately headed towards her over the uneven grass, almost bumping into the tray. Rose took a step back, off balance. The woman's eyes were large and pale, and her hair sprang out round her head.

'Lindsay?' said Rose, uncertain and the woman's expression faded, from eager to palely affronted. She looked over her shoulder towards the figures grouped on the lawn then back to Rose. 'No – is she—' waving her hand at the other mourners with vague impatience.

'No. I'm Martha,' she said, and the smile was back, in the certainty of being recognised now.

'Martha,' said Rose, hoping that was enough, edging

sideways to where a small rickety table sat on the veranda's rippling red tile and carefully setting down the tray.

And Martha was nodding. 'Kate's – birth helper? Doula, if you like. She certainly told me about you, I knew you straight away.' Looking Rose up and down: Rose wished for Jamie, as protection, or justification, but he was drowsing in his big buggy at the other end of the veranda. He looked quite pale, in the shade. 'Yes,' said Rose, 'Yes, of course.'

'She was marvellous,' said Martha, wistful, her pale eyes bulging with emotion. 'Both of them were—' turning to look for Evan. There he stood, right up against the reeds on the edge of the gathering. 'So determined to have their own experience of birth. And look how he turned out, little James. And then they came to this magical place.' She spread her hands wide, and the pale light of the wide horizon was reflected in her broad freckled face. 'What better beginning to a child's life?'

'I knew it was a home birth,' Rose said, numbly, although she had only just remembered. She had shied away from the detail of it: what was it to do with her? If she went on listening to Kate talk about it eventually the implication would be clear. She must do it herself, find a nice man, have a baby. Kate always shied away from actually saying it. But Martha was talking.

'Oh, that hardly does it justice. Evan was marvellous. The two of them: everywhere she went he was there, holding her up, encouraging her. And she was so determined.'

Rose thought of Kate, wandering through the rooms while it happened to her, that awful thing, roiling inside

114

her, imagined her standing at the window of the bedroom Rose still hadn't seen. She couldn't imagine what it felt like, beyond harbouring an alien that needed to burst through your skin. Something prickled her scalp, not fear, but something fiercer.

'You're a qualified midwife?' said Rose. Something told her she didn't want to start a fight at Kate's wake. She made herself smile. 'I mean, as well? A doula doesn't have to be, does she? Or he.' *Christ*, she thought, Christ.

But Martha was colouring. 'I am,' she said, stiffly. 'I work as a private midwife and birth companion. It's illegal to give birth without qualified medical intervention.' She reached for a glass abruptly.

'Your sister was a very brave woman,' she said. 'Many's the time I've asked myself, could I have known, could I have seen? But there were no adverse signs, nothing unusual. It was a long labour but Kate was completely calm.'

Martha looked down at her glass, which was already almost empty and Rose automatically reached for the bottle and refilled it for her. Wanting to shut her up, to demolish her – something. 'How did Kate find you?' she said, quietly. Martha's freckled cheeks were still flushed.

'Online,' she said. 'They found me online. There's quite a network, in the natural birth movement. We're not cranks. I know people – there are people who disparage the movement, but it's based on facts, about stress levels and cortisol and we have our safeguards. Who talk about the dangers and there are dangers, but life has many dangers, doesn't it?'

The eyes Martha lifted to Rose were pale as gooseberries. 'If she'd gone into hospital to have him, or to the

GP for her appointments,' said Rose. 'If she'd had all the scans. They might have seen it.' Martha flushed darkly. 'They might,' she muttered.

And abruptly she stepped back from Rose and her tray. 'If you'll excuse me, I must go and give my condolences to Evan.' But then she turned back. 'She loved you very much, Rose,' she said, but there was something reproachful in the way she said it and it was Rose's turn to flush but Martha had turned her back again and was stomping away, her big rounded back in its flapping cardigan still expressing hostility.

Rose looked at the glasses, and the tray, with a sinking heart. I loved her too, she heard her own small voice saying in her head, and then there was a pale darting shape at her elbow, springing out from behind her.

'Serena,' she said sharply and the girl turned, her small oval face unreadable, clouded. Reckless suddenly, Rose took her by the elbow. 'Could you take this tray around, sweetheart?' she said, using Kate's word and seeing the small dark face change. 'I've just got to – got to—'

But to her surprise Serena obeyed, reaching for the tray, and Rose didn't have to complete the explanation she didn't have. *I've got to hide.* Serena stood upright in front of her for a moment, pushing the tray out towards her in a little motion.

'No thank you,' said Rose, seeing the gleam of mischief in the girl's eye. 'I'll have one later.'

Coming blindly round the side of the house the sound of the falls was suddenly a din and Rose pushed her way inside to get away from it, past the cinder-smell of the boiler, the indistinct shapes that she knew were stacked

116

wood and recycling but could be anything as her eyes adjusted to the dim interior, and then she was in the kitchen.

At the stove someone stood. A woman, with cropped black hair, not Kate, bigger, looser in outline than Kate but with her hair. The woman she'd seen examining the flowers in the crematorium.

'You're Lindsay,' said Rose and suddenly the woman had moved, clumsily, and Rose was so close to her she caught her scent, and her scent was Kate's too, mixed with wine and it happened, it happened at last, in the presence of a stranger, who wasn't a stranger. It escaped her. She howled.

Chapter Thirteen

It was almost dark by the time they had all gone.

Jamie had woken and been fed and run around between the legs in a brisk, sharp wind that had sprung up, mourners bending to pet him, to cluck and tut and look around. Rose, watching from the veranda, knew they were looking for her, to see who would be his mother now.

She'd had a drink, now and the effect was that she felt no obligation to talk to anyone else, at all. Not even Gerald who stood tall and fair and hesitant on the edge of everything since climbing out of his car. *Gerald*. She could still hear Serena's voice, high and fond and fake.

'You've been here before,' she said in the kitchen, when she had stopped crying.

Lindsay shook her head, looking around the room, her gaze pausing on a row of coffee pots dusty on a shelf, frowning. There was a bottle of white wine on the table and two tumblers: Lindsay filled them both and put one into Rose's hand. Apart from the hair she registered that Lindsay didn't look like Kate, in fact, she had the short dark hair but she was looser, somehow, less put together, less neat. Older: close to, her face was soft and lined.

'Never been here before,' she said, looking around the kitchen still frowning as if she was trying to make sense of it. 'I just – I was nosy.' She turned, took a gulp of the wine, kept turning, looking. Her hands were small and roughened, with bitten nails and they reminded Rose of Kate's, pricked from sewing.

'I can't see her here. I can't. It's so – not Kate. She'd have had those coffee pots down and cleaned. And where's all her blue-and-white china?' She wiped her nose furiously, and it reddened. Rose had felt her stiffen under the hug, the onslaught of tears, trying to hold herself still and trembling with the effort.

Lindsay sighed, angrily. 'She asked me out here, once,' she said, and the edge of truculence was still there. 'Back at the beginning, when she – to see the baby.'

'Jamie,' said Rose, feeling a prick of unfamiliar tenderness at his name. Lindsay took another gulp of her wine and stared at the glass that was empty now and reached for the bottle. *People don't come to funerals to get drunk.* But it was the first time since she got here that Rose had felt like something real was happening – and dangerous. Lindsay might just grab the bottle and run outside shouting things.

'Twice, she asked me,' said Lindsay and her chin went up, defiant, her eyes were wide and wet, staring at something Rose couldn't see. 'The second time I didn't even answer. I didn't come.' When she looked again at Rose the tears had been blinked back. She spoke clearly. 'I went

119

quiet on her when she got pregnant and then I didn't come when he was born because I couldn't have babies myself. That's pathetic, isn't it? What kind of friend is that?' Lindsay didn't wait for an answer. 'I had it all out when I was thirty-seven. Kate knew that. Christ, everyone knew that, I'm the kind of woman who tells people on the bloody bus they've had their bits out.' She took a deep breath. 'My grandma died of breast cancer before there *was* genetic testing and my mum died of ovarian, because she didn't *believe* in genetic testing.' She looked straight at Rose. 'I'd had the test. I tried to say, to Kate, when she told me about her mum. *Your* mum. I tried to make her take the genetic test.'

'Don't,' said Rose, her mind skittering, because it was suddenly unbearable. 'Please don't. Blame yourself, I mean. I could have visited, I'm her sister. It's just—' but she broke off so as not to have to listen to herself making excuses. *I had no idea.* 'I wish I'd come. It's not your fault she died. It's not your fault.' *Not my fault. But what if it is?*

'Why didn't she understand?' said Lindsay. 'Why didn't she listen? They even met, didn't they, her and him, they met on a cancer thing. A charity thing. I mean, I get that you don't always want to know—' turning red suddenly, sitting down abruptly at the table. 'It's the menopause,' she said. 'It's part of it, losing your bits, they artificially induce the menopause. Don't listen to me.' She wouldn't look up: Rose saw the flush hot on her neck, behind her ears.

'But she never said. She must have been feeling like shit for months. She never *said*.' Rose sat down beside her and gingerly took another drink: the wine was tepid and sour, and didn't soothe anything. 'People thought she was just, you know, this sort of arty-crafty social worker type, but she had two degrees. Did you know that?'

Lindsay nodded, looking down at the glass between her hands. 'I worked with her, remember. I should have – I should have thought she might need friends. Being stuck at home with a baby, when you've been used to – the world. I should have come. She didn't ask me again, but I should have just turned up.'

'I know,' said Rose.

'So *why*—' Lindsay's anger had built instantly, it had just been waiting – and then there was a sound and there he'd been, in the door. Not Evan, but Gerald, stooped and apologetic and somehow dusty-looking in the doorway, looking from one to the other, panicked at the sight of both of them. Which one had he wanted to find alone? They stared back at him and he began to flounder.

'I'm sorry, I was—' his eyes alighted on the bottle, 'I just wanted to – is there any more wine? To take outside, I mean?' Two spots of red on his parchment cheeks.

They walked back out together, Gerald awkwardly carrying two bottles from the fridge, Lindsay cradling her glass and then Jamie was wriggling and thrashing awake and they separated as if by agreement. Leaning down to unfasten Jamie from his buggy Rose saw Lindsay talking to Martha the midwife but looking across at Evan. He was standing with his hands by his sides and looking at nothing, or something too far off to discern, between two elderly women in hats and a man in a dog-collar. He looked as though he wanted to be there, where he was looking, wherever it was. With Kate, thought Rose, wherever *she* was and her heart squeezed, guiltily glad to be alive and warm, even if Kate wasn't. Then Jamie seized her arm, pinching, surprisingly strong, and she lifted him out.

She shadowed the small figure as he ran on the uneven grass, propelled like a wind-up toy, running for the fun of being able to. Jamie tripped and stood and tripped again, escaping anyone who tried to detain him. Only once, when his hands smacked down flat on a paving stone did he look around for a familiar face – *that* face, his eyes passing over her and then as she ran Evan was between them and kneeling, kissing the small red hands, Jamie's eyes round and wet fixed on him.

'He's hungry,' she said. 'Shall I?' And Evan sat back, quiet, and let Jamie go to her.

Out of the corner of her eye she saw Gerald watching her, as she swung Jamie up and headed inside but when she came back out almost an hour later his car had gone. She looked around for Lindsay and couldn't see her either: she'd expected – hoped for – her to come back in, but when the soft sound came from the boiler room it was only Serena, flitting past without a word and back upstairs.

Holding out a piece of ham sandwich to Jamie in his high chair she had wondered suddenly, *And where was he?* Evan, cold and lost and mute and grieving. Jamie had grabbed and she had the sharp, vivid sense that she could walk back out there and find him gone, folded into the reeds and gone. And when she came around the house she didn't see him straight away but then he *was* there, still, he was kneeling at a flowerbed and patting something down under a bird box, before turning, as if he knew she had emerged.

Nobody seemed to notice, or think it was odd, that he was on his knees weeding, or whatever, people walking about his garden drinking wine. Rose felt a guilty pang, remembering the gin bottle carefully removed from the fridge. They knew him better than she did, of course, maybe he was always like this, shy, awkward. Of course it wasn't what she thought, what she dreaded, that he was just waiting for all their backs to be turned to die himself, to lie down and let the tide wash over him. She knelt and let Jamie go to him, and sheepish he stood up, brushing down his knees.

And then abruptly the last stragglers: the old ladies and the stooped vicar and a woman with a child, a girl smaller than Serena who Rose had been aware of only dimly. The woman introduced herself as another parent from Serena's school only as she was shaking Rose's hand goodbye. Anna, Annie, something like that. A woman tall with long lank hair, wide flat hips and an anxious, pouchy face. Rose stood suddenly too tired to speak. She stood under the veranda, weary and cold in a mist that seemed to be gathering at the corners of the garden, unrolling softly across the grass, softening Evan's outline as he walked towards them carrying Jamie.

She saw the woman – Anna, Annie – look round once, up at the house whose grey outlines were already softening in the twilight before hurrying after her daughter to her car, so eager to be gone suddenly that she slithered momentarily on the stones. Rose had the distinct impression none of them wanted to linger and she felt only dull relief, longing to be quiet, to be in bed and sleeping and for all of it to be over.

Evan seemed to guess because he was there, taking Jamie from her gently and she saw him focus, at last, looking at her.

'Where did Lindsay go?' she said.

'She had to run,' he said, helpless, apologetic. 'Gerald was going and he offered her a lift. She said to say goodbye.' He looked at her, bewildered. 'I didn't know you knew her so well.'

'Oh I – no. I don't, it's just—' She couldn't work it out. 'Who is Gerald?' she said. He passed a hand over his forehead and Jamie reached for it: for a second he looked down at Jamie.

'He's my partner in the business,' he said, then, drily, 'An old-fashioned gentlemanly sort. Lindsay was asking about calling for a taxi and he insisted.'

'It's OK,' said Rose. Lindsay must have heard all about her from Kate, she thought, resignedly. The feckless little sister, not worth giving time to – and after all, there was an element of truth in that. She hadn't wanted to know Kate's friends.

Evan seemed to detect her unhappiness. 'I'm sorry,' he said. 'I'm sorry you had to do all that,' he said and his eyes were kind on her, grateful. 'I don't know how I'd have managed without you.' He shifted Jamie round and put a hand on her shoulder, so soft she hardly felt it but warm, so warm in the cold grey evening she had to resist an impulse to bring her cheek down to it. But instead she looked back at the house, up to where the school mum had looked, but the windows were dark.

Evan didn't look. 'Early to bed,' he said, and then his hand was gone.

Weary Rose plodded up the wide stairs in the last of the greyish light falling through the cupola, and the red hall soft and dark below her. It seemed to glow with a queer kind of warmth. She was almost at her door, already anticipating the dark and the quiet and the deep comfort of the good night's sleep she hadn't had, it seemed, in weeks when a door opened ahead of her, the last door on that side of the gallery and there was Serena, standing framed in it. The room behind her was not quite dark.

'Do you want to see my room?' she said, and her head tilted, sly. She was wearing an old-fashioned nightdress, not too small for her but too big, this time, smocked and gathered.

'Oh, Serena—' Rose began, wanting to say, *Not now, tomorrow, please. Not now.* She saw Serena's small face watching for it, pale in the gathering dark.

'Sure,' she said, instead and followed the girl inside. The room was big, bigger than hers, on the corner of the house: she could make out a big old-fashioned bed and a small china basin in the corner. A pair of heavy dark curtains that hadn't yet been drawn hung either side of one of the big windows and on impulse Rose went straight there.

There was the bridge, then the rusty black shape of a big old graveyard yew almost as tall as the windowsill standing this side of it, below Rose a bit of the white fretwork of the veranda, where she had stood to say goodbye; where the teacher had looked up, fearfully. The

125

fog had rolled in closer since and now the garden's outlines were gone, only the feathered tips of the reeds were distinguishable, only the upper curve of the bridge's brickwork: as Rose watched it seemed to shift and swirl. Abruptly she reached for the curtains. 'Shall I—' but as she turned to ask Serena she saw her busy with something at the dim shape of a chest of drawers. She also saw that the door had been shut behind her.

'Serena?' And a match flared, and she saw Serena's sharp little face lit by it before she moved the flame to light a pair of candles. 'Oh, *no*,' escaped Rose and then she saw Serena's eyes shine, and stepped over to her, wanting to forestall it, whatever it was.

'It's just − it's just my—' said Serena, hissing and then she made a sharp sound and Rose saw it was because she had still been holding the match and it had burned her fingers.

Rose moved fast, seizing her by the shoulders marched her to the little sink, taking the burned fingers and putting them under the cold tap but something drummed in her head. The candles. Beside the sink were tiny Post-it notes in a column up the wall, pink and green and yellow, with writing on that Rose couldn't read in the dim light but looked like dates. Revision? At twelve she surely didn't have exams, but what did Rose know?

Looking back nervously over her shoulder she saw that the candles were either side of some framed photographs, and a litter of little objects, she could make out a tiny china box, a little bowl. One hand holding Serena's fingers under the water, another on her shoulder Rose could feel her rigid under her grip, as if strung on wires.

Girls made shrines. Rose had never done it, but it was normal, wasn't it, it—

'I'm all *right*,' said Serena and pulled away from her violently. Rose took a deep breath and turned off the tap. Serena moved across the room, the nightdress floating pale in the dark and Rose followed her.

'Look, Serena,' she began but Serena turned on her, in an instant.

'No,' she said, savagely and the white oval of her face shone with anger. '*No. You* look.'

Rose stiffened, holding back. There were four or five framed photographs on the scarred surface of the chest of drawers, one of a woman with Evan, holding hands, one of her cradling a small fierce baby that must be Serena, one of her holding up a grey cat, a cat as sleek and high-cheekboned as she was, tolerating the manhandling. At just the sight of the animal Rose felt it, the old familiar prickle, her throat, her nose, her eyes, and sneezed. She saw interest grow in Serena's face as she pulled out a tissue from her pocket and blew her nose.

'You don't still have the cat?' she asked. Serena stared at her.

'Daddy doesn't like cats,' she said. Tilting her head as if Rose was a specimen, 'Do they make you sneeze?'

'I'm allergic to them,' said Rose, her lips tingling.

'It's only a picture,' said Serena, disdainful, and then in a darting movement she grabbed the biggest of the photographs and thrust it at her, up close. A pointed chin like Serena's, tilted sideways, slanted eyes, splintered like quartz, long pale hair parted in the centre. Rose stared at Serena's mother, mesmerised. Not just because she was as beautiful as a painting, or startlingly young but because she could not have looked less like Kate: sturdy practical Kate with her warm dark eyes, who would have taken off her glasses and blinked if anyone had tried to paint her, *poor Kate, poor Kate* – and before she could stop herself Rose had taken Serena's wrists. Only for a second, but long enough.

Then Rose let go and in that second she saw that the candles, guttering, were burned almost down, clean of drippings but the wooden top of the chest showed where they had fallen. She must do this every night.

Rose took in the other photographs, 'There,' Serena said. '*That's* my mother. Not you, not you or your stupid ugly sister.'

Rose took an involuntary step backwards under the force of her hatred, but the face in the photograph held her and they stared at each other, Serena white-lipped, the hollows dark under her eyes.

'My sister wasn't ugly,' said Rose, finding her voice, finding something else with it. 'And she wasn't stupid.'

Serena looked at her, disdainful, then carefully she set the photograph down flat on its face, and all the others after it. 'You can't look at her,' she said. 'She's just mine.'

'Serena,' said Rose, suddenly pitying, remembering how young she was, how little she had. 'I'm so sorry about your mum, it must have been—'

'Oh, I was too young for it to matter,' said Serena, in her precise little voice. 'I was five. Children forget about things, everybody knows that.'

'I don't think they do,' said Rose, and abruptly Serena stepped back from her, into the dark, and then she was at the door and tugging it open.

128

'You can go away, now,' she said, and half her face was hidden by the door but her voice jeered, 'She's dead and you can go back to your boyfriend in Italy. I'm better at looking after Jamie than you anyway.'

Rose's scalp prickled, with all the things the girl knew, she felt the dark of the room close around her and she moved, before she could do something stupid, like shake the girl or slap her, three, four steps and she was on the threshold, the glowing dark of the red hall below her.

'She was a liar.'

Not sure if she'd heard or imagined the words, hissed softly as she passed out of the room, Rose turned back.

'Your stupid. Ugly. Sister,' said Serena, her face at the crack. 'She was a liar, too.' And as the crack closed Rose saw a last flicker of the red candles behind her.

Chapter Fourteen

The fog didn't lift all weekend. Rose learned things – not many, but enough – about Jamie, as she carried him or followed him padding from room to room downstairs, around the shrouded furniture, into the green dim sitting room or – anxious – out on to the grass where he would straight away begin to wander in search of the sound of the water. He kept her occupied, and exhausted her: every time she wanted to break away, he cried out for her.

Of Serena, who stayed upstairs, mostly in her room but occasionally walking the gallery, softly, Rose learned almost nothing, except that she was secretive. And of Evan? That when he wasn't working in the green sitting room, he liked to go out into the garden and stand motionless on the edge of the reeds, looking at the house. That he said almost nothing, but he watched her. She caught sight of him, as he looked in to the kitchen from the yard, or standing motionless behind the crack of a door, as she passed through the hall. She supposed he wanted to give her time alone with her nephew, without feeling she was being judged.

Rose did feel it, all the same, whether it was him, or poor lost Kate, or herself doing the judging. But as she navigated the strange quiet spaces with Jamie's warm weight in her arms, without being conscious of having made the decision, Rose allowed the realisation to sink in, that she had to stay. For as long as they needed her.

At intervals, she found herself taking her phone out of habit and then just staring at it, all its apps useless. *No service.* Once or twice a ghost sort of signal appeared briefly then disappeared. She looked through her photographs, old emails, searching for what it had used to mean, this magic object. There were new photographs appearing: Jamie in Serena's arms. Evan on his knees by the flowerbed. Evan clearly didn't like having his photograph taken.

She had to say something, and she did, seizing a moment in the kitchen the next morning, but even as the words – 'I had a dress' – spilled out of her mouth, the story seemed frivolous, selfish. He looked at her as she blundered on. 'There was a tiny blob of red wax, and in Serena's room—' but then his face was so pale and drawn and Rose still felt the aftermath of the funeral in her own bones, that long exhausting confusing day, like the after-effects of illness, that she faltered. 'It doesn't matter,' she said. 'I'm sure she didn't mean – it couldn't have—'

'I'm sorry,' he said, simply, and Rose thought, *His heart is broken as it is, and the poor child's just unhappy* and she smiled, shook her head, blinking back tears.

'I've got go in to work,' he said then, helpless, 'I've got so much to catch up on, since . . .'

'Of course,' said Rose. 'We can get to know each other properly,' she said. 'Me and Jamie. And – and Serena.'

But Serena avoided her almost completely, appearing for meals, her face bland and composed whenever Evan was watching: when Rose saw her something else crept in, a secret, malicious, watchful look, like a spy. She didn't offer to help with Jamie, leaving Rose to flounder. Once, when he'd thrown his food on the floor and Rose was grovelling under the table to scrape it up she saw Serena's bare brown feet in the doorway, and knew she was watching. One foot set on the other, a toe curling: Rose could imagine the expression of satisfaction, and as she shifted back she saw the feet disappear, noiseless until the small soft sound of the green baize door closing behind her came.

A liar. The words came back to her. Kate had been, to Rose, the most honest person she could imagine. Upright and straightforward and truthful. It could mean anything, though, on Serena's lips.

At one point, coming into the hall in search of Evan to ask where the dustpan was because she'd broken a jam jar, Rose had glimpsed him upstairs on the gallery, at the door of the room he had shared with Kate. She had retreated, with a keen sense of having intruded on something, to look for the dustpan on her own. Couldn't she have just called up, *where's the dustpan?* And couldn't she even have said, *is that Kate's room* while she was at it, and waited to be asked up? But she could see him, in her head, turning to look at her from the gallery, sorrowful.

She couldn't. So she had gone back to the kitchen while Jamie shrieked from his highchair and the unfamiliar sense of her own incompetence was so dampening, like the fog, disorientating, that Rose had to be reminded, by Evan, calling her pale and kind from the top of the stairs on the Saturday evening, that the hour of internet had arrived. He took Jamie, who squalled and reached for her, and told her to go and make the most of it.

'I don't want to exploit you,' he said, bravely, as Jamie wriggled, and made a sweeping motion, sending her up the stairs.

Feeling strangely aimless and lopsided suddenly without Jamie's counterweight Rose ran up to her room and got out her laptop, logged on, dialled. As the strange peeping sounds started up, the icon with Deb's curly head on it, waiting for her to answer she looked around at the little room, wondering what Deb would make of it, out of focus over her shoulder. A framed watercolour Kate had done, a patchwork cushion, the writing desk by the window.

Serena might have been lying, of course: with the memory of the mutilated dress not yet erased although she'd folded it carefully and put it away, that thought occurred to Rose. Just out of malice to point out what a bad sister she was and at the same time to jeer at Kate's delusions, that her little sister would ever get it together to visit. But it felt true: the objects whispered to her, *sister*, and a knot tightened in Rose's belly. The sonar peep went on, unanswered.

Deb wasn't there. The screen still said, offline. There had been no arrangement made, in the end, and it was Saturday night. Deb did have a life, after all. Downstairs

Jamie's bellowing was reaching a crescendo. An hour of internet was nothing, was it? It didn't matter. She logged off then, on impulse, logged in to Facebook, searching back for Kate. For clues: those first months with Jamie, the desperation she remembered: because there must have been comfort, too, happiness, Kate getting to grips with motherhood as she always got to grips with any task. Achievements, lessons learned.

Rose knew there might be other clues too, clues she might not want to see. Pain, or worry, a visit to the doctor, a symptom unexplained. The silent killer. Her own page appeared, faded and out of date as an old newspaper: she hadn't been on Facebook in months and months, it was all old news, other people's pictures, chats with students or fellow teachers dwindled into nothing.

Had she thought Kate's page might magically have reappeared? It was still gone. Nothing.

The sound downstairs changed, Jamie's howls were something else. He was sobbing, sobbing, inconsolable, a sound that set up an unbearable vibration and Rose stood so suddenly from the bed where she'd sat with the laptop that it bounced to the edge but she'd just left it where it was, and run.

On Sunday morning Evan went to the supermarket, without telling her. She assumed he was working upstairs until she heard the car crunching back across the bridge and felt her heart flip at the sound, the thought of a visitor. But coming outside to see him hauling shopping bags out of the back of the battered orange car, she had to suppress a feeling of frustration.

Why couldn't *she* have gone? She could drive – or

there was the bicycle. She could have been in a super-market, in the aisles, in the bright real world where people were. And then Serena was behind her, brushing past soft and light with her strange outdoor smell, bonfires, smoke and leaves, to stand by her father. Gravely handing her a bag to carry Evan was smiling at Rose, like a child wanting approval, and Rose had to squash her disappointment. Because after all, it was just a supermarket shop, and besides, she had no money to pay for it.

'School tomorrow?' Because it was Sunday night, and she mentioned it only in passing, not thinking – although afterwards she knew it was not by accident that she said it – turning round from the sink where she was washing the pan she'd used to make risotto – after Serena had left the table.

Serena had sat at the table reading her book while spooning the rice into her mouth, too absorbed to be rude. Seeing her do it, her finger on the page of a book Rose had loved herself, the pinched frown of concentration, Rose couldn't see the other Serena at all, the vindictive, jealous, dangerous Serena. But then as if she could read Rose's mind Serena had looked up, from one of them to the other, closed her book and marched out.

'What does she do up there for hours on end?' The problem with risotto was always the sticky pan, and she was scrubbing when she asked the question, prompted by the sound of a door closing above their heads. Evan had looked at her, clouded, and she had remembered the calendar and changed the subject quickly, saying it. *School tomorrow?* He murmured something and stood to clear the plates, Jamie drooping half asleep in his high chair.

135

Jamie had quietened down immediately, the night before, just at the sight of Rose in the doorway to the green sitting room where he sat on the floor. Evan had been sitting beside him with his elbows on his knees and his hands in his hair, his face hidden. Jamie's sudden stillness was only interrupted by a last hiccupping sob before his arms lifted to her. The heavy feeling his dependence gave her was shifting, Rose had realised then, leaning to take him up, the less she resisted it the more it settled into something easier. She had touched his warm streaked cheek and as if she'd pressed a button his head had tipped sideways on to her shoulder.

She looked across at him now, his sleepy head jerking upright, and she set the clean pan on the draining board and went across to get him.

When Rose had got back to bed, eventually, her laptop was on the floor: it must have fallen off although she hadn't heard it. It wouldn't turn on for the longest time, and when it eventually did the battery was almost dead.

'So Serena goes back to school tomorrow?' she said, settling him on her hip. Evan looked at her, despondent.

'I suppose so,' he said.

Hearing her silence, he sighed. 'I just can't stand the thought of people—' and he looked at her quickly, his dark eyes fixing on her for a warm moment then looking away, knowing she knew. She did know. 'In the playground. Other parents talking. You know. Feeling sorry for her, for us. I—'

'I'll take her,' Rose said, abruptly, and he looked up at her, startled. 'You need to give her a chance to deal with it, at least. I'll take her, and I'll see off anyone who tries to look sorry for her. For us.'

And for the first time since she had seen him at the airport, it seemed to Rose, Evan's face cleared: he made a small movement. And for a moment she saw what he wanted to do out of sorrow, or gratitude or – like her, like Rose, just the need to touch someone who understood, the one person who understood – so clearly that she almost moved first.

But he stayed where he was. And barely daring to consider what it was her old anger with him had become, so did she.

'I'll tell her,' he said. 'Tomorrow, then.'

When Rose came to, she was at the door to the back staircase, her face was pressed against it, and she was listening.

Something had woken her, a sharp sound: it always took a sharp sound, or sensation, stubbing her toe against the table or knocking something to the floor and sometimes she couldn't tell which it had been. Rose hadn't sleepwalked in a decade, but she remembered the feeling immediately, the transition. The sense that there was another world in between the real one and the sleeping one, where words crept in, faces crept in, orders were issued.

Help me.

She knew there were reasons. She'd started sleepwalking in the phase when she wasn't eating, after Mum's death. Her body at night insisted it needed nourishment and Rose had used to sleepwalk to the kitchen and open the fridge door and cram slices of ham into her mouth, drinking milk from the carton to wash it down. The milk would rouse her and seeing the bright interior of the fridge she would wipe her mouth and go back to bed, sedated by food.

Later it was other things, exams, leaving home, leaving Dad. Up and out of bed, a puppet pulled by invisible strings. There were scientific explanations.

The brain, though. Science didn't quite cover what the brain could do, the corridors it could trace, the shadowed alleys. Rose stood there in the velvet dark, feeling the draught from downstairs curling round her bare legs, seeing her hands against the old wood of the door in the pale light that fell on her through the cupola, silvery moonlight. The soft pulse in her ear against the little door was the sound of her own blood, and that was all the brain was, blood and chemicals except that it could tell you stories. What science put together in the daylight, the brain's secret passages reconfigured in the dark.

The dream, or the state halfway between dream and waking that had brought her here sat, secretive, behind her eyes. It shifted and swirled, it was Deb's face accompanied by that sonar ping, Deb at the bottom of an ocean; it was Lindsay in the kitchen, pressed back against the stove and her angry mouth moving; and it was the sound of Evan talking softly to Serena behind her bedroom door.

Quick. It was as if she heard the word, but it was in her head. She ran, back round the gallery, heart thumping, into her room. Close the door, *quiet,* into bed. *Listen. Listen.*

She put her hands to her ears to stop the low, hoarse, hopeless sound, but it was there. Muffled behind doors, hiding behind curtains, under the sheets. Somewhere,

138

someone was crying, a sound that was so strange, so deprived that Rose didn't know if it came from man, woman or child, or her own head.

Once Kate had been home when Rose sleepwalked and had been there when she woke, right there in front of her but not daring to touch her, for fear. Waking a sleepwalker was dangerous, they said, and Kate was careful, always careful. Only when she saw Rose focus, when she heard her bleat, *What, what?* then Kate had put her arms around her and led her back to bed.

She slept.

Chapter Fifteen

They said the house was haunted from the word go.

It made Evan actually angry: he hates that kind of thing. Astrology, ghosts, auras, crystals: even psychology, dream analysis. The estate agent said it bluffly, smiling, offering it up as a joke. Saying, *Well, look at it this way, it means it's cheap. And available.* Dangling the keys, a big old rusty one to the front door that wouldn't work even if you tried to turn it with both hands. Evan glowering in the corner.

And when we came around the corner he wanted the house straight away, of course. *Oh darling, oh darling,* he said breathless, running up to me, throwing his arms around me.

I asked if we could redecorate when I saw the hall. That colour, the dark dark red, the hall is never light, not even with the sun streaming down. You only need to look up at the great brass hook to wonder, *Was it here?* But the girl who died, the girl whose ghost was supposed to haunt the place hadn't hung herself, hadn't died in that big strange shadowy space. The estate agent just smiled when I asked, standing under the cupola in that strange light; he was uneasily hearty, beginning to regret having mentioned it. It was all a long time ago, he said, but he was quite sure it wasn't hanging, wasn't here. Him looking over at Evan as if to say, *these women and their stories*, but Evan stalked off, refusing even to go near the subject.

I couldn't forget it, though. History is history; we'll all be history some day and we all want our stories to be told, don't we?

The difficulty is when you ask around, you get versions, with stories like this that are handed down. A ghost story is supposed to be embellished. A man in the boatyard has one version and someone's grandma has another. I did ask around, and I googled, and the version – the greengrocer's as a matter of fact, a miserable old biddy as a rule but she warmed to this subject – that felt right to me eventually as the house came to settle around me was: she wasn't a young girl but the vicar's housekeeper. An old maid, seduced and foolish with love, unexpectedly pregnant and then discarded, her last hope of love gone. She took poison. Took poison and crept away into the warm dark to die and there they found her curled like a mouse, stiff and dead and white, on the back stairs.

I'll re-paper the hall, when I've got the energy, I'll get the front door key to work. Let them tell their stories about that, about how I threw the doors open, and the light came in and filled my beautiful house.

'You look pale,' said Evan, looking sideways at her from the driver's seat. 'Are you sleeping?' She glanced away, feeling herself soften under his warm, steady look.

141

From behind them came a sarcastic grunt from Serena. They were on their way to school: a compromise arrangement. Evan would drive, and park around the corner. Rose would walk Serena in.

'I'm not a flipping baby,' Serena had said when the plan had been outlined to her at breakfast, glaring and Evan had said sharply, *Serena*. She'd looked at him long and hard and stalked off, but when the time came she'd appeared with her hair brushed and her school bag packed. *He's all she's got*, thought Rose. Itching to say it, *Try having the dad I had*. She looked back at Serena now, between the seats, and with a small shock of recognition what she saw was herself. Bad-tempered, ungracious, stroppy. Frightened. She withdrew her head.

'I'm fine,' said Rose. 'I slept fine.' He glanced again then quickly looked back at the road: they'd come to the junction with the tarmac and a truck thundered past.

There was something persistent, though, in that look, even now he was pulling away, checking his wing mirror, she could tell he wanted to examine her face for clues. She'd heard them arguing the night before: maybe that was it. And then, only then, she remembered, waking up around the gallery with her cheek to the secret door. Perhaps he'd heard *her*.

'What about you?' she said, lightly. No sound from Serena, this time: she could hear the tinny hiss of something in headphones. Jamie was quiet too, sleepy as a little owl after a bowl and a half of porridge, his head turning mechanically as the hedges flashed past.

'Well,' said Evan, 'you know.'

'Um, not really,' she said, avoiding his eye.

It was his turn to glance into the backseat to see if Serena was listening. The tinny sound hissed on. Looking back he shook his head, wearily. 'I don't sleep,' he said, weary, and his voice cracked. 'Not since—' He tried to smile, out of the corner of his mouth and at the sight of that lopsided look, with the hoarse sound of his voice, something turned over inside her.

'Maybe you should go back to – your bedroom,' she said. 'I could always take a turn with Jamie, you know? It can't be easy to relax in there.' The picture of him came into her head, him lying alone on the narrow bed, staring at the ceiling while Jamie slept evenly and soundly. Perhaps it had been Evan who'd made the sound that woke her. Perhaps he had heard her gasp, as she woke.

But he just shook his head.

When Serena climbed out of the car, Rose, waiting on the pavement, saw her tug the skirt down, saw the uniform was getting too small for her. No one could have mistaken her for Kate's daughter, she was all legs and elbows, like a grasshopper. It seemed as if she'd grown an inch even since Rose's arrival – Rose remembered going on stubbornly growing herself after Mum died, when by rights she should have shrunk into nothing.

'All right?' she said, reaching for Serena's elbow as her stuffed school backpack slid sideways, almost pulling her over. Serena drew away and stalked off ahead of her.

'You're not holding my hand,' she'd said as she came back into the kitchen and there was no chance of that. Rose followed her though, stubborn, along the pavement.

The school was a low Seventies building with blue glass panels and a garish new sports hall: no playground,

Rose remembered that herself, when you went to big school you looked in vain for a space to run around and be stupid. But there was a strip of grass and pupils – some gangly in their blue-and-grey uniforms, some still looking like little kids with sleeves too long – were milling around, in gangs. A space seemed to clear for Serena, and Rose remembered that happening after Mum. Like there was something wrong with you. Serena's head was held up high. Nobody looked at Rose: grown-ups were invisible.

The teacher was waiting at the classroom door to take her in. She wore glasses, ugly block heels and tights, a hand descending on Serena's shoulder a second then lifting and released, Serena went inside. 'Is there anything we should know?' the teacher said in an undertone to Rose, stared and hurriedly added, 'We are aware of the – of the—'

'Nothing,' said Rose, siding for that moment with Serena against the nosy intrusiveness of dumpy teachers. With Serena, and Evan. 'She's— I think she'll be fine.' The teacher pushed her glasses back up her nose and stared herself, a moment, then went in after Serena. The door closed.

Walking back out through a long wide lino-tiled corridor, listening to the hum of teachers' voices behind doors, Rose found herself almost hypnotised by memory: the school she and Kate had attended, years apart, had been so similar, a low Seventies construction of coloured glass and flaking laminate, it had even smelled the same. The corridor echoed: she heard footsteps somewhere behind her, hasty, and hurried, but then there was a loud scraping of chairs that filled the space, and immediately after that singing began. She took a wrong turning and found herself at the foot of some stairs.

Shit. She turned and almost immediately a woman came around the corner and was hurrying towards her. A tall woman with lank hair and wide flat hips in jeans. A woman she knew or at least had seen before. Anna, Annie.

Her hand was out as if she was worried she might trip, her hair flopped. She came up to Rose, panting. 'I'm sorry,' she said, catching her breath.

'Is it – Annie?' said Rose and the woman grimaced.

'I wasn't following you,' she said, then, 'Well, I was,' and let out an abrupt laugh. 'We didn't get a chance to talk at the – the—'

'The funeral,' said Rose, thinking, *We didn't even do it properly enough for her to know what it was.* Everything had been wrong. That awkward gathering of people.

'Right,' said Annie, holding her ground.

Rose knew immediately that this woman had been Kate's friend. She seemed to doubt every word that came out of her own mouth, and there was Kate, steady and certain and kind.

'I'm lost,' she volunteered, sheepish, smiling. 'Can you show me how to get out of this place?'

Annie smiled, a wide grin. 'Oh yes, oh yes, of course.' Patting Rose on the shoulder, a kind gesture. 'This way.' She walked briskly, as if the school corridors were a place she needed to escape. Rose had to hurry to keep up.

'Your daughter's Serena's friend?' It was her turn to be breathless.

145

'Yes, well, yes. They have their moments but – yes.' Annie examined her, thoughtfully. 'This way.' A sharp left-hand turn and they were at a small side door, and out. Annie stopped abruptly in a pool of sunshine on the concrete forecourt and breathed out.

'You don't like it in there?' said Rose. Annie shook her head, laughing sheepishly.

'I wasn't happy at school,' she said, tugging down her sweatshirt over her hips. Shrugged. 'I was – overweight. And – I hated it, in fact. I think Evie – that's my daughter – caught it off me.' She made a face. 'Serena's very bright,' she said, regarding Rose. 'Evie worships her. I hope – I hope – Kate always said you—' and a bright flush came to her cheeks, her eyes abruptly brimmed.

'Kate was your friend,' said Rose softly. Suddenly she found herself not wanting to hear what Kate might have said about her. 'She was always a good friend.'

Annie's head bobbed up and down. 'Such a good friend. Such a good friend. She said Serena was kind underneath, she'd just had an awful – well, you know.' She took deep breaths of the cool damp air. There were trees on the grass in front of the school, and their leaves were just beginning to rust and turn.

'I don't really know,' said Rose tentative, 'actually, I don't. What happened to Serena's – her mother?'

Annie frowned. 'She died,' she said abruptly. 'Didn't you know that? She died, too.'

'Yes, well, I—' Rose hesitated. 'I assumed. When Serena was small?'

'Eight years ago.' Annie's wide flat face was grave. 'Serena was only four, or five.'

146

'I knew that, I knew Serena was small. Was it—' the word wasn't *easy*. And this felt intrusive: what business, after all, was it of hers, it was ghoulish, it was – but she wanted to know. It seemed important, she didn't know why. 'Was that cancer too?'

Annie stared, her head tilted.

'Oh, no,' she said, eventually. 'Although—' hurrying, catching herself up. 'Kate thought that, too, I suppose cancer is what you worry about.' She frowned down at her hands.

'Well, or a car accident,' said Rose, slowly. Hadn't they met on some cancer fundraiser? She must have got that wrong. 'So what was it?'

Annie rubbed at her upper arms defensively. 'Yes, I suppose. In a way it was. A kind of accident, anyway. Has Serena talked to you about it? About her mother?'

Rose opened her mouth, feeling the flush rise at the memory of the candles, the little shrine. She shook her head. 'Not really.'

'She was very clever apparently, very beautiful. A lot to live up to. A lot for Serena to live up to and – Kate, too.' Annie sighed, heavily. 'Such a horrible shock it must have been. She had a fit and fell down the stairs. Evan was—' a minute pause, 'her dad was at work.'

Something there, that tiny hesitation prompted his image in her own imagination, dark and fierce and sad.

'Look,' said Annie impulsively, 'do you need a lift? I—'

'Oh, no,' said Rose quickly, 'Evan's waiting for me—' she saw Annie's head snap round, looking. 'No, he's round the corner,' and Annie drew her head back in.

'I see,' she said, and after a moment's frowning hesitation, 'I can bring Serena home after school now and again,' she said. 'If you've only got the one car. I used to offer but Kate always said no.'

'Serena seems to want to be independent,' said Rose warily.

'Kate was so determined,' said Annie, abruptly, 'that Serena should be able to trust her not to leave her, never to leave her, because her own mother, well, children, you know; death maybe looks like you have a choice, they think adults always have a choice.' Blinked, blinked. 'And then Kate died, too.'

'She's angry,' said Rose, frowning, not sure where this was going. 'Yes.'

'You're so good,' said Annie, biting her lip. 'You're so good to step in, but—'

'Annie,' said Rose, because what Annie meant came clear, before Rose understood herself how she would answer. The decision that had crept up on her in tiny steps over the hours and days – it seemed like weeks – since she'd come back, since she'd stepped inside the house where Kate had died, since she'd taken Jamie when he was handed to her. 'I won't leave them.' And then. 'I've got to go now,' and turned, blinded, into the sunshine.

Walking back to the car across the wide forecourt, empty now of students, she could still feel the weight of Annie's hand on her arm, wide and bony like her hips, trying to convey some message to her. Thinking confusedly of Jamie, who needed her, who wouldn't let her out of his sight, and of the house, drawing them back in. The house folding them into itself among the mist and the reeds, its corners and corridors, its secret places she hadn't even seen yet.

At the corner Rose turned back, feeling as though they were all watching her from the rows of school windows, just like Evan had said. Annie was still standing there, tall and spare as a scarecrow in the pool of sunlight, impossible to think of her as the overweight schoolgirl.

And Rose came around the corner and there was the car and there was Jamie, his face at the rear window, his hands flat against the glass.

Chapter Sixteen

It was a week: a week from the funeral, Friday to Friday. It took that school week, and the mist clung on for most of it.

The fog was part of the geography of the place, Evan told her when it persisted, as he packed his bag for work in the kitchen. She had observed it. A slim new-looking laptop, a particular kind of technical pencil, a big battered notebook. The fog was to do with the marsh and the weir and the estuary, the moisture always in the air, the collision of warm and cold fronts. She had only half listened, looking out through the kitchen window into the drooping black mist-hung branches of the yew tree.

The days fell into a pattern very quickly. It wasn't that Rose wanted to take charge, to establish a routine – *her* routine – it just fell out that way. Evan taking Serena to school at eight every morning, leaving Jamie with Rose. He would knock on her door, tentative, soft, at seven. The first day he was apologetic, the next, she was waiting at the door so he wouldn't have to be, holding out her arms for Jamie, still yawning.

The first couple of days he came back after the school run to make sure she was OK, got his stuff and went. Then she told him he should go straight from the school to work, it made sense. He flushed and she wondered if she'd said the wrong thing but then his head bobbed, grateful. Watching him disappear again in a cloud of dust she wondered about his day, the office, Gerald on the next desk.

Very soon Jamie's nap was what she looked forward to, always with a pang of guilt. She would take him out in the big three-wheeled pushchair after she'd given him lunch, along the road towards the town because the surface was smoother than the other direction towards the weir, where it wasn't much more than a footpath knotted with roots that disappeared between hedges. And thinking perhaps she might get all the way to town, but she never did: the moment she saw his head droop she would wheel round and hurry back to explore the house.

It might be a routine already, but it was just temporary, of course it was. Rose kept reminding herself of that: the world was still waiting for her, a job, a life, coffee in bars, and people.

She still kept her phone charged, got it out and looked at it out of habit, but there it was. *No service.* She could hear Deb putting a positive spin on it, digital detox, change your life. There were some books on art and architecture on the half-empty shelves in the green sitting room that she thought must be Evan's – eco-housing, modern art

– and she browsed through them there when Jamie was asleep, after dinner. The boxes beyond the staircase remained unpacked: it all felt provisional. Would Evan sell the place? And they'd all move on. He said nothing about it, work seemed to wear him out to silence. Give him time.

But putting the phone back in her pocket for the hundredth time, walking briskly back down the lane in the mist, with the strange diffuse saturated light where the sun glowed far off and invisible and feeling the buzz of the hour and a half of freedom awaiting her, it was the old life that began to seem like a dream. She sank down in the sofa absorbed in stories, instead, occasionally looking up in a daze to register the news on the TV.

And there were Kate's things. 'I packed them up because – it seemed easier,' Evan had said, about the boxes. 'Every time Jamie saw anything of hers—' and he had moved his head as if something was hurting him. 'It got so difficult.'

'I understand,' said Rose, and she did: Dad had done the same thing. She still thought it was wrong.

'It's all there, though,' Evan said humbly. 'I kept it for you.'

There wasn't as much of it as she expected. A few boxes of books, witness to Kate's passions, the ones that lasted and the ones that didn't: books on stained glass, stencilling, watercolours, art history. A wicker basket of Kate's needlework – tapestry cushion covers and wall hangings, all neatly folded and packed in tissue, with old mothballs in between – that made Rose sit back on her heels and wonder why they'd never been brought inside, before replacing them carefully, stricken with the thought that perhaps she never had the energy. Boxes of things that hadn't been unpacked.

Putting them back in, a flash of pink nylon surprised her, pink never Kate's colour, and she pulled at it. One of those things people wore on charity runs. She sat back on her heels, frowning. The logo made it clear, a charity rally for cancer, so she'd remembered that bit right. And it was the kind of thing Kate would do, for Mum, and Rose had just managed to mix it up somehow with her meeting Evan. She wished she could remember. She wished she had *listened*.

She put the tabard down.

In another box she found a small battered paperback that surprised her, a self-help manual on creative writing. It was soft and worn, as if Kate had pored over it, and Rose held it in her hands a moment, wondering, and then she had heard the sharp interrogative shout from the buggy which meant Jamie had woken up, and freedom was over for the day. She took the book with her, though: it felt warm, somehow, and when she lifted the pages to her face, along with the mustiness of damp paper she smelled Kate, a smell of grass and flowers and something of earth, too, earth under her fingernails from gardening. The thought constricted her throat, Kate not buried but burned, as she lifted Jamie out of the pushchair and she pressed her face to his little neck, breathing him in instead.

Once she experimented with taking him out of the pushchair, painstakingly unclasping the straps with fumbling fingers, laying him warm and unresisting against her shoulder and carrying him inside up to his cot in hopes it might prolong the sleep. He settled back and straightening, she looked around the little room, the narrow bed where Evan was still sleeping. It made sense to her now, him in here. Jamie was what was left of Kate.

She didn't know what he'd done with the ashes. They weren't in Jamie's room because that was what she'd been looking round for, hoping Evan wasn't keeping them in there, because somehow that would be wrong, as though they might escape their urn to be breathed in. Reversing carefully out into the hall, watching his small chest rise and fall in the cot, she half closed the door. She was standing then on the corner of the gallery, between Jamie's room and Kate's, or Kate and Evan's bedroom, the master bedroom.

She'd seen the windows from the outside: it had a double set. She could almost make out the pattern of the curtains, and she knew, because it was one of the few things she remembered from those long-ago emails, that Kate had made them herself. Kate had been making curtains since she was barely out of her teens, she could have done it for a living.

Rose had tried the door. It wasn't the first time she'd done it, covertly, but it was still locked. In case the door got left open and Jamie cried to be let in.

'It's why I keep her— our room locked.' Although she'd seen Evan, in the evenings, up there on the gallery. He went in there. Rose knew why, he would be touching her things, like she'd done herself, looking for what was left of her, pressing his cheek against the curtains. That was what he did when he couldn't sleep. It was what she'd do.

The list of things Rose wanted to ask Evan when he

got back grew. Could she drive the car, was there a big town anywhere near, were there any language schools she could teach at there, when, when – well, at some unspecified time, what was Lindsay's phone number?

She wanted to suggest that maybe she could come and see his office, bring Jamie and a picnic lunch. She had pored over the brochures at the kitchen table while feeding Jamie one time, a lot of statistics about carbon neutrality and heat exchangers, an artist's impression of severe little wood-lapped houses on the edge of the estuary, a gleam of water and some new trees and – elegant in a shroud of artistic mist – a wind-generator.

Rose could imagine Kate loving that picture, like she'd loved those books when she was a kid, the *Little House* books all about the American prairies and wagon trains and self-sufficiency and maybe those little houses Evan was building had been for Kate, really. She couldn't ask.

Maybe she could go and see them. See him at work, at that drawing board: the thought warmed her, she couldn't quite articulate why. The thought of watching him doing something he was good at; it felt like an escape from – all this.

There were so many questions she couldn't ask. *What was it like? Finding the person you loved dead.* She couldn't ask that. She'd been a thousand miles away.

Why didn't they know she was dying? Why did no one see?

On the Thursday it rained. It came down in sheets, steady and constant. Looking out from an upper window with Jamie, watching it stream down the glass, it seemed as though there was no division between land and sea, it was one great grey watery waste, broken here and there by the black skeleton of a tree or the marsh grass ruffling the water's surface.

It was still raining by the time Serena was due back from school and she spent half of her freedom walking to the bus stop to take her an umbrella with Jamie asleep under a rain-cover. They walked back in silence, Serena's shoulder only occasionally bumping against hers in the proximity enforced by the shared umbrella.

Serena spoke only once. 'She did, you know,' she said, stopping in the middle of the lane. 'She did do that room just for you.' Glaring at her from under severe eyebrows. 'Why didn't you come?'

Rose looked at her, trying to work out if this was more hostility or something else. Wondering if she would ever get an opportunity to tell Serena she understood, to tell her she knew, she forgave her, for the dress.

'I would if I'd known,' she said, simply, leaving out all the excuses about not having enough money or being too busy. 'I was stupid, and selfish.' Rose made herself say it. 'Little sisters are like that sometimes, they don't realise how they're behaving until it's too late—' It wasn't about her. 'I would have come if I'd known how hard things were for her.' She hesitated under the steady glare. 'For everyone.' Serena's lips tightened at that and she began to walk again, marching.

And back in the room, listening with half an ear to Serena along the corridor unpacking her schoolbag, she stood and let her eyes roam over the little blue-and-white room, the room Kate had decorated for her. And there they were on the top shelf, the *Little House* books, in

156

order, tattered but intact. The turquoise glass lamp at the bedside that Rose had never seen before coming here, but she loved. She took down one of the books – the first one, its cover had a hand-tinted engraving of a log cabin beside a lake that made her close her eyes a sudden moment, against the weird stir of memory. She put it down abruptly, beside the bed, under the lamp.

The rolltop desk. Rose passed her hand over it and tried it again, easing her fingertips under the pale varnished wood, but it didn't budge. There were three drawers beneath it, she pulled open each in turn but they were all empty, releasing only the faint sweet mustiness of old wood.

She made stew for supper that day. She had used almost all the food in the larder and had planned to cycle Jamie to the town for more that morning but the rain had stopped her and instead she'd raided the freezer and used up the last wrinkled vegetables from an organic box that had been there since her arrival.

The freezer had given her pause, kneeling there in front of stacked plastic boxes and bags, all with Kate's writing. Mushroom soup; chilli; lasagne. Rose could have thawed that out but it looked precious, something *she*'d made and labelled, and the idea of using it seemed sacrilegious, at least now. Rose wondered what it would feel like in six months' time, when it would only have to be thrown away. Six months: what would their lives be like, in six months? Would they have learned to love her? It didn't really matter, she realised: she was staying, either way. She took out the stewing beef and closed the door.

Eating steadily, Evan was appreciative: he always was. Marvelling, grateful, although he never took more, never looked more than hollow-cheeked. He saw her looking, and smiled shyly.

Serena pushed food around, ate just enough to be allowed to leave the table but this time, hauling Jamie out – at first he struggled, then, delighted, went limp – to take him with her she left an expectant feeling behind her with the soft sound of the green baize door, a pause. The kitchen was warm, the light outside the long window fading, the pendant lamp over the table cast a glow that made it all look comfortable, settled, not just a provisional arrangement any more.

'I was just—' they both spoke at once.

'You first,' she said quickly, reaching to stack the plates, feeling the heat in her face. She didn't even know which question to ask, so many had bubbled to the surface over the slow wet day.

'I was just wondering,' said Evan, looking at her from under dark brows with a constrained expression. 'If you'd rather— I mean, being stuck out here, with us, it's—' he stopped, sighed, started again, looking down at his hands. His sleeves were rolled and she could see the fine tendons in his wrists. 'If it's too much. I mean, you're in at the deep end, aren't you?' Risking a look up at Rose, then back down. She felt a stir of alarm. 'I was thinking. You could always go and live in one of my— on the development. One of the houses is almost finished.'

'What?' She didn't know why it was a shock, like cold water, but it was. Hadn't she wanted to see those houses? The little pioneer house. Almost finished was not what she'd expected from the brochures – but still. She stared. 'I don't understand,' she said, faltering.

'I don't want to trap you here.' His head moved, side to side, unhappy, the thick dark hair falling over his face. Impatiently he pushed it out of his eyes. 'I mean, we haven't talked about the longer term. But you've got a life. You've – I can't—' his voice cracked and he rubbed his chin fiercely, making as if to stand up from the table.

'No,' Rose said, standing to meet him, pulling the stack of plates towards her. With an effort she kept her voice steady. She stood too with her stack of plates. 'I'm not trapped here. I want to be here with – all of you. I can't leave Jamie, now, can I?' He wasn't looking at her. 'Or Serena for that matter, however much she wishes I wasn't here.'

Evan looked across at her then and she saw his eyes gleam, brimming. 'She doesn't mean to—' he said. 'She's just—'

'She's just miserable,' said Rose. 'She's angry. I understand that.' She felt it like a weight, though, intractable, unbearable, and faltered. Who was she to think she might shift it? She cleared her throat. 'And she's only twelve.'

'So you—' he reached across the table for the plates and it was as if he didn't dare meet her eye.

'I want to be here,' Rose repeated. 'I want to be with you. All of you.'

There was that pause again, a kind of hum in the air, but that finished the conversation. They cleared the table together quickly: plates, bowls, cutlery, but their fingers never even touched.

When she went up to bed the beaded glass lamp was lit, though she couldn't remember having turned it on. She peered under the bed but there was her suitcase,

159

pushed back still. The house was quiet, or not quite, muffled. Rose could hear Evan's deep voice talking somewhere, around the gallery, across the dark red hall. The back staircase coiled there, twisting like smoke in the darkness: she didn't use it, she realised, when she could be seen to use it. She picked up the book on the bedside table, automatically, wondering why. It was her hiding place, and you couldn't be seen to enter your hiding place.

Rose was very tired, suddenly: it was like a sedative, or a cosh, the tiredness of responsibility, all day, every minute and she hadn't asked Evan any of her questions but it didn't seem to matter. Being a family wore you down. You could resist but it wore you down. She laid her head back on the pillow: it wasn't an awful feeling. It was restful, it went along with the low sound of Evan's voice across the dark space.

When she woke with a start the light was still on, and the book had fallen from her hands: a scrap of paper had fallen out of it. She picked the book up, and put it on the table with the piece of paper on top of it and turned out the light.

Chapter Seventeen

I do wonder if I'm going mad sometimes.

Writing notes to myself, like a mad person. And not just to myself. When we were small – well, I was ten or something and Rose was just a toddler, not much more, I used to invent those games for us. It was like the childhood I hadn't really had, when Rose arrived, games to play. *We have to leave clues.* She'd stare up at me, round eyes, no idea what I was on about.

I don't even mind it, that's my secret. The baby madness, I mean. I embrace it, the secrecy of it, the privateness of it. Me and Jamie in our own little world, the further away from everyone the better. When Serena's at school and Evan at work, sitting for hours just looking at the sun moving, or the tide coming up or the mist creeping in. I've read about it. How many books have I bought about being a new mum, a new *old* mum. Who was I to think *I can hack it* when all those other women sink down and can't climb out again? *Kate can back anything*. Is that why Rose doesn't come and see me?

The health visitor came to the flat in London, while we were packing to leave. God knows what she'd have thought here, nothing properly unpacked and the windows showing the dirt, dust everywhere. She gave me a questionnaire about how I was feeling that made me laugh. *How many times today have you felt like ending it all?* That kind of thing. She cheered up when I laughed and said, *Well, baby's doing awfully well*.

Evan comes home, to make sure I'm all right. I hear him tiptoeing in the hall. I know he's there.

Rose thinks I was born grown up and bossy but until I had him, Jamie, until that wrinkled red-and-purple little creature I was still a child. I know that now, however much I had going on, committees and groups and outings and making, until I had *him* I didn't know.

I can write it for her. In my book, or a little letter on tissue paper, fold it small like we used to do. I wish she was here, to talk to. I wish she was here.

Rose didn't know if it had been her, or him. She tried to work it out, afterwards, going over the detail. Over and over.

The rain had stopped in the night, and Friday, that strange new Friday, first Friday since the funeral, dawned with cold piercing brightness. It woke Rose early: she hadn't drawn the curtains and it flooded in, it dazzled her as she sat up sleepily. She got out of bed and went to the window, the four big panes of glass all glowing, that same window she and Jamie had looked through with the rain battering it. The house was soft and silent around her and the world spread out, gleaming like mother of pearl, the sky wide and pale, it was like the moon, or a new world, something untouched and alien.

She didn't remember the book, and the paper that had fallen out of it but something like her movement out of bed must have displaced it again and it lay there on the boards beside the bed. Rose picked it up. She didn't know what she'd expected – an old drawing of hers or Kate's, something from long ago. But the paper wasn't old, the writing wasn't faded – and it wasn't something a child would have written. It was Kate's handwriting, which hadn't changed since she was twelve, neat and small and regular, but the ink was still bright. It was a number: from the order and spacing, a telephone number, from the prefix, London. Rose looked at it a long moment. She put it back in the book and – after a moment's hesitation – instead of replacing it on the bedside table, slid the book back into its place on the shelf.

At breakfast Evan was quiet, reading something on his laptop. She examined him covertly, sideways, as she was feeding Jamie. He was frowning. She found herself looking at the stubble on his chin, his square-nailed hands.

'Can we come and see you sometime?' she said before she could stop herself, and his head jerked up. 'Me and Jamie? I could come on the bicycle. I'd like to see your— the houses.' And then stopped abruptly, feeling herself blush, thinking of the night before, for some reason.

Evan looked at her, the frown still there. *This is stupid*, she thought, *this is awful*. 'Of course,' he said, awkward. 'Of course you can.' Then there was the sound of Serena on the stairs, clomping.

163

'Next week?' she said, lightly, and with the words knew she was setting something in motion, that went with the blush, and the fact that it was not quite under her control was a part of it.

'I'll have a look at the diary when I'm in,' he said, then quickly, 'I'd love that,' the tips of his ears reddening. Jamie lurched for the spoon and she gave it to him. And by the time Serena came through the door Evan's head was bowed over the computer again.

Rose came out to say goodbye to them, Jamie batting with his hands on the roof of the car. Evan waited until Serena was inside the car and strapped in, earbuds in her ears and then came round to the other side where Rose waited. For an unsteady moment she thought he was going to kiss her goodbye — just on the cheek — but he took one of Jamie's hands instead.

'You talked to Kate's friend Lindsay at the funeral, didn't you?' he said, hesitant, his voice lowered. 'What's she like?'

'Nice,' said Rose automatically, although it wasn't the right word. Lindsay had been angry, she had been defensive. 'Funerals don't always bring out the best in people. Don't you know her?'

Evan shook his head. 'Never met her before,' he said. 'She and Kate fell out, something to do with her mother dying, I don't even know what.' He rubbed a hand over his forehead, tugging the thick hair back and his exposed forehead looked vulnerable. 'She was drunk. Did you see that? Was she drinking in the kitchen?' He frowned. 'I think she might be an alcoholic.'

She opened her mouth and then closed it again. She

164

wondered if Kate had told him about Dad. Rose didn't tell people.

Evan was still talking. 'It's why she disappeared just like that, without saying goodbye, Gerald – well, he offered. I didn't want to say in front of Serena. It was Serena said we should put an announcement in the paper and I didn't want her to feel guilty, you know.'

And then he turned, the door banged and they were gone, splashing through yesterday's puddles.

Jamie had a tantrum, late in the afternoon, shocking her, it was uncontrollable as a firestorm.

Rose thought she'd seen that side of it already, mistakenly, foolishly, she thought she'd weathered tantrums, the banging of hands on the kitchen table, the turning of his head to refuse food, the strained shout of denial he'd give when he didn't want to do something. Arching his back as Rose tried to strap him into the trailer.

Perhaps they'd spared her – Rose had, after all, heard him in the night, once or twice. She didn't have him all the time, she heard herself talking to Kate in her head, *It's all right. Evan gets up in the night if he needs to, he takes him after he's got in from work, even Serena's helping out.* Serena would take him with a look of triumph at chosen moments, when he'd just thrown food at Rose and she was spattered and irritable and had to smile, thank you.

They were all home, and when she heard the car Rose had felt a small stir of the possibilities of Friday night, a heightened feeling, the sun sparkling off the water down-river, beyond the reeds and the thought of a weekend. Perhaps they would go somewhere, a walk together, perhaps she could go somewhere on her own. On her own! Serena had been back for an hour, more, upstairs in her room taking advantage of the internet and Evan, who had climbed out of the car weary but cheerful was in the outhouse, doing something to the bicycle.

'We'll have to get you on the insurance for the car,' he had said as he knelt to examine it and she felt a surge of something, warmth, gratitude, relief. 'Just for—' looking up, not smiling because he never really did, but with the shyest of his frowns, 'you know. Whatever. Emergencies.' And had bobbed his head and wheeled the bike off.

They'd been in the garden, she and Jamie, at the furthest end. She didn't understand, not before or after, what had sparked it, just her stopping him doing something he wanted to do. A bird box on a pole that was already at a tilt, loosened by a high tide, and he strode into the flower-bed to haul at it, little fat fists around the pole and swinging, straining to get up to the little house perched on top of it, trampling the beds a clump of pale pearly tall anemones – that Rose knew and particularly liked already, the cleanest brightest thing in the garden – snapping under him.

It was going to hurt him, it was going to fall – and beyond it was the bank down, steep, to the rising tide. Rose had also been impatient, nettled by the knowledge that Serena was on the internet and why couldn't *she* be the one? Rose the little sister, used to being the one who got what she wanted.

And always, always, always, underneath it the dead heavy knowledge that Kate was gone, because grief they didn't tell you was anger, half anger at least. What makes you think I can manage without you? *Come back.*

And the look Jamie gave her as she seized him – probably too hard, probably she herself wasn't smiling, probably
she had looked as angry as she felt – rocked her back,
she felt her mouth open in shock. His face was a kind of
stiff blank, wiped by rage, with just a flush of triumph
around the edges as if this was an opportunity he had
been waiting for, as if something had been gathering, a
demonic euphoria that he needed to vent. Rose felt him
stiffen under her hands and then without warning he
arched and flung himself backwards out of her grasp. His
head hit the pole and she saw his eyes roll white.

Lunging, Rose grabbed and caught him back: he writhed
with furious strength and she begged, panting, *Jamie, Jamie,*
not knowing what she was saying, for him to breathe, at
least. A beat, another, and then he did breathe, he roared.
His lips pinked, his mouth opened, his eyes round and
unblinking, staring mutinous at her as if it was all her
fault, all of it, everything he wanted and couldn't get,
everything that was gone for ever. She hung on as he
thrashed and kicked, and it felt as though she had dropped
him in the river and was fighting to bring him back, to
find him under the water.

Struggling, he flung his hands out and yanked at the
anemones, he drummed his heels in the damp earth
until they were both showered in dirt, Rose's knees
muddy, earth under her fingernails. She couldn't have
said how long it went on but eventually Rose managed
to get back to her feet, staggering upright still holding
on to him because she knew for absolutely certain that
if she let go he *would* find his way to the water: he had
no fear, only determination, only energy. As she turned

167

at the edge of the flowerbed for a second she glimpsed Serena, the ghost of a profile in the upper window that was hers, the shadow of a smile on the face that disappeared, and then she was gone and there was Evan, coming round the corner, hurrying, a smudge of oil on his cheek.

In her arms Jamie went limp. She lowered him to the ground and he lay still a second then rolled over and ran, with his little clockwork run, his arms windmilling. Evan scooped him up and stood there: Rose saw Jamie look up into his father's face and then as if a switch had been thrown he laid his cheek down and was motionless.

Unsteadily Rose walked towards them, loose-jointed and weak from the struggle, everything in disarray, shirt untucked, knees dirty, hair straggling. She saw Jamie's muddy thumb make its way to his mouth, the plump backs of his legs under Evan's forearm, and she stopped. *I don't belong. I don't belong.*

'I don't − I don't know what—' she heard herself, helpless.

Evan was looking at her. 'He does it,' he said, sadly. 'It's − part of the whole − it just happens. It's not you.' His hand went out, hovering a few inches from her. 'Are *you* all right?' On his chest Jamie's head shifted, sideways, a wet-lashed eye blinked and looked at her.

She said nothing.

When the sound came in the night Rose knew it, in her sleep. She walked towards it in the soft darkness that cushioned her dreams.

The dreams had primed Rose, dreams that weren't of

any man she recognised any more but only the sensations, of his hand at the back of her neck rubbing softly in the small hairs.

When Rose woke this time she wasn't at the back staircase, she had stopped short of it. She was outside Jamie's room, her hands at the door again, the back staircase to her left, the locked master bedroom at her back and for a second it was like a game, a puzzle, which door should she open? Blinking, she listened, couldn't hear anything – and then she could. He was stifling it, so that Jamie wouldn't wake but she could hear it, through the door, through whatever was muffling it. His hands at his face. A low awful sound, she'd heard before, not in this life but in the old life, a twelve year old listening at doors. She put her hand on the cracked porcelain of the doorhandle: she didn't make a sound but he stopped.

She pulled back her hand, she turned and pressed herself, her back, against the panelling. Overhead the diffuse light of the moon shone through the cupola, pale out of a clear sky a black branch silhouetted, moving, scratching softly. And then, beside her cheek, the door opened, she felt the movement of air and he was there.

Oh, please.

She didn't even know if she heard it in her head or spoken out loud. And then she felt him, his hands, warm on her face, his face, his lips. His eyes, open, dark and open, looking at her. Searching her out.

'I'm not, it's not, I'm not Kate—' she heard herself whisper and he said, '*I*—,' only that, and then his voice cracked and his head came down. She held him against her, his face was pressed against her neck, mouth and nose as if he was trying to breathe her in. His lips on her skin and his body pressed against hers, connected at the breast, at the hip, at the thigh. He stepped back but his grip on her tightened, and she moved with him, back into the room.

It was dark, muffled by heavy curtains but they got to the narrow bed, clinging to each other, without falling. Without knocking into anything, beyond the edge of the bed. They both knew where the cot stood, with Jamie in it.

'I'm sorry,' he kept saying, 'I'm sorry.' But he didn't stop. She didn't want him to.

Chapter Eighteen

There was a letter on the mat: it was the first thing Rose saw when she came down the stairs.

Getting out of bed she couldn't trust her legs straight away, she felt shaky all over. Remembering it. She felt bruised, in places, a soft ache while all the time her brain was going *fuck fuck fuck*, like a burglar alarm.

Jamie had stirred around four and she had sat up immediately, pushing back the covers, although she had been pretty much awake in between, lying on the edge of the single bed in the dark, staring at what could be seen of the outlines of the room, the cornicing. While she lay there – her brain ticking and hurrying *fuck fuck fuck* – Evan had slept. Lying beside her, on his back, motionless, unconscious, but when she sat up he woke instantly.

'What is it, what—' and he subsided against her, his cheek against her shoulder.

He had reassured her, over and over, the night before, soothing her, stroking her, whispering to her. Afterwards. During, he hadn't said anything, but at the last moment he let out a sound like pain, dampened instantly – and they both went still, holding on to each other, waiting for Jamie to wake. He hadn't, then. 'Oh,' he had whispered, into her neck. 'Oh, oh.'

'I've got to go,' Rose said, as under the window Jamie turned and the cot creaked and gathering herself, pulling down the shirt she slept in, suddenly shy, she escaped.

The letter must have been there since the day before. The post arrived at odd hours when it did arrive – she'd seen a postman once, surly in the lane climbing out of a van in the early afternoon to hand her a bunch of circulars – but never this early.

After Jamie stirred she'd gone back to her own bed, swift across the floor, silent through the door, silent closing it after her. If he'd woken properly, she wouldn't have known it, she was asleep before her head hit the pillow. And she slept and slept and slept, a deep luxurious sleep like she hadn't had in weeks.

Now coming down the stairs it was eight thirty, but the house was silent.

Rose was still wearing the shirt, as she stopped on the stairs, frowning down into the hall at the oblong on the mat. She'd put on knickers, with difficulty, tangling in them as she sat on the edge of the bed, all fingers and thumbs. She looked down at her legs now, pale against the red carpet, toenails bare, the skin on her knees dry and rough. They must all still be asleep: Rose moved on down towards the doormat. It was only as she leaned down to pick up the letter that she remembered it was Saturday. Something eased: good. No school run, no hurry. And then tightened again: a whole weekend. Serena would know. She would know straight away.

I love you. He had said that, and not in the heat of the moment, either. Whispering afterwards into her skin, the soft skin where her breast met her armpit. *Since I saw you in the airport. Since then.* She had lain, so still, feeling her scalp prickle, the wrongness of it, all of it, like a chill in the air around them. And then the light seemed to change, to warm, something shifted in her head and she felt Kate, there in the house like a breath. Kate who loved them both, her and Evan: she had shifted then, on to her side in the narrow bed, and slept.

The letter was fat, as though several sheets of paper were folded in it – four or five. The name of a company of solicitors was printed in the top left corner of the envelope.

Kettle on, Rose propped the envelope on the dresser behind cups. The dresser made her think of Lindsay, and Kate's blue-and-white china and she knelt to retrieve some from the cupboard where she'd seen it.

She could easily have missed the letter yesterday, she didn't look out for post as it wouldn't be for her. She supposed Deb might write, eventually.

She had planned to Skype Deb tonight – to clear it carefully with Evan and Serena, to phone her on the landline this morning and fix a time, but the idea receded, it felt awkward. How could she tell Deb what had happened? How could she talk about anything else? She cleaned the kitchen, instead. Washed up, put away, sorted the recycling, emptied the bins. Found a space on the dresser for some of Kate's plates. She was scrubbing the table when she heard Jamie, and there was Evan in the doorway.

Did he look different? She didn't know. He smiled. She felt a fierce flush rise, burning. He still smiled.

'I'm not going to say I'm sorry,' he said.

'We can't,' she said. 'We can't, we—'

'Shh,' he said, parking Jamie in his high chair and coming over to her. Jamie's eyes were on them, beady as Evan reached and gently moved her hair back, away from her face and he leaned in, his lips brushing her under the ear. 'We can,' he said, into her hair and the slight unsteadiness in his voice touched her, made her reach up and take his hand that was on her shoulder. His fingers wandered in her hair. Upstairs a door banged.

'Serena mustn't know,' she said quickly, stepping back, away from him. He just looked at her, quizzical, then he was looking past her, at the dresser.

'I found it on the mat,' she said, smiling, 'It looked official so I thought—'

'Solicitors,' he said and she wondered if she'd made a mistake, somehow. 'It's just about Kate's – it's just the—' He rested a hand on her shoulder, patted once, twice, reassuring her. 'I know what's in it already.'

Rose's heart sank, for reasons she couldn't identify.

He lifted it carefully off the dresser. 'You put some of her plates out,' he said, 'that's what I noticed,' opening a drawer and when Serena pushed her way in, glowering, he was closing it and Rose was setting the teapot on the table.

The letter must have been about Kate's will. If she

knew Kate, once she'd had Jamie, she'd have gone straight to the solicitor. Kate loved paperwork – loved ordering and sorting. Rose stuffed bank statements in the back of a drawer and was afraid of them. Evan hadn't looked afraid, he'd just looked indifferent.

'Why's it so tidy?' said Serena rudely, scraping a chair out, and Rose had to turn away under her cool suspicious look, before she understood everything.

The phone had rung, startling and loud, in the hall.

'It's for you,' said Evan, standing in the doorway, smiling at her.

At the table, Serena looked from one of them to the other, then looked away.

That night, he came to her.

The day had passed, in a dream. Walking on air, and it did feel a bit like that, Rose a hovercraft gliding over everything, just grazing the ground, not feeling the bumps.

It had been Annie on the phone. Business-like, but with a pleading edge. 'I thought maybe we could go on an outing or something, tomorrow.' Hurrying on. 'Evie hasn't seen much of Serena lately.' And underneath the briskness Rose heard her anguish, the same guilty pain she felt herself. Annie went on bravely. 'The weather's supposed to be good. Just, you know, a walk on the prom or a picnic or something.'

Serena had just shrugged, spooning cereal into her mouth at the table. 'Evie's your friend, right?' Rose said, and although she didn't stop eating Serena made a small grunt of assent which was as close, Rose thought, as she got to enthusiasm.

Evan thought it was a good idea. 'I've got stuff to do,' he said agreeably as she stood there in the doorway. 'Sure, yes, why not.' He smiled. 'You don't need to ask my permission, anyway.' Wrongfooted, Rose paused. She didn't think she'd been asking permission.

Annie would come in her car to get them, she'd make a picnic, and Rose just agreed to everything: she would make some sandwiches. Other possibilities presented themselves.

A bottle of wine, scoping out the town for an internet café, shopping, even. The thought of the supermarket was like sunlight.

All things seemed possible, suddenly. *You don't need to ask my permission.*

It was easy. Now they understood each other, now the prickly tangle of feelings, misunderstandings, anxiety had been erased, overnight. The way he smiled at her – when she cleared the table, when he caught her humming to herself, when she plucked Jamie from the high chair – was the sign, the green light.

Jamie still seemed to want to go back to the bird box: there were no tantrums but he did stop, in the afternoon sunlight on the edge of the flowerbed where it had all kicked off, and look up at her as if expecting something. She went round the bird box warily, peering through the little circular hole but there was nothing, at least, no nest.

It wasn't just going through the motions, waiting to see what would happen once Jamie had been put down, once Serena had flitted back to her room, it was more like a

176

dream, all day. It might be once had been enough, a release for both of them. She told herself that would be fine. She made no attempt to talk about it, and nor did Evan. Evan just smiled. She didn't even ask him anything, not, did they need anything at the supermarket, not what was the stuff he planned to do while they were out the next day, not, would it be OK, the money and everything, the will and all that. Maybe there'd be time for that.

So it was just like the previous day, except everything had been different then. All those days, since she arrived, looked chilly and anxious now, like a shrouded room, and now the covers had been pulled off, the curtains opened. Rose did at one point think of something, in the soft dark of her memory of last night, as she sat beside him on the sofa, something that made her lay her head a second on the cushioned back and although she *didn't* sigh happily, and although Evan didn't turn to look at her, when she lifted her head again, he was smiling, at the TV.

Rose was almost asleep when he came, and she didn't think she'd been expecting it, by then.

She knew the soft sound though, not what it was — a footstep or the door moving over the carpet — but what it meant, and she lay still, she didn't sit up, she lay there in the bed and heard him move inside the room and felt her heart beating faster and waited, almost faint with wanting whatever it was. And then there he was, the whole length of him against her, and his stubble scratching her cheek, and his soft mouth, kissing her eyelids in the dark.

Rose slept, afterwards, deep and heavy and pressed

warm against Evan's back although the bed was bigger than his, an old-fashioned double built for days when people were smaller or slept closer, when there was no heating or something. Sleeping soundly: sound meant whole, safe, a boat was sound when it didn't leak, you needed the night to close up the gaps, to seal you off: those were the thoughts she drifted off to. She woke to the soft noise of the door closing on him and although there was no other sound, no crying from Jamie, she didn't take it personally, she lay back luxuriously in the warmth he'd left behind, waiting for sleep. When it didn't come she looked at her phone by the bed for the time and saw it was just after midnight, and felt the creep of something.

She recognised it: it had happened enough times. Waking in the night with the horrors, wondering if she'd made an awful mistake, somewhere, somehow. Rolling over to find some guy gone in the early hours, to remember she'd talked too much at a party, drunk too much. That feeling of finding yourself too far from home.

In the dark, feeling the creep, Rose resolved to talk to Deb, tomorrow, but that didn't help.

In the bed she stirred, uneasy, frightened. It couldn't last, it wouldn't work, it was wrong. If it wasn't wrong, why did she want to keep quiet about it? Evan didn't. 'I don't know what you're worried about,' he'd whispered against her cheek when she'd shushed him, for fear of waking them. Waking Serena, next door. 'She loves you.'

Rose had almost laughed when he said that, but he seemed serious. She let him talk on, lulling her, and then she had slept. Now she turned it over and it looked ridiculous again: fierce angry Serena.

Then Rose heard something. She stiffened. Not inside the house, outside. She didn't move, straining to hear. Then softly she swung her legs out of the bed and went to the window, hesitated behind the curtain then moved it aside, just a fraction, and with the movement the sound, whatever it had been, a murmuring, a whispering, something more guttural mixed in, had gone. She moved close to the glass, she could feel the cold from it. The moon's light was dim, diffuse behind cloud, there was no light shed from anywhere in the house and she could hardly make out anything at first. The pale rushes: further off where some moonlight filtered there were splotches of marsh grass, a gleam of mud, the deeper dark of water stretching off away to the black of the estuary.

Something moved, just beyond the edge of the garden, where the river curved and met a hedge, at the end of their land. Something made of shadow, bigger than a person, it separated and came together again to form a different shape. There was a sound, as it moved, but not more than a sigh, that could be wind. Rose let the curtain fall and stood behind it for one beat, two. Another, then she looked again.

There was nothing there.

By the time she got into the bed her shared warmth had almost gone and she lay there, stiff, a long time telling herself she'd imagined it, before sleep swallowed her again.

I was worried about him meeting her. He's so shy, you see, people don't see that. They think he's arrogant, but it's not that, it's more – he doesn't believe people will understand him.

Evan doesn't have brothers and sisters, he doesn't know what it's like.

I told him – I still tell him, until he almost rolls his eyes and finishes the sentence for me. Rose's the one who knows me, better than anyone else in the world.

Chapter Nineteen

Evie and Serena ran in circles on the close-cropped tough grass, their hair streaming. You didn't have to watch long for it to become obvious that Evie was the needy one and Serena was trying to escape her, Jamie zig-zagging in their wake. Rose retrieved him and – worn out by the excitement – he fell abruptly asleep beside them on the rug.

'Poor little thing,' said Annie, leaning back on her elbows, giving Rose a sidelong glance. 'You have to feel sorry for her.'

Rose returned her look. 'Serena?' and felt immediately guilty. She'd been on the point of telling Annie about the dress and was glad she'd held back. 'I know.'

The boats clinked on the tide, their rigging slapping metal masts, and Annie waved as a little plastic yacht came past them motoring jauntily and a neat family, boy, girl, mother father waved back, cheerfully. The horizon opened out, broad, empty, a nice day, a peaceful Sunday.

They were in town, or rather out the other side of it, out along the promenade past the arcades and beyond, where it petered out into marshland alongside the curve of the estuary. The town scrambled up a modest bit of hillside behind them. It was bigger, more rambling than Rose had grasped when she came on her own, to the undertakers'. Then she'd thought it an ugly, dismal place.

It *wasn't* ugly, though, it turned out; it wasn't miserable, not altogether. Turning right at the fork whose left branch had taken Rose to the undertakers', they found themselves at the top of a hill and there was a glimpse of red roofs, a small spire, the silver curve of the river. Rose must have made a sound of surprise because Annie at the wheel had eyed her sideways and said, 'Not so bad, is it?'

Rose had answered, meaning it, 'No, it's – it's lovely.'

It was. But was it home? Not yet: the thought that she'd have to make it into home herself, made Rose shift in the passenger seat and glance over her shoulder at the children. Jamie beamed back at her, and the thoughts chased themselves, thoughts involving Evan, involving the house, pulling off dustsheets and cleaning windows and opening doors. When Rose got to the picture of herself in Kate's apron she stopped. *Don't.*

There was a tiny car park near the promenade. In the back as they drove there had been whispering, and at one point a giggle and when they stopped Serena flung open her door straight away and they were off. Annie opened the boot and lifted out a proper picnic basket, lined with a checked cloth, and filled with the right things. Cold chicken legs, and apples, and tomatoes, and fresh bread.

'That's just what Kate would have brought,' said Rose,

'and the nice clean tea towel and everything.' And Rose saw her frown, lip between her teeth before turning to smile.

'Of course she would,' she said.

'You don't think of her like that?' said Rose casually as they hauled the stuff along the path.

Annie gave her a thoughtful look. 'I— at the beginning yes,' she said. 'To be honest that seems like such a long time ago, now. But yes. I remember her bringing a Christmas cake to sell at the first school bazaar after – after they arrived and she confessed to me it had cost four times as much in ingredients as they were charging for it and Evan couldn't believe it and I should buy it.'

'That sounds like Kate,' said Rose although there was something about the story that prodded at her, unhappily. Had they been poor? Evan had given her twenty pounds for shopping that morning, when she said they might go to the supermarket. In fact, he'd taken out ten then added another ten. 'Did you? Buy it?' she said.

The out-of-town supermarket didn't open till twelve on Sunday: they were going to go on the way back. Rose clung gamely to the prospect, but it had faded somewhat, with wondering what she could buy with twenty quid.

Annie smiled grimly. 'Yes. But at the school May Day thing she wasn't feeling well enough, we thought – well, I don't know what we thought. I mean, people get ill, don't they? I think she told me it was the flu. I took Serena, that time, and I made some fairy cakes for her to hand in to be sold, too.'

They came past a small cluster of sideshows, a shooting gallery, rows of arcade games and some swingboats but considering it was Sunday the place was quiet, with a fug of spicy dope smoke giving a clue to its customer base. One tall boy dressed in Goth black on a game and another looking over his shoulder who turned and made a pistol at them with his thumb and forefinger, and even he had a mobile in his other hand. Always on their phones, thought Rose, realising with an uneasy shock that she hadn't even remembered to bring hers. It was good, she was weaning herself off it – but. Damn. She'd left it on the kitchen table, jumping up when she heard Annie's car in the lane, distracted by Evan's wide smile at her excitement.

'In our time,' Annie said, nodding at the boy who'd turned away, 'it was arcade games that were the devil. Do you remember that?'

Rose did. Mum forbidding them going anywhere near, for the boys that hung out at them more than the danger of addiction to shoot-'em games. She glanced back over her shoulder but the tall boys, plus two others that might have been male or female in coats that trailed the ground, had drifted out from the arcades and were mooching back along the river towards the town, tugging and pushing at each other, a black shape that formed and reformed. The sight of them reminded her of something vaguely.

'Does Evie have a mobile?' she asked, as they laid down a big tartan rug. Evie and Serena had taken off their shoes and were up to their knees in black mud off the end of the prom: there was a smell of sulphur, and the brisk salt wind blowing in off the sea. Taking out plastic plates, a bowl of salad covered with clingfilm, two glasses, Annie sighed.

'Well,' she said, 'she does, yeah. We gave in when she

184

went to secondary school, I mean you can't stop them—' she broke off. 'I know Kate and Evan had other ideas.'

'I quite like having to live without it,' said Rose, gamely. How many times had she got it out of her pocket and stared at the words *No Service*. Annie eyed her.

'Really?' she said, dubiously, and they both laughed and Rose thought that she hadn't even had that conversation with Evan. She had acted like it was – fine. But it wasn't really, was it? It was a pain. Surely Kate must have found it a pain, too? And worse. A nightmare, by the end. Rose shifted, uneasy.

'Of course I'd be back hooked again in five minutes,' she said as Annie knelt over the basket, fishing in it for something. 'I have no doubt.' It nagged at her. If she'd remembered the phone she could have called Deb. *Forget it.*

Annie straightened, a bottle of wine and a corkscrew in her hand. 'Oh,' said Rose. Thinking of lunchtime wine on her breath when she got back, she hesitated.

'Just a glass,' said Annie, firmly. 'It's your first proper weekend here, after all.' She poured half a tumbler each, and corked the bottle back up again. 'I should have thought,' she said, 'Kate did tell me about your dad. She didn't drink, did she?'

'Well—' Rose hesitated again. *Didn't drink?* Over by the water, in silhouette, some kind of pantomime was being performed by the two girls. Evie, smaller and slighter, was leaning backwards, arching her spine, a hand in the small of her back. For a moment her mind went blank. 'Sorry,' she said, 'Oh, oh. Yes. Kate drank, I mean, a bit—' A bottle between them on special occasions, on the pine table of her cosy little flat.

'Evan doesn't,' she finished, leaning back, 'doesn't drink.' Closing her eyes with the taste of wine on her tongue. *And he thinks I shouldn't,* drifted into her head with the memory of the gin bottle carefully removed from the fridge, and out again. The grassy bank under her was firm, the air was soft and damp, and the clink of the boats was like music.

'What are they up to?' she heard Annie mutter and blinked her eyes back open to see Evie doing it again, sticking her belly out, hand in the small of her back and her meaning was quite plain, she was imitating a pregnant woman. Serena lurched towards her, shouting something into her face, chin up in anger. 'Evie,' said Annie sharply and Evie crouched and ran, her hair flying, Serena following her. They disappeared over a hummock of marsh grass.

'Such a weird age,' said Rose automatically, finding excuses while at the same time scrambling upright a little. She didn't know what the little pantomime meant, but it bothered her.

'You're not—' she couldn't help a glance at Annie's belly, flat beneath her sweatshirt.

'What?' Annie drained her glass and picked up the bottle, contemplating another. 'No way,' she said. 'Not me.'

'What do you think that was about, then?' Rose said, nodding towards the edge of the marsh where the girls were invisible but audible, muttering. And then she felt the heat under her hair, of panic. Serena had heard them, last night. Serena, finely tuned to a batsqueak of betrayal, or intimacy. Luring Rose in to see her little shrine, her photographs of her One, the one who loved her and only her. The red candles, the spot of wax on the dress. Even the sound of their murmured talk in bed, Rose and Evan whispering to each other, would have been unmistakeable to Serena's sharp ear.

Annie was refilling their glasses. 'Oh, kids,' she said, vaguely, frowning, then defensively, 'They're very small glasses,' not meeting Rose's eye. They *were* small. She took another sip. Glancing sideways at her Annie corked the bottle back up and stowed it in the basket. And sighed.

'Kate told me, a while back that Serena – wanted another baby brother or sister,' she said thoughtfully.

'Serena did?' Rose was taken aback. 'After Jamie?' Beside them on the rug he stirred, pale in sleep, his mouth opened then closed again.

'Serena adores Jamie,' said Annie taking a sip, leaning back on her elbows with the glass upright in one hand. The girls' heads had reappeared, at the top of the hummock and looking back at them, their bodies invisible. Annie tipped herself on to one side, leaning on one elbow so she was facing Rose and angling her body so the girls were behind them. 'I suppose you're her rival, now,' she said.

'She told me she was better at looking after Jamie than me,' said Rose. Then blurting, childishly angry, 'God knows, I didn't ask to be here, did I? Fucking useless as a mother-substitute. I could be in bloody Italy without a care in the world—' but she sounded like a baby. And it wasn't true: it didn't even sound true. When she'd watched that little happy normal family heading out into the estuary on their boat she'd been thinking about the house. Thinking of the mist and the moonlight through the cupola and the secrets, their secrets together in Evan's narrow bed, and Rome drifted further off, lost. She sat up abruptly. What was she thinking? Could she really make this work, taking over Kate's life, just moving in? The children needed her and Evan – Evan wanted her. Maybe he just wanted Kate back, maybe this would – change into something else. Things did. She rubbed her face with her hands, hard.

Annie who was looking at Serena, didn't seem to notice.

'She'll get over it,' she said, easily, as if the outburst had relaxed her, rolling back so the girls came into view again. Giving Rose another sideways look. 'She just needs to be able to trust someone not to disappear. It'll get easier.'

'Does she talk to Evie?' Rose said, abruptly. 'Serena? Because she doesn't talk to me. Or Evan, much.' She remembered the muttered argument, at night. She sighed. 'And I can't ask either of them, really. Well, not yet.' Something occurred to her. 'Does Serena have grandparents? I mean, she must. Her mother was so young.'

Annie was lying, leaning on one elbow, watching the girls. 'That's a good question,' she said, hesitating. 'Kate did mention something. I mean – you know what she was like, she didn't gossip. She wasn't ever unkind about people—'

'Yes,' said Rose, clearing her throat. 'But?'

'I got the impression the relationship with the grandparents – Serena's mother's parents, that is, I think his are in Australia or something – was not good.' She tipped the glass and emptied it. 'I suppose—' scrambling to her feet, 'Kate was taking their daughter's place, maybe they didn't like it.'

'And they'd be grieving,' said Rose, almost to herself, but Annie had her hands cupped either side of her mouth and was calling.

'Hey,' and the girls turned, their hands black with mud. 'Hey. Do you want this picnic or not?'

By the time Annie dropped them in the lane – 'I won't come up to the house,' she'd said as she slowed, 'Evan— it's hard to turn in the tight space and when he watches me,' her mouth set in a line, 'I always do something stupid' – it was getting dark.

One of the things Rose was remembering, after so long away, was how long English summer evenings were, until suddenly they weren't, and autumn closed round you like a thick curtain and it was dark at five. In the back, Serena had bestowed a quick, hard hug on Evie, climbed out and run in, calling her thanks – to Annie – over her shoulder.

They'd had fun: not just the girls, Rose too. Fresh air, or something, and the picnic, that they'd all guzzled as if they were starving. Although Serena steadfastly ignored her as they ate Rose had caught a look from Evie more than once, a curious, questioning look. She didn't know what went on in their heads.

The birds had started up, in the hedgerows and under the trees that shadowed the little bridge, when Rose climbed out of the car with her bag of shopping. Jamie was still asleep in his car seat: she unbuckled him and then straightened, listening.

'Wow,' she said, 'Annie? Listen to this,' leaning down to the driver's window, and after a moment's hesitation

Annie climbed out. Through the big yew Rose saw a light come on in the house.

'In Rome you hear them, when the sun goes down they go mad in the trees, but it's not like this,' Rose said, in wonder, looking up into the dark branches. The bird-song in Rome was harsher, a noisy, rowdy twittering, but this was liquid, softer than liquid. It went on, and on. She couldn't imagine how such a sound could come out of a bird. The two women stood there looking up, and then Annie said something, mumbling, about how good she was, to take them on, about it not being easy.

Rose turned to look at her. 'To tell the truth, I thought—I hadn't really registered that Serena's mother had died, too. I suppose I vaguely thought he had custody because—' she frowned, trying to remember what Kate had said about him, in her emails, when they'd been introduced in the pub. 'I suppose I thought it would be just Jamie,' she finished, biting her lip. She went around the car and opened the back door and lifted him out of the car seat. He was getting too big for it, she registered. His face was sticky, upturned and pressed into the cushion. He didn't stir.

Rose walked back round to Annie, lugging the car seat.

'Serena's a good girl, really,' Annie began.

'You said it was an accident,' Rose said, interrupting her. 'Her mother. An accident and Evan was at work. I thought it was cancer, but I don't know why, now. I can't remember why I thought that. What kind of an accident?'

Annie's face was pale, in the long shadow of the big tree. 'She had an epileptic fit,' she said. Rose noticed again Annie's odd way of talking, her hand coming up nervously as if she always wanted to cover her mouth: at lunch, outside on the prom the tic had disappeared. 'She fell down the stairs. Serena had just started at school and when her mother didn't arrive to collect her someone else took her home. She was lying at the bottom of the stairs and—' she stopped, and overhead the birds sang on, oblivious, beautiful.

'And,' said Rose, feeling a tightness along her jaw, where she'd been clenching it.

'Serena saw her, Serena was the one who saw her,' she spoke in a hurried undertone. 'They couldn't stop her, she looked through the letterbox and saw her, on the floor. They couldn't stop her looking—' Annie stopped abruptly, turned her head as if listening.

'No wonder then,' said Rose, almost to herself, 'shit. No wonder.'

'Yes,' said Annie, 'yes,' leaning to open the driver door but Rose wasn't listening properly, she only registered the high forced note in Annie's voice a beat too late because she was hurrying on, the gathering dark made it urgent, she'd had all day with Annie and now she was going.

'You talked to Kate,' she said. 'I don't know anyone else she talked to – and that's not like her, she was so – such a joiner in, she was so gregarious.' Annie was climbing into the driver's seat and Rose was talking to her hunched shoulders. 'She had no idea? That she was so ill?'

There was a sound then, she heard it, a distinct crunch on the gravel.

Annie leaned across her to pull the door closed and

Rose had to step back. She saw Annie's face, pale, saw her shake her head, quick and mute before she bent it over the key in the ignition, and the car was moving off.

Rose watched it, arms across herself, she had time to register that the birds had gone quiet and then she heard Evan's voice from behind her. 'Rose?'

She didn't know if he'd heard. Had Annie shut up because she'd heard him, before Rose had? Because they'd been gossiping. It occurred to her that Annie probably knew Evan better than Rose did: she probably knew that he hated gossip.

Behind her Evan spoke again. 'Darling?' She felt herself unclench and almost in the same moment his hands were on her, soft on her upper arms and he leaned in from behind and she felt his mouth brush the hair below her ear. She turned and he was examining her, frowning. His habitual expression – but all the same she was relieved when he smiled.

'Supper won't be long,' he said, a hint of reproof in his voice, but no more.

'I bought some things,' she said. But in the kitchen the table hadn't been laid and Rose put the shopping bag down carefully on it, so as not to make the wine bottle clink. Reckless on the glass she'd drunk at lunch, egged on by Annie: determined to make the supermarket visit the sunlit pleasure she'd anticipated, she'd sauntered in the aisles, avoiding organic veg, tinned tomatoes, eyeing up crisps. She'd ended up buying the cheapest bottle of rosé, and some chocolate, and a plastic pack of six peaches. Evan came in behind her, lugging Jamie in his car seat and she leaned against the table to let him past, holding the bag's neck closed. She smiled as he set Jamie down and went into the hall to call Serena.

There was pasta bubbling in a saucepan on the stove and some sauce.

Rose unpacked hurriedly: the things she'd bought looking cheap, suddenly, tacky treats for a girls' night in. Wine in the fridge, chocolate – her hand hovered over the drawer but she left it out in the end, it wasn't a secret.

The table hadn't been cleared, there were the same papers that Evan had set down carelessly at breakfast, the fruit bowl with wrinkled apples: Rose tried to disguise the bright peaches among them and lose their carbon footprint, stuffing the packaging hurriedly under the sink.

And then Rose saw her phone. She stopped, the empty plastic supermarket bag crumpled in her hands.

When they sat here eating breakfast she'd been sitting at the end of the table nearest the door into the boiler room, her back to the door, the window on her right, facing the stove. She could remember her position quite clearly – and when she'd realised she'd left her phone behind, lying out on the strand with Annie that afternoon she had visualised it exactly, lying half under a newspaper, half hidden which would be why she'd forgotten it. The newspaper was there, still: she lifted it up, but she knew the phone wasn't there because she'd seen where it was now. The phone was at the other end of the table.

Well, of course. Plenty of reasons for it to have moved.

And when Evan walked in he could see, straight away, he knew, straight away.

'I ran after you,' he said. 'I saw you'd left it and I ran out but—' he shrugged, rueful and a lock of the thick dark hair flopped across his eyes and he smiled, he put a hand to her cheek, mock mournful. 'You'd gone.'

Then at their feet in his car seat Jamie, pink – too pink – from the sun, stirred and looking up at them his face contorted into a wail.

From that point on the evening turned chaotic. Rose walked Jamie up and down while Evan set the table and drained the pasta and poured on the sauce and served it up then they took turns to eat. Serena was quiet, subdued. Evan tried to ask her how her day had been over the sound of Jamie's howling – it went on, and on, beyond the eating of the food and the clearing of the plates – but she just shook her head, looking from him to Rose from under her fierce fine eyebrows. Her mother's eyebrows, Rose saw now, not Evan's.

She knows, all right, thought Rose, Jamie bellowing in her ear as she held him. *Serena knows.*

Eventually Jamie fell asleep on her in the green sitting room, in the dark, and she stayed in there, at the window, not daring even to sit down, for a long time, swaying slightly, to and fro. He was getting heavier, even since she arrived and when he had struggled she could feel the physical effort it took to wrangle him. Rose swayed, side to side, side to side. It worked, if you thought of the baby like this, flesh of your flesh, joined at the hip, at the breast: it calmed them both at once. It must be evolution, persuading you to protect them. To save them.

The dangers were everywhere, once you had a small child, Rose knew that now, they were there in the sound of the rising tide on the edge of the lawn that was the background to Jamie's soft breathing. And suddenly Kate was in her head, Kate pacing these rooms, growing weaker as her baby grew and struggled. How could she not have known? How could *they* not have known?

Of course, Kate never liked to ask her help, never had. As she defended him in her head, Rose heard Evan's footsteps padding soft in the hall and she heard him pause, then begin to climb the stairs.

She didn't have a lock on her phone, never had. The married man, she remembered out of nowhere, had used to keep his hand over his phone, if it was out on the table. Had kept it in his hand when showing her anything on it. Guilty conscience? She had nothing to hide. And Evan had told her, after all, what had happened. He'd run after her with it, too late. She saw him in her mind's eye coming back into the kitchen, setting it down. Hesitating, picking it up again, holding on to it.

Was that it? She saw him, clear as day, sitting in his chair with her phone in front of him on the table with his hand resting on it, not looking, just knowing, it was her, in there, her life, her secrets. His lover. The thought settled, of his wiry body against hers, his hand sliding the length of her.

She hadn't sent a message to anyone in days. She had nothing to hide, did she? Against her breast Jamie gave a little shudder and she rested her chin against his warm downy head.

It must have been, he had just wandered back into the

kitchen, impatient with having missed her and put it down without thinking, anywhere, and walked away.

When she pushed the door to the nursery open with one fingertip he was asleep with the bedside light on. Lying on his back in T-shirt and boxer shorts, one bare leg dangling off the bed as if ready to jump up but his face wiped blank and mysterious in sleep, a stranger. He didn't open his eyes at the door opening or at the creak of the board as she leaned to lower Jamie into his cot. Jamie gave a little sigh as he settled, but Evan still didn't stir.

Straightening Rose looked around the room, just once, just quickly, then she turned the light out, and left.

Chapter Twenty

He looked so lost, I told him, *You looked so lost*, among those women in lycra with their pink tabards, jostling him, joshing him. There weren't many men, you see. 'They were offering to make me casseroles,' he said and he looked as if he was going to cry.

I found the tabard this morning, with the number still pinned to it. I'm not much of a runner, but I managed it. I was embarrassed when he caught my eye because I knew how red-faced I must be, scarlet. It was the same at school coming in after hockey, one of the many reasons the boys didn't go for me, prodding each other and laughing as I sat at the back of the class trying not to be seen.

'Are you here for – someone, too?' he said to me and I told him, Mum. He gave me a handkerchief to mop my forehead with and when I gave it back to him he did something strange, he held it for a moment, up to his face, as if he was breathing it in. And then he looked embarrassed, and laughed.

Rose would have been better at that run than me, she's got Dad's physique, though she won't thank me for mentioning it, built for speed, all those nerves. I get nervous too: she'd probably be surprised to know that. Maybe when I'm old I'll come into my own, they do say. Maybe the cheekbones will emerge.

I'm losing weight, actually. I am. That didn't happen last time.

A night of undisturbed sleep was remarkable. Rose woke out of it at seven with that delicious heavy feeling, and turned on the pillow. The pillow that was her friend, not an enemy to be wrestled with all night.

Evan hadn't come. Rose lay still thinking about that, looking at the grey light coming round the curtains, and found it didn't bother her, not a bit. They were living together. They were bringing up children together. It wasn't like, *Is he going to call? Has he changed his mind? What's he thinking?*

He might have come, she supposed, and found her asleep. She thought of him asleep last night, the deep sleep of the dead tired, and thought not. She wondered what he had done yesterday: something physical, to wear him out. She lay, and listened: Jamie must be up by now, but she couldn't hear him. The house was quiet – but not silent. She could hear Serena's movements next door, they were mouse movements, surreptitious rustlings and tiptoe-ings. Nothing mouse-like about Jamie waking up. More of a lion, greeting the day, and as she thought of that she did hear something, but far off, and getting up from the bed she understood that it wasn't from inside the house.

198

She crossed to the window and saw Evan, in the same T-shirt and boxers he'd been sleeping in, out on the lawn with Jamie struggling in his arms. The grass was silvered pale with dew, but Evan was barefoot: as he leaned down to set Jamie on the grass he gave a shout and a cloud of rooks rose from the spindly trees beyond the garden. The air was suddenly full of their black shapes, like broken umbrellas, and the sound of their cawing, and Evan looked up and saw her.

She ran down, and out on impulse and met him there, in the cool damp green outdoors. Evan barked a laugh, as she hopped, and grimaced when her feet froze in the grass.

'What about you?' she protested, pointing at his feet. Jamie, staring down with interest at his feet as he stood there in pyjamas and a sagging nappy, seemed unbothered by the cold.

'We're English,' said Evan, giving her a grave look. 'Warm-blooded, unlike you European types.'

'What are you doing out here?' she said, and looked around curiously. He must have come out in a rush, too, without shoes, without changing Jamie, and the answer came to her just as he said it.

'I thought you needed the sleep,' he said, smiling, kind, and she thought he must have realised even as Jamie woke him, that she had slept well, slept long.

He must have woken up thinking of her, of looking after her. Rose hugged herself against the chill and then Evan was closer, and suddenly she was very aware of him, of his warmth in the cold morning. And of herself, in the too-short shirt she slept in, she looked down and saw goosepimples, the fine hairs raised. And then his hand,

199

stroking her there: Rose felt her throat tighten and she took a step back, awkward and hurried.

'We *can't*,' she said, 'We can't. Not—'

Not yet, but she couldn't say that, either, because what if this was it? A — fling. Temporary . . . comfort, for both of them. It would confuse Jamie and Serena, and besides there were other considerations, there was a feeling of it all going too fast. Evan was just looking amused by her, as if she was a child. 'They're grieving,' she said stubbornly. 'It's too soon after, too soon. They'll be shocked by it.'

He was still close to her, looking somewhere beyond her, above her, at the house behind her. But she didn't turn around and she didn't move away, she wanted him to understand. Eventually he just shrugged.

'If you want it that way,' he said. 'We won't tell them.' He smiled. 'Not yet.'

Yet. The word did a funny thing, she smiled uneasily because he'd known what she was thinking but a shiver overtook her and then they did break apart. Evan turned so his shoulder was to her, his hands shoved under his armpits and he was looking off into the corner of the garden where Jamie was kneeling at the edge of the flower-bed. Beyond him were the rounded bushy shapes of the shrubs that had moved and shifted in the dark as she watched from her window, two nights before.

'Oh,' she said, 'yes, I was going to—' Evan turned his head back, she saw his lips, the shadow of his stubble, so dark, and she hurried on. 'The other night I thought I saw, I thought I heard voices out here.'

He turned right back around and studied her, quizzical. 'And you thought — what? That it might be ghosts?' his

200

eyes narrowing, head tilted and then abruptly he took her by the hand and led her, like a child, over to the corner. They sidestepped Jamie who barely looked up.

'He needs his nappy changing,' she said, 'he needs breakfast,' but Evan ignored her, he led her on, across the turned earth of the bed to the shrubs. Beyond them was some rusted barbed wire that barely marked the edge of the garden. Of their property, she assumed.

'There,' said Evan, pointing. She leaned, trying to make out what he was pointing at, a flash of orange, and he leaned down across the barbed wire to retrieve it. 'They can roll joints, our ghosts,' he said cheerfully. 'I've told them to fuck off out of here more times than I can count,' he said. 'Kate – Kate didn't mind them,' he finished. The orange paper was part of a Rizla packet and she flushed, feeling it to the tips of her ears.

'I think I saw them,' she said, and the image of the black-clad Goth kids came back to her, the smell of dope smoke that hung over them. 'I saw them out there on the prom, on the arcades.'

Evan spread his hands. 'See?' he said, cheerfully. 'They come out here to do their Saturday night devil-worshipping, or whatever.' He glanced back up at the house. 'They're harmless.'

Rose remembered the cocked thumb and finger pointing at her, the dead-white faces looking at her without a smile. 'Sure,' she said, but Evan was scooping Jamie up from where he stood shaking the bird box again, and if he heard the doubt in her voice he didn't answer it.

*

201

From where she sat in the Promenade Tea Rooms Rose could see both ways along the river. The day was still cool and grey but the long clapboard-trimmed pre-fab that housed the café was flooded with the pale light that came off the estuary, and it was quiet. Monday: it could easily have been closed, Rose had thought too late as she pushed the buggy up the prom past the shuttered and deserted arcades, but it opened at midday, and all she had to do was wait, wandering with Jamie's hand in hers then sitting watching the passers-by. Mostly old people, a couple of lads in stonewashed jeans, swaggering and shoving each other, glancing back at her and the buggy with brief indifference.

It occurred to her, pushing doggedly, that it would have suited Kate, this role, this quiet invisible role that involved a lot of hard work. She'd have loved it, all the organising and sorting and planning, making baby food, stepping into Mum's shoes at last. If she'd been given a chance. Even Mum got twenty years at motherhood. And at the thought Rose put her head in her hands suddenly. Kate had *been* there, Kate knew how Mum had died. Did she not recognise a single one of her own symptoms, had she not even wondered?

In front of Rose was a metal teapot and a cup and saucer in institutional pale green china that she remembered from a hundred years ago and school fêtes. The tea was very strong. An elderly couple dressed for winter sat in a corner bickering over a battered iPad. She'd got Jamie out of his buggy when they arrived and set him down on the floor thinking perhaps of Italian children running between restaurant tables; he'd straight away begun to totter over to the old couple, who hunched immediately in recoil, a pair of old tortoises, and she'd had to retrieve him with profuse apologies. They sat stiff and distrustful and said nothing in reply, just pulled the iPad towards them in case Jamie might make a grab for it. He was on her knee now, reaching for the tea, and pushing it out of reach. Rose got a surreptitious digestive out of the packet she'd bought on the way down.

She knew what Evan would think of digestives, and Kate too, although she knew Kate liked them despite herself. Fat and refined flour and refined sugar. He was right, of course. They'd cost fifty-two pence and the tea cost one pound ten and that left her with a handful of coppers in change from Evan's twenty. Her little stash. Carefully breaking the biscuit in half Rose found herself thinking of the roll of money. Kate's money. She knew it was Kate's with ever greater certainty: the tight careful roll of it. The idea of using any of it was impossible: it was more than money. It was *hers*, it was a reminder of her, it was – something else. A sign.

There was wi-fi, astonishingly. The stocky girl behind the counter had shoved a scrap of paper with a handwritten password on it across to her grudgingly. She had pink dreadlocks: she wore Indian printed trousers whose crotch drooped to the knees like a nappy and she had a few studs: one in her eyebrow, one in her nose, big metal ones like beads of mercury. She'd hardly looked up as Rose came in: but now, as she was wiping the sides down desultorily with a grubby cloth and fiddling with the radio, she kept looking over.

Rose had brought her laptop and it sat open on the

table. Smuggled it out, was what it felt like, stowed in her big cloth bag while Evan loaded the buggy in the back.

'Sure,' he'd said, taken aback when she asked if he could drop her in town on his way to drop off Serena. He had hesitated, and she knew he wanted to know where she was going.

'I thought I'd walk back, with Jamie, you know, for the exercise.' Serena was the one gave her that sideways look: Evan just nodded.

The first thing Rose had done when she'd got a signal – well, when she was unloaded and Evan had driven off, not even then, when the car disappeared round the corner – was to text Deb and tell her she was going to try to Skype. And then, on impulse, scrolled through her photographs of the house, to show Deb what her life was like for the moment: she'd taken dozens. That was what happened when you kept getting your phone out and it was no good for anything else. Rose selected one that showed a bit of the house itself – a grey brick corner, a window, the ornate white fretwork of the veranda in front of the pale dry reeds and a gleam of water – and sent it. She wanted Deb to see it: to get it. Looking down at the pictures herself, she saw the strange, magical, not quite safe place.

She was trying to work out how to top up her phone credit online while stopping Jamie tipping tea over himself and all under the gaze of the dreadlocked girl who by now had stopped wiping and was leaning with her elbows on the counter, her chin in her hands. Then the screen came up and began to ping, calling Deb: Rose shifted slightly so the girl couldn't see her or what was on the laptop and then suddenly, miraculously, Deb's face appeared, blinking in her cloud of dark hair and her mouth made a sound, suspiciously like a sob and her hand appeared on the screen.

The old couple were up and shuffling over to pay, interrupting the girl who was on her phone now, just as on Rose's knee Jamie began to bob excitedly, and his hand went out to meet Deb's on the screen. Rose hung on to him until the door had closed behind the old couple and then set him down. Free. Free.

'Deb,' she said.

'Was that your nephew?' said Deb, peering at her. 'You look thin. Are you ill?' Rose glanced at the little fuzzy image of her own face inset on the bottom of the screen and saw herself grimace, jerkily. She looked away quickly.

'I'm fine,' she said, 'I'm just tired.'

'Have you found anything out?' Rose caught a glimpse of the familiar surroundings of Deb's flat behind her – the long window, the shutters, the white curtain in the sunshine – then Deb's face lurched closer, blocking it out. Out of the corner of her eye Rose saw Jamie careering from chair to chair in the long narrow space and she saw the girl come out from behind her counter and crouch, at his level.

'Rose!' Deb's finger tapped loud and impatient on her microphone, recalling her.

'What's the address there?' There was a smell of dope in here, too. 'Found anything out?' Rose's head began to ache. 'About your sister. About how she could have not known she was dying. I can't stop thinking about it.' Deb

205

was fierce. 'And you're not well. I knew it. Something – there's something—' she pushed her face close to the screen again. 'That house looks weird. Is there something in the water there? That makes people ill?'

Rose put her hands up to her head, one on each temple, rubbing but all she really wanted to do with them was cover her ears.

'People don't get ovarian cancer from stuff in the water,' she said, feeling weary just at the thought of Deb, at her fierceness, her insistence, then revised down. 'At least, not in two years they don't. And anyway there's nothing in the water.' She didn't know that, she realised. The water supply could easily be contaminated, out there beyond civilisation. She wondered if she could ask Evan. 'It's not weird,' she concluded lamely, except it was. It was weird and marvellous. It wasn't like any place she'd ever been.

'I think you should come back to Rome,' said Deb firmly, sitting back. 'We will work it out. You can live with me.'

Behind her counter the dreadlocked girl had Jamie on her hip now, swaying, wandering round to the door and looking out down the prom, pointing at something. Jamie was absorbed, he'd forgotten her. For a second Rose had the oddest feeling that she shouldn't be here, that she had ceased to exist, that the girl was Jamie's mother, that if she turned around from the window and looked into her café it would be empty in the pale clean light off the marsh. She cleared her throat and the girl turned with Jamie still on her hip, studying her. She *did* exist.

'But there's the baby,' Rose said. 'There's my – Kate's

– stepdaughter, too. Serena. And there's Evan – he's Jamie's dad, after all.'

Deb grew thoughtful, sitting back.

'Was that her,' she said, 'your stepdaughter? In the picture?'

Rose picked up her phone. 'What?' she said. She must have sent the wrong picture – but she hadn't thought she had any pictures of Serena. She looked at her message thread with Deb and there it was, the corner of the house, the window, the reeds, the white trelliswork of the veranda.

'I don't know what you mean,' she said, peering down at the picture, trying to enlarge it. 'Deb?'

Deb said something but it distorted, crackled. The laptop screen flickered, froze, unfroze.

Over at the door Jamie whimpered suddenly, as if something had frightened him and in the same moment a cloud passed over the pale sun and the light in the long room changed, the pre-fab walls with their faded posters turned grey, the sheen left the yellow formica table-tops. The girl glanced back over her shoulder at Rose, and jiggled him again, pointing through the glass.

'At the window.' Deb's voice was abruptly distinct, and the screen sharp, but she repeated the words anyway. 'At the window.'

Rose felt the creep of something with the words, cool fingers on the back of her neck, raising the little hairs because she didn't need to look back at the screen to know that the window was in Kate's room, the marital bedroom, the room that had been locked since she arrived. She lifted the phone to her face again, not wanting to look, not wanting to see the face. And Rose remembered now with a clarity that tightened her scalp, that when Mum died – a month, maybe two months after she'd died, to be accurate – remembered lying awake at night thinking, *if she came back – what would I do, to have her back?* Aged twelve and imagining her mother, underground for two months, in the coffin in the dark, for two months, imagining her at the front door, with dirt in her mouth.

'Is that her?' said Deb, and Rose blinked, and looked. Nothing, nothing – and then something. So faint it might have been a trick of the light on old windowpanes but there it was. The face behind the glass, half a face at the window, the white oval, the dark hollows of her eyes. 'Yes,' she said, but her lips felt numb. She stared, fascinated, then put the phone down, face down on the formica.

'Yes,' she said, 'that's her.'

What had she been doing in Kate's room? How had she got in?

'She looks like—' Deb's mouth twisted. 'What's your expression? A piece of work.'

'She's lost two mothers,' said Rose. 'What do you think she's like? She's grieving. She's jealous. She's—' she picked up the phone again to look, at the burning eyes in the window. 'She's angry.'

'Two mothers?' said Deb. 'His first wife died too?' But as she said it the room darkened further, the girl had stepped back from the door as it opened and set Jamie down on the floor, running to her. Three, four, five of them came inside, dressed in long black, clomping in their big boots. The dreadlocked girl leaned up and kissed one of them, on the mouth, a long kiss and when they separated, triumphant, Rose saw that it was the girl she'd kissed. They all looked the same, male and female, pierced and pale with rusty dyed black hair. She leaned down sideways, one eye still on the screen, to receive Jamie as he tottered towards her.

'How did she die?' said Deb, and her face sharpened as she leaned abruptly close to the screen. 'Rose. *Rose.* Was it cancer? Was it an accident?' The screen froze, unfroze. 'Was he *there*? ROSE!'

Her implication was unmistakable, and shocked, Rose recoiled.

'Look, I've got to – got to go,' said Rose. Jamie clung to her arm, his fingers digging in. 'I've got to go.'

Chapter Twenty-One

They shuffled round her table on their big boots, and Rose saw they were just kids.

'Told you,' said the pink-haired waitress to her girlfriend, or whatever, her arm draped over the black studded shoulders. Straps and laces hung off the girlfriend's long black coat and her eyeliner swooped, beautiful, up to her hairline. 'Haunted house lady.'

The waitress must have phoned them. How had she known who she was? Rose had barely been there two weeks, even if it felt much longer. 'I'm Rose,' she said, looking up at them. Jamie was on her knee with his face buried in her T-shirt, fingers clinging. 'Do you want to sit down?'

The boys shuffled backwards, awkward, but the girls held their ground. The Goth girl set a hand on the table and leaned to inspect Rose, head on one side. 'That's not her name,' she said, and frowned. 'Haunted house lady's Kate.'

Rose's heart jumped in her chest. 'You knew her? You knew my sister.'

The girl frowned, pulling out a chair, and sat, not answering. 'I'm Caitlyn,' she said finally. 'Thass Ellie.' Nodding towards the pink-haired waitress, who was at the chiller cabinet dishing out Cokes to the boys.

'It's true then,' said Caitlyn. She stared at Rose, her thin pale face taut and hungry. 'She died. Kate did.' At the sound of his mother's name Jamie's grip slackened on Rose's T-shirt and she felt him shift, turning against her chest to look out with one eye and in response Caitlyn extended a finger to him across the yellow formica, a shiny black fingernail. His grip tightened again, but he didn't hide his face.

'Yes, she died,' said Rose. 'Two weeks ago. I've come to help – them. How did you know her?' She wanted to buy them their Cokes, tea, chocolate bars, chips, anything to keep them there but she didn't have the money. Pink-haired Ellie pulled out a chair and sat and the boys came over to stand behind the two girls, like centurions.

'She was nice,' the taller boy said. He was so tall and thin it might be a developmental thing, thought Rose disorderedly. She tried to work out how old they were, and settled on seventeen. They shouldn't be smoking dope.

'She told us we shouldn't be smoking,' said Caitlyn and Rose sat up abruptly, and blinked. A mumble passed between them and they shuffled, sheepish and defiant at once.

'Well, you shouldn't,' she said, 'it's – dangerous. At your age. For your brain.' They stared at her expressionless and she sighed. 'She told me the same, when I was your age.'

'Didn't do you any harm then,' said the shorter boy,

trying to leer at her and Caitlyn jerked her head sideways hissing at him.

'Shut up, Nathan.'

'I stopped,' said Rose, and flushed, remembering the conversation, remembering after all this time. Kate taking her by the shoulders, furious for once. 'You're smart,' she'd said, 'Don't mess with your brain, Rose. You're going to be so smart.' She hadn't told Kate she was going to stop but she had. She had said no, next time it was offered, even though she got stick for it, and a reputation for being a stiff, and even though Kate never mentioned it again, as if she'd known.

'When was this?' Rose said, quickly, to interrupt her own thoughts. Where was her brain when she needed it? 'When you talked to her? How long ago?'

'Ages ago,' said Caitlyn. 'She came out to see us. Not long after they moved in.' She stopped. 'It used to be our place, see. No one lived there, not for years and years. Belongs to the water board, see, and what with there being no signal and just a dirt track and that, we used to go out there and hang out, wait to see the ghost.'

'There's a ghost?'

Pink spots appeared on Caitlyn's cheeks.

'They say. We never saw 'ut. Lady ghost.'

'There's no bloody ghost,' said Ellie. 'They went out there to smoke an' that's all.'

'Boy did die in the weir once,' put in the tall boy. 'An' now—' he stopped. 'She was nice. Your sister.'

'Anyway,' Caitlyn shot him a narrow glance, not unkind, 'we saw her in the window that firs' time and we was stoned and we thought, you know, *there she is*. The ghost.

We made such a racket—' looking sideways at Nathan, 'as she come out. He weren't there that time, I think thass' why. She come out, carrying the baby, an' he was just tiny—'

At this she leaned down so low looking at Jamie across the table, her chin was almost resting on the formica, her finger crept out again and this time Rose felt him joggle delightedly on her knee and reach for it.

'You was, wa'n't yer?' And sat back up, frowning. 'Jamie, he's called, is that right? You taking over, then?' she said gruffly. 'With him?'

'Taking over?' said Rose, 'No. No.'

'Aw right,' said Caitlyn, sitting back, equably. 'Keep yer 'air on.'

'What did she say?' said Rose.

'She asked if we wanted hot chocolate,' chipped in the tall boy, then blushed.

'Yeah,' said Caitlyn, 'only then *he* come back, and we run for it.'

'Evan,' said Rose.

'Yeah,' said the girl and her eyes were dark. 'And next time he tell us to fuck off. Not his land though, is it? Not after the fence, it's not. So we can come back, whenever we want.'

'And you did?' said Rose. Caitlyn nodded.

'Not every night, issa walk out there. Well—' with a thin smile, 'I s'pose you know that, don't you? He's got the car and you got to walk, like she had to.'

'I have a bike,' said Rose slowly, but what she was thinking was, these kids had known Kate. They assumed because Rose was living out there with Evan, that the

213

same rules would apply to her. The same life of walking the baby, of solitude, of seclusion. Caitlyn didn't seem to hear.

'So we only go once in a way. Now and again. Just to, you know. Wind 'im up.'

'He weren't always there,' said the tall boy, whose name she didn't know. Who she thought had wanted Kate for his own mum, and who wouldn't? The other boy, Nathan, had wandered to the window beside the entrance and was shielding his eyes as if trying to see something.

'But she only come out but the once more,' said the tall boy, and he swallowed. He had long fingers, bone-white, and they twined and untwined as he spoke. 'That was a few months back.' The pink-haired girl, Ellie, pushed her chair back impatiently and went to the door to stand next to Nathan.

'Did she talk to you, that time?' Rose could feel her heart flutter in her chest.

'She never talked to us but the first time,' he said. 'And that time – there was something wrong.' He looked away, pained.

'Something wrong?' said Rose. Across the table Caitlyn's head was bowed over her hands, and she lifted it at the words, and the darkness was back in her eyes.

'It was like—' she spoke softly, as if she'd only just remembered they were talking about Rose's sister, her sister who she loved. She grimaced. 'Like she was pissed, or had gone a bit—' her finger raised to her temple twirling, then stopping, 'you know. Not quite right in the head.'

'Months ago,' said Rose. 'So – in the summer?' Caitlyn thought a moment then nodded.

'Beginning of the summer,' she said. 'Like when the nights go on and on? End of May, June.' She took a breath. 'Whatever. We come out and it just wouldn't go dark. Better when it's dark. Like, to spook 'im.'

'Evan?' The girl's animosity unsettled her. 'Does he – spook easily?'

Caitlyn's mouth twitched, sardonic. 'He's wound up already, in't he? So it's not hard.'

'He's lost his wife,' blurted Rose. 'You were out there two nights ago. You think that's a nice thing to do?'

Behind Caitlyn, Nathan shifted, uneasy on his feet. 'We never knew,' he whispered, but Caitlyn just folded her arms over her chest, not sorry.

'You want to hear about your sister or not?' she said bluntly.

'What do *you* think?' said Rose, holding her stare, then felt the anger go out of her. Why should she care what they thought of Evan. They liked *her*. They liked Kate: that was all that mattered.

'Aw right then,' said Caitlyn. 'Well, it was getting dark at long last. All green all round, you know them evenings, like, *glowing*, and the tide was very high. It was coming up the side channel – when that happens you can't get across, that place, it's like an island. That happens, couple times a year.'

'Right,' said Rose, not impatient suddenly, she saw it in her head, the rising tide, slow-moving, and the green evening. She could smell it, even, the hedges and the grass. 'You were—'

'We was smoking, hunkered down like, behind the big bush there. Like the other night. We'd seen him go out so we wasn't hiding. It was late, like ten, eleven. And she come out.'

At the window Ellie and Nathan had turned around, listening. Nathan's eyes were very round.

'Kate,' said Rose.

'She give me the fear,' said Nathan, from where he stood, seventeen, eighteen maybe but shorter than Ellie beside him, an advert for smoking stunting your growth. Caitlyn gave him a sharp look and he was quiet.

'It was like she was – floating,' Caitlyn said. 'Long white dress, shirt or summat. She came round the house all quick, like she was being chased. Came right over to where we was, she was stood just the other side of the flowerbed.'

'But no one else was there? Not Evan?' said Rose, then, 'The children?'

'They'd 'a been asleep, I s'pose,' said Caitlyn, impatient, but pale still. 'He weren't there, no. We saw him come back – later. He passed us in the lane.'

'He come very close,' said the tall boy, 'Yeah,' Nathan began to chip in, 'He—' but Caitlyn shut them up with a wave of her hand.

'And then she began talking. Kate did. Like I said – like she was pissed or on something.'

'Talking to you?'

Caitlyn considered, looking off, away. 'More like she was talking to herself. Very quick, though. I think she knew we were there but—' her mouth twisted, uncertain, 'like she didn't know who else was listening. Or she was pretending to be talking to herself, or like when grown-ups say things to little kids and really it's for someone else.

216

You know, like,' and she spoke in a high voice, '*Mummy's been silly*. She didn't want anyone to know she was telling us something.'

She fell silent, uncertain after the long speech as to whether it made sense.

'What did she tell you?' said Rose, and the words went out softly into the silence.

'She wanted to post something, she said.' It was the tall boy who spoke. 'She had something in her hand and she was going on about where had they put the post box and it used to be here and she didn't know if stamps went out of date.'

Caitlyn nodded. 'That's right. He's right.'

'A letter?' He shrugged.

'Or something.'

'Did you say anything? Did you – offer to help?' The thought of Kate, wandering, desperate, barefoot in the twilight, filled her head. 'Like, I don't know. Take it to the post office for her?'

Shamefaced, the tall boy shook his head. 'Nathan were scared shitless,' and at the window it was Nathan's turn to flush, but he said nothing. 'He told us not to move, not to talk to her.'

'She weren't normal,' said Nathan, then, sullenly. 'She weren't right in the head.'

Caitlyn turned her face away, pale, ashamed.

'So what *did* you do?' Rose spoke to her cheek, unsteady. Because they were just kids. Because where had *she* been, when this was happening? Off in another country, fucking around.

'We watched,' said Caitlyn, stiffly. 'We watched her, she

217

went into the flowerbed and she tried to post the – whatever it was, in a tree or summat.'

The tall boy stepped forward, his hands on the back of Caitlyn's chair. 'Then she stepped back on the grass and she stood there, straight up, and said out loud like she knew we were listening, *Mustn't tell.*'

'Who mustn't tell? You?' They stared at her, all four of them, mute, and eventually Caitlyn shrugged.

'Was that the last time you saw her?' As she spoke, Rose saw pink-haired Ellie turn back to the window.

Before anyone could answer Ellie was moving fast, heading behind the counter. 'Yer dad's coming, Caitlyn,' she hissed and Caitlyn shifted her seat so abruptly it began to tip. She scrambled upright. 'Out the back,' said Ellie and they began to troop past her, to a door behind the counter, tucked away beyond the big old fridge.

Rose got to her feet, Jamie a sleepy dead weight as she lifted him off her knee and saw a man walking up the prom, no one she knew, a stocky man in a donkey jacket. She held Jamie against her, watching him approach.

'We see her once more.' The voice was low, but distinct, it was Nathan, still flushed and sullen, lurking behind the fridge. 'Just once, but she never said nothing, she just stood there looking down from the window. I said it weren't her, she looked smaller, like she'd shrunk to a kid. But it were her.'

The others were gone, but the door beyond the fridge stood open.

'How long ago?' said Rose, faltering.

'Nathan,' hissed Ellie, jerking her head sideways. 'I don't want the aggro.'

He didn't seem to hear her. 'A month? Mebbe,' he cleared his throat. 'Mebbe less.' He held up his hands. 'She were standing at the window like this,' he said and the colour had gone from his face, it was white and drawn, his palms facing her. 'An' her face, pressed up against it.'

'Like she wanted — someone to help her?' said Rose.

But he was gone.

Rose passed the man on the way back down the prom, blunt-faced with a high-vis vest under his donkey jacket. He didn't look like a bad guy, but then how would you know? He barely glanced at her.

By the time she got back to the house it was well into the afternoon.

As she approached the bus stop on the main road, she slowed as it had occurred to her that if she waited Serena's bus would arrive before too long. They could walk together.

The picture of Kate at the window, her hands pressed against the glass, the memory of the boy's pale anguished expression imitating hers, had haunted her all the way. Leaving the houses behind, Jamie asleep at last in the buggy, walking in the road now with the late hedgerows high to either side, smelling damp after the rain, feeling the chill of approaching autumn as the sun dipped — Rose thought of Kate's face, in the summer twilight.

To know you wouldn't see spring again — and still Kate hadn't phoned. She hadn't emailed. Rose tried not to calculate, at what point the evidence must have turned, symptoms that could no longer be ignored. Her hands up against the glass.

Poor Evan, she thought, resolutely. Poor Evan, tormenting

himself now. And Serena – well. Rose knew all too well what it was like, living in a house with someone dying, how hard you work to deny it to yourself. Poor Serena, she told herself. Poor kid.

If she walked back with Serena Rose considered that she might have a chance to find something out. She looked up at the bus stop, which was by a quirk of progress equipped, even where mobile signal faltered, with one of those illuminated signs. FORTY MINUTES, it said. And just like she'd avoided googling symptoms so she'd avoided asking Serena – because how could you? – what it had been like. How Kate had been. What mystery was she trying to solve, anyway? She pushed that question away, and kept walking.

Forty minutes alone.

The first thing Rose noticed, pushing Jamie into the yard, was a faint smell of burning. She remembered getting a whiff of it that morning, vaguely assuming it was the boiler. But it was outside, not in, and it was more acrid than the woodsmoke or solid fuel, it was a bonfire smell, a hint of burning plastic, too. She stood a moment and sniffed the air, turning. It came from the barn – no. From behind the barn.

Leaving Jamie where he was she walked slowly around the tarred board flank of the building, pushing goosegrass and nettles aside. She hadn't been round the back here since she arrived: she came out into a half-cleared space and saw that she'd come the wrong way – there was a path she hadn't seen. And someone had been burning rubbish.

Well, not someone. Evan, obviously: he'd said as much

220

yesterday. He'd told her cheerfully on their return from the picnic that he'd got things done. Rose stood there and looked. There was a heap of ash. Papers, books, she could see the ghost of them, a wodge of them turned to ash and as a breeze came round her ankles they lifted and blew into dust. Beside the ash was a steel drum on a kind of trestle that had clearly been used as some kind of makeshift incinerator and inside it more ash, but of clothing, it looked like. Peering in Rose saw something that looked like a buckle and when she reached in for it saw that was exactly what it was. A coat buckle she half recognised, an old thing of Kate's. She stared down at it and felt a prickle at her scalp. Something shrivelled and pink that had once been nylon.

Perhaps he hadn't known whose it was. Perhaps it got caught up in other things. Slowly Rose walked back around into the yard: Jamie was still asleep in his buggy.

Books and papers: *Perhaps it didn't occur to him*, Rose thought, appalled, disbelieving, staring blindly down at Jamie's sleeping face, *perhaps he didn't think. That I might want it all, all her stuff.* Men did have this urge, she knew, to chuck things out. Dad had always ranted at them as kids for hoarding. Ribbons and cards and old schoolbooks. Rose took an abrupt, stumbling step back, as she remembered, as she wondered. Thought about clues, childhood games, and hiding places.

Kate had chosen what went in that room for her, hadn't she. Down to the old books on the shelves. Rose ran, quick, fumbling with the back door, through the kitchen, up the big staircase.

She'd stopped using the back staircase, although it was

221

on her radar, always, her mental map of the house's places. It was as if she was saving it, hiding it.

Round the gallery, into her room. The first book she took down was the wrong one, and then Rose remembered she'd chosen the second in the series, as a better hiding place. Less obvious. Although she hadn't known what she was hiding – or who she was hiding it from. The little scrap fluttered to the ground, Kate's writing. She snatched it up and ran down, to the old-fashioned telephone in the hall, at the foot of the stairs. She dialled.

Listening to it ring Rose felt the house around her, listening. Watching. The shrouded shapes in the neglected back parlour with its high ceilings and etched glass, the green light that filtered through from the sitting room, the shadows of leaves behind the coloured glass of the front door that never opened. You'd better be careful, they warned. She had the strangest sensation that the house wasn't just on an island, it was like a ship unmoored, it could drift away from land.

It rang and rang, her heart beating hard and fast to the same rhythm and Rose thought of Kate sitting right here, of Kate wandering outside in her nightdress with a letter to post and finding her house had cut its moorings in the night, and she was alone. There was no answer: Monday afternoon, was someone at work – and then there was a click and an answering machine cut in.

Lindsay Macrae can't take your call at the moment.

So the number was Lindsay's.

There was a beep. Startled, Rose said nothing for a second, then babbled her name, *Kate's sister* her mobile number, took a breath, *though of course there's no signal here,* reading the landline number off the telephone. *It'd be so nice to – talk.*

When she hung up Rose thought that of course Lindsay must have that number, they must have called each other, she and Kate. Lindsay had said they'd fallen out over her own mother's death, which didn't sound like Kate at all, Kate who was all compassion. Except that increasingly she could only see Kate as alone, cut off.

Standing up from the phone table and walking through the red gloom of the hall back towards the kitchen Rose wondered not for the first time how Lindsay's number had ended up on a piece of paper hidden in a children's book. A secret message. A summons: a clue.

Or it could mean absolutely nothing. Kate, with no mobile phone, didn't want to lose her best friend's number, however estranged they had become.

As she came into the kitchen Rose heard murmurings from through the kitchen window and that little startled shout of Jamie's that she was beginning to recognise: the sound of him waking.

Hurrying out through the back door Rose saw Serena, kneeling beside the buggy with her school backpack by her side on the ground, and unbuckling Jamie, who was reaching for her face. *She adores him,* Annie had said that. And the face Serena turned to her was in that moment so bright and open that Rose understood that it was true, and that alongside the tricky, malicious Serena there was also the Serena that was just a child, still. She loved her brother. She'd wanted another sibling. She wanted Lindsay to come to Kate's funeral. Had Kate left Lindsay's number in a children's book for Serena, in emergencies?

There was a second in which they were both smiling, and then there was the smallest adjustment in Serena's expression, a kind of shutter that was her little private mechanism, and she stood, hauling Jamie up with her. Rose, trying to hold on to the moment, held back, smiled still.

She stopped, and in front of her Serena swung Jamie round on to her hip, and Rose saw that soon enough he would be as big as her. Now though she stood upright and strong, watching for what Rose would say.

'You're so good with him,' was what Rose said, but Serena only swivelled coolly, lifted him back off her hip and plonked him in Rose's arms, where he began to bawl.

'I saw you in Kate's room,' Rose said. 'At the window.' Serena's face was a careful blank. 'So?' she said.

'Have you got the key?' said Rose. Serena shook her head, biting her lips together.

'I was in there with Dad,' she said quickly, 'he goes in there to— he goes in there sometimes.' Then grabbing her school bag off the dusty ground Serena sidestepped them and disappeared into the house, leaving Jamie reaching after her, thrashing.

In the kitchen Rose calmed him with a digestive, remembering to stash the packet out of sight, opening a drawer. Only as she opened it did she wonder if it was the same drawer where Evan had put the solicitor's letter, but if it had been, it wasn't there any more, there were only some of his brochures, pencils, the red stubs of candles. She carefully pushed the biscuits to the back and closed the drawer again, thoughtful.

Upstairs Rose could hear Serena moving around and

Jamie reached towards the sound with sticky fingers. She put her mouth to his soft hair. The house around them was so silent, it rested, like a house in a story, gathering dust, the leaves coming in at the windows. Why were so many people kept out? Even at the funeral only drunken Lindsay had gained entry. It wasn't healthy, she should talk to Evan – Rose quailed at the thought. His parents in Australia. What had Annie had said about Serena's other grandparents, that they'd fallen out with Kate about something? And pursuing the thought she found herself shaking her head. Not Kate. Kate would never have excluded anyone. She would have felt pity for an old couple whose daughter had died. And turning that over in her head she sat up, alert, listening for something. For the sound of Evan returning. But it was quiet.

The door to Serena's room was ajar.

'Serena?' There was a silence. 'Can I come in a minute?'

Then Jamie lunged for the door and it opened and there was Serena, tense and watchful, at the window. Rose took another step and Serena said nothing. She set Jamie down and he tottered to Serena's bed where he began to bat at the cover with his hands.

'You gave him a biscuit,' said Serena, but not accusatory, more wondering.

'Serena,' said Rose, not wanting to waste time, 'is there anyone you can talk to? I mean, apart from your school friends?' She hesitated. It felt dangerous: Serena might tell Evan she'd asked. But something told Rose she would not. 'Are your mother's parents still alive?' Serena's eyes slid away from her, over to the chest of drawers where the little red candles sat unlit, then back to Rose. She gave a little shrug and her face drew together, tight, eyes black. Rose persisted. 'Do you ever see them?'

Serena sat abruptly, leaning down to push her fingers towards Jamie's across the coverlet and muttered, 'No. Yes they're alive and no I don't see them. They don't like us.'

'They don't *like* you?'

'They don't like us. Me and Daddy and Jamie. They didn't even like Mu— my mother.' Now she was walking her fingers across the bedcover towards Jamie, not looking up.

'Did they meet Kate?'

'I haven't seen them since I was small,' said Serena still not meeting her eye. 'They live a long way away.' And then she stood up as suddenly as she'd sat down, and slotting her hands under Jamie's arms began to walk him to the door. 'And if you *don't* mind I've got to do my homework.'

The door banged after them and shut out on the landing with Rose, Jamie began to cry.

No, thought Rose, *I don't believe it*, and wearily she lifted Jamie into her arms.

Chapter Twenty-Two

I'd never been in love. Before Evan.

I remember Lindsay laughing when I said that, and then she covered her mouth because she knew she was laughing *at* me for talking about love, at my age. I watched them together, her and Evan, the only real time they met, and I was jealous. I've never been a jealous person, the idea seemed ridiculous to me before Evan, I mean, if someone wants to be with someone else then you let them go.

But *in love* makes you watch the other person so closely you can see their thoughts. I saw Evan talking to Lindsay, I saw all the things about her that weren't me – her easiness, her softness, her impulsiveness, her smile – and I wanted to get in between them. I stood at the bar buying the drinks and I itched to stop them talking, I turned right back into the pushy girl I was at school. That was why I didn't have boyfriends, I talked too much, I asked too many questions: in love sends the questions away. Because you just *know*.

(Does writing this down make it real? I have to write it because there's no one to tell it to. I tried phoning Rose but she was busy, she was distracted.)

He liked Lindsay, I could see, the way he saw she understood when he explained the eco-houses. She liked him, she can't deny it now, whatever she says. You can tell.

Love is a bubble and you climb inside the bubble, it seals you in with the magic. Evan looks at me and only me and the bubble closes around us and it's just the most delicious feeling. The surrender. The rest of the world doesn't matter, nothing matters but the way he looks at me. We don't need other people.

And I think Lindsay was jealous of *me*. Of us. When she said I should go for the tests, I think she was trying to burst the bubble, just because she has the gene doesn't mean I do. And then I got pregnant and now of course she must hate me.

I don't know how to get out. I don't know how to get back.

It got late, and later, and Evan didn't appear. When it got dark Rose made scrambled eggs for her and Jamie and Serena and they sat around the table together, in the warm. Serena didn't seem at all fazed by her father's absence: when she caught Rose glancing at the clock she said, pushing her plate away, 'He's often late. Well he was, till – Kate died, then he had to be here with us, obviously. I s'pose now you're here—' and she shrugged, as if Rose was a piece of equipment she didn't care about one way or the other, and got up from the table.

Jamie was half asleep in his high chair as she cleared

the plates and lifting him out, feeling him lean against her, Rose took him upstairs. She got him washed and stood beside him in his cot as he swayed sleepily on his knees, putting up resistance. And then at last, abruptly, he turned himself over, bottom in the air, cheek against the sheet, and slept. Turning to the window Rose saw the garden in the twilight, and the bushes where the Goths smoked. There was no one there. She saw the bird box.

For a second she saw Kate, standing in the flowerbed, holding out her hand.

The phone rang, loud, downstairs, and she ran. It wasn't Evan, though. It wasn't Lindsay, either. It was Gerald.

'Gerald?' she said stupidly into the phone in the dark hall and as she said it there was a creak from upstairs, a shard of light quickly extinguished. Serena had opened her door then closed it again.

It must have been Serena.

For a moment she couldn't remember who Gerald was then she remembered Serena saying his name in that simpering voice.

'Oh,' she said, 'hello. No, he's not here. I assumed he was still at work.'

There was a pause. 'He might be,' said Gerald eventually. He sounded tired and anxious and upper-class. 'I left early myself,' and cleared his throat, apologetic. 'I've been breaking myself back in gently.' She didn't know what he meant so she just waited but what he said next was, with a kind of urgency, 'You're all right there? Are you? All right?'

'Yes,' said Rose, startled into alarm, 'I'm – well. You know considering – it's – Evan's being— We're managing,' she said.

'I was so sorry about Kate,' said Gerald then, and he did sound it, there was a break in his voice, guilt and grief, a gentleness when he said, 'Your sister.'

'Thank you,' Rose said formally, thinking that would be everything now, she wanted suddenly to get him off the phone, this strange broken disembodied voice. But it wasn't everything. 'I couldn't understand it,' he said, and something else had crept into his voice, panic or fear. 'I don't know how we – how no one saw she was getting ill. I don't know how – that house. The children alone with her in that house.' He drew a breath abruptly as if regretting what he'd said.

'Anyway,' he said, clearing his throat again and his tone had changed again, become formal. 'When Evan does get in, perhaps you could tell him I phoned.' And was gone.

Rose found herself walking to the back door and outside.

The night was cool and silvery, the moon casting deep shadows. Almost sleepwalking Rose came around the side of the house under the wisteria that had lost almost all its foliage since she arrived, leaving just a few dry leaves translucent in the moonlight and the bare trunk lying in thick grey coils around the veranda's ironwork. She ducked under it and on, knowing where she was going without knowing, her feet taking her there.

The grass was wet underfoot and Rose had the sense again of being on shifting ground, the sodden marsh that could so easily turn back into sea. She could smell the mineral scent of the river, see its gleam between the black-feathered tops of the rushes and she could hear it. She stopped and listened: the sound was many small sounds, a kind of sucking and lapping, advancing and retreating as the water crept up, between reeds, between blades of grass. She walked straight across the grass in the moonlight and when she got to the flowerbed she turned immediately to look back up at the house.

No one was watching her. Serena's curtains were drawn and no light showed through, but it seemed to Rose that the blank black window that was – had been – Kate's bedroom, the central window, looked down at her, and waited. He must go there to grieve. To cry, perhaps. She wondered if he went alone, or with Serena, because that was where Deb had seen her in the photograph, the pale face looking down at the garden in the dusk. Kate's room, then, was the one they both retreated to in secret, the place where Rose couldn't find or follow them. But now the window was empty.

The soil of the flowerbed was sticky between her toes: she sank into it, feeling a sudden anxiety. She'd bring dirt into the house, they'd know, and she felt unsteady at the thought – but the bird box was within reach and she put her hand out to it. In her head she saw Jamie, straining to reach up to it, shaking the pole that supported it.

Perhaps Jamie was the message. Kate had left him for her, to tell her. Rose peered down, one hand on either side of the box. It was in the shape of a little house and was old, the wood rough with creosote, the little shingles flaking and peeling: there was a circular hole at the front for the birds to go in and out. She leaned down and peered into it: she couldn't see anything but there was a musty scent, of disuse, dead leaves. She tried to insert her fingers inside the hole, but it was too small and she pulled them back out, scraping the knuckles. Frustrated she shook

231

the pole, like Jamie, but it was embedded firmly in the soil and then – something shifted.

Blindly feeling around the underside of the box, Rose felt a ridge and tentatively investigating it with her fingers, detected the movement again. There was what felt like a little panel: she pushed and it slid, stuck, slid again and was open. Something half fell out of the aperture: she felt it brush her grazed knuckles, pulled her fingers out and it half came with them.

Curled at the corners and soft with damp, half the underside still stuck to the wood, Rose pried at it with careful fingers until it came away. Kate had wandered out here looking for a post box in her nightdress, white as a ghost in the dark, and had found something that looked right. She'd posted her letter – postcard – and Rose was holding it.

She heard the car. It was coming slowly.

For a moment the scrap of mouldering card in her hands was an offering for Evan, a clue for him to Kate's state of mind, but in the next moment she saw his face, in her head, his face frowning at her and his hand reaching for it. Her clue. Rose turned and ran, awkward on the gravel in bare feet across the yard.

The words on the card swam before her eyes in the bright kitchen and she had to sit down. Just an old post-card. Just – she peered down, brushed birdshit from a corner. There was no stamp, but the card was addressed to Rose in Kate's neat, careful writing and it was dated months earlier, before the summer.

Just the sight of the writing gave a sharp twist to Rose's insides: Kate's schoolbooks had stayed in the spare room for years after she'd left home, Dad hadn't cared enough to tidy anything or get rid of anything. Rose had used to go and open them now and again, pages stuck together with damp that were covered with tiny neat writing, exercise books it used to be then, no online homework, a special pen and here was the writing again, precise and small as typing.

She'd written it in the spring. *We won't be going anywhere this year, just getting used to the house, who needs a holiday house when you've got a place like this? You've got to see it, Rosie, it's like nowhere else. Evan's frantic with work, I offer to help but he says the children need me and they do, I suppose they do. Serena's a handful – remember what you were like—* then something crossed out, the lines as neat and precise as the writing. *Anyway we'll need the money. Because I've got news.*

Rose realised she was holding her breath but she couldn't let it out. *I mean, pretty much a miracle at my age.* For a second Rose stared not understanding, thinking was this a whole year old, this card, then she focused. *Martha did say once you've had one, the body is primed.*

What?

I'm pregnant again.

And breathe. Outside the kitchen window the car crunched across the gravel and Rose got up quickly from the table with the card in her hands. Distractedly she grabbed the kettle and filled it and when Evan came in she was standing beside it with her back to the door.

'You waited up,' he said, his voice warm and Rose gave him the corner of her smile over her shoulder as she reached for mugs, playing for time while she held on to this new information, just a moment longer while she tried to understand what it meant. Carefully she poured hot water on to teabags. 'We've eaten, but I can make you something—' she began and heard falsity in her voice and in the next moment she knew he heard it too because he said, 'What's wrong? Has something happened?' and turning she stopped there with two scalding mugs in her hands. She felt a tremble and set them down gently.

'I found this,' she said, giving the curled piece of card a little push towards him. Evan looked down at it but didn't pick it up, didn't lean to read it.

'What is it?' he said, wary.

'It's a postcard from Kate to me,' she said. 'From months ago.' She was trying to understand. 'She never sent it. She says she was pregnant.'

Evan had sat down, so abruptly the surface of the tea trembled in the mugs. He was very pale. And then he reached for the postcard.

'No,' he said, she could see him scan the words once, twice, going over them as she had, his lips moving. 'No. It's not – she—' and he raised his eyes to hers, searching her face. 'She couldn't have been,' he said, eventually. 'She couldn't have been.'

'She didn't tell you,' said Rose, slowly. His hands were at his temples, tugging at his hair.

'I don't understand,' he said, and his eyes were wide. 'I don't understand.'

'You didn't notice anything?' Slowly he shook his head. 'There was no baby,' he said, and his eyes still stared off, past her. 'When they did the post-mortem.'

'Did she miscarry?' said Rose, trying to make sense of

it. 'And not tell you?' Another possibility occurred, it twisted and turned, eluding her. 'Or did she just – make a mistake?'

Slowly Evan's focus shifted, he was looking at her now. But it was as if he hadn't heard.

'I told them at the post-mortem,' he said. 'I was working so hard on the site, everything was happening at once.' His mouth was set. 'I should have seen. I should have seen something.' Rose's hand went out to his arm: he didn't seem to notice. 'Kate was looking so pale, all the time, I did mention anaemia to her, I know with breastfeeding and all that – but she wouldn't go to the doctor.'

'Why *not*?' Rose couldn't stop herself.

He still didn't seem to hear. 'There was a stomach upset that seemed to go on for ever in the summer – she didn't say anything to me. The last month, when Serena went back to school I was taking her every day, Kate always seemed to be still in bed.'

In her head Rose saw it, Kate in the bedroom she'd only seen from the lawn, had only imagined. The dark window and behind it a big bed and in the bed Kate, turning over, trying to get comfortable, trying to find a way out.

'But why didn't she tell you, Evan? Why didn't she go to the doctor?' she insisted, because she'd held back too long. She should have asked him days, weeks ago. She should have asked him when she first heard and not stopped asking. 'Kate was always so practical – she hadn't turned into some kind of Christian Scientist, had she? If she thought she was pregnant she should have gone to the doctor. They could have seen she was sick. And then it was too late and she was *dying*.'

Slowly Evan's head turned, his eyes rested on her. 'It's my fault,' he said. 'It's all my fault. There was one bad experience waiting in a hospital when she was pregnant with Jamie, and I couldn't get there for the scan and the consultant was – cold, or rude, or something about her age and she turned against – the system, I suppose. I could have talked her out of having Martha, for Jamie. It's what started her off on it. Hating conventional medicine. And wanting to live out here, away from the modern world. She was so euphoric, after Jamie.'

She gazed at him, the last sentence ringing in her ears, because it did sound like Kate, that did. Kate's triumph when she had pulled something off, finished something without anyone's help. Helpless, knowing it would hurt him but she had to say it, she let out a long breath.

'Maybe,' she said. 'Maybe. But I still don't understand why she didn't tell *you*?'

Evan was staring back at her, with a dawning certainty, but without hope.

'It's – it's all my fault,' he said again. And his face was back in his hands. She stood up and as she did his arm came out sideways, around her hip pulling her towards him, turning and pulling, then suddenly burying his face there in the concavity between her hips, his breath warm against her through her skirt. He was saying something, his voice muffled then she understood. *Let's go upstairs. Please. Please.* He shuddered against her, and when he looked up she saw that the gleam of tears in his eye. 'Not your fault,' she murmured, feeling something unfamiliar stir in her, Kate's first impulse always, never Rose's, the urge to protect, or comfort. She bent to lift him, closer.

236

They left the tea there on the table. After, in her bed, she felt him ticking away to sleep beside her, ticking down, but inside her another rhythm beat, and drowsily she remembered.

'Gerald called,' she said, murmuring and the last thing she heard as she fell asleep was the level tone of his voice repeating the name in the dark, like a stone dropped in a well.

Gerald.

Chapter Twenty-Three

It was before dawn when Rose woke, stiff from lying squeezed against the edge of the narrow bed. The light leaked grey and dull around the curtains and she could see Evan's head tipped back on the pillow: shifting gingerly she saw his clothes in a heap on the floor. She didn't know what had woken her but the house didn't seem quite quiet, somewhere there were creakings. For a second Rose thought it might even have been the telephone, she half remembered it, ringing in the night – but then she remembered Gerald.

She lay back. Something had come to her in the night that had felt like a fact, a memory, a screenshot but in that half-asleep state where you couldn't trust anything, where you could panic over test results that didn't exist, or imagine yourself flying. If she lay still it might come back to her.

And it did. The silent killer: the frantic, terrified Google search she'd done before she left Rome. Wanting to know what had killed Kate, and not wanting to know. *Ovarian cancer and its symptoms, missed diagnoses.*

She eased herself off the bed, looking down at her body pale in the dim room and suddenly she felt very naked, she shivered and reached for Evan's T-shirt by her feet. It didn't help: it smelled of him, alien, and she didn't know, anyway, if he would mind, he might look at her in that way he had. Dropping it Rose tiptoed to the small low chair at the window where one of her own lay.

When Rose emerged from her T-shirt, tugging it down, Evan was looking at her from the bed, and slowly she returned, tentatively she laid herself against him. She didn't fit, not quite: she wasn't small enough to get under his arm comfortably and for a second he felt all elbows and knees against her. With a conscious effort Rose made herself relax, and she felt Evan rest his chin against her head, keeping her down.

'What is it?' Rose said, suddenly unwilling. The phrase, in her experience, was never good. Just the need to ask. But there was something. He sighed, into her hair.

'Kate,' he said dully and with the name, the faded words on the postcard came back to Rose and suddenly, unaccountably, she wanted to cry. 'Kate thinking she was pregnant, and saying nothing to me.' His voice was cold.

Rose cleared her throat, nervous suddenly. 'I – I searched online for ovarian cancer.' Silence. 'Anyway. I googled, after you'd called. I couldn't really focus on it, it frightened me—' Rose had stopped reading because it had made her sick with fear. She started again. 'But it came back to me, just now.'

'What did?' said Evan, and she turned her head to look at him. He was frowning.

'It's one of the symptoms of ovarian cancer,' she said and her mouth was dry. 'It can mimic pregnancy.'

Evan was staring down at her, very still. 'No,' he said and there was an edge in his voice now. Rose saw the glitter of his eyes.

'No?' she said, not understanding. 'Did she do a test?'

'She can't have even imagined she was pregnant,' he said. 'At least—' and Evan looked at her as if he was testing something, some possibility.

In the silence Rose heard the house again, the shifting or creaking. She waited, the silence extended and Evan said flatly, 'I think she didn't tell me because she knew that if she *was* pregnant, I wasn't the father.'

A silence followed that deepened and lengthened and then Rose came to herself and said, 'What?' then beginning to protest, 'Kate? No. *Kate?* No, you're wrong. And – how can you be so sure of that? How could she?'

Evan had turned his head and was looking at her, and his eyes were very dark. 'Because I had a vasectomy,' he said, flatly.

'You got a—' Rose felt her eyes widen and in that second last night came into her head, the something furtive and hurried that had been in it. Evan had been very quick, making himself come inside her and Rose had lain quiet, understanding his distress, or thinking she did. And also thinking about when her prescription for the pill would run out, realising that he hadn't asked her at any point about contraception.

'I don't understand,' Rose said stubbornly and Evan looked at her a long moment before speaking.

'Jamie's birth was hard,' he said and his voice was low and sad. 'Kate didn't make anything of it but—' he hesitated, 'sometimes not much is made of what it's like to – watch that. Someone you love going through that, and her insisting on Martha and not being in hospital. And money—' he made an angry, impatient sound, 'money was tight, we didn't have enough *money* for another child. I know Kate wouldn't have – I couldn't have said any of it to her because she would have made any sacrifice – *any* sacrifice.' Evan laid his head back on the pillow again. He spoke dully. 'So I just went and got it done. I couldn't lie to her.' He turned his face away on the pillow. 'She was very angry. I suppose I never knew – *how* angry.'

'You mean,' said Rose, pulling away, sitting on the edge of the bed. 'You mean she was so angry she had an affair with someone else?' Swallowing. 'And then got pregnant?' Corrected herself. '*Thought* she'd got pregnant?'

Evan brought his hands up to his face and rubbed, then took them down and looked at her. 'That postcard,' he said. 'Lying awake last night, I kept forgetting it wasn't real, that pregnancy. I found myself thinking, I would have let her have the baby, she could have told me, why didn't she trust me. Except there was no baby, was there? There was only cancer.'

'But—' Rose lay staring up, trying to make sense of it. 'So – just *thinking* she was pregnant, even if she wasn't, must have meant—' she swallowed, because it felt like a slap in Kate's face. 'That she was sleeping with someone else.'

Evan was sitting up against the wall, one knee up, his shoulders broad and strong, the faded old wallpaper behind him. He was looking at her. 'But who?' she said, and the idea was absurd all over again. Who would Kate even meet? 'Do you know – do you have any idea who?'

Evan shook his head, looking down so his shaggy hair obscured his face. 'The world's full of men,' he said flatly. 'If you want to find one. Maybe she needed to have another baby that badly.'

'Maybe,' said Rose, but it just didn't fit, somehow. Kate did want another baby, Rose had understood that much before their communications petered out – and why, her brain insisted, over and over again, why *had* they petered out? – but had she wanted it that badly? And on cue, it came, Jamie's high, certain shout of command from along the gallery and Evan was clambering across her out of the bed, pulling on his trousers, T-shirt.

Rose followed him as far as the door but some instinct told her, once there, to hold back, to wait, just one beat, to let him cross the landing on his own. Just in time to see Serena's door begin to open, just in time to step back and close hers quickly, silently. Just in time – or just too late. Rose stood inside her room with her back to the door, waiting for her heart to stop thumping, listening for a conversation that never came.

But how? Stuck out here. A dad from school, a man with a car, a place of his own, and what did she do with Jamie, leave him with Annie? And another thought came to her: Kate must at least have told *him*. Told her lover that she was pregnant, or thought she was. And why didn't *he* help her?

If there was a lover.

There was no trace of the conversation at the breakfast table: Evan sat motionless frowning over his laptop, and if Serena had seen – or heard – him emerge from Rose's room she gave no sign of it. Outside it was grey, the colours all gone from the trees, the sky low and heavy and the kitchen stuffy. Jamie was sniffling and irritable, refusing his breakfast, straining away from her when she held out the spoon, and all the time it ran round in Rose's head, driving her mad.

Kate had been having an affair. Emptying Jamie's cereal into the bin with her back to the table Rose had to stifle a desire to scream at them, *Just go.*

Her back still to them Rose crossed to the sink and began washing up. Her hands were beginning to suffer: her nails were cracking and her knuckles were red. Perhaps Kate had blamed herself for coming here, wilfully cutting herself off, perhaps Kate had wondered, increasingly, if this had all been a terrible mistake. And with the thought Rose felt a creeping sensation at the back of her neck and in that moment didn't want to turn around because she knew they'd all be staring at her. *It's all been a terrible mistake.*

Rose had slept with people she shouldn't have, before. Evan was different. When Rose thought of Evan she thought of his arms, wiry and strong, containing her. She thought of the fierceness of his need, and it made her shiver. A terrible mistake. Was it? Rose had never lived with a lover. She didn't know if this feeling – of panic, of claustrophobia – was normal or if she was just immature.

Kate had been stronger, she had been grown up. But it must have come to her, too, in the end, the need to run outside, to escape. Why else would she have wandered in the garden in her nightdress, looking for help? By the end it must have become urgent: she must have wondered if she had the strength to cycle to the hospital, if she could give in and tell Evan, she needed to get to the doctor, to the emergency room. At some point she must have realised that she wasn't young and strong any more, that her body was betraying her. Rose felt it rise in her throat, choking her.

'Come on then, Serena.' His voice behind her was level, almost cheerful. Rose waited, not hearing what he said to her, not seeing whether he was smiling or not, deliberately letting him blur in front of her eyes so that he couldn't see her, either. Like children hiding their eyes think it makes them invisible.

And then they were gathering their things and they were out of the door and Rose was lifting Jamie out of his high chair and they were outside in the yard and she was telling him to wave goodbye.

The car disappeared into the lane. The air was strange and muggy and lowering her cheek to Jamie's downy head as he lay limp against her Rose registered that he was warm. She lifted him, looking into his face but he drooped and wouldn't look back, only pushing out his lower lip miserably and whimpering.

Shit. Rose stood a moment, trying to work out what

to do next. She had no clue what you gave small children if they had a temperature – then she thought of Annie.

'I'll come straight over when I've dropped Evie,' Annie said when she finally answered, her voice muffled behind car noise. 'Are you OK? Look, I'm sure it's nothing to worry about. The stuff's Calpol, anyway, even Kate surely must have had some somewhere – but I'll bring some. Pink stuff.' And hung up.

Jamie wouldn't be put down, he clung, hot and sniffling, wanting only to lay his head on Rose's shoulder. Her arm was beginning to ache. Where did people keep stuff like that? *Even Kate?* What had she meant? Maybe Kate hadn't even believed in paracetamol either, these days. There hadn't been any in the upstairs bathroom when Serena had found the bandage and the iodine for the cut on her leg.

Rose went along the side of the staircase to the back room, the high-ceilinged room that was cluttered with stuff under dustsheets. She lifted one at random and saw a crate of box-files: GREEN SPACE was printed on their spines, and dates, three, four years back. The name made no sense to her and the room suddenly felt claustrophobic, its nameless shapes looming over her and letting the cloth fall back, Rose reversed hurriedly out into the hall.

Turning back to look down the hall on her right was the downstairs toilet: she'd used it perhaps once, a long dim room that smelled of damp with an ancient wooden-seated lavatory that didn't flush properly. Rose pushed at the door, which had an old hand-painted sign on it saying CLOAKROOM and Jamie slipped down: she hoisted him back up feeling a sweat break on her forehead, trying not to think of Kate, ill, dragging herself around this strange house.

She moved into the long, narrow room and it closed around her, dank and dismal, the toilet bowl brown with ancient scale, the smell of ringworm and damp in her nostrils and she knew, keenly, suddenly, that there'd come a time when Kate had wanted to get out of here, too.

And there it was: an old-fashioned cabinet over the scale-stained sink. *Maybe here, maybe here.* And she opened the cabinet and there, among a lot of stuff that looked as if it might have been there since the war – old bandages in rust-marked packets, a bottle of something that had separated out into water and chalk – was a bright new box, purple and white. It said, INFANT PARACETAMOL, but even as she reached out and took it Rose heard the sound of a car. Hurrying in her relief she barely had a chance to close the cabinet behind her.

'You found it then?' Coming hesitantly inside Annie looked around the kitchen, frowning. 'It feels like for ever since I was here last.' She stationed herself stiffly behind a chair. 'Looks like a new bottle.'

'Yes, it's – weird,' said Rose. 'It was hidden away.' Annie reached for the bottle.

'You hold him,' she said. 'On your knee.'

Rose was surprised by the force necessary, Jamie stiffened and tried to move his mouth away from the spoon, but Annie – practised – got it down him. 'Horrible sticky stuff,' she said, cheerfully, and it was, when Rose stood up again she seemed to have got it on herself and there was a saccharine smell that went with it as she wiped them both down that Rose suddenly remembered from her own childhood so vividly she almost gagged.

Annie looked around the kitchen and said abruptly,

'Let's go for a walk, shall we? He'll fall asleep in the buggy, and we can keep an eye on him that way. It's probably just a cold but well – you know.' And looked at Rose a moment, her expression clouded, then she sighed. 'Fresh air,' she said.

After the bridge, instead of heading into the lane, Annie turned sharply and there was a narrow path that Rose hadn't seen before, so narrow the buggy barely squeezed through. As they came around the big brick pumping station the roar of the weir was suddenly amplified, it was like a physical thing – but either the throb of the water or the medicine must have had a soothing effect on Jamie because he was asleep, pale now against the buggy's cushioned back, his mouth a little open. The path widened, between great towering mounds of bramble and elder and field maple: the light was strange and flat under the low sky and it was like a lost world, an overgrown Sleeping Beauty place.

'We used to come down this way for walks,' said Annie, raising her voice against the roar of the water. 'When Kate and Evan had just moved here. Kate was so—' she frowned, 'she was so exhilarated by it. Loved it. She thought it was like a fairy tale.' She stopped and turning they saw the chimneys of the house rising out of the wild tangle of trees. 'The way the tide comes up and down around the house,' said Annie, 'reminding them, she said, anyway, that nature was bigger than them. Something like that. That they were temporary.'

It didn't sound like Kate. 'It freaks me out,' said Rose slowly, 'if you put it like that. It could drown you, couldn't it? Looked at that way.' They came around a corner and there it was, the source of all the noise, the wide expanse of water flowing fast over concrete with a rusted rail along the top. Just a weir: but the relentless rush of the water, the dark swirl of it where it met the pool below, made Rose take a step back. There was a wooden bench marked with initials, bleached and flaking, and they sat.

'Coming here with small children, though,' Rose said, averting her eyes from the bubbled pool. 'It's not really safe, is it?'

'Kate liked a challenge,' said Annie, trying to sound upbeat and Rose drove herself forward, elbows on her knees and buried her face in her hands. She felt Annie's hand tentative on her shoulder.

'I think it was all they could afford,' said Annie eventually, with a sigh. 'And it *is* beautiful.'

Rose stared at her. 'All they could afford? I know it's a long way from civilisation but – surely,' and she glanced towards the house, invisible from where they sat, the great rambling magical strange place, and for a second Rose imagined that it wasn't real at all, that they would walk back down the lane and it would be gone. 'Surely it must have cost a fortune?'

Annie looked at her, uncomprehending, then her face cleared. 'Oh,' she said, 'oh, no, they didn't *buy* it. It's rented. From the water board, I think, and a peppercorn rent because no one wants to live out here, like you say.' She tugged her cardigan around herself, although it was not cold.

The new situation presented itself, as if out of a mist.

Rose still didn't understand. 'But Kate was always so careful with money,' she said, the café she'd turned a profit with, the little antiques shop she'd run, the flat she'd bought and paid for before she was thirty. 'She was always so independent, she was – it was never about romance for Kate.'

Or that's what Rose had always thought, carelessly: the way Kate steered herself away from the kind of untidiness and now she saw it might have been something else, it might have been that she wanted it so badly she was afraid. 'It was about getting her life sorted.' Then slowly she said, because it might be banal but it was true, 'She was always adamant about not renting.'

Annie said, 'You must miss her.' Rose looked at her, almost bewildered by the understatement.

'It's more than that,' she said. 'I need to *know*. I need to know why she died. It doesn't make sense.'

Annie twisted her head as if something was hurting her. 'And you think *I* know,' she said. 'Don't you think I've asked myself, over and over again, why I didn't ask her, why I didn't just come out here and ask her – when she stopped coming to the school gates? Ask her how she was, what was going on?'

'When did she stop?' said Rose, scenting something. Thinking of Evan, lying beside her before dawn, telling her how it had been: she felt the sudden need to sidestep his account, to find someone *else*. Annie dipped her head, unhappy.

'Before the summer holidays. Weeks before. The end of May? I don't think I saw her after half-term.'

'You saw Evan?' said Rose quietly, her skin prickling

suddenly at the thought of all those months. 'Did he give you any explanation?'

'He's not the talkative sort,' she said. 'I asked if she was unwell, once or twice, and he just glowered at me.'

'Well,' said Rose, hesitating, 'that sort of makes sense.'

'What do you mean?' said Annie, frowning. The gurgle of the water over their speech was hypnotic, lulling. It was, thought Rose suddenly, like in spy movies, people going somewhere to talk where they can't be overheard.

'Did she tell you – did Kate tell you she thought she was pregnant?' Annie's eyes, widening, gave Rose her answer, and then she leaned abruptly close.

'What?' she said. 'No. I thought – I knew she wanted another baby. She was *hoping* for one. I didn't like to tell her that at her age—'

'I found a card from her to me, that she never sent, telling me,' said Rose. 'Listen. It must be why she didn't go to the doctor about her symptoms, because she thought it was pregnancy. And then maybe she'd been brainwashed by that awful midwife Martha into not talking to doctors about it. It doesn't sound like the Kate I knew but Christ – there's so much I don't know.'

Annie was frowning fiercely. 'I didn't know them when Jamie was born, it was before they came but – look – the truth is, I envied them, her and Evan. Doing it all together, managing without the outside world. I had no help from my ex when Evie was born, it all went tits up in hospital and whatever the doctors might have told them Jamie was safe and healthy and – who was I to say it was a mistake?'

'It was, though,' said Rose. 'It was. If she'd had proper

250

hospital follow-up for example. She was over forty. If she'd had all the scans—'

'I know,' said Annie, anguished, 'but she was so jubilant. To have done it. I should have asked more questions. That Martha—'

'You don't know her surname?' said Rose. Jubilant? That was at odds with Evan's account of a traumatic birth. 'I'd like to talk to her.'

'Perhaps there's some kind of a directory,' said Annie, 'I'll see what I can find out. I know — Kate told me about the internet situation here. I'll have a look and call you.'

Rose stared down at Jamie in the buggy, she saw the dried sweat on his forehead and she sat up. 'Shit,' she said, 'what about vaccinations, though — she didn't—'

Annie put a hand on her arm. 'It's all right,' she said. 'Jamie's up to date. I had to drive her to the doctor's myself and make her get them done. I only persuaded her because I told her the health visitor would be on their case day and night if they didn't. It wasn't long before — before. Before she stopped coming to school.'

There was a silence. 'There's something else, isn't there?' said Annie timidly. 'Isn't there? Something you haven't told me.'

Rose looked at her. 'Evan thinks she was having an affair,' she said, abruptly.

Annie laughed then, a horrified, startled sound that made Jamie stir uneasy in the buggy, and she got up from the bench.

'He's mad,' she said, shaking her head. '*Kate?* She loved him. They loved *each other*. Most people don't have that.' She spoke bitterly.

'Perhaps he thinks it's his fault,' said Rose quietly. Annie stopped pacing.

'What d'you mean?' she said.

'He had a vasectomy. He couldn't give her the baby she wanted, and when she found out she was so angry she went and had an affair,' said Rose. Annie sat down abruptly.

'No,' she said, 'no, he—' she shook her head. 'How could he do that?' She leaned back.

'He did, though,' said Rose. There was a silence, Annie staring at the water.

'How *could* she have an affair, stuck out here?' she murmured. 'I mean she didn't *know* any men.'

'What about at the school gates?' ventured Rose. 'She thought she was pregnant back in – back in February, March. Around then, was there anyone, did you see her talking to dads, say?' Rose cleared her throat. 'She never asked you to – have Jamie?'

Annie looked at her incredulously. 'Well, I know it's not always the obvious ones – but – no. I never – if Kate was having an affair she was keeping it very quiet.' She frowned. 'Kate didn't even go to the school Valentine's disco, that's where you usually see – you know. Flirtations. Didn't go to the pub like most parents did, while they waited. Dropped Serena off, and Evan picked her up.' She was still frowning though.

'No one else,' said Rose, quietly.

'Well—' Annie's shoulders dropped. 'She just – I never saw her with a man, I just wouldn't have said she was interested in hanging out with men.' She paused. 'Even their solicitor was a woman, I always thought it was because Evan didn't like other men.'

'You knew the solicitor?' Rose jumped on that. 'Was she at the funeral?' Annie shook her head.

'There's only one practice in town, way over the other side of London Road.' Rose's heart sank at the thought of how far away everything was, but it was Annie who sighed.

Her face was quite pale suddenly. 'Besides, if he'd found out—' her voice stilted, trying to make light of it and failing, 'he'd have killed her, wouldn't he? Evan would.'

'What?' Rose stared at her, impossible thoughts colliding in her head. *Cancer killed her first.* 'Was Evan – violent?'

There was a silence.

'I never saw anything like that,' Annie said, not meeting her eye. 'But there was something about the way she made excuses for him, his house rules – he was quite controlling.' Rose thought of the excuses she had begun to make for him herself. 'Yes,' she said.

Annie cleared her throat. 'The only man I saw her with was Evan – and the old guy Evan worked with.'

'Old guy?'

'You know,' said Annie patiently. 'He was at the funeral. Took that woman home, the friend. The one who was the worse for wear.'

'Lindsay,' murmured Rose, but for a second she still couldn't work out what old guy Annie meant and then the penny dropped. 'Gerald,' she said and she heard his name, Evan saying it. Serena saying it, in that jeering voice. *Gerald.*

And Annie said, 'That's the one.'

Chapter Twenty-Four

'It's all right if I phone you here, then?' Annie asked, looking at her hard, her hand on the car door. The roar of the weir still hummed in Rose's ears. 'About the— if I find a number for that midwife, Martha?'

'Why wouldn't it be?' Rose said. Annie compressed her lips.

'Just – well. Kate stopped coming to the phone.' They looked up at the back of the house, its chimneys looming. Some slates were coming loose: Rose wondered that Evan hadn't fixed them, she could imagine Kate pointing, shaking her head.

'Of course it's all right,' she said to Annie, but in that moment she knew why Kate would have stopped coming to the phone. Evan's head turning at the ring, the dislike on his face at the intrusion: the suspicion. And then listening, from behind a crack in a door. Rose felt cold.

254

As Annie's car disappeared into the lane Rose wished she could have kept her, just half an hour longer, an hour, for lunch – but she'd gone in a sudden hurry. Rose knelt beside the buggy and put the back of her hand to Jamie's forehead. It was only warm, but that could be the fresh day, the cool damp air of the weir, and she felt a prick of panic at not knowing where she'd put the medicine bottle.

Kitchen table: hurrying inside, parking Jamie, still asleep, in the corner Rose saw it straight away.

Too many things. Too many questions.

If Kate was going to have an affair, in order to get pregnant – Rose supposed it might be with someone like Gerald. A safe, quiet, dusty person, who wouldn't cause any trouble. It struck her then not for the first time that Evan wasn't Kate's type, not really. More Rose's, truth be told. Handsome, brooding, difficult: not comfortable. Not safe.

How had Kate ended up with him? And what – and that question troubled her somehow even more, because it made her feel guilty – had he seen in *her*?

The hall was dim and red around her and from somewhere there was a sound, a breath of something, coming closer. Rose hurried, along the side of the stairs, back into the cloakroom where the sight of the old cabinet's door standing open brought the same shiver of foreboding she'd felt when she saw Annie leave, when she panicked over leaving the bottle on the table for anyone to see. Which was silly as it wasn't even lunchtime, she'd be on her own for hours yet.

But as Rose reached to put the Calpol back in the cabinet – feeling that there was something else on the

255

shelf stopping it sitting back in its place, something that must have been concealed behind the bottle – she heard him. The unmistakable rattle and clank of the old car. And Evan, calling her name.

He seemed cheerful, plonking his work bag down on the table. For some reason Rose assumed he'd been to see the solicitor – the woman on London Road – and things were moving, things would be sorted out. Money would be sorted out.

But Evan said nothing about the solicitor. He was unpacking his bag.

Something fell out, tiny, a little yellow paper packet, smaller than a matchbox; unhurried, he picked it up and dropped it back into the bag. She had no idea what it was: if it rang a bell it was a far-off, ancient one.

'Did you forget something?' Rose asked, and he looked up, blithe, and smiled. She didn't like it. She didn't like his smile: its angles seemed all wrong, as if it had arrived a fraction too quickly. And with the glimpse something began to unravel.

'No,' he said, and the smile widened. 'Working from home today. I haven't been able to since – well. The whole idea was that Gerald would manage the day to day and I'd be free to work where I'm happiest. Now he's back – well. You'll be seeing a lot more of me, I'm afraid.'

'Back? You mean Gerald? Back from where?'

'Oh, he didn't go anywhere,' said Evan, with a hint of impatience, 'he just needed—' he hesitated, 'time out. Trouble is, small businesses like mine – there's not much leeway for key people to go on sabbatical.' His smile was forced. 'But he's back now. That's all that matters.'

256

'I've sorted the insurance on the car,' he said instead, cheerfully. 'You're on the policy now.'

'Oh!' Rose felt a curious mix of feelings, a prickle on the back of her neck, an eagerness and then an immediate caution. 'That's so — that's fantastic!'

But why? Why now? Rose had a sense of something edging forwards, a loosening, a recklessness. Was it because she was his lover? She took a step back, swallowing. 'Do I have to sign anything?'

She didn't want to sleep with him again. It came to her with a dull thump of certainty. The certainty that was physical, that came from that lopsided smile of his, from knowing that she'd gone down the wrong path, she had to turn around. She saw the car keys on the kitchen table.

Evan shrugged. 'They definitely said you could drive the car immediately,' he said. His smile broadened and he held out the keys. 'If you'd like to, that is.' Their hands touched as Rose reached for the little bunch and he looked up at her from under his eyebrows and when she took the keys Evan moved his hand, his finger on the tender inside of her elbow, stroking. Rose felt something climb inside her, like panic.

'I thought it might be nice,' Evan said softly, and she kept herself still, 'to be here a bit more. Keep you company.' Her eyes must have flicked sideways, to Jamie in his buggy because in that moment Evan turned, seeming to notice Jamie for the first time. He took his hand away.

'He doesn't usually nap in the morning,' he said, stiffly.

Rose let out a breath, one she felt she'd been holding

for minutes. 'No,' she said, 'he felt quite warm, quite—' she didn't mention the Calpol, in case. In case the weird ideas about medicine were his, and extended to refusing his child medicine, in case Kate had hidden it from him. Horrible thoughts radiated out from that one. 'I think he's coming down with a cold, or something.' Evan turned away from her, beginning to rifle through papers on the table.

'They've always got something,' he said, sounding bored.

Over his shoulder Rose glimpsed something that might have been the envelope from the solicitors', and then it was gone and he was turning back and she was smiling, smiling. 'Well,' she said, as gaily as she could manage, 'I might go out for a little – you know – cruise around?'

'Well, take Jamie, will you?' said Evan, his back to her still. 'I won't be able to work with him here.'

She didn't need telling twice.

The car was even dustier than when she'd last been in it, and littered with rubbish. Evan, absorbed in something on his laptop at the table, had left her to haul Jamie in his car seat – but in that moment, almost holding her breath with the chance of getting the car, she didn't want him to touch the baby, to know how warm he was.

Rose turned the key in the ignition and it whined and coughed, raising a sweat on her forehead, expecting Evan to come out at any moment and take the keys back – but then it fired.

The brakes were soft, the suspension shot, but Rose kept her foot down.

Annie had told her where to find the surgery, while they sat at the weir. 'I'm not sure Evan would know,' she'd said, hesitant, and Rose knew they were both thinking that he would be angry, if you asked him. And that was wrong Surely it was?

It was a low modern building: in the car park Evan's ancient estate car looked as if it had come from another world beside the bright little hatchbacks. Rose felt like she had walked out of the bush.

The receptionist, a woman with candyfloss hair and an annoying voice, stared at her before peering over the desk to inspect Jamie, who was still asleep. 'And you are?' Then she disappeared through a door, there was muttered conferring and she returned.

'We're not sure about the legalities – you're not registered as his carer—' at which point Rose lost patience and said she'd go to casualty instead and the candyfloss woman told her tightly that she couldn't guarantee anything but to come back in an hour and there should be a doctor free.

Back in the car, with Jamie beside her in his car seat stirring now, uncomfortable, Rose sat, irresolute and angry, until she remembered. Her mobile.

There'd been a panicked moment or two turning on to the main road when she'd wondered if she'd left it behind again but it was in her pocket, although only half charged, it had slipped down in her list of priorities now she barely used it. Rose dialled Deb's number, thinking, breathless with anger, *fuck it, fuck it, fuck those people.* The woman with the frizzy hair especially. But all of them.

It only took the sound of the familiar voice for it all to pour out – in the wrong order, but all there, things she'd told Deb before, and things she hadn't. The ear infection, the roll of money in the cupboard, Kate thinking she was pregnant. Evan.

Evan.

'You're sleeping with him?' Deb sounded deeply shocked. She had listened to it all and this was what shocked her.

'Deb—' she tried to explain, hearing the tired wheedle in her voice and hating herself.

'Oh, to hell with that,' said Deb, righteous as always – and right as always. 'You know what? I don't like this guy, what's his name, Evan, with all his rules, who's sleeping with his dead wife's sister,' Rose stiffened, but Deb kept going. 'Evan, who didn't see his wife dying under his nose? Do you know how his first wife died yet? What's his surname? You could look online, you know, if you don't dare ask him. Or I could.'

'Evan Lloyd,' said Rose, in a whisper, feeling cold.

'I mean, you're sleeping with him and you don't trust him enough to tell him you're taking his kid to the doctor's?'

'It's just that – he – he and Kate did things their way. They loved each other, Deb, he's grieving, I don't want to upset him, I want to—'

Deb interrupted, talking over her. 'They did things their way – and yet she had an affair? And yet she could have been pregnant by another man? You're hiding things from him. You don't dare to ask him things. He's burning your sister's stuff while you're out?' Rose heard her draw breath. 'You know what this looks like?'

'I—' Rose felt choked suddenly, she squeezed her eyes shut under the onslaught. She felt panic overwhelm her, and guilt; she tried to cast about for anything to defend herself with.

Deb let out a long breath. 'He controlled your sister and now he's controlling you. You do this, Rose, I've seen you do it. You try to turn yourself into a different person, for one guy after another, you dance around trying to be what they want.' Rose was dumb: Deb had never been anything but sympathetic over her rubbish love life. 'And what did *you* want, Rose?'

'Just because, just because—' Rose knew she had to stop herself before she said something that would change it all.

But she was too late; she knew it in the pause before Deb spoke. 'Just because I don't have a man?' said Deb. Her voice was tight with disappointment. 'I think we'd better stop this now, don't you?'

Rose was numb, tingling with fear at what she'd done, waiting for the click that meant Deb had cut her off, not daring to speak.

'You know what you need to do next, don't you, Rose?' Deb said, sounding bitter, and weary. 'You don't need me to tell you.'

And she was gone.

Clutching the phone as if it was a hand grenade or something, holding it against herself, Rose heard herself make a sound, a strangled sort of sob. She hadn't even told Deb the worst of it. The worst of it was, she was sleeping with Evan because she was afraid. Afraid of hurting him? To begin with. Afraid he'd hurt himself? Maybe. But now that fear was something new, something different. The gin bottle put away. The doors she couldn't open.

261

The ashes in the yard. She was afraid of what he'd do, when she said no. She was afraid of that moment when he heard her say it, and turned, and she saw his face.

The seconds ticked down and she heard Deb's last words, over and over.

Think, Rose. Think. What do you do next?

Chapter Twenty-Five

The phone. Rose had never imagined she would find the technology so miraculous. It took only seconds to find the address of the solicitors' on London Road, and a name. Two male partners and one woman. Rose dialled the number.

Jamie barely woke as she lifted him out of the baby seat. He made a small whimpering sound and then laid his hot head against her neck.

The solicitors' office was a modest semi set back from the road: there was a reception desk but it was unmanned and Estelle Janeway – a brisk-looking middle-aged woman with short white hair and no make-up – let Rose and Jamie in herself. Rose, balancing Jamie against her shoulder with some difficulty, found the hand Janeway offered her firm and dry and warm and thought for a second, that the woman was like Kate, or Kate would have been like her, if she'd grown old.

On the phone Janeway had shown no surprise at hearing

from her: in fact, it was as if she'd been expecting her. Rose had started saying something about the doctor's and being registered as a carer for Jamie, but the solicitor had cut her short. 'Yes, yes – I'm free now if you'd like to come, we'll go through it all.'

'So, your— Mr Lloyd has filled you in,' Estelle Janeway said, seating herself behind a wide leather-topped desk.

'Mr Lloyd—' Rose was bewildered, 'no – oh. You mean Evan. No – we haven't, he hasn't talked to me about – anything really. I mean, I saw he'd had a letter from you, it's how I knew who to come to. He's – we – he's still grieving.' Rose was suddenly aware of making excuses for him, of not being entirely straight with this woman, but she felt trapped, this was a legal situation, and she was dimly aware that Janeway had a duty of – something. Confidentiality? Or the opposite – a duty to involve the authorities if she thought— Rose sat up straight, feeling guilty for no reason except she was in the presence of someone with legal powers, and she needed to proceed carefully.

Janeway leaned abruptly across the desk. 'There'll be no problem with the doctor's,' she said straight away. 'I can write a note. Your sister made a formal statement in her will that she wanted you to have parental responsibility for Jamie in the event of her death.'

'She did?' Rose stared, trying to process the information – and its implications. 'So she didn't want Evan to look after him?'

'I tried to persuade her to outline her reasons, formally,' said the solicitor, 'for not wishing her husband to have responsibility for his son. But she was – reluctant. She became agitated.'

264

'Frightened,' said Rose, almost to herself. 'She was frightened of what he'd do, if he found out. If she put it down in black and white.'

Janeway nodded. 'That was my impression,' she said. 'Irrational, as he'd only see it in the event of her death but—' She sighed. 'I said, he could contest it if she didn't set out her reasons, and she said, she whispered it as a matter of fact . . . ' she hesitated, 'I wondered if she thought I was recording her – she said, *He won't care. He doesn't care about Jamie.*'

She looked at Rose, a direct, inquiring look. 'I'm not so sure about that,' Rose said, slowly. 'He doesn't like people telling him what to do.' She felt a chill of fear run through her and she said in a low voice. 'Does he know?'

Janeway sat back in her chair. 'He knew,' she said. 'I wasn't sure, for obvious reasons, if your sister had discussed it with him. But then of course after Kate's death—' the solicitor frowned, 'he came to see me. Quite soon after her death, in fact.'

'She didn't write,' said Rose, numb, barely registering what she was saying. 'But maybe she didn't think—' she felt something burn behind her eyes.

'She thought she'd have time,' said Janeway, but she was still frowning. 'Most people do. Most people don't believe they're going to die. Your sister was unusual in being prepared—' she hesitated and Rose sprang in.

'She was unusual,' she said, 'she was, Kate was so—' and at the thought of Kate, who never thought she was exceptional in any way – who was only loving and sensible, who covered all the options – Rose put her face in her hands and stopped herself sobbing, because Kate would have hated that. Because she needed to keep her head clear. She sat up.

'He knew all along,' she said, numb. The solicitor was watching her. 'He knew and he didn't tell me.'

Evan on the phone to her, broken, Rose stunned in her little room in Rome with the swallows swooping behind her, hearing for the first time of her sister's death. *Come. We need you.* When would he have told her? When she was in love with him? When she had been brought into line? *Think*, she told herself.

'I imagine he's the – what's it called? – the executor.'

Slowly Estelle Janeway shook her head. 'He was originally,' she said, 'But now it's me.'

There was a shift in the air, barely perceptible, as if an avenue had cleared in mist. 'All right,' said Rose carefully, as she saw that what this meant was that this was the person Kate had chosen to trust.

She hesitated in the chair, feeling Jamie's forehead clammy against her skin. 'I – I've got to get to the doctor's, you see, I need to ask—' and she blurted it. 'Did she leave it all to Evan?' Then because it sounded greedy, and bald, hurriedly, 'I mean, I'm sure that would be appropriate, they weren't married, you see, and she'd want to make sure – make sure—'

Estelle Janeway was looking at her, her face clouding.

Rose stopped, started again. 'It's just that there are things I don't understand,' she said, bluntly. 'About the money.'

'It's all right,' said Estelle Janeway slowly, 'it's a natural question. It's the question everyone asks.' It was her turn to seem hesitant. 'But in this case— I don't know how

266

much money you're thinking of, because—' she paused, shuffling papers on her desk, taking a stapled sheaf out and holding it between her hands.

'Well,' said Rose, 'she ran two successful businesses in her twenties and thirties. She had bought her own flat – in London, mind – and paid off her mortgage by the time she was thirty.' *And sent me money whenever I needed it. Thoughtless, heedless, little sister.*

The solicitor was watching her, saying nothing.

'I don't *want* the money,' Rose said, leaning suddenly, fiercely, across the table, 'it's for Jamie—' and as if on cue he stirred, wailed. She stood up. 'Maybe I'd better come back and do this another time,' she said on the verge of tears, of frustration and anxiety and simple grief that it boiled down to this, to money.

'I think that might be best,' said Janeway, standing too, looking worriedly at Jamie's scarlet cheeks, his bleary eyes. She put out a hand, then hesitated. Opened a drawer and took out an envelope, handing it to her.

'It's a copy of your sister's will – for you. In case Mr Lloyd – well, always good to have two copies, isn't it? Janeway sighed. 'There were two accounts: one in her own name, and she specified that all the money in that account should be left to you. It amounts to . . .' and she looked down at the papers in front of her, '. . . a little over £10,000.'

'And the rest?'

'She and her husband had a joint account,' said Janeway shortly. 'She had effectively already given him the rest. However much that was: I gathered from her that it had dwindled considerably.'

'So he didn't—' Rose paused. 'He wouldn't have needed to rely on her leaving it to him in her will.'

'He would not,' said the solicitor and looked Rose in the eye. She knows, thought Rose. She knows what kind of man he was: not after her money, he had wanted her *life*. Her life in his hands. 'When did she come to you, and do all this? How did she seem, did she look ill?'

'In the spring,' said Janeway, 'Six, seven months ago.' She shrugged, helpless. 'She was a little pale, perhaps. Anxious.' A pause. 'I'm sorry. Of course, I wish I'd known. But I'm not a doctor, I'm just a solicitor.'

'No,' said Rose, taking pity, and she stood to go.

'I'll help you,' said Janeway, getting to her feet. 'If he contests anything in the will, anything at all. I'll help.'

As Janeway spoke Rose thought of Serena. She thought of what would happen if she took Jamie and left them alone together and for a second an awful image entered her head, she didn't even know where it came from, of what would happen if she stayed. Of that narrow back staircase and all of them on it and the house winding tighter around them, holding them inside.

The candyfloss-haired receptionist at the doctor's told them to wait, and Rose sat, Jamie's hot weight against her, watching the minutes tick by. The longer she took, the more certainly Evan would know she'd been up to something behind his back. Had giving her the keys been letting her out on a lead, for the pleasure of tugging her back? She saw the faces, peering not too discreetly, at them, she felt sweat trickle down her back, and for a moment she could see Kate's life, as if she'd looked through a window, as though she *was* Kate. After only two weeks she knew, on instinct but quite certainly, that Evan would have had a reason for her not to take Jamie. *Let his body fight it on his own,* or something like that. Natural immunity.

Kate must have changed the will before she began to think she was pregnant, and then that took over, consumed her, distracted her, gave her a reason to ignore her symptoms.

'Jamie Lloyd?' Rose stood up abruptly as the doctor who had appeared in the doorway scanned the heads.

It was an ear infection, for which the doctor – young, male, nervous – prescribed antibiotics and infant paracetamol.

Having received the information and the prescription Rose (who suddenly no longer cared what she was or was not allowed to say to people in authority) remained stubbornly in her seat in the airless room with its window looking on to anonymous shrubbery and its high, narrow, ominous bed against the wall. Rose knew what Deb had meant: she'd known it herself, all along, she'd been trying. She pleaded with Deb in her head. *You have to ask all the questions.*

The doctor was looking at her, impatient. She said, 'Did you treat my sister? Were you her doctor? She died two weeks ago of ovarian cancer that wasn't diagnosed.'

The man informed her that he was a locum and had been there under a week.

Still Rose sat, unwilling, unable to move, wanting to throw things. *Why didn't you help her?* Until the locum's gaze hardened into something unfriendly and then, finally, she stood and went, without a word.

In the car park the battered old car felt stuffy and

claustrophobic and Jamie on her knee fretful, letting out a weak plaintive cry and batting at his ear.

Just an ear infection. Holding him awkwardly she administered first another dose of Calpol then the antibiotic, a yellow liquid that smelled chemically of banana (if it had been pink, would it have been synthetic strawberry? she found herself asking, the world of babies was so weird). Jamie spluttered miserably but he was too feeble to struggle now and most of it went down. *Good boy. Good boy.*

She knew she should go back, now. She had the will in its envelope and she had the antibiotics. She didn't even know, did she – beginning to excuse him – if Evan would be angry about the antibiotics, it was Kate, he'd said, or implied, wasn't it Kate who'd been adamant, been against? And yet with a grim certainty she could see him take the bottle and up-end it. It wasn't worth the risk.

Instead of heading back Rose turned the other way, towards the eastern edge of the town, towards the sea, and out there somewhere, strung along the grey estuary, the little settlement Evan had planned. A place of clapboard houses built in the traditional style, clustered on the edge of the marsh with tough marine grass sloping gently down to the water. Evan, of course, would not be there, because Evan was working from home today. She wasn't going to see Evan, though.

Thinking of it as she drove, leaving the town behind her, the bungalows and pre-fabs and bright municipal roundabouts, and imagining it instead, remembering the pictures, Rose could feel a kind of calm descend, like a mist, and behind her Jamie was quiet too, sedated, babbling gently, inquiringly. Not quite his normal self, lulled.

It seemed distant to Rose, now, the plan she'd had, for surprising Evan with a picnic lunch. Soon it would be winter, after all, and where would they go, she and Evan and Jamie? It was quite unreal: a rug laid out, set with the food Evan wasn't interested in. Had he and Kate had lunches like that together? Had they made love in the trees? Rose blinked, feeling sick again.

And then there was a sign, rather attractively hand-made (by Kate?) SALTCOTE ECO-HOMES, where a narrow newly made tarmacked lane met the main road. So newly made its edges had not been finished, nor road markings applied, but it was unmistakably the right place. The road wound between sparse trees, down towards the water.

But where? But where?

There was a gate, and the field did slope down to the brown river but it wasn't green, there was no meadow, there was no cluster of houses. It was churned earth down to the water's edge and a rusting digger sat just inside the gate. She could see a portakabin and a single dwelling facing the estuary, lapped in wooden weatherboarding. Was that the house he'd offered her to live in? He must have known she'd say no. He had calculated it all from the outset, then. She was a dupe. She pulled up in the rusty shade of a tree with yellowing leaves.

Slowly Rose climbed out of the car, leaving Jamie, awake now but quiet, looking around with a faintly glazed expression, in his car seat. The gate was padlocked: she climbed over.

'Gerald?' Rose called, one hand on the gate, and her voice echoed. There was no answer, and no sign of a car, and walking, with sinking heart past more traces of the building site, the footprints of other dwellings laid in concrete — but was concrete allowed, for an eco-house? — across the trodden earth to the portakabin, she tried the door. It was locked. She stood there a moment, looking from the gate to the river, The scheme was a failure, or a scam, or just a vanity project: Evan's real ambitions were elsewhere. Inside the house where he'd confined his family, and the tide coming up around them.

The car started only on the third go, by which time Jamie was whimpering in the back as if he felt her heart thudding. *So much for freedom,* thought Rose, turning laboriously in the narrow lane for home. For *not-home.*

And as she turned in from the lane, bumped over the bridge, moving slowly, more slowly there he was, waiting for her. Smiling.

He told her Lindsay had called, while she was out.

Chapter Twenty-Six

I think she likes me. Estelle. The solicitor. She did say, when I came in to ask her, that I should tell them about the codicil, and of course I said I would. *Straight away*, I said. But I didn't write to Rose. It would freak her out so I didn't write. I'll put it all in the diary. And of course I didn't say anything to Evan.

I mean, it's just – there's time to change it, isn't there? It's not like I'm going to die tomorrow. If I don't die they'll never know, he'll never know.

I don't know what's in Evan's will, after all.

Today's such a beautiful day. I think that's what made me go. Evan had already gone when I woke up – I'm just so sleepy these days, it's ridiculous, I seem to have no energy. He says it's normal, it's hormones. Sometimes I think he knows more about me than I do myself, but then that's love.

The odd thing is I love *him* because I *don't* know him, because he's mysterious. They do say, you need to keep mystery, it's one of those things they say in magazines that I thought would never apply to me. Anyway, the sun's out. When I stand in the window and look out across the marsh and the light is all silver and the land is all bronze and there it all is, the world, there's everything in the air, and I put my hands on my belly and I can feel it there, heavy. Her – I think it will be a girl this time. I feel so much bigger.

Sometimes – just sometimes – I want to ask someone. I know Martha's busy but she'll be around in time for the birth, and there's plenty of time. Plenty. These are the months when nature does her work. That sounds like a magazine article, too, but when did I last read a magazine, or a newspaper?

I could have asked her. Estelle. She'd have laughed at me, or worse. *What do solicitors know about pregnancy?* she'd have said. I wanted to tell her, to confide, to boast but she just stood there looking at me and I wanted to get it done so I didn't give her any excuse to stop me.

The taxi took for ever to arrive. I wondered if— it's a small town, after all, Evan's always saying that, complaining about them, the small-town mentality, they gossip, they pass information on, he doesn't even like me talking to Annie, when did I last see Annie? Too long – anyway, I wondered, but it's madness – I wondered if they'd called Evan at work and said, *you do know your wife – she's not my wife,* he would have said proudly then so their small-town mentality would have had to swallow that – *you do know your wife has called a taxi.*

Silly. Of course they wouldn't. It arrived in the end and a woman driver.

This doesn't fit, does it? If I phoned Rose and talked to her, told her it all, she would have questions. *But why? But*

274

why? Why won't you tell people how it is? Why don't you want Evan to have Jamie, if you die?

Because. There are compartments in the brain – magazines say that too but I know it's true now. And Rose knows I've always liked compartments and neatness, things folded and put away. You put some precious things away for safe-keeping, while you're sorting out bigger stuff, big unwieldy stuff, like arguments, like freedom, like being in love.

Oh, Rose. Oh, Rose, I love you. You were my first baby, really. Your wild hair and your silliness and the way you used to fall asleep against me, after Mum died, after you'd worn yourself out sobbing. I love you and I miss you and if anyone's going to love Jamie for me, it's you.

The house feels cold, now. Isn't that strange, so warm outside and so fresh and new and the smells of spring, coming on summer and the house is so dark, so cold. It took it out of me, the taxi, the solicitor, the worrying about Evan and the cost of the taxi and him finding out. I'm just tired.

If I lie here still I'll get warmer. If I lie here with my hands on my belly, I can feel our heart beating.

But sometimes I want to ask someone if this is normal.

Rose wondered if she'd been seen. If anyone would tell him she'd been seen down there at the site. Why would they? People gossiped.

Walking from the car with Jamie on her shoulder, smiling back at him, she had to cut it all out, the clamour of the morning in her ears. The bottles of medicine in her bag, the will thrust down underneath everything.

They wouldn't have told him *yet*. She certainly wasn't going to.

And it was nonsense, Evan knew nobody, she realised, was friendly with nobody. The tall trees whispered, beyond them the weir rushed, on and on. It was getting colder and she stopped for a second, wondering about this place in the winter, the wide horizon, the grey and green, the pale sky. The emptiness.

'Shall I get the bags out of the back?' Evan said and Rose turned, bewildered.

'Bags?'

He frowned. 'You mean you didn't go to the supermarket?'

'I—' her throat felt choked suddenly. 'No – I—' her heart thudded. Rose forced a smile. 'I didn't have any money,' she said.

Which was true. He was frowning still but smiling at the same time, as if she wasn't to take it seriously.

'I just went for a drive, you know,' said Rose. 'It's ages since I—' she shrugged. 'Look how much better Jamie's feeling.' She turned him, and the warmth of him against her made the thud of her heart in her throat more urgent.

Evan didn't look at him. 'Petrol costs money too,' he said, easily. And the smile and the frown were there together, so she didn't know what she was supposed to think. Had she done the wrong thing, or not?

She hoisted Jamie higher and turned to go inside.

'Rose?' he said from behind her. She made herself turn back: his hand was out. 'The car keys?'

Inside the house folded round her, cold and dim, as her heart thudded in her chest.

She had dropped the keys into his open palm and his

other hand had come out and taken her by the wrist, gently. He had tugged her towards him, gentle still but firm, until her face was close to his, she could see the flaw in his dark-golden eyes and the stubble on his chin. She felt sick. His mouth so close to her ear she felt his breath, his lips on her neck, but then Jamie strained and she had a reason to pull back. Evan had turned away, impatient.

She could hear him start the car. She stood in the hall. 'Down,' said Jamie, quite distinct in her ear and Rose looked at him. A word. His first word. She almost laughed. 'Down?' she said and he grinned and bounced and kneeling, she set him down.

Off he went like a clockwork toy, down past the wide stairs, into the dark, the red and dark towards the cloak-room and she followed, slowly. Outside the car was still running: it was going nowhere. Evan must be sitting there, running the engine and for some reason the thought turned her insides over. Thud, thud went her heart: *Go, go*, she thought, *go if you're going*.

When he went she would be able to phone Lindsay. She had for a second wondered if he would follow her inside the hall to the telephone and stand there while she called. *The number.* Where had she put that piece of paper? With sudden clarity she remembered setting it down upstairs on the little table in her room and making the calculation that Jamie was safe, for thirty seconds he was safe, she dropped her bag and ran, two steps at a time, into her bedroom.

It wasn't there. In the little room Kate had set out for her Rose went to the bookcase and found the book with its picture of a little prairie house – she flipped the pages, turned it upside down but nothing fell out. She pulled out all the books, riffling through them one after another and still outside the engine ran, idling in the yard. She turned, in the room. The writing desk? Could she have put it on the rolltop and it had fallen through a crack? She pushed at the rolltop in vain but it wouldn't budge. Something caught her eye, at the little brass lock: scratches as though someone had tried to force it.

This was stupid. Stupid. The phone could tell her the last number it had called, or she could ask Evan. But someone had taken it. Someone was looking for her secrets.

It could only have been Evan. Perhaps he didn't know whose number it was. Perhaps— downstairs came a thump and a small cry and Rose ran.

Jamie was sitting solid on his bottom, a comical frown in place. He raised his arms, and spoke again, eyeing her craftily. 'Up,' he said, unmistakably, 'up, up.' He was asking to be lifted – and also to be taken somewhere. To the little medicine cupboard on the wall. Jamie must know, she thought, that that was where Kate kept her secret stash of Calpol. She thought of the antibiotics in her bag and running, retrieved the bag from where it lay, open for anyone to see, at the foot of the stairs. She got out the little bottle of yellow liquid, opened the cupboard – and something stopped her. What? What? Outside the car's engine stopped.

Rose stared at the shelves. Something. The Calpol was still there – but when she put the bottle back last time, there'd been something else, hadn't there? – she reached up with the antibiotic solution and pushed the packages and bottle aside to make room – and there.

'Rose?' Evan was somewhere in the house. Quickly she felt around, back on the little shelf, gritty with dust. A keyring, two keys, brass, one tiny, one large. She flipped them into her pocket, put the medicines back, silently closed the cabinet door, swooped for Jamie and her bag and was out in the hall as he came through the green baize door.

'Can't keep up with him,' she said, smiling, smiling. Evan was studying her in the dim red light and she knew he knew. He knew something. 'He said a word,' she said gaily, brightly, a distraction. 'He said, *down* and then he said *up.*'

'Up,' said Jamie, on her arm.

Evan didn't seem to have heard. 'Lindsay said—' he paused, looking at her and Rose thought, *Lindsay said you'd called her.* And he would know Rose had called and hadn't mentioned it to him. 'She said she was just calling to find out how you were doing.'

And now, Rose thought, *he knows both of us are lying.* 'That's so sweet of her,' she said. 'Did she say I should call back?'

'Down,' said Jamie and without thinking she set him down. The keys chinked in her pocket. Evan could ask, *What was that noise?* because it had been distinctly audible, but he didn't.

'I'm sure she meant you to,' said Evan, smiling pleasantly. He didn't offer her the number, though. And sighed. 'If you enjoyed the ride so much,' he said, 'why don't you pick Serena up from school?'

Rose stood there, not moving. *He doesn't want me to call Lindsay, he's not giving me the number.* 'We're out of milk, too,' Evan said, 'maybe you didn't notice, and I don't know what you were thinking for supper?'

The way he spoke. Rose felt it flare inside her – *I'm not your fucking slave* – but kept very still: she had to keep control, she had to plan ahead, for what would happen after supper. There was no lock on her door. 'I'm afraid I haven't got any money in my account,' she said. 'I must do something about—'

About escaping, Rose thought. 'About getting a job, perhaps?'

Getting back.

Evan's smile returned. 'Good idea,' he said. 'I'm sure there's something round here – I mean, it wouldn't be what you're used to. It might be seasonal. This is a fairly low-rent part of the country, in case you hadn't noticed.' Rueful. His hand came out to her again, resting on her upper arm. 'I can look after us for the moment.'

Jamie was looking at the hand on her: he put out his own small one with a comic frown and shoved at Evan's and Rose felt a prickle, a stiffening of dislike then Evan took his hand away and Jamie laid his head down, satisfied.

Evan felt in his pocket and took out a crumpled tenner, thrusting it at her. 'There you go,' he said. Rose took it. Perhaps the money would be halved each time, she thought, until they were down to nothing and she saw a future, her working the arcades in the summer, chip shop for the winter. Would Kate have done that? For love, she might. 'Thanks,' she said.

'Better get going,' Evan said, the smile abruptly gone, 'school's out in half an hour.' And held out his hands for Jamie. 'You can leave him with me,' and when she hesitated, he went on, 'I missed my son's first word,' lightly reproachful. 'Let me catch up a bit.'

Again the car took its time starting: Rose saw that the petrol was low but she'd have to hope her card worked, if it came to it. The empty back seat whispered to her. *My son*. Nothing Evan said was accidental: this time he was reminding her that Jamie wasn't hers, whatever the will said. She couldn't just put her foot down and go, not on a tenner and no petrol – had he sat in the car running the engine for that? – not on an empty bank account. And not without Jamie.

Once on the main road Rose pulled in, to check her phone. To see if Deb had texted, forgiven her, said anything at all even to reprimand her, to tell her what to do – but there was nothing. The battery was at fifteen per cent. *Shit*, she thought, *shit* and she knew somehow, she knew that this was Evan's doing too. Shoving her back out of the house without a chance to recharge the thing. And the house drained the battery fast, as the mobile searched and searched in vain for signal.

Rose was early to the school gates: she could see other parents in their cars, heads bowed over their mobiles. She could see the bus stop from where she sat, she wouldn't miss Serena. Rose got out her phone too, uselessly and then, to her astonishment, it rang. She almost dropped it.

It was Lindsay.

'Oh my God, oh my God, thanks for calling back—' the words tumbled over each other: Rose felt as if she was on the verge of tears. 'I – I wish we'd had a chance to talk properly at the funeral but—'

'Yeah, yeah,' Lindsay interrupted her drily, Rose heard the slurred edge to her voice and her heart sank. 'But your brother-in-law – well, he isn't *that*, not technically, is he, and thank God for small mercies – he had me seen off the premises, didn't he?' Gerald hadn't exactly given her a lift, then, thought Rose, numb. Lindsay was still talking. 'Before I could – what did he say – embarrass myself. How d'you get my number?' Her voice was harsh. 'Because he sure as fuck didn't give it you, did he? Was it the girl? The little girl? She's the one said I had to come to the funeral. She phoned me.' Her voice softened then. 'Poor little cow. I mean, imagine. Been through two mums already and—' she stopped, dead, as if something had occurred to her.

'Lindsay?'

'You're next, aren't you?' Lindsay said, and her voice was sharp now. 'I spoke to him, y'know, he answered the phone. I knew something was going on, the way he talked about you.'

'What?' said Rose, '*What?* There's nothing—' it would be a lie, though, wouldn't it?

'Look, forget it,' said Lindsay. 'I'm not interested in talking to you if you're going to tell me how bloody great he is, how gentle, how kind, how thoughtful,' and she drew a harsh breath. 'How good he is at fucking.'

Silence. 'I'm not,' said Rose. More silence. 'What did he say about me?'

An angry laugh. 'Just the way he said your name, babe. He wanted me to know.'

And suddenly Rose had had enough. 'All right,' she said. 'I did – but now I'm scared. Is that enough for you? I'm scared, Lindsay. I think – I think—'

Her phone made a sound and she held it away from her face: *Low power mode* it told her. 'What were you going to tell me?' she said. 'Why did you and Kate fall out?' Then she spotted Serena, her slight figure, tangled hair, alone at the gates. Not even Evie with her, walking apart from the others. 'Hold on,' she said and climbed out, calling Serena's name. Serena turned, Rose waved, and Serena turned and began to plod, reluctant, head down, towards the car.

'Lindsay?' There was a warning sigh.

'You want to hear this or not?' said Lindsay.

'I want to hear it,' said Rose.

Chapter Twenty-Seven

They were at the top of the lane before Rose realised that she had been supposed to go to the supermarket. There was too much in her head. Too much: it buzzed at her angrily. She pulled up. Reached for the bag and pulled out the envelope from the solicitor. It was Kate's will. The words ran into themselves: her name caught.

Sole guardianship. Then further down: *bequests.* There was the ten thousand pounds – and her writing desk.

'Serena?' She turned to look into the back seat. Serena had come up to the car and seen Rose on the mobile and climbed into the back seat in a silence that was more tense than sullen, as if she knew something was happening and she didn't want to be involved. She hadn't said a word, and now she looked back at Rose, frozen, eyes large and dark.

'That was Lindsay on the telephone, wasn't it?' Serena said 'telephone' when most kids would have said 'mobile', like she hardly knew what it was. But there was an edge to her voice, and Rose wondered how much she'd heard. She looked like she was holding her breath, pale.

Lindsay.

'You phoned her to ask her to the funeral,' said Rose. 'You, not your father. How did you know her number?'

'I phoned her,' said Serena, shifting in her seat. Not answering the question. Then, 'He thought she'd seen the notice in the paper.' She pressed her lips together. 'She doesn't like Dad.'

'Like your grandparents?' said Rose softly. Serena folded her arms across her body and tentatively Rose said, 'You know – people don't understand him,' she said. 'And maybe it's because they should try harder, but sometimes maybe – he could explain things to people. Be more—'

'Friendly?' her voice was scornful again. 'Why should he be friendly to stupid people. People who don't understand anything.'

Rose sat, knowing she was one of the stupid people, stupid to panic over what Lindsay thought, over the distance between her room and Evan's, suddenly dizzying: the narrow balustraded gallery in the wide red hall, the tiny winding back staircase beyond his door, that tight space with its worn-down wooden steps, its smell of whitewash. Rose was holding it in reserve, she realised. She didn't use it because she was saving it for when she needed it.

Stupid. They were civilised human beings. She only had to say no. She said, instead, mildly, 'Shall we go to the supermarket?'

Then a solution occurred to her. Risky but. 'We could

have something special for supper tonight. Something with a bit of flavour.'

Serena stared at her with dark eyes, and Rose knew she knew there was a plan but she couldn't work out what it was. 'All right,' she said eventually.

The supermarket was on the edge of town, towards the dip that led to Evan's development, and as they pulled in and Rose climbed out she looked but it wasn't visible. You could see the water, though, the grey-green marsh ruffling the wide estuary: the tide was low and the creek was brown mud, at its centre a snaking silver trickle of the turning tide.

Rose let Serena run on ahead of her with a trolley although with ten pounds to spend a basket would have been enough. As Serena disappeared inside, she slowed her pace but her heart didn't slow, didn't calm.

How long had Rose known, and ignored it? Ten years, perhaps, and if she'd known, Kate must have too. A news item on the breast cancer gene appeared in the papers with awful regularity: sometimes it was a celebrity 'coming out' with the news of a diagnosis, or radical, terrible surgery, that made you want to cry. Sometimes it must contain good news, breakthroughs in the treatment but Rose wouldn't have known, she would have let the words blur.

'We fell out over my mum's death,' Lindsay had said, and not waiting for a response. 'My mum had the BRAC1 gene, and after her death, when I thought about how my nan died of ovarian, my cousin got the cancer gene – I got myself tested.'

'And Kate—'

286

'And Kate wouldn't do it.' Lindsay spoke flatly, then gave a long sigh. 'I think I made it worse. I tried to bully her.'

Mum's older sister had died before her, before Rose was even born. Her own mother, and her aunt, aged fifty and forty-seven. Two ovarian – three if you counted Kate – and one breast. Tough women who never complained, but looked away from the coincidence. Rose had picked up the information here and there: mutterings at the funeral, as she sat under the table hiding. Dad ranting and raving.

There must have been limits, then, to Kate's good sense, her practicality. Her courage. Didn't that apply to everyone? And maybe there was courage in not having the test, in going on with it, too. There'd have been no Jamie, if she'd had her ovaries out, her womb, her breasts. And at the thought, now, Rose stopped dead in the supermarket car park, realising her hands had gone up to touch herself there and dropped them.

She'd pleaded with Lindsay that she didn't have much time, the battery was going and Lindsay had drawn a quick sharp breath. 'Did he stop you charging it? Have you lost your charger cables? It's part of it, you know, it's all part of it—'

'Just tell me,' said Rose. 'Do you have proof of – anything? That he – that Evan— She thought she was pregnant,' she said. 'That's why she didn't tell anyone about her symptoms, she thought it was the pregnancy.'

She didn't know if Lindsay hadn't heard, or hadn't taken it in, because she was still talking, talking over Rose. 'Keep hold of your stuff,' she said. 'Keep hold. What did his first wife die of? Who got her money? Where's *her* family?'

'She—' but Lindsay was still talking. 'Ask him how they met, her and Kate. You ask him that, then tell me. Then tell me I'm being—'

The mobile had died. She hadn't had a chance to say goodbye, or to ask Lindsay what she meant, or to tell her what it was like, out there.

Now Rose couldn't see Serena. It wasn't a big supermarket: eight aisles, the size of a barn, and she walked at first from one to the next to the next, telling herself not to be stupid because – because. Because Serena was sensible? She was twelve. And as she roamed it occurred to Rose that Serena had as little freedom as she did, that she might want just to run, on the off-chance that might get her back to another life, too.

Or into the arms of a security guard, the police, care officials – or a child abuser with a van waiting, just out of sight of the CCTV.

Tins, cold counter, freezer section – and there. A trolley without an owner – but crouched below it, examining something – there was Serena. Without thinking Rose grabbed her, rough, relieved, folded her into a hug.

'I thought I'd lost you,' she said, into Serena's hair and inside her arms the girl stayed very still, not resisting and suddenly Rose felt something else in the compact narrow body, a fierce longing, a need. But Serena said nothing, did nothing and Rose released her gently, looking down into the sharp-chinned little face. 'I thought I'd lost you,' she said again.

'Can we get one of these?' Serena was holding a bar of chocolate, her longing then ridiculously modest unless it was a cover for all the things Rose might give her and

Rose was nodding yes, but thinking of the money when Serena's face changed. She was looking over Rose's shoulder and when Rose turned she saw Gerald, stooped and tall, at the end of the aisle.

'Put it in the trolley,' Rose said absently, but Serena was disappearing round the corner.

Rose got to her feet, awkward. He was walking towards her with purpose.

The supermarket had a cafeteria, a dismal place with a single waitress in a yellow tabard, grey tables and an all-day breakfast. They sat at a table in the window, watching the exits: Serena had refused to come with them, eyeing Gerald with distaste, and Rose had given her a basket and told her to fill it with anything she needed.

'Not want, need,' Rose said, with a half smile, 'I've only got a tenner, remember. And don't talk to strangers.' She was rewarded with a scornful look and Serena ran off, her school blouse untucked, her stringy hair flying, sandals slapping on the supermarket tile. Sandals, in October. She'd need new shoes and where would that money come from? Rose thought of the roll of cash and alarm jumped. Was it safe?

Gerald was coming back with two cups of oak-brown tea and the memory of coffee, proper coffee – a creamy-bitter mouthful in a thick white cup in a bar where the machine hissed and people talked – sparked briefly in Rose's head before she extinguished it. His hands trembled: she could hear the cups chatter on their saucers: at the counter the waitress watched without interest.

'I've been trying to track you down,' she said, and

Gerald's head moved, scanning the glassed-in room, the supermarket beyond before returning his gaze to her.

He pulled the cup towards him slowly. 'Yes,' he said, grimacing at the dark liquid, she could see grey hairs in his eyebrows. 'I wanted to talk to you.' As if the two things were connected, as if he knew what had been happening inside the house. He knew Evan, after all, better than most. And perhaps Kate – perhaps that had been what had drawn Kate to him. Someone she could confide in.

His face was long, pale. She could see a trace of stubble: in his basket on the floor beside their table he had bran cereal and semi-skimmed milk. He must be in his fifties, she thought. Middle-aged – but not old.

'When did you last talk to Kate?' she said and Gerald drew back from the tea that he'd been about to drink.

'Kate?' he said. He seemed baffled – but then perhaps he would. He would deny it. Gerald was an old man's name, Rose thought, tormented suddenly, why would she have an affair with him? How could she? Unless she needed the gentleness, the kindness.

'Did she tell you she was pregnant?'

Already pale, Gerald turned paler, with horror. A kind of fastidious fear that Rose couldn't help but feel was genuine. 'No,' he said, then with greater urgency, 'No, *no*. She couldn't have been.'

'She wasn't,' said Kate, 'but she thought she was.'

'But Evan—' he stopped.

'He told you, then,' she said. 'About the vasectomy.' Gerald's face was stiff, embarrassed.

'No,' he said. 'Not willingly, he didn't. I – I—'

He stopped abruptly because then Serena was there between them, with her basket, accusing. The basket held a bottle of shampoo. There was a movement on Gerald's side of the table and he brought out a twenty-pound note.

'I forgot,' he said mildly, addressing himself to Rose, 'I borrowed this from Evan.' And Serena's hand came out and snatched it, gleeful.

'So I can—' she said, 'I can.' Rose took the note from her.

'Get whatever you want,' she said, for an instant smiling at Serena's face, and then the girl was gone again. Where she'd stood was the view, beyond parked cars, of the estuary now, sun glancing for a second down from low cloud, bouncing off the rising tide.

And suddenly she knew what the tiny yellow envelope that had fallen out of Evan's briefcase had contained. Razor blades: he used an old-fashioned razor, and kept them out of harm's way. Except when he needed them to slit fabric, from the breast to the navel? And there were red candles in the kitchen drawer. She'd seen them.

Gerald was staring at her, and she went on, numb.

'Evan said she didn't tell him she was pregnant because she must have been having an affair, because it wasn't – obviously it wasn't – his baby.' Rose placed her hands flat on the table, either side of her untouched cup of tea, the light off the river in her eyes and then gone. 'The baby that never was.'

Opposite her Gerald's bushy eyebrows were drawn together in confusion. 'But if she didn't tell Evan why on earth do you think she would tell *me*?'

Rose sat back, said nothing, he stared, silent, and then coughed a laugh, an incredulous, miserable laugh.

'Oh, no,' he said, and began shaking his head, 'oh, no, no, no. Kate and I?'

Just that phrasing, the pronoun, Kate and I, so old-fashioned, so courtly, so precise, and the theory began to crumble. Gerald leaned forward. 'Do you know how I knew, about Evan's vasectomy? Do you know why I've been off work for the last nine months—' both of them thinking, *nine months.* The term of Kate's last nine months, waiting for a baby that never came.

Something had been released, though, in Gerald, the tension had gone, he spoke rapidly. 'Off work and coming back to – God knows what, now. Kate's the worst of it, poor Kate. Of course I was fond of her – who couldn't be—' he broke off and Rose stared, with wonder, thinking, *Well. Well. So he did love her.* 'I thought no wonder, Evan must have been off his head with worry, no wonder he didn't see – no wonder the accounts—'

'I don't understand,' said Rose quietly. 'You're not making sense.'

'I've been having treatment for aggressive prostate cancer,' he said. 'That's how I knew about Evan's vasectomy, it was my initial consultation – I saw him in the hospital corridor. He swore me to secrecy, didn't want anyone to know, not even Kate.'

'He said he changed his mind about that,' said Rose, her mind whirring, but Gerald went on.

'So – I had surgery that has left me – well. Not a great prospect for an affair, let's say, even if I would have an affair with my business partner's wife—' he drew himself

292

up, giving Kate the dignity of the official title she had never wanted. 'Even if *she* would have for a moment entertained the idea.' Rose flushed, to the tips of her ears, knowing he was right, he knew Kate. 'Then chemotherapy that turns you into a menopausal woman, sweating into the sheets at night,' he said, with finality and without bitterness, only rueful. 'Did you know, a man with that much gonadotrophin in his system can turn a pregnancy test positive? Evan thought that was very entertaining. *Let's try it*, he said.'

What? thought Rose. *What?*

But Gerald came up short, breathless, anguished suddenly. 'Kate,' he said. 'Poor Kate. Poor girl.'

And he stared at her, and as he shook his head the loose skin below his unshaven chin wobbled. *Gerald*. She heard Serena's voice in her head, mocking him, but that didn't come out of nowhere, did it? She was copying someone. 'I don't understand,' he said. 'Not Kate, she wouldn't. Not with – everything.' He ran a hand through his thinning hair. 'She *loved* him.' As if that was the most incredible thing of all.'

'Everything?' said Rose, quietly.

And panic came into Gerald's eyes.

By the time Serena reappeared, Gerald was on his feet, gathering his things in a hurry, backing away from the table. Rose felt as if she'd walked into a swarm of flies, they buzzed and glittered, forming shapes she didn't want to see.

Serena's expression was uncertain as she stood stubbornly silent, watching Gerald disappear, his hunched, shuffling shape melting into the elderly shoppers with their tote bags leaving after their all-day breakfasts, as if he was one of them. An old man, with his dodgy prostate and his anxiety and his strong tea – and his secrets. Rose watched Serena.

'Evan told me . . .' she hesitated, *as good as told me* but would Serena understand that? 'I had a dress,' she said. 'I was going to wear it to the funeral but when I went to get it, it had been cut, all the way down.' Her hand moved, from her breast downwards and she saw Serena's hand go to her mouth, her eyes darkening in fear. 'It wasn't you, was it? I know that now.' And reached for her, Serena's head was against her shoulder a brief second and then away.

And Rose nodded. 'So,' she said. 'Piri piri chicken? Something like that?'

It turned out Serena never went to fast food places, or chicken places, or out for a curry.

'Well,' said Rose, hesitating, 'it'll be an experiment.' She bought ingredients for fajitas, and a vegetable curry for good measure, her plan forming cautiously. There was even seven pounds left, which she spent on petrol.

Back at home Evan was nowhere to be seen, but the house was open and there was a smell of smoke in the air and a blue haze drifting from behind the open barn. Rose could feel her heart pattering, anxious, and then there was Evan appearing from out of the smoke.

'You were for ever,' he said, apparently cheerful. 'I was beginning to wonder if you'd run off with the circus.'

'Oh, *Dad*,' said Serena, uncertain, not sure if he was serious and it was true, Evan never said anything funny. 'No, we were just—'

Rose put out a hand and touched her elbow, gently.

Evan saw. He'd done it to keep them apart, slash the dress and let her think it was Serena.

'Where's Jamie?' she said calmly and he tilted his head a moment as if he might actually not tell her.

'Asleep upstairs,' he said. She nodded, smiled, turning to retrieve the bags from the back of the car. He made no attempt to help her: as she lifted them the car keys fell from her hand to the ground and then he did bend, swiftly, to scoop them up.

He stood watching as she went inside, but made no move to follow.

The first thing she did was run upstairs to the bedroom, Lindsay's insistence in her head. She couldn't remember where she'd left it, that was all. Her phone charger. She could have sworn it had been plugged in beside the bed, but there was nothing there.

That's part of it.

She pulled the suitcase out from under the bed where she'd pushed it, far back. Out of sight. Had she done that on purpose? Had she always known?

In that instant she thought of Evan bending to pick up the car keys. *We should have gone while we could. Me and Serena and Jamie.* Then she dismissed the thought, *Madness. Gone where?*

She opened the suitcase and there was the charger, the plug, the adaptor. She slid her hand into the silk pocket and there was the money. Kate's money. Thinking a moment she reached for the cloth bag she used as a handbag and slid the money in, and the charger, there with the medicine.

The kitchen was empty and swiftly Rose plugged the phone in to charge in a plug that stood behind a tray cluttered with bottles of condiments, ketchup and vinegar. Pushed it down so it was less visible. How long did she have, unobserved? No way of knowing.

Rose made herself chop vegetables and crush spices before she did anything else. Kate's old spice jars were still half full, if a little dusty, although she'd always loved hot food: Rose thought she wouldn't mention what she was cooking to Evan in case he said he didn't like curry, but he didn't come in. He'd started the car up and she heard it moving, then the sound stopped: it was like earlier: it was as if he had to reclaim it as his, after her occupancy. Peering out of the window she couldn't see any sign of it but she could hear his voice, and Serena's answering one, murmuring somewhere out of sight.

The kitchen filled with the old smells, comforting: frying onions, chilli, garam masala, mustard seed, cayenne.

The food on the go and Serena and Evan still outside, Rose washed her hands carefully and slipped out of the kitchen. At the door to the back staircase she rested her cheek on the narrow panelling: it gave a little and she got that particular smell – warm wood, old plaster – before she stepped away and through the green baize door. She took the main staircase, up out of the red hall into the silvered light that fell through the cupola and felt the house folding in on her as it must have folded round Kate, the doors softly closing, one by one, the windows turning blind eyes to the wide grey marsh, a box of tricks closing itself. Was it outside, the danger? Was it in the brown water? It was closer. She almost felt her way forward, to Evan's room and stopped at his door.

For a long moment she stood and listened: there was

no sound. Pushing the door open a crack, then wider, she saw that he was there, Jamie, asleep in his cot. She stepped inside warily, one step over to him and another – then a board creaked and she stopped, lowered herself to peer at him through the bars of the cot. His cheeks were flushed, streaked with something, tears and snot.

When he woke would be time enough for the next dose of antibiotics. Rose would tell Evan, of course she would. She could say she thought she'd already told him, hadn't she said she'd been to the doctor's? Maybe tomorrow she'd tell him. Tomorrow loomed, though, it seemed somehow impossible. She needed to get through tonight.

Jamie looked as though he had cried a long time. Thinking, Rose went to the chest of drawers where his little clothes were kept and pulled his drawer open. She looked down: worn, soft things, old things. Second-hand, even, perhaps although she couldn't imagine Kate buying her only child's clothes from charity shops.

Kate's savings. All gone.

Everything except a tight roll of banknotes, at the bottom of Rose's bag.

'I don't know how he can have let it get this bad,' Gerald had said, hopelessly. 'All the money we put in. The down payments on two houses and the buyers asking, when they can move in, when they can visit, letters un-answered. There's nothing in the bank and two lots of builders unpaid.'

He'd stopped then abruptly and sensing something Rose had turned and there Serena had been, looking from one of them to another with her black eyes, her little frozen face.

The voices had moved from the yard, had they come round the house? Into the kitchen? Evan's voice low but not gentle, Serena not answering. Rose tiptoed backwards out of the room and fled, along the corridor into her room, closing the door behind her and putting her back against it. She could feel her heart going like a hammer: it seemed to have been doing that for days.

The room seemed undisturbed, the books on the shelves, the cover on the bed, but she knew he'd been in here. The – wait. The desk. Rose felt in her pocket, a bubble of sudden excitement rising in her because that was what it was for, wasn't it? The small key. The small key on the flimsy keyring— hold on. Had she put them in the other pocket? She turned and turned, on the spot, as that might make them appear but the keys were no longer in her pocket.

Shit. Shit. But he can't— even if he had heard them chink, when they stood there together in the yard, Evan couldn't have picked her pocket, he wouldn't— they must have. They must have fallen out in the car. That would be it.

Rose went to the sink, where her sponge-bag sat, an old floral thing Kate had given her in another life, she must have been sixteen and here it still was, grubby and worn. She took it on her knee on the bed and scrabbled through it, looking, looking. Lipgloss, paracetamol, hotel soaps. Impatiently she upended the bag on the bed and there. There.

Deb had given them to her, had bought them from a private doctor on a trip to New York when the jetlag had killed her and she wanted to sleep on the way home. Given them to Rose when it had all gone tits up with the married man and she'd ranted and raved for forty-eight hours without sleep. There were four of them. 'Be careful,' Deb had said back then, awe-struck, 'they knocked me right out.' In the end Rose hadn't dared take them.

There was no packet, only the little blister pack. Temazepam.

As she reached for them, the phone rang, and with the sound the door opened a little, amplifying the clang of the old-fashioned bell, and although Rose knew, somewhere in her rational brain that it meant a door had opened downstairs – Evan going for the phone, the air coming inside had found its way upstairs – it was also as if an invisible hand had pushed it, inviting her. Summoning her. Screaming for her.

And her bag was in the kitchen, her bag – she couldn't remember where – with the envelope from the solicitors' in it, the money, the medicine. And Rose was on the landing without even knowing how she'd got there.

Evan was already there, answering, he had the phone in his hand and he was turning a little on the spot as if he was looking for someone and – although he lifted his head to the gallery, although he must be able to see her feet through the balustrade, although he must have heard her run out of her bedroom – Rose listened to him saying, quite distinctly, 'I think she must have gone out.' And then there was the shush of the green baize door opening and Serena stood in it, looking up, straight at her.

'No, Daddy,' she said then, quite distinct, looking up at Rose. 'There's Rose, I can see her.' Pointing. Loudly enough that whoever was on the phone must hear, must know and then they were both looking at her, Serena pale and defiant, her slender finger quivering. Brave Serena: Rose saw that, in the same instant as she saw the stairs between them. Her mother had died on the stairs. She'd had a brain haemorrhage and fallen down the stairs.

What Lindsay had said came then into her mind, *Ask him*. Ask him how they met, him and Kate – except that Rose already knew because Kate had told her, long, long ago. Only three years ago, in fact, but time enough, for a life to run its course. Her life.

'No, here she is,' said Evan, pleasantly, into the phone but his face was stiff with anger as Rose came down the stairs, hand out for the phone. 'It's that woman from the school.' Annie must be able to hear it, his casual, deliberate rudeness. It was for her. 'What's her name? Annie.'

'I got her number,' said Annie but Evan hadn't moved away. He was standing so close he must be able to hear.

'Yes,' managed Rose begging for her not to say the name. Martha.

'It was a bit of a pain, she's not on any registers though she does seem to be qualified—' and then from upstairs came Jamie's wail.

'Hold on—' began Rose, seeing alarm in Serena's face, seeing her looking from Evan to Rose, 'I've got to—' and something like a smile appeared on Evan's face.

'I'll get him,' he said and the smile broadened. 'You talk to your friend.' He turned and set off up the stairs, slow.

Serena was looking at her, a hand to her mouth, shaking her head. Pleading. 'I can't call her,' said Rose. 'I can't—'

'It's him, isn't it?' said Annie. 'I told her. It's Evan. I

asked Kate what he was like, I told her it didn't seem right. She wouldn't listen.'

'Can you call her for me?' said Rose, interrupting her. 'I just want to know if she knew about the pregnancy. If Kate was in touch with her, or – or Evan.'

'But I thought he didn't know?'

'He says he didn't,' said Rose, lowering her voice, 'but I think – I think—' although what she thought had only just come to her.

Annie was talking, urgently, her voice too loud, while all around Rose the great lofty space of the hall turned dark.

'I already spoke to her,' said Annie. 'To Martha. I called because I wanted to know it was her, it was the right number. I told her – what you told me, that Kate thought she was pregnant. She was shocked.'

'Because of the affair? That Kate must have had an affair?'

'No,' said Annie, patient. 'Shocked because she had no idea Kate thought she was pregnant. None – and Kate would have told her, she insisted, she would have wanted Martha. But no one had told her anything.'

'You believed her?' Rose was whispering.

Upstairs the door opened and she looked up. Evan stood at the balustrade, Jamie in his arms and a small sound came from Serena in the depths of the hall, her back to the deep soft green of the baize door, the dark red of the walls and the carpet enfolding her small figure, a doll in a box.

'Yes,' said Annie, 'yes, I did. I—'

'I've got to go,' said Rose.

Chapter Twenty-Eight

It's getting dark.

I hear him turn the key in the door.

I used to stand at the window and look out and my heart would fill up with it. The endless light, the salt smell of the rising tide, the tiny sounds of water coming up. Seeing the horizon, the edge of the world. No one to spy, no one to ask questions, no one to tell us what to do, or how to do it, we only let in those we choose.

The world is wrong, and we're right. Our bodies know what's good for them. Was that Evan, or was it Martha? My body is a stranger, it's an enemy. My arms are like sticks and my belly bulges, it slops and stabs me. I don't know if I can get to the window, now. It's like after I had Jamie and I tried to stand up, my legs slide off the bed but they won't take the weight of my belly. What's in there? What's in there?

I have keys. I hoard them, try them in doors. I lock

precious things away, for the future to find. But I hid the key to my bedroom for her, and now I can't get out.

There's another life of mine – with work to go to, with flowers on a windowsill and cars in the street outside and meetings in cafés – it's like a room filled with hazy sunshine where the old me might have stood and observed this woman who scuttles from room to room, hiding keys and notes, squirrelling clues away, afraid of noises, afraid of things that don't have shape. A figure on a fuzzy television screen, seen through a closed-circuit spy camera, monitored and assessed and judged.

I have keys but I don't remember where I put them.

The key has turned in the door and the light is going. I don't know any more if that's in my head, the way it turns dark from the corners.

He'll unlock it in the morning.

If there is a morning.

As she hung up the phone with deliberate care – putting the smile on her face first for Serena, to reassure her there where she stood in the frame of door and flock wallpaper, her velvet padded box, with her fists clasped together at her mouth – Rose realised she was still clutching the silver blister pack of sleeping pills in her free hand.

Serena took a step forward as if released and Rose turned the smile wider, more rigid, up at Evan, who was standing on the gallery with Jamie in his arms and facing outward, legs dangling, just Evan's forearm across his small belly between Jamie and the deep void of the dark red hall.

The great high space around them settled into darkness and no one spoke: it was too dangerous. Rose only smiled, until her jaw ached. And casually folded her fingers around the blister pack of pills and let her eyes slide across to Serena, holding her gaze, until she understood. Serena stood very still.

The time for being reasonable was gone. Now the only thing to be done was to lie. To pretend everything was all right, everything was normal, to stall and prevaricate. To pretend they *hadn't* thought, she and Serena, that unless he got what he wanted, Evan would let his child fall, into the deep dark hall.

'For heaven's sake,' said Evan, taking a step forward on the gallery and peering down at them, Jamie straining, reaching over the banister towards them. 'Cat got your tongues?' Rose saw Serena tremble again at the weird unfamiliar jokiness.

'Serena's shivering,' said Rose, the first thing that came into her head that resembled normal speech, bright and hollow and artificial. 'I don't suppose we could—' and she grimaced, pleading, obsequious, 'get the heating on?'

For a second it all hung suspended and then Evan let out a small dry laugh and turned away, was moving back from the balustrade and towards the wide staircase and Rose was moving too, shepherding Serena ahead of her into the kitchen.

Once inside Rose positioned herself between the table and the boiler room to be in a position to intercept him as he passed to light the boiler, just casually to reach out her arms to take Jamie from him. There was hesitation, just a second, and Evan let her take him.

What did he know? He knew something. He knew *she* knew something.

What did she know? That Kate's savings were gone. That she'd been hiding money from him. That he'd had a vasectomy and as far as Gerald knew, Kate had no clue. Because if she *had* known, she'd have known she was sick, not pregnant. They had only Evan's word for it, didn't they? That he'd told her about the vasectomy, that she hadn't told him she was pregnant. Kate, having an affair? The idea was laughable.

Turning back into the room Rose took in her bag, still on the floor under the table where she'd dropped it, and saw Serena's face. 'What?' Rose mouthed, and she saw Serena turn pale, paler.

'He's going to—' said Serena, 'I don't know what he's going to do.' Rose reached back and flipped the door, just a little, so it creaked closed. He wouldn't like that, if he saw, and they both knew that this had to be quick.

'I told him we'd seen Gerald in the supermarket,' whispered Serena, 'I didn't mean to, I was just saying what we—'

'Did you say I had tea with him, talked to him?' said Rose, quailing, and seeing the look in Serena's face, said quickly, 'It's all right.' And then was pulling away, dropping Jamie into his high chair because she could feel the door opening, she could feel Evan coming back into the room. There was a soft whump as the boiler came on behind him.

'That's better,' she said, composing her face into a grateful smile. 'Thanks, Evan. Supper in – half an hour?'

He looked from her to Serena, who was standing half

turned away at the stove, prodding at the vegetable curry. 'Smells good,' he said, but his expression said different. 'Sure, whatever.' His smile was professional. 'I've got a few things to do. Serena, perhaps you'd like to help your auntie Rose?'

Auntie Rose: he hadn't used that expression before, either, but Serena just nodded obediently and he went, closing the door behind him with care.

In his wake the room hung a moment, the glitter of what had been – might have been – in the air, and then was ordinary. They were a family, making the tea.

A sound came from the hall, a soft grunt, a chair or something moving and with the sound a sudden shocking image flew through Rose's head, a picture of violence, of things hanging, things dead, and then she heard his foot-steps on the stairs, quick and light and she swallowed.

'How about helping me with some chopping,' she said to Serena. 'Peppers? If you give a bit to Jamie that might keep him quiet for a bit.' She found a board, a small knife, and sat Serena at the table. Jamie was uncharacteristically quiet: he watched, eyes moving from Rose to Serena and back again.

Having located a dusty pestle and mortar at the back of a cupboard Rose positioned herself carefully, with her back to Serena. She ground coriander seed and cumin first, scrupulously fine, before – after a quick glance over her shoulder – extracting the blister pack from her pocket. She popped one, then two of the pills and then with a tightening in her chest, the other two, into the mortar. She ground them carefully small then, hesitating, licked a finger, dipped it so a grain or two stuck, and tasted. It was bitter. Behind her Serena had got up from the table and was moving about, opening cupboards, getting out plates but Rose didn't turn to check on her, to betray her mission, she was methodical, she was calm.

When Rose did look around – one hand protectively covering the mortar and its contents as she scanned the room for something to transfer them to, something small, discreet, pocketable – she saw that Serena had chopped all the vegetables and was sitting at the table she'd laid, up close to Jamie, her fingers reaching to his. She looked at Rose, and Rose saw her child's face, her frightened face.

'It's all right,' Rose said, mechanically, but it wasn't, and they both knew it. Then she leaned and took the plates. 'I think I'll serve on the side, not at the table. Less messy.'

Serena's eyes were on her, wide and round and dark, and she nodded.

As if by silent agreement, they didn't call Evan. They sat and waited, the chicken and peppers cooking, the curry bubbling, and Rose fed Jamie carrots and little bits of cheese. She didn't turn round to look at the stove, to look at the plates stacked and ready, to seek out the eggcup holding the fine white powder that looked like neither sugar nor salt. And then they heard him.

Rose was on her feet quickly, silently, she was at the stove, she heard his voice behind her, talking to Jamie. *Now then, young man.* She hadn't noticed before that voice he had when talking to Jamie, the too-loud voice, the parent who just wants to be overheard.

The voice held no love. It held tension, a kind of greedy anticipation. *He didn't love her. He doesn't love his children.* Not turning round Rose stirred, tasted, then finally dared a look over her shoulder.

'Hungry?' She was looking at Serena.

She served them. Serena first, the chicken in a flatbread and some vegetable curry. The curry was spicier, she held her breath as she asked Evan casually, so casually, which he'd like.

'Oh, everything,' he said and just at that moment Jamie, her small ally, batted his hand on the table and a fork clattered to the floor. Evan leaned after it and swiftly, her throat tight with the fear of what she was doing, Rose tipped half the contents of the eggcup into the curry she'd served him, stirring, stirring.

It would be enough, she didn't want him to taste it. *Stop,* she told herself.

Something stirred, though, a dirty, muddy thing, the truth she knew and didn't quite know, she felt towards it in the dark, it wanted her to tip the whole lot in, to stop him, quiet him, keep him away. She set the eggcup back quickly, pushed it in among the bottles of oil, the jars of old herbs.

She turned, and he was setting the fork back on the table. He reached for the plate she offered him and looked into her face, and he looked almost amused, a smile hovering as if he knew something she didn't.

There was nothing she could do now, though. If he knew — well. She'd find out soon enough. Rose served herself, sat at the table. Raised her glass of water: '*Buon appetito,*' she said, and saw Evan's little smile at her pretension, her thinking she was sophisticated, or clever, before he inclined his head, saying nothing.

They began to eat. She deliberately didn't look at his plate: she concentrated on Serena, bravely swallowing. It was very spicy — not disastrously, unless you weren't used to it, but hot — and Serena's colour rose abruptly.

'Milk,' said Rose, catching a glimpse of Evan's plate, half eaten, a fork lifted to his mouth, as she tuned to the fridge. 'Milk's good for that.' When she turned back, the glass of milk in her hand, Evan was holding his fork out, across the table, towards Jamie, loaded with curry.

Rose felt the hairs go up on the back of her neck: she saw Serena's eyes widen in panic. She'd seen. Seen the powder, seen the sleight of hand, and said nothing. Serena knew. And wouldn't say.

He knew. He knew. The options presented themselves: shout, grab the spoon, give yourself away. She dropped the glass, Evan turned at the sound, and suddenly Serena had lunged across the table, she was pushing the fork back at him.

On the floor, scrabbling for the broken pieces of glass, her knees in a puddle of milk, Rose heard Serena say, 'Daddy,' shocked and outraged, fierce, 'You can't give him that, it'll burn him.'

She half rose to see Evan sitting back, quite equable, quite mild in his chair, Serena scarlet with fear.

'Goodness me, what a fuss about nothing,' said Evan, shrugging, forking the food into his own mouth. Clearing the plate.

Rose watched him from her hiding place, up between the chair backs. He *didn't* know. He had done it to hurt

Jamie. He only wanted the fun of burning his child's mouth, of seeing the tears come into his eyes. And he was pushing them to see if they'd stop him. And then he could respond, then he would be justified.

If she'd had any doubt, she knew now at least that cruelty was in him, hardwired.

The room was close, too bright, too hot. Kneeling back down to clear up the milk and the broken glass she felt it bear down on her like a weight. There was a long shard she looked at a moment before carefully setting it in the others in newspaper, putting it in the dustbin, returning to the table.

They ate in silence. It seemed to go on for hours, the lifting of glasses, the dull clinking of cutlery against plates and then abruptly Evan was on his feet. Rose saw him sway, knew it must be her imagination, it was too soon, and indeed he was just leaning down to get Jamie.

'Bit of fresh air,' said Evan, turning a look on her. She could see a bead of sweat on his forehead. 'Come along, Serena,' his eyes sliding over Rose. 'You don't mind, do you, sweetheart? Clearing, I mean?'

Serena was watching them like a hawk, must have caught Rose flinching at the word 'sweetheart'. Rose was on her feet, hurriedly. 'I can do that later, can't I?' Wiping her hands on the apron she was still wearing, and he sighed, as if she was a clumsy servant, dismissed.

'I'd rather be on my own with them,' he said easily. 'It's all a bit — we're all a bit overwrought.' Smiling down at Serena who had got up quick and agitated, darting a glance at Rose, about to plead — but his look silenced her. 'If that's all right with you?'

Keep pretending. 'Of course,' said Rose, looking at Serena as he turned away, nodding at her, yes. Meaning, *I'll follow. Don't worry, I'm here.*

She waited, as they moved into the boiler room, she heard his voice, explaining something, instructing and heard the boiler's whump as it went out. *Wait*, she told herself, *wait until he's moved off, out of the door, into the yard.*

At what point do you say, *No. No, I won't do what you ask?* The point at which you fracture it, the relationship, the truce, the uneasy accord: do you wait until the children are safe, the key is in the ignition? Rose waited: she began to clear, mechanically. She saw them move past the kitchen window, slowly, across the yard. She hoped he wouldn't take them to the weir.

A minute, two, five. She put the plates down, she took off the apron, she crept out into the boiler room, through the cluttered silent dark, she put her hand soft to the doorhandle.

He'd locked the door.

Chapter Twenty-Nine

It took a moment, first fear. Outrage, then the fear again. Rose couldn't even rattle the handle, because then Evan would hear, he would know she'd turned, she was against him. And he had the children.

Men didn't kill their children unless they were cornered, did they? Humiliated, found out, exposed. Rose couldn't be sure if that was always true but she knew she couldn't waste time. She ran, heedless of noise, like wind, through the house, the baize door banging behind her, straight for the glazed front door. The hall was dark around her, the air felt thick. There was a key in the door's lock, a big rusted key – using both hands Rose managed to turn it, then took hold of the old brass knob, turned and tugged. A squeak, no more: swollen with the damp, it didn't move. Rose tugged again, feeling the tendons pull between her shoulder blades, felt her feet slip on the mat. It didn't budge an inch. She could hear their voices, Jamie babbling something and that low reasonable monotone that was Evan.

Not reasonable. She could feel panic lapping, lapping, the tide coming up.

Up. Up. She needed to get out of this – this dark, this thick red swarming gloating dark, she needed to find a vantage point. She ran fast, to the stairs, up, round the gallery, into the room. Her room, the room Kate had chosen for her: she went straight to the dark window, past the desk in the corner, the writing desk Kate had left her felt her, it seemed to address her, but she couldn't stop for it. She went to the window, her hands went up to the glass and she was Kate, she was Kate, signalling for help.

And there they were.

The three of them, at the edge of the water, a dark three-headed silhouette beyond the reeds. She pressed her face against the glass so she could see: there was the shape of Jamie's head down on Evan's shoulder, she could see Serena on the end of Evan's arm, pulling away.

At what point? At what point do you smash the glass and call for help?

No one can hear. She stood, hands flat on the window-pane, holding her breath ready to shout and then, slowly, slowly, the shape changed, turned and they were black figures against the grass that had grown long and wintry, silvered with dew and the light from a rising moon somewhere out of sight. The figures were walking back towards the house, Evan slow as a sleepwalker, Serena tugging, tugging. Rose ran for the door, and as she passed the writing desk snagged on her again, the desk Kate had put

313

in here for her, Serena had told her as much. *Come back,* it seemed to say.

Someone had tried to get into it. Evan had. The keys had been left for her by Kate. But Rose didn't stop, she ran out on to the gallery and saw the doors along it, all closed, she was locked blind in the house. She ran back downstairs, into the green sitting room without turning on the light, listening for them, hearing the monotone.

Then she heard Serena, her voice sharp with fear. *Shhh,* Rose wanted to say, *don't give it away, don't give yourself away.* 'Daddy, Jamie needs to go inside, he's not well, he's not—' and the monotone again, saying words she couldn't hear, only their dull, bullying insistence.

Heard the footsteps on the gravel, *Don't, don't –* she hardly dared think of the turning to the weir, down the side of the brick outhouse then dark between trees, and the footsteps stopped. As if the someone whose footsteps they were was wondering, had forgotten what they'd come out there for.

When the key turned in the lock to the boiler room she was back in the kitchen, drying up.

'Was that nice?' she said, looking into Evan's face, not into Serena's. He yawned, stupid in that moment and she took advantage of it to take Jamie. Evan gave him over carelessly, barely waiting till she had hold of him to turn away saying something about going to watch the news, throwing back the door so it banged, and he was gone.

Jamie's hot hand was on her face, he babbled: Rose felt Serena come up, close and quiet, felt her press herself against her side.

'All right?' she whispered, and Serena nodded uncertainly, white-faced.

'Up you go and run a bath,' said Rose, still whispering, holding her gaze. 'I'll be there to tuck you in.'

Waiting for the sound of the water, when it came she moved into the hall, holding Jamie still to quiet him though he hardly needed to be quieted, he was limp.

There was no sound of the television. Had Evan fallen asleep before he could even turn it on? She must be patient, make sure.

She must be methodical. She must think.

Jamie needed his medicine. Phone. Keys. Car. Serena. Was that all?

Overhead the water had stopped running. Quickly she sat Jamie on her knee and – no time to prime him, or hesitate – she administered his medicines, one sticky yellow spoon, one pink. He let out a feeble wail, his mouth turned down piteously, but he didn't have strength to protest. They padded back into the hall where she paused at the closed door to the green sitting room.

What if. What if she'd killed him? Evan. Rose examined her responses but found only a quickening, not fear exactly, but adrenaline: it was a risk but still one worth taking. The thought of him still and silent felt perilously exhilarating, the thought of those eyes closed, even if he was pale, even cold.

But Rose still had no proof of the story she was beginning to reconstruct, it could all turn back again, she could see them ranged against her, incredulous in their white coats: doctors, policemen, experts.

But there was Gerald, baggy-eyed in the supermarket café,

315

mournful and certain. There was Martha who'd been told of no pregnancy. There was Lindsay saying, *Ask him. Go on, ask him how they met.* And there was Kate, whispering to her in corners, leaving traces for Rose to find, in the will, in cupboards. None of them trusted Evan, not even Kate, who'd put her faith in him, loved and pitied and wanted to believe and then one day she found she was being held so tight she couldn't turn around. *How had he done it?* The trail must be here, in the house that had become her prison.

Her ear was at the door to the green sitting room, waiting for a sound, when she heard something, an impatient sigh. She crouched, her eye to the keyhole and saw the flicker of the screen, so it was on, but he must have turned the sound down, or off. He wanted to listen. He wanted to hear, to monitor their movements, to follow every footstep, to identify every door opened.

Not yet. Be patient. And then there was a sound from upstairs and looking up she saw Serena in a faded night-dress that was too short in the arms, a little ghost peering down at them. Rose began to climb the stairs, feeling a chill swirl and gather behind her.

'Where is he,' said Serena, in the door to her room, 'where is he?'

Rose held a finger to her lips, pulling the door to behind her and gesturing to the bed. She climbed in beside Serena and pulled the covers over them, all three. 'Did your mother make that nightie?' she said and Serena nodded, lips tight – and then she spoke.

'He was going to hurt Jamie, wasn't he?' she said. Rose hesitated a second, then nodded and Serena lay back a little on the pillow, staring at the faded wallpaper. 'I know how he – is,' Serena said, in a small choked voice, not meeting her eye, 'he's one person then he's another person. He was like that with Mu— with Kate.' Her eyes brimmed suddenly. 'I don't know how he was with *my* mum, maybe he was the same. When he wants you to like him he— You have to like him. Then when he doesn't care, it's like you're somewhere very dark and cold and you can't get out.'

There was a palpable silence, it tiptoed around them in the house, creeping from room to room, peering in. The three of them in the bed held very still in that instant, and then the moment passed.

'She was nice,' Serena whispered. 'Kate. She only wanted – she wanted to make me happy. Us happy. And when she said she couldn't tell me but there was going to be good news.' A beat, then another, waiting for the words. She saw Serena swallow with difficulty and between them, sleepily, Jamie turned, settled against her.

'About – another baby?' said Rose, holding her breath. 'You knew? She told you?'

Serena's eyes were very dark on hers and she pulled the covers up, to her chin, to cover her mouth as if she didn't want it to be seen and then she shook her head. 'I heard them talking,' she said. 'I didn't mean to listen but – I heard them talking. I heard her telling him, downstairs in the sitting room. They were whispering but I heard. I wanted it to be a baby and it was. Kate said it was. She kept saying, *oh darling*, to him.'

'Your dad.'

'He was pretending to be pleased,' said Serena, 'but he wasn't.'

'She told him.'

'She sounded so happy,' said Serena, her voice choking up again, her eyes wet black buttons, then she made a sudden convulsive movement, as if to get out of the bed, and Jamie, whose eyes had drooped, jerked awake.

'What is it?' said Rose, as the implications whirled like dust, began to settle, whirled again.

'I want to talk to Nanny and Grandpa,' Serena said, sitting up.

'Your mother's parents?' Serena nodded, calmer, quieter, the bright black eyes intent, on something far off.

'I remembered them, he thought I didn't but I remembered them. I remember Grandpa's moustache and his suitcase, I remember Nanny's smell, of flowers.'

'Does your father—' Rose swallowed, thinking of drawers she would need to go through. The mobile phone she'd never seen him use, that would be locked. 'Has he kept their number?'

Serena's eyes were bright. 'I've got it,' she said. And pointed at the little chest of drawers, and whispered, 'I hid it in the back of the photograph.' The photograph of her mother, standing on the veneer.

She pointed. 'They came one time to our old house and Daddy shouted at them on the doorstep and said he'd call the police and Nanny knelt down and put her arms around me and put something in my pocket, and when I looked later, it was a telephone number.' She nodded at the little cabinet on the chest of drawers, beside her mother's picture. And let out a long shivering breath, as if it was a secret she'd held too long.

'Do you remember what the argument was about?' said Rose, gently.

318

Serena looked at her, pale, a long second, then shook her head, pressed her lips together. She knew. She remembered. Rose looked at her a second then very carefully so as not to disturb Jamie, eased herself out of the bed. He gave a small sigh and spread an arm, but he didn't wake and Rose pulled the covers back up over him.

She stood a moment. 'Serena?' Serena, her eyes on Rose, unwavering, tipped her head up, waiting. 'Serena,' said Rose again, 'I'm coming back. OK? I'm coming *right* back. But I need you to look after Jamie until I do. Keep him with you.' Her black button eyes fixed on Rose, Serena nodded again.

Tiptoeing to the chest of drawers, Rose picked up the photograph, turned it over quickly: the back unclipped and there it was, a soft scrap of card, a number blurred and faded, tucked into the frame. Rose prised it out and the photograph came too, the face looking up at her, so young, fair, fine-featured, laughing, the tiniest trace of Serena in the pointed chin, the delicate nose.

At the door Rose thought of something, paused. 'Have you got a key to your door?' she said. Serena's face clouded, cleared and uncertainly she nodded.

'I found one,' she said. 'I didn't know how – it was just there one day on my chest of drawers, I thought – well. I knew Daddy hadn't put it there. It was—' and her voice congested, 'about a week before Kate – before she—'

'Before she died,' said Rose, feeling the sadness like a flood rising, to her waist, to her neck.

'I was scared of her,' said Serena in a small, sad voice, 'she got – she was strange. She sort of began – sleep-walking. She looked like she didn't know where she was

319

and sometimes I heard her in her room and I didn't dare – Daddy said not to—'

'Don't—' said Rose quickly. 'Don't – none of this is your fault, Serena. Just – use the key if you think – if you think you need to. But I'll be back soon.'

She closed the door behind her with extreme care. The great lofty space of the hall was almost completely dark around her, there was only the lightest silvering of surfaces here and there from the moon somewhere out of sight. The banister, the top of a picture frame, the edge of the low table by the front door and on it, the gleam of the curved receiver of the old phone, in its cradle.

Rose felt it as she ran, soft on the stairs, the cool of a draught curling in from somewhere and when she got to the bottom, to the table, she stopped, turned. Had someone opened a door? And her heart was hammering, instantly: she turned, backed against the front door, the great key in her back. The door to the green sitting room was still closed: she knelt to the keyhole and saw the flicker of the screen but his head was no longer visible above the sofa.

Perhaps – perhaps – as she turned she felt almost as much as heard the smallest soft sound of movement, the green baize door, not opening but shifting, shifting. Shifting in a draught. She followed the sound, as noiseless as she could be, through the door.

The kitchen sat, looked back at her, bright and still and undisturbed, some plates still stacked on the table where Rose hadn't cleared them: she moved on to the boiler room and there stood the back door, wide open. A black rectangle, and then something moved in it, her heart jumped again and then she saw it was leaves – a bush that grew beside the door, rustled by the same stiffening breeze that she could feel around her ankles – that had stirred the baize door.

She couldn't remember. Evan walking back into the kitchen with the children had been like a shockwave, the flash from a camera bleaching everything out, deafening her. She didn't remember the closing of the back door before they came in. Perhaps. Perhaps.

If he was outside she could lock the door and keep him there. But the thought of him out there in the dark, watching, circling, moving through the bushes, tightened something in her belly. *Don't go out, though,* pleaded the voice in her head. But out there somewhere was the car. The keys that had fallen from her pocket – those keys Kate had left for her to find, like the ones she'd placed ready for Serena, knowing the danger would come. And – who knew? – Evan might have left the car keys there too, tucked under the sunshade, in the glove compartment, and if she had the car keys— Rose went out. Hands out ahead of herself like a blind person, feeling through the dark.

It was windy. She could hear it rushing in the trees, combining with the roar of the weir, like an invisible animal running, running. Barefoot she crossed the sharp rough stones of the yard, awkward, hands still out against falling, against the invisible running animal.

The car wasn't in the yard, it wasn't in the drive, it wasn't over the bridge. She couldn't see much but she could see that, the hazy moon revealing grey space between hedges. And there was the brick outhouse, the building she had thought was part of the water board's occupancy, a pump house. She turned a second, looked back at the house, dark against a congested sky of pale cloud moving over black. No lights came on, Rose could hear nothing over the roar of the wind and the water. She thought of Serena and Jamie huddled in the bed, Serena creeping to the door to lock it.

Coming into the lee of the outhouse the cold dark smell of water rose to meet her, somewhere close, getting closer. She put up a hand to the blistered paint of the old double doors – and it gave. Cautiously she got her fingertips between the doors, eased them apart and the smell changed again. Petrol, rubber. Yes. Then she was inside, and the car was in there with her.

She remembered her phone only when she was inside it. The driver door unlocked and there she was in the stale-smelling interior, something gritty under her feet. She remembered not because she might use it to phone the number in her pocket – she'd practically forgotten that purpose though she did glance, into the corner of the screen as it illuminated to check that it still said, *No service* – not for that. For the light. She shone it first into the glove compartment, then, flipping down the sunshade, looked there and the light glanced back at her in the mirror. No car keys. And then she remembered the other keys. The keys she'd found in the medicine cabinet – did she have time to look?

Feeling down to the side of the driver's seat, Rose shone the light down into the footwell – hastily, because those other keys seemed an irrelevance, a distraction, what did they matter – and something winked back at her. A

322

gleam of brass. She reached, fumbled, extracted them from under the seat. A tiny triumph. Pocketing them she clambered out.

It was only once she was halfway back to the house, heart thumping, the stones sharp under her bare feet that she paused to wonder why Evan had put the car there. All day he had been playing games with her, letting her out on a long leash then tugging her back. Take the car keys, give them back. And then the car disappears, behind locked doors. Other possibilities jumped at her, dangerous. A car in a locked garage, engine running. She turned back and ran the last few feet, then, stumbling, suddenly sure she would find the door closed, find herself locked out with God knows who, or what.

But it stood open. Was he inside, or out? Had he woken – Rose turned and set back off through the yard, skirting the house. At the veranda something brushed at her face, cobwebby soft, something crawled and panic jumped and she raised her hands to bat at it .

Kate had always been the one to protect her from spiders – the spidery time of year, this, those big grown striped ones – gently extracting them from where they'd got caught, in Rose's hair once, *Don't look* and a giant rage inflated inside her, like a disease. She controlled it with an equal ferocity, *Wait. Wait until you know. Then fly.* She moved on, brushing sharply at the cobweb, around the house to the long silent window where the light flickered.

The curtains were half shut.

Why wait? It hammered in her head. *Why wait? Don't wait. Get them out, run.*

For a second the sofa seemed empty, half her view of

it blocked by the large old-fashioned television, no one had televisions any more, did they? They had internet, they had the world at their fingertips. And then she saw a leg, a foot, a shoe on the floor, and stepping further into the window, there was his head. He looked smaller there, he barely occupied the length of the sofa, but his face looked back at her, even with eyes closed it was as if he was coiled, ready. The gleam of teeth between lips just parted. The eyes could just snap open, she had the sudden powerful sense that he was waiting for her to move full into view and the eyes would snap open, he would run at her. She held her ground – and nothing happened.

Now. Now. Get them out and run. You don't need the car. You don't need the evidence. But she quailed, she thought of them running, in the lane, the sound of the car starting up behind them. The thought of what he would say.

She could call Annie. She could call the police. And say what?

In her pocket something crackled. The photograph, the telephone number of her parents, the first wife's parents because with a sour dread she knew. *What did the first wife die of?* And Lindsay had asked, how they met, Kate and Evan. Those things were connected.

And she remembered the pink flash of a tabard, shrivelled in the bonfire, an email from Kate gushing about him. 'Who are you running for?' Kate had asked him.

Just one last piece in the puzzle, and they could answer it. The parents of the first woman to leave Evan a widower. Rose would get her answer – and *then* they'd run. Out into the dark, along the lane, run, run, run while he sleeps.

She locked the back door behind her, and kept the key. Coming round the kitchen table she stepped in something slimy, Jamie must have dropped food on the floor and she grabbed a tea towel, rubbed it off, saw the little mound under the table like dog's mess and recoiled.

The hall was silent. Tiptoeing to the phone, carefully she lifted the big old-fashioned thing, all of it, clutching it to her chest, she eased the cable free from behind the small table and as she did so heard a soft snore from behind the door. Moved away from the sound, two steps, three, there must be plenty of cable, crouching she hid herself in the shadow of the big staircase, the phone on her knee, she got out the number, she lifted the receiver. There was no sound.

No dial tone. Rose depressed the button, released, was about to do it again, looking back to where she'd come, to the door she expected to open at any minute, and saw it.

Things to do. And that was what he'd been doing, after dinner. The grunt of satisfaction from behind the green baize door, as they'd sat obedient at the table. That was why the telephone's extension had followed her so easily.

Because there it lay, between her and the door to the green sitting room, on the red carpet that was black in the moonlight, the telephone wire. A flash of white was exposed in the old cabling, where it had been cut.

Chapter Thirty

Fuck you. Fuck you. Fuck you. The rage swelled, but along with it a terror that raised the hairs on her head. Rose scrambled to her feet and the telephone rolled to the ground, letting out a sharp *ting*.

Holding her breath as the sound hung in the air, Rose waited for the groan, the footsteps, the door opening – but nothing came. And then she was at the door and opening it – trying to be quiet but trying mostly to be quick. And besides, something in her wanted him on his feet, so she could fight, she could take him on but then at the last minute, when she was inside the room with him, his body on the sofa, his face turned away now, into the cushions, so he had moved, he *had* – she quailed. Thinking of his black, black eyes, the strength in his arms, the pale gleam of his teeth.

And then she saw it. He was lying on his side, one leg drawn up underneath him and there in his hip pocket the frayed corner of a leather fob Rose recognised because it had been attached to the keys to the car. Edging as close as she dared, crouched down against the sofa, she reached across him and pulled gently, so gently, easing them out. They were almost there when the groan came and with it an upheaval of shoulder and leg and she felt him turn against her hand. The keys came out, they were at her fingertips and she had to choose, grab or hide – and it was too late.

The keys were in her fingers, and then Evan's hip turned, tugged them from her grasp and with a soft clink they fell, down between the cushions, he rolled and they were underneath him. And as Rose tipped, off balance, back on one hand at the foot of the sofa for one second he was looking at her.

She felt her mouth open, but then his eyes rolled back, his eyelids fluttered as he let out a strange rough sound, a kind of growl from deep in his throat and abruptly he was still again, his back arched slightly against the cushions, his mouth open. He snored.

Fuck you. Rose stood over him, stiff with frustration, with rage, with fear, then it came to her. She backed, carefully, out of the room. *Think.*

Her phone was in her back pocket. Fully charged. She withdrew it, and the number with it – and the brass keys she had just retrieved from the car. *Hold on. Hold on.*

She took the stairs two at a time. Why not run? Because once they'd gone they could never come back. It'd all go on the bonfire, every stick of furniture, every shred of evidence.

Think. If you're going to leave – what do you take with you? Had Kate had the same thought?

Children first. If necessary only them – but if there's five more minutes of time? She listened, heard nothing. If there's time: evidence.

Rose ran, past Serena's door into the bedroom, and there it sat, in the corner, the rolltop desk. Fumbling, she fitted the key into the lock, seeing the scratch marks again, and with a click it turned. She eased the shutter up, gently, gently. Empty. She stared, furious – with herself, with Kate, what was this wild goose chase – and then she saw a little curved lip, almost invisible, on the front edge of the leather writing surface, she slid her fingers under it and it came up. And there lay an exercise book, the kind you bought for school, scuffed green paper, a dotted line for the name and class, but nothing was written on the cover. Suddenly afraid, she slid it out of the secret compartment. With trembling fingers, she opened it, at the first page.

I've got such plans, it read. Kate's neat careful handwriting. And suddenly Rose couldn't read any more: she backed out of the room with it pressed to her chest, slid it into the bag and the two keys and in that moment all she could see was the door she had not yet opened. The room she had not entered.

And then she was standing in front of it. The door to Kate's room, that was always locked; the room where she must have taken her last breath. Like a sleepwalker Rose fitted the key into the lock, and pushed.

The room was empty. Empty except for a big bedframe, not even a mattress, its surfaces shone back at her, silver-blue in the moonlight. Rose turned, looking, closed her eyes a second as if it might come to her that way, what had happened, how it had happened. But the room felt sterile, evacuated, and with hysterical relief Rose opened her eyes again. What did it mean? That he'd taken every trace of her away – or that it didn't happen here? Or that it was all superstition, fantasy, ghost stories.

Ghosts were real. Rose could feel them beyond the door, pressing, whispering, their hands against the walls, their fingertips on the windowpanes, they walked with soft steps – they just weren't in here. And then she saw it. She saw it blink. She knelt, crouched, under the bed frame that cast a latticed shadow on the dusty floor and nothing – no, not nothing this time. There.

Not green but red, the faintest glow from what looked like the skirting board but when Rose got up close it was a cupboard built in to an alcove beside the bed, a key in the door. And there it was inside, just a plastic box with an antenna. She felt along the side, found a button, slid it upwards and held her breath. The blinking red turned to green, two, three green lights, and Rose slumped beside it, her back against the wall, and opened her phone. She had logged on once before, she prayed to the little rectangle of plastic and metal in her hand that it would remember – and then, like magic, it did. The sign appeared, the striped cone in the corner of the screen. With trembling fingers she extracted the scrap of paper, the photograph, she propped the photograph against her knees and dialled.

Something happened to her screen. Half blinded by the fear she didn't know even know what button she'd pressed, but the ring was not the one she knew, blurred images came into focus. FaceTime? Was that what this was? And it was a face that appeared, a frightened face, peering up at her. A woman's face she half knew, an older version of the photograph she held on her knee right now, and a tinny voice. *Hello? Hello? Who is this? Do you know what time it is?*

'You're Serena's grandparents,' she said, that name, their granddaughter, her only hope. 'My name's Rose Bateman,' and she swallowed. 'My sister was called Kate.' She held the photograph up to the face gone silent on her screen. 'Please,' she said. 'Please help me.'

'Rose Bateman,' the voice repeated slowly. Then, 'Your friend phoned us.' The mouth moved jerkily. A small face, short silver hair, her daughter's pointed chin, and two deep lines of sadness etched to either side of the mouth. Another face appeared, indistinct, behind the woman's, said something Rose couldn't hear but the elderly woman didn't waver, she didn't turn. 'Your Italian friend. She found us online – there was a newspaper article about Jenny's death, we tried to challenge the coroner's verdict. She told us you were with him now, and she was afraid for you.'

Rose felt her head fall back, against the wall. 'Deb,' she whispered. Deb, who always followed everything through.

'He took all our Jenny's money,' said the woman.

'What's your name?' whispered Rose. The woman pushed her face closer to Rose.

'Helen,' she said. 'My name's Helen. He took all her money and he killed her, and now he's killed your sister too.' Her mouth was trembling, unless it was the screen.

'Kate died of cancer,' said Rose, numb.

'And Jenny had a fit,' said Helen. 'They said she hadn't been taking her medication. He was at work when it happened, there were witnesses, but she always took her

330

medication, always. Never missed it. He told her not to take it or he gave her something else instead. She left it all to him. Her savings.'

'How did they meet?' said Rose, suddenly and Helen's head tipped, frowning, and the figure behind her on the screen loomed closer, then it was him. An elderly man, his eyes baggy, high forehead.

'She was working for an epilepsy charity,' he said, his voice shaking as he came closer, Rose could see white stubble on his chin. 'She always helped other people first, before herself. He met her on a fundraising walk. He told her his brother had been epileptic and had died.'

Who are you running for? The blackened shreds of that tabard, in the bonfire's ash. 'He told Kate he was running for his dead wife,' she said.

The two faces were squeezed side by side on the screen now. 'It's how he got her,' said Helen, bitterly. 'Pretending to be all heart, knowing she was sick, knowing how easy it would be, how much she wanted to believe someone would love her. Is that what he did with your sister? With you? The police won't listen. Someone dies of natural causes, none of their business. Too hard, too complicated. We have no rights. He's kept her away from us, little Serena, he's told her lies.' Rose saw her take a deep ragged breath, saw her eyes open wide.

'You can call the police now,' she said. 'You can.'

'Where's Serena? Is she safe? Where's our granddaughter?'

'I'm going to get her out of here,' said Rose 'But if I – if I—' but as she said it she heard the sound. A soft sound, careful.

'The town's Reydon, it's the old pumping station or

331

something,' she said. 'Get the police here.' And she hung up.

When she got out on the landing, the green light winking behind her, there was silence. But she knew she'd heard something, downstairs.

Rose crept along the landing, tried Serena's door: it gave, she didn't have to knock, she didn't have to speak – clever Serena, clever girl, she thought. 'It's me,' she whispered and from the bed against the wall heard the sound of breath let out. Into the dark Rose felt her way towards the bed and found them, hoisted Jamie's small warm weight on to her shoulder as gently as she could, reaching for Serena's hand, cool, clammy. *Now.*

Still silence: the wide staircase yawned below them, down into the red dark, into the shadows that held the ghosts and their reaching hands. She felt Serena stop, turn and tugged her gently. 'This way,' she mouthed, to the dark hollows of Serena's face in the thin moonlight.

In here. She didn't know if she'd said it, or if it had been said to her.

'In here,' and she pushed the narrow door to the back staircase, the secret door, she smelled the old wood and plaster inside, felt the warmth – and something else. *In here. In here.* She felt resistance, Serena stubborn, pulling away from her.

'No – not – not there,' in a mumble, the small head shaking. 'That's where she – where Kate—'

And on the threshold the soft secret space that twisted down below them, narrow and dark as a chimney, spoke to Rose again as it had the first time only now she understood, it spoke to her as Kate's bedroom had not. It had happened in here, all along. Kate had crept here, like an animal, to hide. To die. And with the realisation, Jamie on her shoulder and Serena close at her back Rose felt a sudden vertigo, she bent to Serena, fighting it.

'It'll be OK,' she whispered and abruptly Serena gave up her resistance, shifted, stepped inside. The door closed behind them.

Down in the dark, one hand on Jamie, one on the wall. One step at a time, down, down. Beyond the walls something silent, invisible in the house paced, up and down, up and down, waiting. And then they were at the bottom, and there was the narrow door and the cold creep of the house finding its way up to them from under it. Rose pushed it open onto that space between the green baize and the kitchen doors – and then she heard it again, felt it as much as heard it. A vibration, a footstep, a warning: she didn't know where it was, behind or ahead of them, in the hall or the kitchen.

'Wait,' said Rose, and turning, transferred Jamie to Serena, on the last step of the staircase. 'Stay there.' The door closed on them, they were hidden – and Rose turned back, into the house.

The kitchen was empty: Rose ran on through the boiler room, and stopped. The back door was closed, where she'd left it open. She put her hand to the knob, knowing what she would find. It was locked.

Stumbling, she backed away from it into the crowded darkness of the room, almost fell, turned. Ran, through the green baize door and into the hall. The door to the green sitting room stood open: beside it in the hall the heavy old telephone had been put back on its little table, almost neat but for the cut wire, dangling. *How?* How could he still be conscious? Remembering the slime she had trodden in in the kitchen Rose knew that like a bad child, like a sick animal, he had let his food fall. He hadn't eaten it all. She stepped forwards, into the doorway, and looked into the green room.

The sofa still held the imprint of his body, but he wasn't there, nothing was there. The keys that had lain under him weren't there. She turned in the doorway, back into the hall, and he stepped out of the red shadows, grinning.

And in the second even before she could think, or plan, Rose leaned sideways, grabbed the heavy telephone with two hands and hit him with it on the side of his head, as hard as she could, and something fell from her, skittering away across the floor into the shadows: the back door key. He went down, and before she could see him get up again, she ran.

Chapter Thirty-One

I don't know what day it is, what time it is, what season it is. I can't taste, or smell, and it's getting dark. The world has become as small as a cupboard and huge like space and all there is in it is a bird singing beyond the walls, where I can't go. This is the last story, contained in me.

Rest, he says, *you rest*. I hear it in his voice, the excitement. He knows it won't be long now: he knows it's safe to leave the door unlocked. I lie quiet against the pillow, I hear my shallow breath like the sound of a sea where I float but I don't rest. I wait.

What is life? That soft mouth against my skin, the feel of his starfish hand patting, the scent of his warm head, my baby, mine. I can get my legs off the bed, I can. Just the last, just the last time, the door opens and it yawns up at me, come down, come to meet me in the shadows, it whispers. *Come here and rest*.

I'm listening for him, my baby, my Jamie, flesh of my flesh. He's sleeping. Let him sleep.

I creep, I creep along the gallery. It's just. It is. So slow. It takes so long.

The narrow door admits me and the little space brings me inside, it curls around me soft as breath, it enfolds me there, where while he sleeps I may be still, unseeing and unseen.

Rose had heard him fall, heavily. She imagined him bleeding, imagined him dead, imagined as hard as she could. Now, in the close warm dark of the back staircase, she listened, heard only the sound of Serena's quick breathing. Rose squeezed her eyes shut, her own heart pattering fast, she mapped out the house around them in the dark of her head, the doors she knew wouldn't open, front door back door, french windows in the green sitting room. All locked. Up. Up? She leaned down to Serena, took her arm and pointed, back up the stairs. In the dark she saw only the pointed gleam of Serena's stubborn little chin. 'Back up,' she said, 'you go.'

And gently she lifted Jamie from Serena's knee and laid him warm and heavy against her shoulder. A plump arm fell against hers and she smelled the sweet-sour smell of his skin – and then heard it. Him. Evan. She seized Serena's arm again, thin as a twig, and turned her.

Something between a groan and a growl from deep in the house, the noise of a cornered animal, red-eyed in the shadows, then the sharp clatter of something falling or kicked against and then, quietest and most ominous, the soft shoosh of the baize door.

He was there. He was on the other side of the door. She heard Serena stop, at the tight bend above her.

And then the kitchen door banged. They would have

no more than a minute before he saw they weren't in the kitchen or the boiler room. Less. 'Quick,' she hissed and heard Serena scrabble. 'Wait for me at the top.'

Something clanked, banged: she turned to follow Serena and he was back, she could hear his ragged breathing. The door between them shivered, with the draught, but it didn't fly open.

He must know. There was no bolt on this door, no lock. She couldn't keep him out.

Another clank. She smelled the boiler room, smoke and oil, and held very still. 'You,' he said. His voice was so close: something moved in the crack of the door and she knew he was there, pressed up. Why didn't he come in?

'She always said you were a little whore,' he said and she saw it, the gleam of his eye at the crack. For a second she trembled on the brink of believing him and then she knew, Kate reasserted herself, 'whore' a word she would never use, not whore not slag, and found her voice.

'You killed my sister,' she said. He wouldn't come in because he was frightened of the place where she'd died. He was a kid in the playground spewing insults, because nobody loved him.

'She'd have been proud, would she, to see you in my bed?'

The jibe was so negligible now she knew, she hardly even heard it.

'You targeted women you knew were vulnerable,' Rose said, hearing her terrible voice. 'I've spoken to Helen—' a rough angry laugh came from beyond the door but still it didn't burst open and she pushed on. 'You found them and you took their money and then you let them die. You

337

told them lies. You never had a brother with epilepsy, you never had a wife with breast cancer. You lied to them, you cut them off from their friends, and you waited for them to die. But Kate was too clever for you. Kate left clues. Kate left evidence. Kate knew – she *knew* I would come.'

A scrape, a lurch, the door trembled again, and she waited for the flood of light that would reveal them there, her and Jamie crouched on the narrow stairs, blinking, helpless. She shifted quietly off the step, rising, turning, setting her shoulder against the door.

'She was pathetic,' he said, raising his voice. 'Pathetic. Half women, they were, less than half, *defective* women, they knew that, all of them, their fat red faces all looking up at me, fucking stupid pink ribbons, I could have had my pick. Bald and titless, women who'd have a fit in the street, piss themselves in front of strangers – they knew no one wanted them. And then I came along. I touched them. Christ, it was hard.'

'You let her die.'

He wasn't listening. 'Of course they all want fucking kids, don't they? And then you're lumbered. It all takes so long, there's doctors poking their noses in unless you find some fool like that Martha – and you. Lapping it up, when I told you she'd had an affair, your dumpy little sister, like that was ever going to happen—'

'You let her *die*.' Rose didn't recognise her own voice, it was deep and rough and Jamie must have heard it too because he reared up on her shoulder and let out a strange high wail. And in the same moment she knew what it was she could smell, and she heard Evan's impatient sigh, the tiny flare of something beyond the door.

And then Rose was tripping, stumbling backwards in her haste to get away from it, Jamie was twisting in her arms as she reached for the rail, the whump came from behind her and immediately the tight space was full of choking black smoke. From above her she heard a frightened whimper and she scrambled desperately, falling and bashing her shin, righting herself and then she was up, bumping against Serena at the top and they burst through, coughing, the smoke billowing out of the narrow door.

From downstairs Rose could hear him, not the words but a kind of high ranting incantation as if he was telling her still what a whore she was, how her sister hated her, spitting his hatred for the women, all the stupid defective women, and in her desperation she shoved Serena ahead of her, through the door to Kate's room that stood there opposite, half open still.

It would take him two minutes, less, to find them. Smoke them out – did he think they would stay in there to die? Like Kate had. Rose crossed straight to the old window, with its many small panes.

'Here—' she shoved Jamie into Serena's arms as she wrestled with the catch, it stuck and then was freed. *Better to die of a broken neck—* she hauled, hauled on the old window, felt it stick, ancient sashes rotted in their grooves, they would die, they would die here – and then it moved. Up – two inches, six. A foot. She peered out and there – a blessing, a mercy, there below them was the old tiled awning of the veranda. There was mist down there, coming up from the river, lit up by something from inside the house.

'You first,' she whispered to Serena and watched as she

struggled under the sash, kept hold of her hand as she tested her weight on the flimsy awning. Jamie was thrashing and wailing and she felt his hot belly as his T-shirt rode up and panic jumped. She reached him down to Serena and turned, to see the room, hazed and choking with smoke, it drifted, uncurled, swaying crabwise into the room.

Halfway over the sill Rose felt a great bang came from somewhere below and scrambled – out of the corner of her eye seeing Serena clinging desperately to a drainpipe with one small hand, the other round Jamie, her feet beginning to slide on the slimy tile. Rose lunged to grab him just as Serena went down, on her bottom, twisted and slipped, fingers scrabbling and was over the edge. Was gone. She hardly dared breathe, her own fingers cramped, her eyes stinging. And then came Serena's voice. *Quick,* she was saying. *Quick. He's – quick.*

Without the words she didn't know if she'd have dared to do it, an effort that seemed beyond her, superhuman, Jamie gone quiet with terror against her, his hands clinging, digging into the flesh of her arm. She crouched, holding on to the sill till the last minute, then flattened herself on the narrow awning, Jamie in the crook of her arm, her hands twined into the creeper that covered it, and let herself slide to the edge.

It happened too quickly. She felt him go. And slithering, hopeless, as if her despair was a wave that had knocked her from the roof, she fell after him.

'No,' she heard, *No, no,* a sob and she didn't want to look, she didn't want to see him, her Jamie, her baby, Kate's baby and then she did look. And he looked back, clinging like a monkey to his sister's neck, round-eyed, and on Serena's face a look of terror and triumph mixed.

Inside the house something exploded, and glass tinkled outwards.

'Run,' said Rose. 'Can you run?'

They knew he'd come. They knew he'd come after them. The bag bumped against her. Phone, money, medicine, notebook. Kate's story. And the first place she ran was the back door – to lock it. *Keep him in. Keep him in.*

At the brick pump house Rose stopped. *No,* she thought, looking between the dark hedges then back to where the sky, plumed grey with smoke, lit with sparks. Not up the lane, he'd come out, he'd get the car, he'd follow them and find them. If they ran towards the weir—

'This way,' she said, seizing Serena by the wrist, hearing his breath in her ears but it was the crackling of the fire. They took the path, where she'd walked with Annie only this morning that seemed a lifetime ago, towards the rush of the weir. It was hardly audible now, merging with the roar of flames. The brambles tugged at them and Serena pulled away, 'He's coming,' she said, whimpering. They stopped. They were in the trees behind the house now, beyond the yard.

'Wait,' said Rose. 'From here—' but she didn't finish the sentence, she didn't want Serena to run. *From here we'll see him, when he comes out.* Hold your nerve. The big window of the kitchen, lit from inside by a reddish glow. The back door still locked. The water roared in her ears, exultant: it wasn't danger after all. It was freedom.

Hold on. She felt her grip tighten on Serena's arm,

341

without seeing it felt the face turn to look up at hers. 'He won't come,' she whispered, and looked down. The small white oval of Serena's face looked back, intent. The window of the kitchen blew out, and smoke billowed out after it, but Serena only looked at Rose, and Rose crouched beside her. 'Think of that smell you told me about,' she said. 'Your nan's smell, of flowers.' Serena's eyes were round and dark; in them Rose could see the reflection of a house in flames, the flicker of sparks. But then Serena nodded.

He had lit the fire at the foot of the staircase, and he was trapped behind it. He couldn't get to the hall, and the back door – and a sound came back to Rose, the skittering of the back-door key flying into the shadows, as she staggered. She couldn't open the door if she wanted to. Evan trapped between the fire he started and the back door she had locked.

Lock him up and throw away the key.

'It's all right,' said Rose and she put a hand down to Serena, firm and sure, and pressed them back into the hedge, stopping her running back towards the fire because they were coming, the blue lights were flashing closer. The sirens. 'It's all right,' she said again.

She held them closer, in the prickly safety of the hawthorn, in the mingled smells of earth and smoke and river. The fire engine thundered past them in the lane and behind it an ambulance, the driver's face turning to look at them, the circling blue lights sweeping across the figures in the hedge.

'It's us now,' Rose whispered, to them, to herself. 'It's just us.' And in that moment Jamie lifted his head from her shoulder, and solemnly – his hair sticking up in comic silhouette, his cheeks gleaming with the snail-trail of dried tears – he raised his starfish hand in the unearthly light, in blessing.

You'll take care of them for me, won't you, Rosie? Like I took care of you.

You'll get that test when I didn't dare, you'll be a mother to them where I can't. You know what to do, you know how it works.

Love.

Epilogue

Six months after the fire that killed Evan Lloyd, Rose tested negative for the BRAC1 gene. She lives with Jamie two streets away from Serena and her grandparents: she'd like to move back to Rome with both children, but has given the choice to Serena.

Acknowledgements

I'd like to thank the wonderful team at Sphere: the ever supportive Cath Burke, buyer of champagne and all round great supremo; the brilliant Kirsteen Astor; my editor and champion Maddie West now going off to pastures more intellectual; her incomparable successor Darcy Nicholson, barely in the saddle before she was applying her own editorial brilliance to making this book as good as it could possibly be; the unflappable, indefatigable, generally terrific Thalia Proctor, and Millie Seaward, sunniest of all Publicity People.

Thanks also to my great and good agent Victoria Hobbs for putting up with me for twelve years and to the literary hero that is Richard Beswick, always kind, always encouraging, always the best fun.

To my dear, permanently worried husband, never less than outraged or delighted on my behalf depending on what is required, thanks doesn't even begin to cover it and last of all my marvellous clever, kind, loving and admirable children, whom I do not deserve.

Did you enjoy *The Widower*?
Then read on for a sneak peek at
Christobel's next gripping thriller...

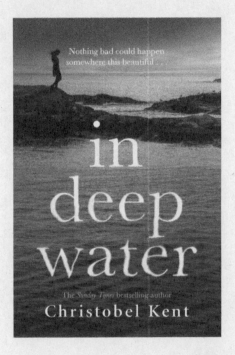

Coming April 2022

Prologue

Heather

At a certain point she thought, *the next thing that happens is, he kills me.*

She'd watched him play his set, the headphones on, one arm raised, she'd gazed. Across the dancing heads, he'd looked back at her.

His smell: sweat and dope. His voice. *It's your first time, isn't it?* Your first time was supposed to be magical, was that right?

The lights off the pier. The music still going on, the moving shadows, the grind and rattle of the stones under the waves, the stones that were under her back. And then his thing white in the darkness, she hadn't even seen one before and it wouldn't go in *I've never I've never* and the words were in her head, she didn't say them because he knew already.

He knew she'd never done it before. And she beat at it with her hands, her knee, and then he hit her. She could taste vomit and blood. He was whispering something, in her ear. She couldn't hear. She couldn't hear.

He was holding her by the throat.

'This is going to hurt,' he said.

Chapter One

Sukie

You can forget your comfort zone. She'd heard someone say that, or had she seen it online? *If you want to find someone, you have to push things.*

It was online dating. She'd done it before, fifteen, twenty, God, could it even be thirty dates?

Some of them awful, Sukie could say that now. Nobody's fault: say that quickly.

Sukie Alexander, whose mother thought she was still a virgin at almost thirty. Twenty-seven was almost thirty.

But it was a numbers game, you couldn't take it personally. The girls from work went on and on about how many bastards were out there, how it worked in a man's favour, how it was all about shagging, Sukie had listened patiently, she'd waited to explain. *The landscape's changing*, she'd tried to tell them that. *You have to do your research, there are sites for that.* For a quick fuck, although she wouldn't maybe put it that way. As a matter of fact Sukie didn't know if she'd ever said that actual word out loud, but she'd thought it. There are sites for people who just want sex, maybe with a different person every night, advertised like that. Down they went, up they came again, dishevelled and dauntless, battered and bruised, ready for another go.

And then there were sites for people who want a relationship: who want marriage, children, cohabitation, whatever. That was the dividing line and although there would be a few who crossed it, ended up in the wrong place – it was in everyone's interest to make sure they were talking to the right market. Right? It was evolving. It was turning into something good: you couldn't always do things the old way.

Was she beautiful? Looking at herself in the mirror and seeing herself fresh-faced with an anxious smile, a bit on the plump side. Some might say pretty. Beautiful? That was a question Sukie shied away from but then most sensible people do, because most sensible people know, *it's not all about that. It's really not.*

He said that. Jake said that.

And there he was now, standing there in this chilly unfamiliar place with his hands in his pockets, he was looking a little away from her, his jaw was moving a little. He was worried about her. Worried *for* her. Of course he was.

You can't go on looking for ever, you can't go on waiting for perfect to come along. You have to get real.

And then when you do – maybe you do have to forget your comfort zone.

The airport wasn't comfortable and that was for sure: dirty and cold, a draught from somewhere that wasn't air conditioning, and the landing strip that sat through the big grubby window beyond the luggage carousel looked bleak.

The carousel was hardly moving now and the whole place looked neglected, a half-built hangar, some bungalows up against a wire fence. But this island wasn't their final destination, Heather reminded herself. Jake was taking her home. To his home.

The carousel had emptied out now, a dusty backpack had been the only thing on it for ten minutes, and the other passengers had collected theirs and gone. Jake had his bag, it was resting against his leg. And his hand was on her shoulder.

Departure seemed like days ago and the big bright UK airport they'd flown out of seemed almost cosy from where Sukie was standing now and shivering, yawning and stiff after three cramped hours in an aeroplane. The sparkling floors in the duty-free – shots of Baileys on a cocktail cabinet and girls holding out perfume sticks, seven different food outlets, the men with pints in a dark bar, at five in the morning. Not the kind of place you were supposed to feel nostalgic for, not when you'd just started on your holiday, just the two of you.

It had been sweet of him to check it in for her and leave her to sit with her latte, but Sukie had felt the jitters set up before he'd even got out of sight and wished she might have gone with him. A woman leaning against the wall in the coffee bar had looked at her from over Jake's shoulder, a look that said to Sukie, what do you think you're doing with *him*? Unsettling her. Sukie had to admit, Jake was good-looking, in a dark sort of way, and the way he wore his clothes – maybe people did think he was out of her league. But then the girl had turned and gone and maybe it had been all Sukie's imagination.

Sukie had been thinking of her mother. Sitting with her latte, thinking about the look her mother would have given her, if she'd been in the airport, passing through and had seen them together.

And she might have been: Sukie's parents did a lot of travelling, since they'd retired. 'You can't take it with you,' her mother would say, at drinks parties, her father looking the other way, mildly. They'd gone to Bermuda last Christmas, and Sukie had stayed at home in her flat, which had suited her fine. She wished she'd known, that was all.

'They didn't *tell* you?' That had been Joey, from work, kind and shocked, and Sukie feeling the need to defend them, or defend herself, had said, 'Oh, of course they did. Don't be silly. I'd forgotten.' But she hadn't. They hadn't.

Her mother had been packing when Sukie had called to ask what time she should come, Christmas Eve or would they rather Christmas Day? And her mother had made an impatient noise. 'Talk to your father.'

Sukie had been born when her mother was twenty-six. 'I gave her the best years of my life,' Sukie had often heard her say, with a sigh, although Sukie, at twenty-seven, did always think but didn't ever feel able to say, that there might be better years.

So she'd been relieved, when they got through the sparkling brightly lit duty-free without coming across Marsha trying on nail varnishes or getting a free makeover while Sukie's father – for some reason she'd never had the same anxiety about what to call her father, he played so little part in either of their lives, just there, on the edge of things, vague and dim and loitering, *my father* – looked at the single malts. And guilty, and longing: Sukie loved her mother. There wasn't really another word for it. Yearned for her, which was how Sukie experienced love, the need for something that was missing.

There was no chance of seeing Marsha in an airport like this, cold and dusty with three rows of plastic seating bolted to the floor and a creaking carousel; Sukie was glad her mother hadn't really been listening when she'd told her on the phone, the words sounding odd and jumbled and rushed, that she was going on a little break. If she'd said it was to Greece, with a man she hardly knew, Marsha would have been all ears, she'd have begun to rattle off an interrogation – *you've known him a month?* – which was why, although it was on the tip of Sukie's tongue to tell her, she hadn't.

Funny thing was, in some part of her, Sukie knew, she'd said yes when Jake had asked her to come because Marsha would have been impressed. She could even hear Marsha's voice in her head as she hesitated, even as Jake looked away, already disappointed, *go on*. Go for it for once, get stuck in, seize life with both hands. Carpe diem. Marsha said that a lot.

Someone spoke.

It was Jake, and he was smiling, protective, looking into her face, and she felt a flood of something, gratitude, and the image of her mother, a painted head on a golf ball, rolled away, into the dusty corner of the airport.

'Sorry?' she said.

'I said, all right, little one?'

'Yes,' she said, squeezing his arm against her. *Little one*, she thought, grateful. I'm his little one.

Coming in to land they'd flown low over a beach and skimmed the roof of a squat hotel, a drained swimming pool beside a link fence, and there they were. He'd given her the window seat, he had insisted, and Sukie hadn't liked to go into how scared she was of flying at that point, it seemed both too late and too early.

'The island, you might – well no, I don't suppose you'd have heard of it. It's pretty wild. Off grid.' Hesitant. 'I want to know if you like it.' And in that moment so much had hung on Sukie's answer, and she knew it.

What would he have said, if she'd said no? Would his face have fallen?

Would she never have seen him again?

She had taken a deep breath. 'So romantic,' she said. 'Let's go. Let's do it.'

So they're doing it. They're going. They're here.

And how being beside the window made it worse: he so wanted to do everything for her, to make it all perfect. She'd taken the seat and surreptitiously pulled down the blind and closed her eyes. She had slept, on and off: at one point she opened her eyes and he wasn't there, for a wild moment she'd thought, he's gone. Mid-air: he's gone. But there he was at the other end of the aisle, talking to a stewardess. The next time Sukie woke it was because he was leaning over her to pull up the little blind so he could see out, she could feel him warm and heavy, his shoulder against her breast as she pulled back to give him room, and they were landing.

They weren't going to sleep together on this holiday. It had been his suggestion and she had felt everything relax when he did, because almost immediately after she'd said yes it had begun to worry her. 'We won't' – hesitating, looking into her eyes until he had been sure she understood. 'Not until you're ready,' he said. Smiling. 'I'm too old these days to rush into anything.'

Forty-something – she'd have quite liked a look at his passport, it occurred to her, to know what the *something* was – wasn't too old. Marsha would have laughed at the idea.

There was a whine and a jerk now, the carousel gave a little jolt and another bag appeared at the top the conveyor belt and Jake was pulling away from her, saying, 'Is that it?' But someone had stepped in between them and she couldn't see where he was pointing and he was moving, had broken into a little jog along the conveyor belt after the bag. She craned her neck to look after him. Sat back. At least he understood – about the sex. About waiting. Most men didn't. She shifted, thinking of those evenings.

357

And now her bag just wouldn't appear and it was the end of the season and it was colder than she'd thought it would be, the wind was blowing through the big airport doors that you could see beyond customs from the carousel if you turned the other way because the airport was so small, so flimsy, a concourse made out of a shoebox. A mangy pigeon had found its way in, through security, right into the baggage arrivals, pecking round an overflowing bin.

And Sukie was cold and tired, and she was worried about work because she'd had to shift a big edit over to Anastasia just like that. At the drop of a hat. And someone else had picked the bag up that Jake had thought was hers, and was walking off with it and it didn't look anything like her one, anyway.

But then Jake had turned and was walking back towards her, both hands spread as if to say, I tried, as if to say, sorry. And then he was in front of her and he said, softly, 'Sorry, darling.' And he held her face between his hands and kissed her, and she felt her eyes flutter closed.

Day one, Wednesday (earlier), Heather

Heather watched her mother go, lifted a hand to wave.

Mum was flying back to Scotland, wittering and anxious at the departure gate, reaching to clasp Heather's hand, her one and only child. Dad died two years ago and Mum was still turning around on the spot like an animal, looking for something that wasn't there any more, something she'd misplaced, not sure if she'd left her shopping on the bus or her husband, last seen in a pine box heading through the hessian curtains at the crematorium.

They'd moved – he and Mum – to Scotland not long before: it all came out of the blue. Well, only out of the blue if you didn't know the relationship between cigarette smoking and lung cancer. He knew it, Mum knew it, they all knew it. They'd tried, he'd tried. And then there he would be again, at the end of the garden, coughing in a haze of blue smoke. And then it was too late.

Heather missed her dad. There were things she wished she'd told him, though it didn't occur to her to tell them to her mother instead. *Bye, Mum*, she mouthed as her mother turned her head one last time from the far side of the barriers, through Plexiglas, stricken. *See you soon.*

And Mum was gone, through a grey door. She'd be all right.

And then Heather turned, and a couple was in her way, young woman, older man, dark-haired, walking across her path to a coffee bar and she didn't know which of her senses triggered it but the world – the wide glass of the windows, the ranked aeroplanes on their stands beyond, the strip lighting, the moving crowd – all spun around her. Dizzy, she stepped back, not knowing what had done it.

Oh, no. No. No.

The lights, the voices, the airport sounds seemed to come from far away, through a fog. She heard a roar in her ears like the sea crashing on stones, long ago, while someone held her down in the dark.

And when the world settled, the girl – the plump, pretty, anxious young woman in her floppy cardigan – was sipping her coffee, alone on a barstool and the man, the man – was walking away, towards a sign that said Check-In.

And setting down her coffee on the ledge – as if she knew what she was doing, as if she had planned all this – Heather pushed herself away from the wall, and followed him.